"Alyson Noël surpassed all my expectations. Not only is *Blue Moon* an amazing sequel, it sets the bar for the rest of this series very, very high! When I reached the last page of this one, all I could say was 'wow!'" —*Teens Read Too*

"It is the mark of a daring writer to defy expectations and Alyson Noël does that to the power of ten in *Blue Moon*. I guarantee you will have no idea what's coming in the second book of the series while Alyson Noël surprises you with a big, fat twist and leaves you wanting more, more, more." —*The Book Chick*

"A mesmerizing tale of teenage angst, love, and sacrifice with plenty of crossover appeal. . . . The startling but satisfying ending shows that Noël knows how to keep her audience hooked. Ever's supernatural struggles are a captivating metaphor for teenage fears about love, relationships, and growing up." —*Publishers Weekly* (starred review)

"One of the best books I've read this year. . . . With immortal lovers, trustworthy friends, betraying fortune-tellers, and freaky identical twins, what more could you ask for? *Blue Moon* has me begging for *Shadowland*! I can't wait for the next in the series." —*The YA Book Blogger*

"Alyson Noël has many talents to share as a writer, and she proves it again and again with her amazing Immortals series. She writes with an intensity and a passion, her words weaving perfectly together to create an overwhelming experience for the senses and the heart." —*Teen Reads*

"*Blue Moon* was incredible. If you thought *Evermore* was full of suspense and unknowns, just wait until you read *Blue Moon*. . . . The plot was insane, and I mean that in a good way. Noël took this novel in a direction I was never expecting, resulting in an emotional roller-coaster ride that I never wanted to end. Fabulous." —*The Story Siren*

"The Immortals series is so unique; it's like a breath of fresh air. . . . Noël knows how to pull you into her world with beautiful imagery and mesmerizing words. *Blue Moon* is a page-turner that will keep you reading until the last page. Just when you think you have the plot figured out, Alyson throws in another twist making it impossible to put this book down." —*Fantastic Book Reviews* (5 stars!)

"Ever is a great character, and this is a highly entertaining series for young adult fans. It's a quick read that is hard to put down. Vivid and intense, *Blue Moon* was a thrilling sequel." —*SciFiChick.com*

"I really got into the book—I felt like I was in it, which is probably why I read it in a few hours. I would get so into *Blue Moon* that I would scream at it. Seriously. My family looked at me like I was nuts. When I finished the book, I almost cried. Not because someone died, but because . . . I love, love, loved this book. I don't know how I'm going to make it until the next one comes out."  —*Shooting Stars Mag*

"Teen angst and the paranormal make a combustible mix . . . Getting hooked on this new series, the Immortals, is guaranteed."  —*RT Book Reviews* (4 stars!)

"*Evermore* will thrill many teen fantasy-suspense readers, especially fans of Stephenie Meyer's Twilight series. . . . Noël creates a cast of recognizably diverse teens in a realistic high-school setting, along with just the right tension to make Ever's discovery of her own immortality—should she choose it—exciting and credible."  —*Booklist*

"Beautiful main characters, tense budding romance, a dark secret, mysterious immortals—what more could you ask from this modern gothic romance?"  —*Justine Magazine*

"When I got a copy of *Evermore*, I sat down to read it, intending to only read a chapter or two. Instead, I blazed through the first hundred pages before I knew it . . . and then I didn't want to put the book down. Except I couldn't keep my eyes open any longer. So I picked it up the next morning and finished it. Now I can't wait . . . for the second book to see what happens next."  —*Blog Critics Magazine*

"Get ready for a wild ride that is filled with twisting paths and mystery, love and fantasy. . . . The writing style, story, and characters are a bit like those of Meyer's and Marr's popular books, but written with a new twist and voice. And after reading the book, you too will probably want your own Damen, even if it means making the ultimate sacrifice."
—*The Book Queen* (5/5 stars!)

"Readers who enjoy the works of P. C. Cast and Stephenie Meyer will love this outstanding paranormal teen-lit thriller."
—*Midwest Book Review*

"I found myself unwilling to put the book down, even though I had to at some points, because I wanted to know what was going to happen. . . . Ever was so real and her emotions were so believable that it was a little creepy. It's like Alyson Noël is actually a grieving, lovestruck teenager. She got Ever completely perfect. And by perfect, I mean delightfully flawed and deep."
—*The Frenetic Reader*

"*Evermore* is a wonderful book that I believe would be a lovely addition to any library. . . . Definitely a book that fans of Stephenie Meyer and Melissa Marr should add to their collections. Definitely engaging and will catch your attention the minute you open to the first page!"
—*Mind of a Bibliophile*

"Alyson Noël creates a great picture of each and every character in the book. I am a fan of the *Twilight* series and I recommend this book to those who like the series as well. It is a very quick read, with all the interesting twists and turns."

—*Flamingnet Book Reviews*

"I loved this book. It really keeps your attention throughout the story, because the puzzle gets pieced together bit by bit, but you don't know exactly what happened until the end. The only thing that disappoints me is that the second book won't be published for a while. I would definitely recommend this to my friends."

—*Portsmouth Teen Book Review*

"*Evermore*'s suspense, eerie mystery, and strange magic were interestingly entertaining. . . . I found Ever to be a character I could really respect. . . . Recommended."

—*The Bookworm*

"*Evermore* was a great way to lighten my reading load this winter and provided me with a creative, magical story that I really enjoyed. This is the first in a series for Noël and I think she may have a hit on her hands. . . . *Evermore* has good and evil, likable characters, vivid descriptions, and a good story."

—*Planet Books*

"I fell into it easily, and loved the world Noël created. . . . The fact that Ever had psychic powers was truly interesting. They flowed neatly through the book and I felt Ever's pain. . . . Trust me, this book was really good. I couldn't put it down. Alyson Noël created an amazing new world, and after this book I am so curious to see where it heads because honestly, I have no idea."

—*Reading Keeps You Sane*

"Ever is an easy character to like. I really felt for her because of all she lost and what she struggled with daily. . . . *Evermore* was a really fast, engaging read with some great characters. It is the first in a series, so I'm eager to see if we will learn more about Ever, Damen, and friends in the next one . . . it's sure to be a great read."

—*Ninja Reviews*

"The writing here is clear, the story well-defined, and narrator Ever has an engaging voice that teens should enjoy."

—*January Magazine*

"Alyson Noël created a well-detailed story that makes it easy for the reader to visualize both the characters and the world around them. *Evermore* has a familiar theme that attracts readers, but inside this book you'll find that the author has added some unique details that set it apart and will surprise you."

—*The Ravenous Reader*

"This young adult novel ponders immortal love and the knowledge that 'revenge weakens and love strengthens.' Fans of the Twilight series should love it."

—*Orange Coast Magazine*

"Noël writes an emotional, thoughtful book that made me cry in a couple of places. *Evermore* was an easy novel to get sucked into, and I wanted to get back to it as soon as possible. If you love Stephenie Meyer, you will LOVE this book."

—*Night Owl Romance*

"*Evermore* is a fresh and original work that . . . branches out and explores new ground. Definitely recommended."

—*Cool Moms Rule!*

"I totally LOVE Alyson Noël's *Evermore*. . . . Noël has delivered a deliciously fresh new series that will be the next new thing that has every teen and even adults everywhere hooked and waiting for more. . . . This is a keeper and a book that you have to go out and buy right now because if you don't you will be missing out. People will be asking if you have been living under a rock if you don't give *Evermore* a try, and that is just not acceptable."

—*Talk About My Favorite Authors*

# alyson noël

# shadowland

st. martin's griffin ❧ new york

SHADOWLAND. Copyright © 2009 by Alyson Noël, LLC. All rights reserved. Printed in the United States of America. For information, address St. Martin's Press, 175 Fifth Avenue, New York, N.Y. 10010.

www.stmartins.com

The Library of Congress has cataloged the hardcover edition as follows:

Noël, Alyson.
    Shadowland / Alyson Noël. — 1st ed.
      p. cm.
    Sequel to: Blue moon.
    Summary: Ever and Damen have traveled through countless past lives and fought off the world's darkest enemies to be together forever, but just as their long-awaited destiny is finally within reach, a powerful curse threatens them.
    ISBN 978-0-312-59044-4
    [1. Psychic ability—Fiction. 2. Immortality—Fiction. 3. Supernatural—Fiction.] I. Title.
    PZ7.N67185Sh 2010
    [Fic] —dc22

                                  2009033861

ISBN 978-0-312-65005-6 (trade paperback)

First St. Martin's Griffin Paperback Edition: September 2010

10  9  8  7  6  5  4  3  2  1

In memory of Blake Snyder, 1957–2009:

*An inspiring teacher, whose generosity, enthusiasm,
and genuine passion for helping others is unsurpassed.
May his spirit live on in his books and his teachings.*

# acknowledgments

It takes a whole team of people to make a book happen, and I'm incredibly lucky to work with such a great one!

Big, huge, sparkly thanks go to:

Bill Contardi—the perfect blend of brains, heart, and sly sense of humor—the best dang agent an author could ask for!

Matthew Shear and Rose Hilliard—publisher and editor extraordinaire—I couldn't have done it without them!

Anne Marie Tallberg and Brittany Kleinfelter—the brilliant brains behind the immortalsseries.com Web site—thanks for your creative ideas and much-needed tech support!

Katy Hershberger, who not only has great taste in music but happens to be a great publicist too!

The amazingly talented people in the art department, Angela Goddard and Jeanette Levy, who design the most beautiful, drool-worthy covers! Along with everyone else in sales and marketing and production and any other department I'm sure I'm forgetting—thank you for all that you do—you guys rock!

Also, hugs and love to Sandy for being a constant source of inspiration, laughter, and fun—my very own Damen Auguste!

And I'd be completely remiss not to mention *you,* the reader—your messages, e-mails, letters, and artwork never fail to make my day. Thanks for being so incredibly awesome!

# shadowland

Fate is nothing but the deeds committed
in a prior state of existence.

—Ralph Waldo Emerson

# one

"Everything is energy."

Damen's dark eyes focus on mine, urging me to listen, really listen this time. "Everything around us—" His arm sweeps before him, tracing a fading horizon that'll soon fade to black. "Everything in this seemingly solid universe of ours isn't solid at all—it's energy—pure vibrating energy. And while our perception may convince us that things are either solid or liquid or gaseous—on the quantum level it's all just particles within particles—it's all just *energy*."

I press my lips together and nod, his voice overpowered by the one in my head urging: *Tell him! Tell him now! Quit stalling, and just get it over with! Hurry, before he starts talking again!*

But I don't. I don't say a word. I just wait for him to continue so I can delay even further.

"Raise your hand." He nods, palm out, moving toward mine. Lifting my arm slowly, cautiously, determined to avoid any and all physical contact when he says, "Now tell me, what do you see?"

I squint, unsure what he's after, then shrugging I say, "Well, I see pale skin, long fingers, a freckle or two, nails in serious need of a manicure . . ."

"Exactly." He smiles, as though I just passed the world's easiest test. "But if you could see it as it *really* is, you wouldn't see that at all. Instead you'd see a swarm of molecules containing protons, neutrons, electrons, and quarks. And within those tiny quarks, down to the most minuscule point, you'd see nothing but pure vibrating energy moving at a speed slow enough that it appears solid and dense, and yet quickly enough that it can't be observed for what it truly is."

I narrow my eyes, not sure I believe it. Never mind the fact that he's been studying this stuff for hundreds of years.

"Seriously, Ever. Nothing is separate." He leans toward me, fully warmed up to his subject now. "Everything is one. Items that appear dense, like you and I, and this sand that we're sitting on, are really just a mass of energy vibrating slowly enough to seem solid, while things like ghosts and spirits vibrate so quickly they're nearly impossible for most humans to see."

"I see Riley," I say, eager to remind him of all the time I used to spend with my ghostly sister. "Or at least I used to, you know, before she crossed the bridge and moved on."

"And that's exactly why you can't see her anymore." He nods. "Her vibration is moving too fast. Though there are those who can see past all of that."

I gaze at the ocean before us, the swells rolling in, one after another. Endless, unceasing, immortal—like us.

"Now raise your hand again and bring it so close to mine we just nearly touch."

I hesitate, filling my palm with sand, unwilling to do it. Unlike him, I know the price, the dire consequences the slightest skin-on-skin contact can bring. Which is why I've been avoid-ing his touch since last Friday. But when I peer at him again, his palm out, waiting for mine, I take a deep breath and lift my hand too—gasping when he draws so close the space that di-vides is razor thin.

"Feel that?" He smiles. "That tingle and heat? That's our energy connecting." He moves his hand back and forth, manip-ulating the push and pull of the energy force field between us.

"But if we're all connected like you say, then why doesn't it all *feel* the same?" I whisper, drawn by the undeniable magnetic stream that links us, causing the most wonderful warmth to course through my body.

"We *are* all connected, all of us made of the same vibrating source. But while some energy leaves you cold and some leaves you lukewarm, the one that you're destined for? It feels just like *this*."

I close my eyes and turn, allowing the tears to stream down my cheeks, no longer able to keep them in check. Knowing I'm barred from the feel of his skin, the touch of his lips, the solid warm comfort of his body on mine. This electric energy field that trembles between us is the closest I'll get, thanks to the horrible decision I made.

"Science is just now catching up with what metaphysicians and the great spiritual teachers have known for centuries. Everything is *energy*. Everything is *one*."

I can hear the smile in his voice as he draws closer, eager to entwine his fingers with mine. But I move away quickly, catch-ing his eye just long enough to see the look of hurt that crosses his face—the same look he's been giving me since I made him drink the antidote that returned him to life. Wondering why I'm acting so quiet, so distant, so remote—refusing to touch him when just a few weeks before I couldn't get enough. Incorrectly assuming it's because of his hurtful behavior—his flirting with Stacia, his cruelty toward me—when the truth is, it has nothing to do with that. He was under Roman's spell, the entire school was. It wasn't his fault.

What he doesn't know is that while the antidote returned him to life, the moment I added my blood to the mix it also ensured we could never be together.

Never.

Ever.

For all of eternity.

"Ever?" he whispers, voice deep and sincere. But I can't look at him. Can't touch him. And I certainly can't utter the words he deserves to hear:

*I messed up—I'm so sorry—Roman tricked me, and I was desperate and dumb enough to fall for his ploy—And now there's no hope for us because if you kiss me, if we exchange our DNA—you'll die—*

I can't do it. I'm the worst kind of coward. I'm pathetic and weak. And there's just no way I can find it within me.

"Ever, please, what is it?" he asks, alarmed by my tears. "You've been like this for days. Is it me? Is it something I've done? Because you know I don't remember much of what happened, and the memories that are starting to surface, well, you must know by now that wasn't the real me. I would *never* intentionally hurt you. I'd *never* harm you in any way."

I hug myself tightly, scrunching my shoulders and bowing my head. Wishing I could make myself smaller, so small he could no longer see me. Knowing his words are true, that he's incapable of hurting me, only I could do something so hurtful, so rash, so ridiculously impulsive. Only I could be stupid enough to fall for Roman's bait. So eager to prove myself as

Damen's one true love—wanting to be the only one who could save him—and now look at the mess that I've made.

He moves toward me, sliding his arm around me, grasping my waist and pulling me near. But I can't risk the closeness, my tears are lethal now, and must be kept far from his skin.

I scramble to my feet and run toward the ocean, curling my toes at its edge and allowing the cold white froth to splash onto my shins. Wishing I could dive under its vastness and be carried by the tide. Anything to avoid saying the words—anything to avoid telling my one true love, my eternal partner, my soul mate for the last four hundred years, that while he may have given me eternity—I've brought us our end.

I remain like that, silent and still. Waiting for the sun to sink until I finally turn to face him. Taking in his dark shadowy outline, nearly indistinguishable from the night, and speaking past the sting in my throat when I mumble, "Damen . . . baby . . . there's something I need to tell you."

# two

I kneel beside him, hands on my knees, toes buried in sand, wishing he'd look at me, wishing he'd speak. Even if it's only to tell me what I already know—that I made a grave and stupid mistake—one that will possibly never be erased. I'd gladly accept it—heck, I *deserve* it. What I can't stand is his absolute silence and faraway gaze.

And I'm just about to say something, *anything*, to break this unbearable stillness, when he looks at me with eyes so weary they're the perfect embodiment of his six hundred years. "Roman." He sighs, shaking his head. "I didn't recognize him, I had no idea—" His voice trails off along with his gaze.

"There's no way you could've known," I say, eager to erase any guilt he might feel. "You were under his spell from the very first day. Believe me, he had it all planned, made sure any memories were completely erased."

His eyes search my face studying me closely before he stands and turns away. Gazing out at the ocean, hands balled into fists as he says, "Did he hurt you? Did he go after you or harm you in any way?"

I shake my head. "He didn't have to. It was enough to hurt me through you."

He turns, eyes growing darker as his features harden, inhaling deeply as he says, "This is my fault."

I gape, wondering how he could possibly believe that after the case I just made. Rising to my feet and standing beside him as I cry, "Don't be ridiculous! Of course it's not your fault! Did you listen to *anything* I said?" I shake my head. "Roman *poisoned* your elixir and *hypnotized* you. You had nothing to do with it, you were just doing his bidding—it was beyond your control!"

But I've barely finished when he's already dismissing it with a wave of his hand. "Ever, don't you see? This isn't about Roman, or you, this is *karma*. This is retribution for six centuries of selfish living." He shakes his head and laughs, though it's not the kind that asks you to join in. It's the other kind—the kind that chills you to the bone. "After all those years of loving you and losing you, again and again, I was sure *that* was my punishment for the way I'd been living, having no idea you'd died at Drina's hand. But now I see the truth I've missed all along. Just when I was sure I'd evaded karma by making you immortal and keeping you forever by my side, karma gets the last laugh, allowing us an eternity together, but only to look, never to touch each other again."

I reach for him, wanting to hold him, comfort him, convince him that it's not at all true. But I pull away just as quickly. Remembering how our inability to touch is the very thing that got us both here.

"That's *not* true," I say, gaze fixed on his. "Why would *you* be punished when *I'm* the one who made the mistake? Don't you see?" I shake my head, frustrated by his singular way of thinking. "Roman planned it all along. He *loved* Drina—I bet you didn't know that, huh? He was one of the orphans you saved from the plague back in Renaissance Florence, and he loved her for all of those centuries, would've done anything for her. But Drina didn't care about him, she only loved you—and you only loved me—and then, well, after I killed her, Roman decided to go after me—only he did it through *you*. Wanting me to feel the pain of never being able to touch you again—just like he feels with Drina! And it all happened so fast, I just—" I stop, knowing it's useless, a total waste of words. He stopped listening just after I started, convinced he's at fault.

But I refuse to even visit that place, and I won't let him either.

"Damen, please! You can't just give up. This isn't karma—it's *me*! *I* made a mistake, a horrible, dreadful mistake. But that doesn't mean we can't fix it! There must be a way." Clinging to the falsest of hopes, forcing an enthusiasm I don't really feel.

Damen stands before me, a dark silhouette in the night, the warmth of his sad tired gaze serving as our only embrace. "I never should've started," he says. "Never should've made the elixir—should've let things take their own natural course. Seriously, Ever, just look at the result—it's brought nothing but pain!" He shakes his head, his gaze so sad, so contrite, my heart caves. "There's still time for you though. You've got your whole life ahead of you—an eternity where you can be anything you want to be, do anything you want to do. But me—" He shrugs. "I'm tainted. I think we can all see the result of my six hundred years."

"*No!*" My voice quivers as my lips tremble so badly it spreads to my cheeks. "You don't get to walk away, you don't get to leave me again! I spent the last month going through hell to save you, and now that you're well I'm not about to give up. We're meant for each other, you said it yourself! We're just experiencing a temporary setback, that's all. But if we can just put our heads together, I know we'll think of a way to . . ."

I stop, voice fading, seeing he's already moved on, retreating to his bleak sorry world where he's solely to blame. And I know it's time to tell the rest of the story, the sorry, regretful parts I'd prefer to leave out. Maybe then he'll see it differently, maybe then—

"There's more," I say, rushing ahead though I've no idea how to phrase what comes next. "So before you assume karma's out to get you or whatever, you need to know something else, something I'm not exactly proud of, but still—"

Then I take a deep breath and tell him about my trips to Summerland—that magical dimension between the dimensions where I learned how to go back in time—and that given the choice between my family and him—I chose *them*. Convinced I could somehow restore the future I was sure had been stolen, and yet all it really amounted to was a lesson I already knew:

Sometimes destiny lies just outside of our reach.

I swallow hard and stare at the sand, reluctant to see Damen's reaction when he looks into the eyes of the one who betrayed him.

But instead of getting mad or upset like I thought, he surrounds me with the most beautiful glowing white light—a light so comforting, so forgiving, so pure—it's like the portal to Summerland—only better. So I close my eyes and surround him with light too, and when I open them again, we're wrapped in the most beautiful warm hazy glow.

"You had no choice," he says, voice gentle, gaze soothing, doing everything he can to ease all my shame. "Of course you chose your family. It was the right thing to do. I would've done the same—given the choice—"

I nod, shining his light even brighter and tacking on a telepathic embrace. Knowing it's not nearly as comforting as the real thing but for now it'll do. "I know about your family, I know everything, I saw it all—" He looks at me with eyes so dark and intense I force myself to continue. "You're always so secretive about your past, where you came from, how you lived—and so one day, while I was in Summerland, I asked about you—and—well—your entire life story was revealed."

I press my lips together and peer at him standing before me so silent and still. Sighing as he gazes into my eyes and telepathically traces his fingers along the curve of my cheek—creating an image so deliberate, so palpable, it almost seems real.

"I'm sorry," he says, thumb mentally smoothing my chin. "I'm sorry I was so shut down and unwilling to share that I reduced you to that. But even though it happened a long time ago, it's still something I prefer not to discuss."

I nod, having no intention of pushing it. His witnessing his parents' murder followed by years of abuse at the hands of the church is not a subject I intend to pursue.

"But there's more," I say, hoping I can maybe restore a little hope by sharing something else that I learned. "When I was watching your life unfold, at the end, Roman had killed you. But even though that seemed fated to happen, I still managed to save you." I gaze at him, sensing he's far from convinced and rushing ahead before I lose him completely. "I mean, yeah, maybe our fate is sometimes fixed and unchangeable, but there are other times when it's shaped purely by the actions we take.

So when I couldn't save my family by going back in time, it's only because that was a destiny that couldn't be changed. Or as Riley said seconds before the second accident that took them again, 'You can't change the past, it just is.' But when I found myself right back here in Laguna, and I was able to save you, well, I think it proves that the future isn't always concrete, not everything is ruled solely by fate.'"

"Maybe so." He sighs, gaze fixed on mine. "But you can't escape karma, Ever. It is what it is. It doesn't judge, it's neither good nor bad like most people think. It's the result of all actions, positive and negative—a constant balancing of events—cause and effect—tit for tat—reaping and sowing—what goes around comes around." He shrugs. "However you phrase it, it's the same in the end. And as much as you'd like to think otherwise, that's exactly what's happening here. All actions cause a reaction. And this is where my actions have brought *me*." He shakes his head. "All this time I told myself I turned you out of love—but now I see it was really out of selfishness—because I couldn't be without you. *That's* why this is happening now."

"So, that's it?" I shake my head, hardly believing he's determined to give up so easily. "That's how it ends? You're just so dang sure you've been chased down by karma you don't even try to fight back? You came all this way just so we could be together and now that we're facing an obstacle, you're not even going to try to scale the brick wall in our path?"

"Ever." His gaze is warm, loving, all-encompassing, but it does nothing to cancel the defeat in his voice. "I'm sorry, but there are some things I just *know*."

"Yeah, well . . ." I shake my head and gaze down at the ground, burying my toes deep in the sand. "Just because you've got a few centuries on me doesn't mean you get the last word.

Because if we're *truly* in this together, if our lives, like our fate, is *truly* entwined, then you'll realize this isn't just happening to *you*, I'm part of it too. And you don't get to walk away from it—you don't get to walk away from *me*! We've got to work together! There has to be a way—" I stop, body shaking, throat closed so tight I can no longer speak. All I can do is stand there before him, silently urging him to join me in a fight I'm not sure we can win.

"I've no plans to leave you," he says, gaze filled with the longing of four hundred years. "I *can't* leave you, Ever. Believe me, I've tried. But in the end, I always find my way back to your side. You're all I've ever wanted—all I've ever loved—but Ever—"

"No *buts*." I shake my head, wishing I could hold him, touch him, press my body tightly against his. "There's got to be a way, some kind of cure. And together we'll find it. I just know that we will. We've come too far to let Roman keep us apart. But I can't do it alone. Not without your help. So please promise me—promise you'll try."

He looks at me, his gaze luring me in. Closing his eyes as he fills the beach with so many tulips the entire cove is bursting with waxy red petals atop green curving stems—the ultimate symbol of our undying love covering every square inch of sand.

Then he slips his arm through mine and leads me back to his car. Our skin separated only by his supple black leather jacket and my organic cotton tee. Enough to spare the consequences of any accidental DNA exchange, but unable to temper the tingle and heat that pulsates between us.

# three

"Guess what?"

Miles gazes at me as he climbs into my car, big brown eyes wider than usual, cute baby face curving into a grin. "No, you know what? Don't guess. I'll just tell you, 'cause you're *never* gonna believe it! You're *never* gonna guess!"

I smile, hearing his thoughts a few moments before he can speak them, refraining from saying: *You're going to acting camp in Italy!* Just moments before he says, "I'm going to acting camp in Italy! No, correction, make that *Florence*, Italy! Home of Leonardo da Vinci, Michelangelo, Raphael—"

*And your good friend Damen Auguste, who actually knew all of those artists!*

"I've known about the possibility for a few weeks but it just became official last night and I still can't believe it! Eight weeks in Florence, doing nothing but acting, eating, and stalking smoldering hot Italian men . . ."

I glance at him as I back out of his drive. "And Holt's good with all that?"

Miles looks at me. "Hey, you know the drill. What happens in Italy *stays* in Italy."

*Except when it doesn't.* My thoughts drifting to Drina and Roman, wondering how many more immortal rogues are still out there, just waiting to show up in Laguna Beach and terrorize me.

"Anyway, I'm leaving soon, just after school gets out. And I have so much to prepare between now and then! Oh, and I almost forgot the best part—well—one of the best parts. As it just so happens it all works out perfectly since my *Hairspray* run ends the week before I leave, so I'll still get my final bow as Tracy Turnblad—I mean, seriously, how perfect is that?"

"Seriously perfect." I smile. "Really. Congrats. That's so cool. And well deserved I might add. I only wish I could go with you."

And the moment I say it, I realize it's true. It would be so nice to escape all my problems, board a plane and fly away from all this. Besides, I miss hanging with Miles. The last few weeks when he and Haven (along with the rest of the school) were under Roman's spell were some of the loneliest days of my life. Not having Damen beside me was more than I could bear, but not having the support of my two best friends nearly sent me over the edge. But Miles and Haven don't remember any of that, none of them do. Only Damen can access small bits and pieces, and what he recalls leaves him feeling terribly guilty.

"I wish you could come too," he says, messing with my car stereo, trying to find just the right soundtrack to match his good mood. "Maybe after graduation we can all go to Europe! We can get Eurail passes, stay in youth hostels, backpack around—how cool would that be? Just the six of us, you know, you and Damen, Haven and Josh, and me and whoever . . ."

"You and *whoever?*" I glance at him. "What's that about?"

"I'm a realist." He shrugs.

"Please." I roll my eyes. "Since when?"

"Since last night when I found out I'm going to Italy." He laughs, running a hand through his cropped brown hair. "Listen, Holt's great and all, don't get me wrong. But I'm not fooling myself. I'm not pretending it's anything more than it is. It's like we've got an expiration date, you know? A full three acts with a definite beginning, middle, and end. It's not like with you and Damen. You guys are different. You're lifers."

"*Lifers?*" I peer at him, shaking my head as I stop at a traffic light. "Sounds more like a prison term than a happily ever after."

"You know what I mean." He inspects his manicure, turning his hot-pink Tracy Turnblad nails this way and that. "It's just that you guys are so in tune with each other, so *connected.* And I mean that *literally* by the way since you're pretty much *always* going at it."

*Not anymore.* I swallow hard, punching the gas the second the light turns green, crossing the intersection with a loud screech of wheels and leaving a thick trail of rubber behind. Refusing to slow until I pull into the parking lot and scan for Damen who always parks in the second best space next to mine.

But even after I set the brake, he's nowhere to be found. And I'm just about to climb out, wondering where he could be, when he appears right beside me, gloved hand on my door.

"Where's your car?" Miles asks, glancing at him as he slams his door shut and slings his backpack over his shoulder. "And what's up with your hand?"

"I got rid of it," Damen says, gaze fixed on mine. Then glancing at Miles and seeing his expression he adds, "The car, not the hand."

"Did you trade it in?" I ask, but only because Miles is listening. Damen doesn't need to buy, trade, or sell, like normal people do. He can just manifest anything at will.

He shakes his head and walks me to the gate, smiling as he says, "No, I just dropped it off on the side of the road, key in the ignition, engine running."

"*Excuse me?*" Miles yelps. "You mean to tell me that you left your shiny, black, BMW M6 Coupe—*by the side of the road?*"

Damen nods.

"But that's a hundred-thousand-dollar car!" Miles gasps as his face turns bright red.

"A hundred and *ten.*" Damen laughs. "Don't forget, it was fully customized and loaded with options."

Miles stares at him, eyes practically bugging out of his head, unable to comprehend how anyone could do such a thing—*why* anyone would do such a thing. "Um, okay, so let me get this straight—you just woke up and decided—*Hey, what the hell? I think I'll just dump my ridiculously expensive luxury car by the side of the road—WHERE JUST ANYONE CAN TAKE IT?*"

Damen shrugs. "Pretty much."

"Because in case you haven't noticed," Miles says, practically hyperventilating now. "*Some* of us are a little *car deprived. Some* of us were born to parents so cruel and unusual they're forced to rely on the kindness of friends for the rest of their lives!"

"Sorry." Damen shrugs. "Guess I hadn't thought about that. Though if it makes you feel any better, it was all for a very good cause."

And when he looks at me, eyes meeting mine in that way

that he has, along with the usual wave of warmth I get this horrible feeling that ditching the car is just the start of his plans.

"How'd you get to school?" I ask, just as we reach the front gate where Haven is waiting.

"He rode the bus." Haven glances between us, her recently dyed, royal blue bangs falling into her face. "I kid you not. I wouldn't have believed it either, but I saw it with my own eyes. Watched him climb right off that big yellow bus with all the other freshmen, dorks, retards, and rejects who, unlike Damen, have no other choice but to ride." She shakes her head. "And I was so shocked by the sight of it, I blinked a bunch of times just to make sure it was really him. And then, when I still wasn't convinced, I snapped a pic on my cell and sent it to Josh who confirmed it." She holds it up for us to see.

I glance at Damen, wondering what he could possibly be up to, and that's when I notice he's ditched his usual cashmere sweater in place of a plain cotton tee, and how his designer jeans have been replaced with no-name plain pockets. Even the black motorcycle boots he's practically famous for have been swapped for brown rubber flip-flops. And even though he doesn't need any of that dash and flash to look as devastatingly handsome as the first day we met—this new low-key look just isn't him.

Or at least not the *him* that I'm used to.

I mean, while Damen is undeniably smart, kind, loving, and generous—he's also more than a tad flamboyant and vain. Always obsessed with his clothes, his car, his image in general. And don't even try and pin him down on his exact date of birth, because for someone who *chose* to be immortal he has a definite complex about his age.

But even though I normally couldn't care less about the clothes he wears or his ride to school, when I look at him again, I get this horrible ping in my gut—an insistent push, demanding my notice. A definite warning that this is merely the beginning. That this sudden transformation goes way deeper than some cost-cutting, altruistic, environmentally conscious agenda. No, this has something to do with last night. Something about being haunted by his karma. Like he's convinced himself that giving up his most prized possessions will somehow balance it all out.

"Shall we?" He smiles, grasping my hand the second the bell rings, leading me away from Miles and Haven who'll spend the next three periods texting back and forth, trying to determine what's up with Damen.

I look at him, his gloved hand in mine as we head down the hall, whispering, "What's going on? What really happened to your car?"

"I already told you." He shrugs. "I don't need it. It's an unnecessary indulgence I no longer care to—*indulge*." He laughs, looking at me. But when I fail to join in he shakes his head and says, "Don't look so serious. It's not a big deal. When I realized it's not something I need, I drove it out to a depressed area and left it by the side of the road where someone can find it."

I press my lips together and stare straight ahead, wishing I could climb inside his mind and *see* the thoughts he keeps to himself, get to the bottom of what this is *really* about. Because despite the way he looks at me, despite the dismissive shrug that he gives, nothing he's said makes the least bit of sense.

"Well, that's fine and all, I mean, if that's what you need to do, then great, have fun." I shrug, fully convinced that it's *not* at all great, though knowing better than to say it out loud. "But just how are you planning to get around now that you've ditched your ride? I mean, in case you haven't noticed, this is California, you can't get anywhere without a car."

He looks at me, clearly amused by my outburst, which is not exactly the reaction I'd planned. "What's wrong with the bus? It's free."

I gape, shaking my head, hardly believing my ears. *And since when do you worry about cost, Mr. I Make Millions Playing The Ponies And Just Manifest Whatever Else I Might Want?* Realizing just after it's out that I forgot to shield my thoughts.

"Is that how you see me?" He stops just shy of the classroom door, obviously hurt by my careless assessment. "As some shallow, materialistic, narcissistic, consumer-driven *slob*?"

"*No!*" I cry, shaking my head and squeezing his hand. Hoping to convince him even though I actually *did* kind of mean it. Only not in a bad way like he thinks. More in a *my boyfriend appreciates the finer things in life* kind of way, and less in a *my boyfriend's the male version of Stacia* kind of way. "I just—" I squint, wishing I could be even half as eloquent as him, but still forging ahead when I say, "I guess I just don't get it." I shrug. "And what's up with the glove?" I raise his leather-clad hand to where we can see.

"Isn't it obvious?" He shakes his head and pulls me toward the door.

But I just stay put, refusing to budge. Nothing's obvious. Nothing makes sense anymore.

He pauses, hand on the knob, more than a little hurt when he says, "I thought it was a good solution for now. But perhaps you'd prefer I not touch you at all?"

*No! That's not what I meant!* Switching to telepathy the moment some classmates approach, reminding him how hard it's been avoiding any and all skin-on-skin contact for the last three days. Pretending I had a cold when we both know we don't get sick, and other ridiculous avoidance techniques that left me feeling deeply ashamed. It's been torture, pure and simple. To have a boyfriend so gorgeous, so sexy, so amazingly awesome— and to not be able to touch him—is the worst kind of agony.

"I mean, I know we can't risk any accidental palm sweat exchange or anything like that, but still, don't you think it looks kind of—*odd*?" I whisper, the second we're alone again.

"I don't care about that." His gaze open, sincere, and fixed right on mine. "I don't care what other people think. I only care about *you*."

He squeezes my fingers and opens the door with his mind, leading me right past Stacia Miller as we head for our desks. And even though I haven't seen her since Friday when she woke from Roman's spell, I'm sure her hatred for me hasn't dampened a bit. But while I'm fully braced for her usual ploy of dropping her bag in my path in an attempt to trip me—today she's too distracted by Damen's new look to play that tired old game. Her unhurried gaze traveling the length of him, from his head to his toes, before starting all over again.

But just because she ignores me doesn't mean I can relax or trust that it's over. Because the truth is, it's *never* over with Stacia. She's made that abundantly clear. If anything she's probably more charged up and vicious than ever—making this little reprieve nothing more than the calm before the storm.

"Ignore her," Damen whispers, scooting his desk so close the edges practically overlap.

And even though I nod as though I am, the truth is—I can't. As much as I'd love to pretend she's invisible—I can't do it. She's in front of me now and I'm completely obsessed. Peering into her thoughts, wanting to see what, if anything, happened between them. Because even though I know Roman's responsible for all of the flirting, and kissing, and cuddling, I had no choice but to watch. Even though I know for a fact that Damen was completely deprived of free will—that doesn't change the fact that it *happened*—that Damen's lips pressed against hers while his hands roamed her skin. And even though I'm pretty sure it didn't go any further than that, I'd still feel a heck of a lot better if I could just get some evidence to back up my theory.

And despite how crazy, hurtful, and completely masochistic it is—I won't stop until her memory gives, and every last horrible, painful, excruciating detail is finally revealed.

I'm just about to delve deeper, travel to the very core of her brain, when Damen squeezes my hand and says, "Ever, please. Stop torturing yourself. I've already told you, there's *nothing* to see." I swallow hard, gaze fixed on the back of her head, watching her gossip with Honor and Craig, barely listening as he adds, "It *didn't* happen. It's not what you think."

"I thought you couldn't remember?" I turn, overcome with shame the instant I see the pain in his eyes as he looks at me and shakes his head.

"Just trust me." He sighs. "Or at least try to. *Please?*"

I inhale deeply, gazing at him, wishing I could, knowing I should.

"Seriously, Ever. First you couldn't get over the past six hundred years of my dating, and now you're obsessed with last week?" He knits his brow and leans closer, voice urgent, coaxing, as he adds, "I know that your feelings are unbelievably hurt. Really, I do. But what's done is done. I can't go back, I can't change it. Roman's done this on purpose—you can't let him win."

I swallow hard, knowing he's right. I'm acting ridiculous, irrational, allowing myself to veer way off track.

*Besides,* Damen thinks, switching to telepathy now that our teacher, Mr. Robins, has arrived. *You know it's meaningless. The only one I've ever loved is you. Isn't that enough?*

He brings his gloved thumb to my temple, gazing into my eyes as he shows me our history, my many incarnations as a young servant girl in France, a Puritan's daughter in New England, a flirtatious British socialite, an artist's muse with gorgeous red hair—

I gape, eyes wide, never having seen that particular life before.

But he just smiles, gaze growing warmer as he shows me the highlights of that time, a quick clip of the moment we met—at a gallery opening in Amsterdam—our first kiss just outside of the gallery that very same night. Presenting only the most romantic moments and sparing my death, which always, inevitably, comes before we can progress.

And after watching all of those beautiful moments unfold, his unabashed love for me laid bare to see, I gaze into his eyes, answering his question when I think: *Of course it's enough. You've always been enough.*

Then closing them in shame when I add: *But am I enough for you?*

Finally admitting the *real* truth—my fear that he'll soon tire of the gloved hand-holding, the telepathic embrace, and seek out the real thing in a normal girl with safe DNA.

He nods, gloved fingers cupping my chin as he gathers me into a mental embrace so warm, so safe, so comforting, all of my fears slip away. Answering the apology in my gaze as he leans forward, lips at my ear as he says, "Good. Now that that's settled, about Roman . . ."

# four

As I make my way toward history class I'm wondering which will be worse—seeing Roman or Mr. Munoz? Because while I haven't seen or spoken to either of them since last Friday when my whole world fell apart—there's no doubt I left them both on a pretty strange note. My last contact with Munoz consisting of me going all sentimental and not only confiding my psychic powers—which is something I *never* do—but also encouraging him to date my aunt Sabine—which is something I'm *seriously* beginning to regret. And as awful as that was, it's only rivaled by my last moments with Roman when I aimed my fist at his navel chakra, determined not just to kill him but to *obliterate* him completely. And I would have too—except for the fact that I totally choked and he got away. And even though in retrospect that probably worked out for the best, I'm still so angry with him, who's to say I won't try again?

But the truth is, *I* know I won't try again. And not just because Damen spent the whole of English class telepathically lecturing me on how revenge is *never* the answer, how karma is the one and only true justice system, and plenty more *blah blah blah* like that—but mostly because it's not right. Despite the fact that Roman tricked me in the very worst way, leaving me absolutely no reason to ever trust him again—I still don't have the right to kill him. It won't solve my problem. Won't change a thing. Even though he's awful, evil, and everything that adds up to *bad*, I still don't have the right to—

"Well there's my cheeky monkey!"

He slithers up beside me, all blond tousled hair, ocean blue eyes, and shiny white teeth, leisurely stretching his strong, tanned arm across the classroom door, barring me from getting inside.

And that's all it takes. The grating purr of his contrived British accent and the complete creepiness of his leering gaze, and just like *that* I'm tempted to kill him again.

But I won't.

I promised Damen I could get myself safely to and from class without resorting to that.

"So tell me, Ever, how *was* your weekend? Did you and Damen enjoy a nice reunion? Was he able to—*survive* you—by chance?"

I clench my fists by my sides, imagining how he'd look as nothing more than a heap of designer clothes and a pile of dust, despite the vow of nonviolence I took.

"Because if not, if you failed to heed my advice and took that old dinosaur out for a ride, then I suppose my deepest condolences are in order." He nods, gaze fixed on mine, lowering his voice as he adds, "Not to worry though, you won't be alone for long. Once the proper mourning period ends, I'll be happy to step in and fill up the void his extinction has left."

I focus on my breath, keeping it slow and steady as I take in the strong, tan, muscular arm blocking my path, knowing all it would take is one well-placed karate chop to break it in half.

"Hell, even if you did manage to hold back and keep him alive, all you have to do is say the word, and I'm right by your side." He grins, eyes grazing over me in the most intimate way. "But no need to answer too quickly or commit yourself yet. Take as long as you like. Because, Ever, I assure you, unlike Damen, I'm a man who can wait. Besides, it's just a matter of time before you come looking for me anyway."

"There's only one thing I want from you." I narrow my gaze until everything surrounding us blurs. "And that's for you to leave me alone." Heat rising to my cheeks as his gaze deepens to a leer.

"'Fraid not, darlin'." He laughs, looking me over and shaking his head. "Trust me, you want way more than that. But not to worry, it's like I said, I'll wait for as long as it takes. It's Damen I'm worried about. And you should worry too. From what I saw those last six hundred years, he's an impatient man. Bit of a hedonist really. Didn't wait for much of anything so far as I could tell."

I swallow hard and strive to keep calm, reminding myself not to fall for his bait. Roman has a knack for locating my weakness, my psychological kryptonite so to speak, and pretty much lives to exploit it.

"Don't get me wrong, he's always been one to keep up appearances—wearing the black armband, appearing inconsolable at the wake—but trust me, Ever, the moss hadn't time to adhere to his shoe before he was back on the prowl. Looking to drown his sorrows in whatever or—should I say *whomever*—he could. And even though you prefer not to believe it, take it from someone who's been there all along. Damen waits for *no one*. And he certainly never waited for *you*."

I take a deep breath, filling my head with words, music, mathematical equations stretching far beyond my abilities, anything to drown out the words that are like carefully honed arrows aimed straight for my heart.

"*Yep. Sawr it wit me own eyes, I did!*" Smiling as he slips into a thick cockney brogue and back out again. "Drina saw it too. Broke her poor heart. Though, unlike me—and, I'm afraid, quite unlike you—Drina's love was unconditional. Willing to take him back no matter where he'd been, no questions asked. Which, let's face it, is something *you'd* never do."

"That's not true!" I cry, voice hoarse, dry, as though it's the first time I've used it all day. "I've had Damen since the moment we met—I—" I stop, knowing I shouldn't have started. It's useless to engage in this fight.

"Sorry, darlin', but you're wrong. You've never *had* Damen at all. A chaste kiss here, a bit of sweaty hand-holding there—" He shrugs, gaze mocking. "Seriously, Ever, you think some pathetic attempts at second base can actually satisfy a greedy, narcissistic, self-indulgent bloke like him? For *four hundred years* no less?"

I swallow hard, forcing a calm I don't own when I say, "That's a lot further than you ever got with Drina."

"No thanks to you," he spits, harsh gaze on mine. "But, it's like I said, I'm a man who can wait. Damen is *not*." He shakes his head. "Shame you're so determined to play hard to get. You and I are a lot more alike than you think. Both of us pining after someone we'll never truly have—"

"I could kill you right now," I whisper, voice shaky, hands trembling, even though I promised Damen I wouldn't do this, even though I know better. "I could—" I suck in my breath, not wanting him to know what only Damen and I know, that targeting an immortal's weakest chakra, one of the body's seven energy centers, is the quickest way to obliterate them.

"You could what?" He smiles, face looming so close his breath chills my cheek. "Slug me in my sacral center, perhaps?"

I gape, wondering where he could've possibly learned that.

But he just laughs, shaking his head as he says, "Don't forget, luv, Damen was under my spell, which means he told me *everything*, answered *every* question I asked—including a good bit about *you*."

I stand there, refusing to react, determined to appear composed, unruffled—but it's too late. He got me. Right where it counts. And don't think he doesn't know it.

"No worries, luv. I've no plans to go after you. Even though your glaring lack of discernment and tragic misuse of knowledge tells me that a quick jab to the throat chakra is all it would take to destroy you for good—" He smiles, tongue snaking around his lips. "I'm having far too much fun watching you squirm to attempt something like that. Besides, it won't be long 'til you're squirming beneath me. Or even on top of me. Either will do." He laughs, blue eyes on mine, gazing at me in a way so knowing, so intimate, so deep, my stomach can't help but heave. "I'll leave the details to you. But no matter how much you may want to, you won't go after me either. Mostly because I *do* have what you want. The antidote to the antidote. I assure you of that. You're just gonna have to find a way to earn it. You're just gonna have to pay the *right* price."

I gape, dry mouthed and slack jawed, remembering last Friday when he claimed the very same thing. So distracted by Damen awakening I forgot all about it 'til now.

I press my lips together as my gaze meets his, my hope rising for the first time in days, knowing it's just a matter of time until the antidote is mine. I just need to find a way to get it from him.

"Oh, look at that." He smirks. "Seems you forgot all about our date with destiny."

He lifts his arm and I start to plow through, then he lowers it just as quickly, laughing as he locks me in place.

"Deep breaths," he coos, lips grazing the edge of my ear, fingers sliding over my shoulder, leaving an icy cold wake in their path. "No need to panic. No need to get all *spazzed* out again. I'm sure that between us, we can come to some sort of mutual agreement, find a way to work something out."

I narrow my gaze, disgusted by the price that he's set, words slow and deliberate when I say, "Nothing you could ever *say* or *do* could convince me to sleep with *you*!" just as Mr. Munoz opens the door, allowing the entire class to overhear.

"Whoa—" Roman smiles, hands raised in mock surrender as he backs into the room. "Who said anything about bumpin' uglies, mate?" He throws his head back and laughs, allowing his creepy Ouroboros tattoo to flash in and out of view. "I mean, not to disappoint you, darlin', but if it's a good shag I'm after, a virgin's about the last place I'd look!"

I storm toward my desk, cheeks burning, gaze fixed on the floor, spending the next forty minutes cringing as my classmates burst into hysterics every time Roman directs a disgusting wet smoochy sound my way, despite Munoz's numerous attempts to quiet them down. And the moment the bell rings, I make a run for the door. Desperate to get to Damen before Roman can, convinced Roman will push him too far and he'll snap—an act neither of us can afford now that Roman holds the key.

But just as I turn the knob I hear, "Ever? Got a minute?"

I pause, classmates piling up behind me, eager to get to the hall where they can follow Roman's lead and taunt me some more. His mocking laughter trailing behind as I turn toward Munoz to see what he wants.

"I did it." He smiles, posture stiff, voice anxious, but still eager for me to know.

I shift uncomfortably, moving my bag from one shoulder to the next, wishing I'd taken the time to learn remote viewing so I could keep an eye on the lunch tables and ensure Damen sticks to the plan.

"I approached her. Just like you told me to." He nods.

I squint, returning my focus to him, gut churning as I begin to understand.

"The woman from Starbucks? Sabine? I saw her this morning. We even talked for a while, and—" He shrugs, gaze drifting away, obviously still very taken by the event.

I stand before him, breathless, knowing I have to stop it, whatever it takes, before it gets out of hand.

"And you were right. She *is* really nice. In fact, I probably shouldn't tell you but we're having dinner this Friday night."

I nod, numb, shell-shocked, the words glancing over me as I peer into his energy and watch it unfold in his head:

*Sabine standing in line, minding her own business until Munoz approaches—causing her to turn and grant him a smile that's— that's—shamefully flirtatious!*

Except that there's no shame at all. At least not on Sabine's part. Nor Munoz for that matter. No, the shame is all mine. Those two couldn't be happier.

This *cannot* happen. For too many reasons to mention this dinner can never take place. One of them being that Sabine is not just my aunt, but my guardian, my caretaker, my only living relative in the whole entire world! And another, possibly even more urgent reason, is the fact that, thanks to my pathetic, maudlin, overly sentimental, ill-advised moment of weakness last Friday, Munoz knows I'm psychic while Sabine does *not*!

I've gone to great lengths to keep my secret from her, and there's no way I'm going to be outed by my love-struck history teacher.

But just as I'm about to tell him that he absolutely cannot, under any circumstances whatsoever, take my aunt to dinner and/or divulge any information I might've accidentally confessed during a weak moment when I was sure I'd never see him again, he clears his throat and says, "Anyway, you should get to lunch before it's too late. I didn't mean to keep you this long, I just thought—"

"Oh, no, it's okay," I say. "I just—"

But he doesn't let me finish. Practically pushes me out the door as he waves me away, saying, "Go on now. Go find your friends. I just thought I should thank you, that's all."

# five

When I get to the lunch table I sit beside Damen, relieved to find everything as normal as any other day. Damen's gloved hand squeezing my knee as I quickly scan the campus, looking for Roman as he thinks: *He's gone.*

*Gone?* I gape, hoping he means *gone* as in *not around*, as opposed to *gone* as in *pile of dust.*

But Damen just laughs, the smooth melodic sound reverberating from his head to mine. *Not annihilated. I assure you. Just— absent—that's all. Drove off a few minutes ago with some guy I've never seen before.*

*Did you talk? Did he try to provoke you?* Damen shakes his head, his eyes peering into mine as I add: *Good. Because we can't afford to go after him—no matter what! He has the antidote! He admitted it! Which means all we have to do now is find a way to—*

*Ever.* He frowns. *You can't possibly believe him! This is what Roman does. He lies and manipulates everyone around him. You have to stay away from him—he's using you—he can't be trusted—*

I shake my head. This time is different. I can feel it. And I need for Damen to feel it too. *He's not lying—seriously—he said—*

Not even finishing the thought before Haven leans forward, eyes darting between us as she says, "Okay, that's it. Just what the heck is going on here? Seriously, enough already."

I turn, noticing how her friendly yellow aura beams in such sudden sharp contrast to the deliberate harshness of her all-black ensemble. Knowing she means no ill will though she's definitely disturbed by us.

"Seriously. It's like—it's like you guys have some kind of creepy way of communicating. Like twin speak or something. Only yours is silent. And more eerie."

I shrug and open my lunch pack, going through the motions of unwrapping a sandwich I've no plans to eat, determined to hide just how alarmed her question has made me. Knocking my knee against Damen's, telepathically urging him to step in and handle this since I've no idea what to say.

"Don't pretend it's not happening." Her eyes narrow in suspicion. "I've been watching you guys for a while now, and it's really starting to creep me out."

"What's creeping you out?" Miles gazes up from his phone, but only for a moment before he's back to texting again.

"Those two." She points a short, black painted nail with a chunk of pink frosting stuck to its tip. "I swear, they get stranger every day."

Miles nods, setting down his phone as he takes a moment to look us over. "Yeah, I've been meaning to mention that. You guys are weird." He laughs. "Oh, and the whole Michael Jackson, one glove thing?" He shakes his head and purses his lips. "*So* not working for you. That look is so played even *you* can't bring it back."

Haven frowns, annoyed by Miles's joke when she's trying to be serious. "Laugh all you want," she says, gaze steady, unwavering. "But something's up with those two. I may not know what, but I'll figure it out. I'll get to the bottom of it. You'll see."

And I'm just about to speak when Damen shakes his head and swirls his red drink, leaning toward Haven as he says, "Don't waste your time. It's not as sinister as you think." He smiles, gaze fixed on hers. "We're practicing telepathy, that's all. Attempting to read each other's minds in place of talking all the time. So we stop getting in trouble in class." He laughs, causing me to squeeze my sandwich so hard the mayonnaise squirts out the sides. Gaping at my boyfriend who's just arbitrarily decided to break our number one rule—*Don't tell anyone who we are or what we can do!*

Calming only slightly when Haven rolls her eyes and says, "Please. I'm not an idiot."

"Wasn't implying you were." Damen smiles. "It's quite real, I assure you. Would you like to try?"

I freeze, body solid, unmoving, as though witnessing a disaster on the side of the road—only this particular disaster is *me*.

"Close your eyes and think of a number between one and ten." He nods, solemn gaze meeting hers. "Focus on that number with all of your might. *See* it in your mind as clearly as you can, and silently repeat the sound of it over and over again. Got it?"

She shrugs, brows merging as though in deep concentration. Though all it takes is a quick glance at her aura, morphing into a dark deceitful green, and a brief peek at her thoughts to *see* she's only pretending. Choosing to concentrate on the color blue instead of a random number like Damen said.

I glance between them, knowing she's baiting him, sure that his one in ten chance of hitting the right number works too much in his favor. Holding her ground as he rubs his chin and shakes his head, saying, "I don't seem to be getting anything. Are you *sure* you're thinking of a number between one and ten?"

She nods, deepening her focus on a beautiful shade of pulsating blue.

"Then we must have our wires crossed." He shrugs. "I'm not getting a number at all."

"Try me!" Miles abandons his phone and leans toward Damen.

Eyes barely closed, thoughts hardly focused before Damen gasps, "You're going to *Florence*?"

Miles shakes his head. "*Three.* For your information, the number was *three.*" He rolls his eyes and smirks. "And by the way, *everyone* knows I'm going to Florence. So—nice try."

"Everyone but *me*," Damen says, jaws clenched, face gone suddenly pale.

"Well, I'm sure Ever told you. You know, *telepathically.*" He laughs, returning to his phone again.

I peer at Damen, wondering why he's so upset over Miles's trip. I mean, yeah, so he used to live there, but that was hundreds of years ago! I squeeze his hand, urging him to look at me, but he just stares at Miles with that same stricken look on his face.

"Nice try with the whole telepathy angle," Haven says, swiping her finger across the top of her cupcake until it's coated with strawberry frosting. "But I'm afraid you're gonna have to try a little harder than that. All you've managed to prove is that you guys are even weirder than I thought. But no worries, I'll get to the bottom of it. I'll expose your dirty little secret before long."

I hold back a nervous laugh, hoping she's just messing around, then peering into her mind only to *see* that she's serious.

"When are you leaving?" Damen asks, but only to appear conversational, having already uncovered the answer in Miles's head.

"Soon, but not soon enough," Miles says, eyes lighting up. "Let the countdown begin!"

Damen nods, gaze softening as he says, "You'll love it. Everyone loves it. *Firenze* is a beautiful, charming place."

"You've been?" Miles and Haven both ask at the same time.

Damen nods, gaze far away. "I lived there once—a long time ago."

Haven glances between us, eyes narrowed again when she says, "Drina and Roman lived there too."

Damen shrugs, expression noncommittal, as though the connection means nothing to him.

"Well, don't you think that's a little strange? All of you living in Italy, in the same *place*, then all of you ending up *here*—within months of each other?" She leans toward him, abandoning her cupcake in search of some answers.

But Damen's solid, refusing to cave or do anything that might give it away. He just sips his red drink and lifts his shoulders again, as though it's hardly worth going into.

"Is there anything I should see while I'm there?" Miles asks, more to break the tension than anything else. "Anything that shouldn't be missed?"

Damen squints, pretending to think, even though the answer comes quickly. "All of Florence is worth seeing. But you should definitely check out the Ponte Vecchio, which is the first bridge to cross the Arno River and the only one left standing after the war. Oh, and you must visit the Galleria dell'Accademia which houses Michelangelo's *David* among other important works, and perhaps the—"

"Definitely hitting *David*," Miles says. "As well as the bridge, and the famous Il Duomo, and all the other items that make every guidebook top ten list, but I'm more interested in the smaller, off-the-beaten-path kind of places—you know, where all the cool Florentines go. Roman was raving about this one place, I forget the name, but it's supposed to house some obscure Renaissance artifacts and paintings and stuff few people know about. You got anything like that? Or even clubs, shopping, that kind of thing?"

Damen looks at him, gaze so intense it sends a chill down my spine. "Nothing offhand," he says, trying to soften the look though his voice betrays a definite edge. "Though any place that claims to house great art but isn't in the guidebook is probably a fake. The antiquities market is loaded with forgeries. You shouldn't waste your time on that when there are so many other, far more interesting things to see."

Miles shrugs, bored by the conversation and already back to texting again. "Whatever," he mumbles, thumbs tapping quickly. "No worries. Roman said he'd make me a list."

# six

"I'm amazed by the progress you've made." Damen smiles. "You learned all this on your own?"

I nod, gazing around the large, empty room, pleased with myself for the first time in weeks.

The moment Damen mentioned he wanted to rid the place of all the overly slick furniture he'd filled it with during Roman's reign of terror, I was on it. Jumping at the chance to clear out the row of black leather recliners and flat-screen TVs, the red felt pool table and chrome-covered bar—all of them symbols, physical manifestations, of the bleakest phase in our relationship so far. Taking aim at each piece with such unchecked enthusiasm that—well—I'm not even sure where it went. All I know is it's no longer here.

"Looks like you're no longer in need of my lessons." He shakes his head.

"Don't be so sure." I turn, smiling as I push his dark wavy hair off his face with my newly gloved hand, hoping we'll get that cure from Roman soon, or at least come up with a less hokey alternative. "I have no idea where that stuff even went—not to mention how I can't possibly fill up this space when I have no clue where you stashed all the stuff you used to have." Reaching for his hand a second too late, and frowning as he walks over to the window.

"The furniture"—he gazes out at his manicured lawn, voice low and deep—"is right back where it started. Returned to its original state of pure vibrating energy with the potential to become anything at all. And as for the rest—" He shrugs, the strong lines of his shoulders rising ever so slightly before settling again. "Well, it hardly matters anymore, does it? I've no need of it now."

I stare at his back, taking in his lean form, his casual stance. Wondering how he could be so uninterested in reclaiming the precious artifacts of his past—the Picasso of him in the severe blue suit, the Velázquez astride a rearing white stallion—not to mention all the other amazing relics dating back centuries.

"But those objects are priceless! You have to get them back. They can never be replaced!"

"Ever, relax. It's just *stuff*." His voice firm, resigned, as he turns toward me again. "None of it has any *real* meaning. The only thing that means anything is *you*."

And even though the sentiment is undeniably sweet and heartfelt, it doesn't affect me in the way that it should. The only things he seems to care about these days is atoning for his karma and me. And while I'm perfectly fine with those occupying the number one and two spots on his list, the problem is—the rest of the page is blank.

"But that's where you're wrong. It's *not* just stuff." I move toward him, voice urging, coaxing, hoping to reach him and make him listen this time. "Signed books by Shakespeare and the Brontë sisters, chandeliers from Marie Antoinette and Louis the Sixteenth—that's hardly what you'd call *stuff*. It's *history* for God's sake! You can't just shrug it off as though it's nothing more than a box of tired old objects you donate to Goodwill."

He looks at me, gaze softening as he trails the tip of his gloved finger from my temple to my chin. "I thought you hated my 'dusty old room' as you once called it."

"People change." I shrug. Wishing, not for the first time, that *he'd* change back to the Damen I knew. "And speaking of change, why are you so freaked by Miles's trip to Florence?" Noting the way he stiffens at the mere mention of the word. "Is it because of the whole Drina and Roman thing? The connection you don't want him to know about?"

He looks at me for a moment, lips parting, about to speak, then he turns away and mumbles, "I'm hardly what you'd call *freaked*."

"You know what? You're absolutely right. For a normal person, that was hardly what you'd call *freaked*. But for the guy who's always the coolest, calmest one in the room—all it takes is the slight narrowing of your eyes and the most minute clenching of your jaw to know you're upset."

He sighs, eyes searching mine as he moves toward me again. "You saw what happened in Florence." He squints. "Despite all its virtues, it's also a place of unbearable memories, ones I'd rather not explore."

I swallow hard, remembering the images I viewed in Summerland—Damen hiding in a small dark cupboard, watching as his parents were murdered by thugs intent on obtaining the elixir—then later, abused as a ward of the church until the Black Plague swept through Florence and he encouraged Drina and the rest of the orphans to drink the immortal juice, hoping only to heal and having no idea it would grant eternal life—and I can't help but feel like the world's worst girlfriend for bringing it up.

"I prefer to focus on the present." He nods, gesturing around the large empty room. "And right now I really need your help furnishing this space. According to my Realtor, buyers like a nice, clean, contemporary look when shopping for homes. And though I was thinking of leaving it empty, to really emphasize the size of the rooms, I suppose we should try—"

"Your *Realtor*?" I gasp, practically choking on the word as my voice raises several octaves at the end. "What could you possibly need a *Realtor* for?"

"I'm selling the house." He shrugs. "I thought you understood?"

I gaze around, longing for that ancient velvet settee with the lumpy cushions, knowing it would provide the perfect landing for when my body collapses and my head quietly explodes.

But I just stand there instead, determined to keep it together. Gazing at my ridiculously gorgeous boyfriend of the last four hundred years as though it's the first time we've met.

"Don't look so upset. Nothing's changed. It's just a house. A seriously oversized house. Besides, I've never needed all this space anyway. I never even use most of these rooms."

"And what exactly are you planning to replace it with, then? *A tent?*"

"I just thought I'd downsize, that's all." His gaze is pleading, begging me to understand. "Nothing sinister, Ever. Nothing meant to hurt you."

"And is your Realtor going to help with that too? With the *downsizing*?" Studying him closely, wondering what's gotten into him, and where this will end. "I mean, Damen, if you're seriously looking to downsize, why not just manifest something smaller? Why are you choosing this conventional route?"

I flick my gaze over him, moving from his glorious head of longish dark glossy hair to his perfect rubber flip-flop–shod feet, remembering how, not so long ago, I longed to be normal again, just like everyone else. But now that I'm getting used to my powers I don't see the point.

"What's this really about?" I squint, feeling more than a little betrayed. "I mean, you're the one who got me here. You're the one who *made* me this way. And now that I'm finally adjusted, you decide to jump ship? Seriously. Why are you doing this?"

But instead of answering, he closes his eyes. Projecting an image of the two of us laughing and happy, frolicking on a beautiful, pink-sand beach.

But I just shake my head and cross my arms tighter, refusing to play until my questions are answered.

He sighs and stares out the window, turning toward me when he says, "I've already told you, my only recourse, my only way out of this hell of my making, is to atone for my karma. And the only way to do that is to forego the manifesting, the high life, the big spending, and all the other extravagances I've indulged myself in for the last six hundred years, so I can live the life of an ordinary citizen. Honest, hard working, and humble, with the same day-to-day struggles as anyone else."

I stare at him, replaying his words in my head, hardly believing what I just heard. "And how exactly are you planning to do that?" I squint. "Seriously. In your six centuries of living, have you ever even held a real job?"

But even though I'm dead serious and not at all joking, he throws his head back and laughs like I was. Eventually calming down enough to say, "You honestly think no one will hire me?" He shakes his head and laughs even harder. "Ever, please. Don't you think I've been around long enough to have honed a few skills?"

I start to respond, wanting to explain that while it's truly remarkable to watch him paint a Picasso better than Picasso with one hand while simultaneously outdoing Van Gogh with the other, I really don't think that'll help him land that coveted barista position at the Starbucks on the corner.

But before I can say it, he's standing beside me, moving with such speed and grace all I can manage is, "Well, for someone who's turned his back on his gifts, you still move awfully fast." Aware of that warm wonderful tingle swarming my skin as he slips his arms around my waist and pulls me close to his chest, carefully avoiding skin-on-skin contact. "And what about telepathy?" I whisper. "Are you planning to ditch that too?" So overcome by his proximity I can barely eke out the words.

"I've no plans to ditch anything that brings me closer to you," he says, gaze on mine, steady and still. "As for the rest—" He shrugs, glancing around the large empty space before finding me again. "Tell me, what matters more, Ever? The size of my house—or the size of my heart?"

I bite my lip and avert my gaze, the truth of his words leaving me feeling small and ashamed.

"Does it really matter if I choose the bus over a BMW, and generic over Gucci? Because the car, the wardrobe, the zip code—those are just nouns, things that are fun to have around, sure, but in the end, they have nothing to do with the real me. Nothing to do with who I *really* am."

I swallow hard, focusing on anything but him. It's not that I care about his BMW or faux French chateaux, I mean, if I want those things I'll just manifest them myself. But even though they aren't important, if I'm going to be honest then I have to admit they were part of the initial attraction—adding to his sleek, shiny, mysterious persona that lured me right in.

But when I finally look at him again, standing before me, stripped bare of all the usual dazzle and flash, honed down to the very essence of who he really is, I realize he's still the same, warm, wonderful guy he's been all along. Which just proves his point. None of that other stuff matters.

None of it has anything to do with his soul.

I smile, suddenly remembering the one place where we can be together—safe and secure and protected from harm. Reaching for his gloved hand as I grasp it in mine, saying, "Come on, I want to show you something," and pulling him along.

## seven

At first I was worried he'd refuse to visit a place that not only requires a certain amount of magick for entry, but that is nothing but magick once you arrive. But just after landing in that vast fragrant field, he wipes the seat of his jeans and offers his hand, gazing all around as he says, "Wow. I don't think I was ever able to make the portal so quickly."

"Please, you're the one who taught me." I smile, gazing at the meadow of pulsating flowers and shivering trees, noting how everything here is reduced to its absolute purest form of beauty and energy.

I tilt my head back, closing my eyes against the warm hazy glow and shimmering mist. Remembering the last time I was here, how I danced with a manifest Damen in this very same field, delaying the moment when I'd have to let go.

"So you're okay with being here?" I ask, unsure just how far his ban on magick extends. "You're not mad?"

He shakes his head and takes my hand. "I never grow tired

of Summerland. It's a manifestation of beauty and promise in its purest form."

We make our way through the pasture, buoyed by the grass just under our feet as our fingers graze the tops of golden wild-flowers that bend and sway alongside us. Knowing anything is possible in this wonderful place, anything at all, including—just maybe—us.

"I missed this." He smiles, gazing all around. "Not that I re-member the last few weeks without it, but still, it seems like such a long time since we were last here."

"It felt strange coming without you," I say, leading him to-ward a beautiful Balinese-style cabana perched beside the rainbow-colored stream. "Though I did discover a whole other side I can't wait to show you. Only later—not now."

I push the gauzy white fabric aside and plop onto the soft white cushions, smiling as Damen lands right beside me, the two of us lying side by side, gazing up at the elaborately carved coconut beams. Heads together, the soles of our feet just a few inches shy—the result of my elixir-fueled growth spurt.

"What is this?" He turns onto his side as I draw the curtains closed with my mind. Eager to shut out all that surrounds us so we can enjoy our own private space.

"I saw one on the cover of a travel magazine featuring some exotic resort, and I liked it so much I thought I'd manifest one. You know, so we could—hang out—and—*stuff*." I avert my gaze, heart racing, face flushing, knowing I'm quite possibly the most pathetic seductress he's met in his six hundred years.

But he just laughs, pulling me so close we just nearly touch. Separated only by the slimmest veil of shimmering energy, a pulsating screen that hovers between us—allowing us to be near without harming each other.

I close my eyes, surrendering to the wave of warmth and tingle as our bodies come together. Two hearts pumping in perfect unison, reaching and retreating, expanding and retracting, the tempo perfectly synchronized as though beating as one. Everything about it feeling so good, so natural, so *right*, I snuggle closer. Nestling my face in the hollow where his shoulder meets his neck, longing to taste his sweet skin and inhale his warm musky scent. A low moan escaping from deep in his throat as I close my eyes and press into his hips, my tongue tipped toward his skin, only to have him spring from my reach so fast I'm met with a mouthful of cushion.

I scramble upright, seeing him move so quickly he's reduced to a blur. Stopping only when he's safely ensconced on the other side of the curtain, eyes blazing, body trembling, as I beg him to tell me what happened.

I move toward him, wanting to help. But just as I get close, he moves again, hand held before him, gaze warning me away.

"Don't touch me," he says. "Please, stay right where you are. Don't come any closer."

"But—*why?*" My voice hoarse, unstable, hands trembling by my sides. "Did I do something wrong? I just thought—well—because we're here—and since nothing bad can happen in Summerland— I just thought it would be okay if we maybe tried to—"

"Ever, it's not that—it's—" He shakes his head, his eyes darker than I've ever seen them. So dark the irises are indistinguishable from the pupils, blending right in. "And who says nothing bad can happen here?" His tone so edgy, gaze so harsh, it's clear he's traveled a very long way from his usual state of infallible calm.

I swallow hard and stare at the ground, feeling foolish, ridiculous—to think I was so desperate to be with my boyfriend I risked taking his life.

"I guess—I just assumed . . ." My voice fades, knowing very well what happens when one assumes. Not only do you make an *ass* out of *u* and *me,* but in this particular case, that very same *u* just might end up dead. "I'm sorry." I shake my head, knowing it's completely inadequate considering the life-and-death circumstances we're in. "I—I guess I didn't think it through. I don't know what to say."

I pull my shoulders in, wrapping my arms around my waist, trying to make myself smaller, so small I'll disappear from his sight. And yet, I can't help but wonder exactly what kind of bad thing could happen in a place where magick comes easily, and wounds are healed instantly. I mean, if we're not safe here, then *where?*

Damen looks at me, answering the thought in my head when he says, "Summerland contains the possibility of *all* things. So far, we've only seen the light, but who's to say there's not a dark side? Maybe it's not at all what we think."

I gaze at him, remembering when I first met Romy and Rayne and how they said something similar. Watching as he manifests a beautifully carved wood bench, then motions for me to sit.

"Come." He nods, urging me toward him as I take a seat at the far end, not wanting to get too close and risk setting him off again. "There's something you need to see—something you need to understand. So please just close your eyes and clear your mind of any random thoughts and clutter as best you can. Keeping yourself open and receptive to any visions I send. Can you do that?"

I nod, eyes shut tight, doing my best to sweep my mind of such thoughts as: *What's going on? Is he mad at me? Of course he's mad at me! How could I be so stupid? But how mad is he? Is it possible to change his mind and start over again?* My usual paranoid playlist set on permanent repeat.

But even after clearing it out and waiting for what feels like a reasonable amount of time, all I've gotten so far is a heavy void of dense solid black.

"I don't get it," I say, opening one eye and peeking at him.

But he just shakes his head, eyes shut tight, brows merged in concentration, as he continues to focus with all of his might. "Listen," he says. "And look deep down inside. Just close your eyes and *receive*."

I take a deep breath and try again, but still, all I get is a foreboding silence and the feeling of black empty space.

"Um, I'm really sorry," I whisper, not wanting to upset him but sure that I'm missing the point. "I'm not getting much of anything other than silence and darkness."

"Exactly," he whispers, unfazed by my words. "Now please, take hold of my hand and go deeper, delve past the surface using all of your senses, then tell me what you see."

I take a deep breath and do as he says, reaching for his hand and pushing past the solid wall of black, but all I get is more of the same.

Until—

Until—

I'm sucked into a black hole, limbs flailing, unable to stop or slow down. Free-falling into the darkness, my horrible high-pitched scream the only sound. And just as I'm sure that this fall has no end—it stops. The scream. The fall. All of it. Everything. Leaving me to hang there. Untethered. Suspended. Completely alone in this solitary place with no beginning or end. Lost in this dark and dismal abyss with no trace of light coming in. Abandoned in this infinite void, a lost and lonely world of permanent midnight. The horrible realization slowly dawning on me—*This is where I live now.*

*A hell with no escape.*

I try to run, scream, cry for help—but it's no use. I'm frozen, paralyzed, unable to speak—completely alone for all of eternity. Purposely held apart from everything I know and love— cut off from everything that *exists.* Knowing I've no choice but to surrender as my mind goes blank and my body limp.

There's no use in fighting when no one can save me.

I remain like that, solitary, eternal, a shadowy awareness creeping upon me, tugging from a place just outside of my reach—

Until—

Until—

I'm yanked out of that hell and into Damen's arms, relieved to see his beautiful, anxious face hovering over me.

"I'm so sorry—I thought I'd lost you—I thought you'd never come back!" he cries, holding me tight, his voice like a sob in my ear.

I cling to him, body shaking, heart racing, clothes drenched with sweat. Never having felt so isolated before—so *disconnected*—from everything. From e*very—living—thing.* Hugging him tighter, unwilling to let go, my mind connecting with his, asking why he chose to put me through that.

He pulls away, cupping my face in his hands as his eyes search mine. "I'm sorry. I wasn't trying to punish you, or harm you in any way. I only wanted to show you something, something you needed to experience firsthand in order to understand."

I nod, not trusting my voice. Still shaken from an experience so awful it felt like the death of my soul.

"My God!" His eyes widen. "That's it! That's exactly what it is. The soul ceases to exist!"

"I don't understand," I say, voice hoarse, shaky. "What *was* that horrible place?"

He looks away, fingers squeezing mine when he says, "The future. The Shadowland. The eternal abyss I'd thought was meant only for me—that I'd *hoped* was meant only for me . . ." He closes his eyes and shakes his head. "But now I know better. Now I know that if you're not careful, *extremely* careful—you'll go there too."

I look at him, starting to speak, but he cuts me off before I can get to the words. "The past few days I've been getting these flashes—glimpses, really—of various moments from my past— both distant and near." He looks at me, carefully searching my face. "But the moment we came here—" He gestures around. "It started trickling back, slowly at first until it all came surging forth, including the moments I was under Roman's control. I also relived my death. Those few brief moments after you broke through the circle, before you had me drink the antidote, as you know, I was dying. I watched my entire life flash before me, six hundred years of unchecked vanity, narcissism, selfishness, and greed. Like an endless reel of all of my actions, every misdeed that I'd done—accompanied by the impact I had—the mental and physical effect of my mistreatment of others. And though there were a few decent acts here and there, the majority, well, it amounted to centuries of me focusing on nothing but my own self-interest, giving very little thought to anything or anyone else. Focusing solely on the physical world to the detriment of my soul. Leaving me no doubt I was right all along, my karma's to blame for what we're going through now." He shakes his head and meets my gaze with such unflinching honesty I want to reach out and touch him, hold him, tell him it will all be okay. But instead I stay put, sensing there's more and it's about to get worse.

"Then, at the moment of my death, instead of coming here, to Summerland—" His voice cracks but he forces himself to continue. "I—I went to a place the exact opposite of this. A place so dark and cold it's more like a Shadowland. Experiencing the same thing you just did. Solitary, suspended, alone—left to stay that way for all of eternity." He looks at me, willing me to understand. "It was exactly like you felt. It was as though I was isolated, soulless—with no connection to anything or anyone else."

I stare into his eyes, an ominous chill blanketing my skin, never having seen him so tired, so jaded, so—*regretful*—before.

"And now I understand the very thing that's escaped me all these years—"

I pull my knees to my chest, shielding myself from whatever comes next.

"Only our physical bodies are immortal. Our souls are most certainly *not*."

I avert my gaze, unable to look at him, unable to breathe.

"This is the future you're facing. The one I've granted you, if, God forbid, anything should happen, that is."

My fingers instinctively fly to my throat, remembering what Roman said about my compromised chakra, my lack of discernment and weakness, wondering if there's some way to guard it. "But—how can you be sure?" I look at him as though caught in a dream, some horrible nightmare with no way to escape. "I mean, there's a good chance you're wrong since it happened so fast. So maybe that was just a temporary state. You know, like I brought you back to life so fast you didn't have time to make the trip here."

He shakes his head, his gaze meeting mine when he says, "Tell me, Ever, what did you see when *you* died? How did you spend those few moments between the time when your soul left your body and I returned you to life?"

I swallow hard and look away, gazing at the trees, the flowers, the colorful stream flowing nearby—remembering that day I found myself in this very same field. So taken by its heady fragrance, its shimmering mist, the all-encompassing feel of unconditional love, I was tempted to linger forever, never wanting to leave.

"The reason you didn't see the abyss is because you were still mortal. You'd died a *mortal's death*. But the moment I had you drink from the elixir, granting you infinite life, everything changed. Instead of an eternity in Summerland or the place beyond the bridge—the Shadowland became your fate."

He shakes his head and looks away, so deeply mired in his private world of regret I'm afraid I'll never reach him again. But just as quickly his eyes meet mine when he says, "We can live an eternity in the earth plane, you and I together. But if something should happen, if one of us should die—" He shakes his head. "The abyss is where we'll go, and we'll never see each other again."

I start to speak, desperate to refute it, tell him he's wrong, but I can't. It's no use. All I have to do is look in his eyes to see the real truth.

"And as much as I believe in the powerful healing magick of this place—just look at the way it healed my memory—" He shrugs and shakes his head. "I can't afford to give in, no matter how safe my desire for you may seem. It's too risky. And we've no proof it'll be any different here than on the earth plane. It's a gamble I can't afford to take. Not when I need to do everything I can to keep you safe."

"Keep *me* safe?" I gape. *"You're* the one who needs saving! It's *my* fault all this happened in the first place! If I hadn't—"

"Ever, please," he says, voice stern, willing me to listen. "You're in no way to blame. When I think about the way I've lived—the things I've done—" He shakes his head. "I deserve nothing better. And if there was any question that my karma was to blame, well, I think it ends here. I've spent the better part of six hundred years devoting myself to physical pleasure and neglecting my soul—and this is the result—the wake-up call, and unfortunately, I've dragged you along. So make no mistake, my concern is for you and you only. You're my only priority. My life is only important in that I stay well long enough to protect you from Roman and whoever else he might hurt. And that means we can never be together. *Never.* It's a risk we can't take."

I turn toward the stream, a thousand thoughts storming my brain. And even though I heard everything he just said, even though I experienced the abyss for myself, I still wouldn't change what I am.

"And the other orphans?" I whisper, remembering how I counted six, including Roman. "What happened to them? Do you know if they turned evil like Roman and Drina?"

Damen shrugs, rising from the bench and pacing before me. "I always assumed they were too old and feeble by now to ever pose a real threat. That's what happens after the first one hundred and fifty years—you age. And the only way to reverse the process is to drink the elixir again. My guess is that Drina stockpiled it while we were married and slipped it to Roman who eventually learned how to make his own and then passed it to the others." He shakes his head.

"So that's where Drina is now," I whisper, overcome with remorse when I realize the truth. No matter how evil she was, she didn't deserve that. Nobody does. "I sent her to the Shadowland—and now she's—" I shake my head, unable to finish.

"It wasn't *you* who did it, it was *me*." He fills the space beside me, sitting so close there's only a sliver of energy pulsating between us. "The moment I made her an immortal, I sealed her fate. Just like I did yours."

I swallow hard, comforted by his warmth along with his wanting to assure me that I'm truly not responsible for sending my number-one enemy through all of my lives straight into that hell.

"I'm so sorry," he whispers, gaze full of regret. "I'm sorry I involved you in any of this. I should've left you alone— should've walked a long time ago. You would've been so much better off if you'd never met me—"

I shake my head, unwilling to even visit that place, it's far too late for looking back or second-guessing. "But if we're destined to be together—then maybe this *is* our fate." Knowing he remains unconvinced the second I read his expression.

"Or maybe I've forced something that was never meant to be." He frowns. "Did you ever think of that?"

I look away, taking in the surrounding beauty, knowing words alone can never change any of this. Only action can help. And lucky for us, I know just where to start.

I stand, pulling him up alongside me as I say, "Come on. We don't need Roman—don't need anyone—I know just the place!"

# eight

We head for the Great Halls of Learning. Stopping just shy of its steep marble steps as I peer at him, wondering (hoping!) he can see what I see—the ever-changing façade that's required for entry.

"So you really did find it," he says, voice tinged with awe as we watch the revolving collection of the most sacred and beautiful places on Earth. The Taj Mahal morphing into the Parthenon, which turns into the Lotus temple, which becomes the Great Pyramids of Giza, and so on. Our mutual acknowledgment of its beauty and wonder allowing us into the grand marble hall lined with elaborately carved columns straight out of ancient Greek times.

Damen gazes around, face a mask of absolute wonder as he takes it all in. "I haven't been here since—"

I peer at him, holding my breath, dying to know the details of the last time he was here.

"Since I came to find you."

I squint, unsure what that means.

"Sometimes—" He looks at me. "I was lucky enough to just happen upon you, ending up in the same place at just the right time. Though more often than not I'd have to wait a few years before it was proper to meet."

"You mean you were *spying* on me?" I gape, hoping it wasn't nearly as creepy as it sounds. "When I was a *kid*?"

He cringes, averting his gaze when he says, "No, not *spying*, Ever. Please. What do you take me for?" He laughs and shakes his head. "It was more like—keeping tabs. Patiently waiting until the time was right. But the last few times when I was unable to find you, no matter how hard I tried—and believe me, I *tried*, living like a nomad, wandering from place to place, sure I'd lost you forever—I decided to come here. And I ran into some friends who showed me the way."

"Romy and Rayne." I nod, neither hearing nor seeing the answer in his head, but somehow sensing it's true. Overcome by an immediate rush of guilt for failing to even think of them until now. Not even wondering how they might be, *where* they might be, until a second ago.

"You know them?" He squints, clearly surprised.

I press my lips together, knowing I'll have to tell him the rest of the story, the parts I'd hoped to omit.

"They led me here too—" I pause, taking a deep breath and looking away, preferring to take in the room than meet his quizzical gaze. "They were at Ava's—or at least Rayne was. Romy was out—" I shake my head and start again. "She was out trying to help you when you—"

I close my eyes and sigh, deciding to just *show* him instead. Everything. All of it. Including the parts I was too ashamed to put into words. Projecting the events of that day until there are no more secrets between us. Letting him know how hard they fought to save him, while I was too stubborn, refusing to listen.

But instead of being upset like I feared, he places his hands on my shoulders, gazing at me with forgiveness as he thinks, *What's done is done. We have to move forward, there's no looking back.*

I swallow hard and meet his gaze, knowing he's right. It's time to get started, but where to begin?

"It's better if we split up." He nods, his words a surprise to my ears, and I'm just about to speak when he adds, "Ever, think about it. You're trying to find something to reverse the effects of the elixir I drank, while I'm trying to save you from the Shadowland, not exactly the same thing."

I sigh, disappointed but having to agree. "I guess I'll see you back at the house then. My house, if that's okay?" I place my hand over his and give it a squeeze, reluctant to revisit his depressingly barren room and unsure where he stands on the whole karma curse thing now that his memory's returned.

And no sooner has he nodded and closed his eyes than he's vanished from sight.

So I take a deep breath and close my eyes too, thinking:

*I need help. I've made a huge and horrible mistake and I don't know what to do. I need to either find an antidote to the antidote— something that'll reverse the effects of what Roman's done—or find a way to get to him, convince him to cooperate with me—but only in a way that won't require me to—um—seriously compromise myself in a way I'm not comfortable with . . . if you know what I mean . . .*

Focusing my intention, replaying the words again and again.

Hoping it'll grant access to the akashic records, the permanent record of everything that has, is, or ever will be done. Praying I won't be shut out again like the last time I was here.

But this time, when I hear that familiar buzz, instead of the usual long hallway leading to a mysterious room, I find myself right smack in the middle of a cineplex, its lobby empty, snack bar abandoned, with no clue of what I should do until a set of double doors opens before me.

I step inside a dark theater with sticky floors, worn seats, and the scent of buttery popcorn permeating the air. Squeezing down the aisle and choosing the best seat in the house, the one halfway down and dead center, I prop my feet on the chair just before me as the lights go dim and a big tub of popcorn appears in my lap. Watching the red drapes retract as the large crystal screen begins to flicker and flare in a profusion of images that quickly race past.

But instead of the solution I'd hoped for, all I get is a series of clips from movies I've already seen. Resulting in a sort of homemade montage of my family's funniest moments, lifted straight from my old life in Oregon and unfolding to a soundtrack that only Riley could make.

Watching a clip of Riley and me, both of us hamming it up on a homemade stage in our den, dancing and lip-synching for an audience consisting of our parents and dog. Soon followed by an image of Buttercup, our sweet yellow lab. Tongue straining toward her nose, licking like mad, trying to get to the chunk of peanut butter Riley had dabbed there.

And even though it's not at all what I'd hoped for, I know it's important all the same. Riley promised she'd find a way to communicate with me, assuring me that just because I can't see her anymore doesn't mean she's not still around.

So I push my quest aside, and sink down in my seat. Knowing she's sitting beside me, silent and unseen. Wanting to share this moment together, two sisters sharing the home-movie version of what used to be.

# nine

By the time I make it back to my room, Damen is waiting, sitting on the edge of my bed, cradling a small satin pouch in the palm of his gloved hand.

"How long was I gone?" I ask, plopping down beside him as I squint at my bedside clock and figure the math.

"There's no time in Summerland," he reminds me. "But on the earth plane, I'd say you were gone for a while. Did you learn anything?"

I think about the home movies I watched, Riley's version of "The Bloom Family's Funniest Videos," then I shake my head and shrug. "Nothing useful. You?"

He smiles, handing over the silk pouch as he says, "Open and see."

I pull on the drawstring, slip a finger inside, and retrieve a black silk cord bearing a cluster of colorful crystals held together by thin gold bands. Watching it catch and reflect the light as I dangle it before me, thinking it's beautiful if not a bit odd.

"It's an amulet," he says, watching me carefully as I take in the individual stones, each of them bearing a different shape, size, and color. "They've been worn through the ages and are said to hold magical properties for healing, protection, prosperity, and balance. Though this particular one, being created solely for you, is heavy on the protection element since that's what you need."

I look at him, wondering how this could possibly help. Then I remember the crystals I used to make the antidote that saved him, and how it really could've worked—if Roman hadn't tricked me into adding my blood to the mix.

"It's completely unique, assembled and crafted with your own personal journey in mind. There's not another one like it, not anywhere. I know it doesn't solve our problem, but at least it'll help."

I squint at the bundle of rocks, unsure what to say. Just about to slip it over my head and give it a go, when he smiles and says, "Allow me." Gathering my long hair and draping it over my shoulder as he reaches behind me and secures the small golden clasp, before tucking it under my tee where no one can see.

"Is it a secret?" I ask, expecting the crystals to feel cold and hard against my skin and surprised to find them quite warm and conforting instead.

He brushes my hair back over my shoulder, letting it fall just shy of my waist. "No, it's not a secret. Though you probably shouldn't flaunt it either. I have no idea just how far Roman's advanced, so it's better not to draw his attention to it."

"He knows about the chakras," I say, seeing the surprise in his gaze and choosing to omit the fact that he's actually responsible for that. Having unwittingly revealed all kinds of secrets while under Roman's spell. He feels badly enough already, so there's no reason to make it any worse.

I tap my fingers against the amulet beneath my shirt, surprised by how solid it feels from the outside, compared to the inside, the part that rests on my skin. "But what about you? Don't you need protection too?" Watching as he unearths a similar amulet from under his long-sleeved tee, smiling as he dangles it before me. "How come yours looks so different?" I ask, squinting at the cluster of sparkling stones.

"I told you, no two are alike. Just like no two people are alike. I've got my own issues to overcome."

"You have issues?" I laugh, though seriously wondering what they could possibly be. He's good at everything he does. And I mean *every single thing*.

He shakes his head and laughs, a wonderful sound I don't get to hear nearly enough anymore. "Believe me, I've got my share," he says, laughing again.

"And you're sure these will keep us safe?" I press it against my chest, noticing how it feels like a part of me now.

"That's the plan." He shrugs, getting up from the bed and heading for the door as he adds, "But, Ever, please do us both a favor and try not to put it to the test, okay?"

"What about Roman?" I ask, taking in his long, lean form as he rests against the jamb. "Don't you think we should come up with some kind of plan? Find a way to get him to give us what we need and be done with all this?"

Damen looks at me, gaze narrowed on mine. "There's no plan, Ever. Engaging with Roman is exactly what he wants. We're better off finding a solution on our own, without relying on him."

"But *how*? Everything we've tried so far has been a total

bust." I shake my head. "And why should we run ourselves ragged, searching for answers, when Roman's already admitted to having the antidote? He said all I have to do is pay the right price and he'll hand it over—how hard can that be?"

"And you're willing to pay his price?" Damen asks, voice steady and deep as his dark eyes sweep mine.

I avert my gaze, cheeks heating to a thousand degrees. "Of course not! Or at least not the price that *you* think!" I bring my knees to my chest and wrap my arms around them. "It's just—" I shake my head, frustrated at having to plead my case. "It's just that—"

"Ever, this is *exactly* what Roman wants." His jaw tightens, his features harden, before meeting my gaze and softening again. "He *wants* to divide us, make us question each other, break us apart. He also wants us to go after him and start some kind of war. You've no reason to trust him, he'll lie, manipulate, and make no mistake, it's a very dangerous game that he plays. And while I promise to do everything in my power to protect you, you have to help me here too. You have to promise you'll stay away from him, ignore all his taunts, and won't rise to his bait. I'll find a solution. Figure something out. Just please, look to *me* for the answers, *not* Roman, okay?"

I press my lips together and look away, wondering why I should promise any of that when the cure is right there for the taking. Besides, *I'm* the one who caused this situation. *I'm* the one who got us into this mess. So *I* should be the one to get us both out.

I switch my gaze back to his, an idea beginning to form— one that might work.

"So we're clear about Roman?" He tilts his head and lifts his brow, unwilling to leave until I consent.

I nod, just barely, but still enough to convince him to head down the stairs so fast I can't distinguish his form. The only hint of his having been here are the stones against my chest and the single red tulip he left on the bed.

# ten

"Ever?"

I close the window on my computer and switch it to the essay I'm supposed to be writing for English. Knowing Sabine would freak if she caught me running a Google search on ancient alchemical formulas, rather than the homework she's expecting to see.

Because as nice as it is lying beside Damen, the beat of our hearts connecting as one, in the long run, it's just not enough. It'll never be enough. I want a normal relationship with my immortal boyfriend. One with no barriers. One where I can truly enjoy the feel of skin as opposed to the way I remember it in my head. And I'll pretty much stop at nothing to get it.

"Did you eat?" She places her hand on my shoulder as she peers at the screen.

And since I didn't prepare, didn't guard myself from her touch, that's all it takes to *see* her version of the infamous Starbucks meet and greet. Which, unfortunately, is not so different from Munoz's version—the two of them acting all happy and giddy, smiling at each other with an abundance of hope. And even though she seems really happy, and no doubt *deserves* to be happy especially after all that I've put her through, I still comfort myself with the vision I had a few months back—the one where she clearly ends up with some cute guy who works in her building. Wondering if I should say or do something to temper her excitement since it's not like this little flirtation is going anywhere. But knowing I've already taken too big of a risk by outing myself to Munoz, I don't say a word. I can't afford to tip her off too.

I swivel around in my chair, releasing myself from her grip. Wanting to avoid *seeing* anything more than I already have, waiting for her energy stream to fade.

"Damen made me dinner," I say, voice steady and low despite the fact that it's not exactly true. Unless you count the elixir I drank.

She looks at me, gaze suddenly troubled as it narrows on mine. "Damen?" She steps back. "Now there's a name I haven't heard in a while."

I cringe, wishing I hadn't just put it out there like that. I should've broken her in slowly, gotten her used to the idea of seeing him again.

"Does this mean you're back together?"

I shrug, allowing my hair to fall in my face so it's partially hidden. Grasping a chunk and twisting it around, pretending to inspect for split ends even though I no longer get them. "Yeah, um, we're still—friendly." I shrug. "I mean, actually, we're more than friends, we're more like—"

*Dating and doomed—destined to spend an eternity in the abyss—madly in love but unable to touch—*

"Well, yeah, I mean, I guess you could say we're back together again." Forcing a smile so wide my lips practically split down the middle, but holding it anyway, hoping it'll encourage her to join in.

"And you're okay with that?" She runs her hand through her golden blond hair, a shade we used to share until I started drinking the elixir which turned mine even lighter, then perches on the edge of my bed, crosses her legs, and drops her briefcase onto the floor—four very bad signs that she's settling in for one of her long, awkward talks.

Her gaze moves over me, taking in my faded jeans, my white tank top and blue tee, searching for symptoms, hints, clues, some kind of telltale sign of adolescent distress. Having only recently ruled out anorexia and/or bulimia when my elixir-fueled growth spurt added four inches to my height and bulked up my frame with a thin layer of muscle even though I *never* work out.

But this time it's not my appearance that's got her unnerved, it's my *on again/off again* relationship with Damen that's rung her code red. Having recently finished yet another parenting book claiming that a tumultuous relationship is major cause for concern. And even though that may be true, nothing about Damen and my relationship could ever be condensed into a chapter in a book.

"Don't get me wrong, Ever. I like Damen, I do. He's nice and polite, and he's certainly very composed—and yet, there's something about that cool self-assurance, something that seems rather odd for a young man his age. Like he's somehow too old for you—or—" She shrugs, unable to place it.

I push my hair off my face so I can see her better. She's the second person today who's noticed something off about him—about *us*. First it was Haven with the whole telepathy thing, and now Sabine's taking issue with his maturity and poise. And even though it's easy enough to explain, the fact that they're even noticing in the first place is what worries me.

"And while I know there's only a few months between you, he somehow comes off as—more experienced. Too experienced." She shrugs. "And I'd hate for you to feel pressured into doing something you're not quite ready for."

I press my lips together and try not to laugh, thinking how she couldn't have gotten it more wrong. Assuming that I'm the innocent maiden being chased by the big bad wolf, never imagining that I'm actually the predator in this particular tale, dangerously pursuing my prey to the point of risking his life.

"Because no matter what he may say, you're in control of you, Ever. You're the one who determines who, where, and when. And no matter how you may feel about him, or any boy for that matter, they have no right to push their agenda on—"

"It's not like that," I tell her, cutting in before this gets any more embarrassing than it already has. "*Damen's* not like that. He's a perfect gentleman, an ideal boyfriend. Seriously, Sabine, you're way off course. Just trust me on this one, okay?"

She looks at me for a moment, crisp orange aura wavering, wanting to believe, unsure if she should. Then she picks up her briefcase and heads for the door, stopping just shy of it when she says, "I was thinking—"

I look at her, tempted to peek at her thoughts, despite my vow to never intentionally breach her privacy like that—unless it's an emergency of course, which this clearly is not.

"Since school's letting out soon, and since I haven't heard you mention any summer plans, I thought it might be good for you to find a job, spend a few hours each day working at something. What do you think?"

*What do I think?* I gape, eyes bugging, mouth dry, at a complete loss for words. *Well, I think I should've peered into your head after all, because clearly this does qualify as a major distress call!*

"Nothing full time or anything like that. There'll be plenty of time for the beach and your friends. I just thought it would be good for you to—"

"Is this about money?" My mind reeling, desperate to find a way out. If it's a simple matter of pitching in for the mortgage and groceries, then I'll gladly come up with whatever she needs. Heck, she can even take whatever's left of my parent's life insurance policy for all I care. But what she can't have is my summer. Unh-uh. No way. Not even a day.

"Ever, of course it's not about money." She averts her gaze as her cheeks flush soft pink. Oddly averse to discussing all things financial for someone who makes a living as a corporate litigator. "I just thought it might be good for you to, you know, meet some new people, learn something new. Get out of your usual environment for a few hours each day, and—"

*And get away from Damen.* Not needing to read her thoughts to know what this is really about. Now that she knows we're back together she's more determined than ever to break us apart. And while I get how concerned she was by all the moodiness and depression I subjected her to when we were apart, this time she's got it all wrong. It's not like she thinks. Though I've no idea how to explain that to her and still keep my secrets intact.

"—and as it so happens, a summer internship just opened up at the firm, and I'm sure it's just a matter of speaking with the senior partners and the job will be yours." She smiles, face radiant, eyes bright, expecting me to join the celebration as well.

"But aren't those positions usually reserved for law students?"

I ask, sure I'm pathetically underqualified to fill those particular shoes.

But she just shakes her head. "It's not that type of internship. This is more of a filing and phone answering assignment. And there's really no money in it either, though you will get school credit and a small end of the season bonus. I just thought it might do you some good. Not to mention how it will really beef up those college applications of yours."

*College.* Yet another thing I used to obsess about but not anymore. I mean, what possible use could I have for all of those classes and professors when all I have to do is place my hand on a book or peek inside my teacher's head to know all the answers?

"I'd hate for anyone else to get in there when I know you're just perfect for the job."

I stare at her, unsure what to say.

"It's good experience for a person your age," she adds, her indignant tone a result of my silence. "It's recommended in all the books. They say it builds character, commitment, and the discipline to show up on time and get the job done."

*Great. So I have Dr. Phil to thank for ruining my summer.* Completely annoyed with Sabine until I remember how she was when I first got here—calm, relaxed, and completely laid back, allowing me all the space and freedom I needed. It's my fault she changed. My suspension, my refusal to ingest anything other than the red elixir, and all the drama with Damen is what sent her over the edge. And this is where it led—to the dreaded summer internship she's bent on securing for me.

But no way can I spend the summer juggling a mountain of files and incessantly ringing phones when I'm going to need all the free time I can get to find an antidote for Damen. And working in Sabine's office, with her and her colleagues snooping over my shoulder, just will not do.

Though it's not like I can say that outright. It'll set off her alarms. I need to play it cool, let her know that while I've nothing against discipline and character building, I prefer to tackle those things on my own.

"I'm totally cool with working," I say, trying not to press my lips together, fidget, or break eye contact, three definite giveaways that I'm not being entirely honest. "But since you do so much for me already, I'd feel a lot better if I could find my own job. I mean, I'm just not sure I'm cut out for office work, so maybe I could look around a little. See what my options are. I'll even pitch in with the mortgage and food. It's the least I can do."

"What food?" She laughs, shaking her head. "You barely eat! Besides, I don't want your money, Ever. Though I will help you establish a line of credit if you'd like."

"Sure." I shrug, forcing an enthusiasm I don't really feel since I've absolutely no need for such conventional things. "That would be great!" I add, knowing that the longer I can keep her mind off this internship, the better for me.

"Okay then." She drums her fingers against the doorjamb as she finalizes her plan. "You've got one week to find something on your own."

I gulp, trying to keep the eye bugging to a minimum. *One week? What kind of a head start is that when I don't even know where to begin? I've never had a job before. Is it possible to just manifest one?*

"I know it's not much time," she says, reading my face. "But I'd hate for them to fill the position when I know you'd be perfect."

She heads into the hall and closes the door between us, leaving me sideswiped, dumbstruck, staring at the flickering remnants of her orangey aura, her magnetic energy field, hovering insistently in the space where she stood. Thinking how ironic it is that I was just making fun of Damen for assuming he could land a job without any experience only to find myself facing the same exact fate.

# eleven

I toss and turn all night. Bed a tangled mess of sweat-dampened pillows and blankets, body and mind exhausted by dreams. Waking briefly, gasping for air, only to be pulled under again, returning to the very same place I fought to escape.

And the only reason I want it to stop is because Riley is there. Laughing happily as she grabs hold of my hand, taking me on a tour of a very strange land. But even though I skip right alongside her, pretending to enjoy the trip too, the moment she turns her back, I scramble for the surface, eager to remove myself from this scene.

Because the truth is, it's not really Riley. Riley is gone. Having crossed the bridge at my urging, moving on to some unknown place. And even though she keeps yanking me back, yelling at me to pay attention, to just trust her and stop running—I refuse to obey. Sure that it's some kind of punishment for harming Damen, sending Drina to the Shadowland, and putting everything I care about at risk—allowing my subconscious to produce these guilt-induced images, so sugar-coated with happiness, there's no way they're real.

But this last time, just as I'm about to run, Riley appears right before me, blocking my exit, and yelling at me to stay put. Standing before a large stage and slowly drawing the drapes, revealing a tall, narrow, rectangular cube—like a prison of glass—containing a desperate and struggling Damen inside.

I rush to his aid as Riley looks on, pleading with him to hang in there while I help him break free. But he can't even hear me. Can't even see me. Just continues to fight until so overcome with exhaustion, with the absolute futility, he closes his eyes and fades straight into the abyss.

The Shadowland.

The home for lost souls.

I bolt from my bed, body shaking, chilled, drenched with sweat, standing in the center of my room with a pillow clutched to my chest. Overcome not only by the feeling of utter defeat, but by the horrible message my imagined sister has sent—telling me that no matter how hard I try, I can't save my soul mate from me.

I run for my closet, changing into some clothes before grabbing some sneakers and heading for the garage. Knowing it's too early to go to school, too early to go anywhere. But I refuse to give up. Refuse to believe in nightmares. I have to start somewhere. Have to use what I got.

But just as I'm about to climb into my car, I think better. Realizing the whole process of opening the garage door and starting the engine will risk waking Sabine. And even though I can easily step outside and manifest another car, bike, Vespa, or whatever else I might want, I decide to try running instead.

I've never been much of a runner. Far more used to dragging

my feet through every forced lap in P.E. than striving for any sort of personal best. But that was before I became immortal. Before I was gifted with incredible speed. A speed I haven't even begun to test the limits of, since the last time I ran was the first time I realized I even had the potential. But now that I'm faced with the perfect opportunity to see just how far and fast I can go before stopping, dropping, or crumbling to the ground with a debilitating case of side cramps, I can't wait to try it out.

I slip out the side door and head for the street. At first thinking I should warm up, start off in a nice slow jog before hitting the asphalt at full throttle. But no sooner have I started than a major surge of adrenaline kicks in, coursing through my body like the highest-grade rocket fuel. And the next thing I know, it's full speed ahead. Running so fast my neighbor's houses are reduced to a visual blur of stucco and stone. Jumping fallen trash cans and dodging poorly parked cars, as I race from street to street with the grace and agility of a jungle cat. Having virtually no awareness of my legs or my feet, just trusting they won't fail me. That they'll get me to my destination in miraculous time.

And no more than a few seconds have passed when I'm standing before it, the one place I swore I'd never return to, prepared to do the one thing I promised Damen I wouldn't—approaching Roman's door, hoping to broker some kind of deal.

But before I can even raise my hand to knock, Roman is there. Clad in a deep purple robe over blue silk pajamas, his matching velvet slippers with embroidered golden foxes peeking out from the hem. His gaze sleek, narrowed, looking me over without a trace of surprise.

"Ever." He cocks his head to the side, allowing for an unobstructed view of his flashing Ouroboros tattoo. "What brings you to the neighborhood?"

My fingers play at the amulet just under my shirt, heart racing beneath it, hoping Damen's right, that it'll provide the necessary protection—should it come to that.

"We need to talk," I say, trying not to cringe as his eyes sail over me, enjoying a nice, long, leisurely cruise.

He squints into the night, then back at me. "Do we?" He lifts his brow. "And here I had no idea."

I start to roll my eyes, but remembering my purpose for coming here, I settle for pressing my lips together instead.

"Recognize the door?" He raps his knuckles hard against the wood, eliciting a nice solid thump, as I wonder what he could possibly be up to. "Of course you don't," he says, lips quirking at the sides. "That's because it's new. I was forced to replace the old one after your last visit. You remember? When you busted your way in so you could toss my supply of elixir down the drain?" He laughs and shakes his head. "Very naughty of you, Ever. And quite a mess I must say. I hope you'll manage to behave better today." He leans against the door frame and waves me in, gazing at me in a way so deep, so intimate, it's all I can do not to squirm.

I head down the hall and into the den, noticing how the door isn't the only thing that's changed since I was last here. Gone are the framed Botticelli prints and abundance of chintz, all of it replaced by marble and stone, dark heavy fabrics, rough plastered walls, and black iron things shaped into scrolls.

"Tuscan?" I turn, startled to find him standing so near I can see the individual dark purple flecks in his eyes.

He shrugs, refusing to back up and give me some space. "Sometimes I get a little hankering for the old country." He smiles, a slow widening of his cheeks, displaying shiny white teeth. "As you well know, Ever, there's no place like home."

I swallow hard and turn away, trying to determine my quickest escape since I can't afford to make even the slightest mistake.

"So tell me, to what do I owe this magnificent honor?" He glances over his shoulder as he heads for the bar. Removing a bottle of elixir from the wine refrigerator and pouring it into a cut crystal glass, before offering it to me. But I just shake my head and wave it away, watching as he carries it over to the couch where he plops himself down, spreads his legs wide, and rests the glass on his knee. "I'm assuming you didn't drop by in the dead of night to admire my latest decorating scheme. So tell me, what's the purpose of this?"

I clear my throat, forcing myself to look him square in the eye without flinching, wavering, fidgeting, or exhibiting any other sign of weakness. Aware of how this whole situation can change in an instant—how easily I can turn from mild curiosity to irresistible prey.

"I'm here to call a truce," I say, alert for some kind of reaction but getting only his penetrating gaze. "You know, a cease-fire, a proclamation of peace, a—"

"Please." He waves his hand. "Spare me the definition, luv. I can say it in twenty languages and forty dialects. You?"

I shrug, knowing I'm lucky to have said it in the one. Watching as he swirls his drink, the iridescent red liquid flashing and sparking as it runs up the sides and splashes back down.

"And just what sort of truce are you after? You of all people should know how it works. I've no intention of giving you anything, unless you're willing to give up something of your own." He pats the narrow space just beside him, smiling as though I'd actually consider joining him there.

"Why do you do this?" I ask, unable to contain my frustration.

"I mean, you're more or less decent looking, you're immortal, you've got all the gifts that go with it—you can pretty much have anyone you want, so why do you insist on bothering *me*?"

He throws his head back and laughs, a giant roar that fills up the room. Finally calming down enough to level his gaze, looking at me as he says, *"Decent looking?"* He shakes his head and laughs again, placing his glass on the table and retrieving a pair of golden nail clippers from a jewel-encrusted case. *"Decent looking,"* he mutters, shaking his head, taking a moment to check out his nails, before returning his focus to me. "But you see, luv, that's just it. I *can* have anything I want. *Anything* or *anyone*. It all comes so easy. Too easy." He sighs, getting to work on his nails, so absorbed by the task, I'm wondering if he'll continue when he says, "It all gets a little tedious after the first—oh—hundred or so years. And while you're far too new to understand any of this, someday you'll realize just how big of a favor I've done you."

I squint, having no idea what he could possibly mean. *A favor? Is he serious?*

"You sure you won't have a seat?" He wags his nail clipper toward the overstuffed chair just to my right, urging me to take it. "You're making me out to be a very bad host, insisting on standing there like that. Besides, do you have any idea how fetching you look? A little—*bedridden*—sure, but in the sexiest way."

He narrows his eyes until they're sleek as a cat's, lips parting just enough for his tongue to escape. But I just stay put and pretend not to notice. Everything with Roman is a game, and taking a seat would be conceding defeat. Though remaining like this, watching his tongue wet his lips as his gaze lingers in all the wrong places, doesn't feel like much of a win.

"You're even more delusional than I thought if you think

you've done me a *favor*," I say, voice hoarse, scratchy, a long way from strong. "You're crazy!" I add, regretting it the instant it's out.

But Roman just shrugs, unfazed by my outburst as he returns to his nails. "Trust me, it's more than just a favor, luv. I've given you a *purpose*. A *raison d'être* as they say." He glances at me, brow raised. "Tell me, Ever, are you not completely fixated on finding a way to—*consummate*—with Damen? Are you not so desperate for a solution you actually convinced yourself it was a good idea to come *here*?"

I swallow hard and stare at him. I should've known better, should've heeded Damen's advice.

"You're too impatient." He nods, smoothing the edges of his freshly clipped nails. "What's the rush when you have all of infinity laid out before you? Think about it, Ever, how exactly would you spend your eternity if it weren't for me? Showering each other with huge bouquets of bloody red tulips? Having at each other so often it couldn't help but grow boring?"

"This is ridiculous." I glare. "And the fact that you see it like this—like it's some chivalrous deed that you've done—" I shake my head, knowing there's no need to continue. He's delusional, insane, determined to see things in his own selfish way.

"Six hundred years I yearned for her," he says, tossing his nail clippers aside, gaze never once leaving mine. "And *why*, you ask? *Why* would I bother with the *same* woman for so long when I can have anyone?" He looks at me as though waiting for the answer, but we both know I've no intention of going there. "It wasn't just her beauty like you think—though I will admit, it did spur things at the start." He smiles, eyes reminiscent. "No, it was the simple fact that I *couldn't* have her. No matter how hard I tried, no matter how long I pined, I was never allowed"—he looks at me, gaze heavy, intense—*"admittance—* if you will."

I roll my eyes. I can't help it. The fact that he wasted centuries pining for that monster is of no interest to me.

But he just continues, ignoring my pained expression when he says, "Make no mistake, Ever, I'm about to share something very important, something you really should keep in mind." He leans forward, arms on knees, voice steady and low, filled with new urgency. "We *always* want what we can't have." He leans back, nodding as though he just shared the key to enlightenment. "It's human nature. We're hardwired that way. And as much as you'd prefer not to believe it, it's the only reason Damen's spent the last four hundred years longing for *you.*"

I look at him, face placid, body still, aware that he's trying to hurt me, prodding the usual spots, knowing this has been one of my fears from the moment I first learned of our history.

"Face it, Ever, even Drina's incredible beauty wasn't enough to keep his interest. I'm sure you're aware of just how quickly he tired of her?"

I swallow hard, stomach like a hard bitter marble. *Since when is two hundred years considered quickly?* But I guess when you're dealing with eternity everything is relative.

"It's not a beauty contest," I say, cringing when I hear the words spoken aloud. I mean, seriously, is that the best I could do?

"Of course it's not, luv." Roman shakes his head, pity in his gaze. "If it was, Drina would win." He settles back, arms spread across the cushions, glass resting on top, daring me to respond. "Let me guess, you've convinced yourself it's about two souls meeting as one, destined for each other, and all of that—*puppy love?*" He laughs, nodding when he adds, "That *is* what you're thinking, right?"

"You don't *want* to know what I'm thinking." I narrow my gaze, determined to get to the point now that my patience's dissolved. "I didn't come here to be bored by your philosophical litanies, I came here because—"

"Because you want something from *me*." He nods, setting down his drink, glass meeting wood with a solid, wet *thwomp*. "In which case, I'm in the driver's seat, which means you're in no position to set the pace."

"Why do you do this?" I shake my head, having grown bored with this game. "Why do you bother when you know I'm not interested? Surely you realize that no matter what you do to Damen and me, it'll *never* bring Drina back. What's done is done. It can never be changed. And, in the end, all of this game playing, all of this nonsense you engage in—all it really does is prevent you from living your life—from moving on." I continue to stare, gaze unwavering, convincing. Projecting an image of him handing over the antidote and cooperating with me. "So, I'm asking you, in as reasonable a way as I can—please help me undo what you've done to Damen, so we can all coexist."

He shakes his head, lids squinched tight. "Sorry, darlin', the price is set. Now it's just a matter of whether you're willing to pay."

I lean against the wall, tired, defeated, but not letting on. Knowing the one thing he wants is the one thing I'll *never* give. The same old game Damen warned me about. "You'll *never* have me, Roman. Never, *ever*, for as long as I—"

Not even getting to the more degrading, insulting part that comes next when he rises from the couch, moving so quickly his breath hits my cheek long before I can blink.

"Relax," he whispers, face looming so close I can make out each flawless pore on his skin. "As much fun as that might be, providing an amusing diversion at least, I'm afraid that's not it. I'm after something far more esoteric than a virginal *shag*. Though, if you'd like to make a go of it, no strings attached, then I assure you, darlin', I'm certainly *up* for the task." He smiles, deep blue eyes boring into mine, projecting the movie he plays in his head, the one starring him, and me, and a king-sized bed.

I look away, breath coming ragged, too fast, summoning every ounce of my will not to slam my knee in his groin when his nose glances my ear, my cheek, my neck, inhaling my scent.

"I know what you're going through, Ever," he murmurs, lips brushing the tip of my ear. "Longing for something so close and yet—you can never quite *taste* it. It's the kind of pain most people will never experience. But we know, don't we? You and I are joined in that way."

I unclench my fists and fight to steady myself. Knowing I can't risk doing anything rash, can't afford to overreact.

"Not to worry." He smiles, slipping just out of my reach. "You're a smart girl. I'm sure you'll figure it out. And if not—" He shrugs. "Well, nothing changes, right? Everything stays exactly the same. You and I with our fates intertwined—for all of infinity."

He slips down the hall, moving so fast it's a moment before I can make out his form. Tilting his head and urging me toward the door, practically pushing me onto his stoop when he says, "Sorry to cut this so short. Though I do so with your reputation in mind. If Damen ever found out you were here—well, that could be rather tragic for you, *couldn't it?*"

He smiles, all shiny white teeth, golden hair, tanned skin, and blue eyes—the ultimate California poster boy beckoning—*Come live the good life in Laguna Beach!* And I'm furious with myself—furious for being so stupid—for not listening to Damen—for putting us further at risk. Handing Roman yet one more thing to lord over my head.

"Sorry you didn't get what you came for, luv," he purrs, his attention pulled by a vintage black Jaguar that pulls into the drive, containing a gorgeous dark-haired couple who head right inside. Closing the door behind them as he adds, "Whatever you do, steer clear of Marco's car on your way out, he'll flip if you so much as smudge it."

# twelve

I walk home. Or at least, that's the direction I originally head in. But somewhere along the way I take a turn. And then another. And another. My feet moving so slowly they practically drag, knowing there's no need to run, nothing to prove. Despite my strength and speed, I'm no match for Roman. He's the master of this game and I'm merely his pawn.

I continue, deep into the heart of Laguna, or the Village, as it's called. Too awake to go home, too ashamed to see Damen, making my way through the dark, empty streets until stopping before a small, well-tended cottage, with flowering plants flanking either side of the door and a woven welcome mat placed just so, making it appear warm, friendly, completely benign.

Only it's not. Not even close. Now it's more like a crime scene. And unlike the last time I was here, this time I don't bother knocking. There's no point. Ava's long gone. After stealing the elixir and leaving Damen to fend for himself, she has no intention of returning.

I unlock the door with my mind and step in, taking a quick look around before I move past the den and into the kitchen. Surprised to find the usually well-ordered room reduced to an absolute mess—the sink piled high with dirty glasses and dishes as the trash overflows to the floor. And even though I'm sure it's not Ava who's done this, clearly someone is here.

I creep down the hall, peering into a series of empty rooms until I get to the indigo door at the end—the one that leads to Ava's so-called sacred space where she used to meditate and try to reach the dimensions beyond. Opening the door just a crack and squinting into the dark, making out two sleeping figures sprawled on the floor. Skimming my hand along the wall and fruitlessly searching for a light, before remembering my ability to illuminate the room on my own—only to find the last two people I ever expected to see.

"Rayne?" I kneel down beside her, holding my breath as she rolls over and opens one eye.

"Oh hey, Ever." She rubs her eyes and struggles to sit. "Only I'm not Rayne, I'm Romy. Rayne's over there."

I glance at her twin at the far side of the room, noting the scowl that crosses her face the second she realizes it's me.

"What're you doing here?" I ask, focusing on Romy again since she's always been the nicer of the two.

"We live here." She shrugs, tucking her wrinkled white shirt into her blue plaid skirt as she gets off the floor.

I glance between them, taking in their pale skin, large dark eyes, and straight, black, shoulder-length hair with the razor-slashed bangs, noticing how they're both still dressed in the same private school uniforms as the first day we met. But unlike in Summerland where they always appear so clean and pristine, now they're pretty much the opposite—sadly disheveled and completely uncared for.

"But you can't live here. This is Ava's house." I shake my head. The idea of them squatting here leaves me extremely unnerved. "Maybe you should think about going home. You know, back to Summerland?"

"We can't." Rayne pulls on her kneesocks, making sure they're of exact equal height, unintentionally providing the only real clue that helps me tell them apart. "Thanks to you, we're stuck here forever," she mumbles, taking a moment to glare at me.

I glance at Romy, hoping she'll explain. But she just shakes her head at her sister, before looking at me. "Ava's gone." She shrugs. "But don't let Rayne give you the wrong impression. We're quite happy to see you. We had a running bet on how soon you'd show."

My gaze darts between them, laughing nervously as I say, "Oh, really? Who won?"

Rayne rolls her eyes and points at her sister. "She did. I was sure you'd abandoned us for good."

I pause, something about the way she just said that—"Wait, you mean you guys have been here *this whole time?*"

"We can't get back." Romy shrugs. "We've lost our magick."

"Well, I'm sure I can help you return. I mean, you do want to return—*right?*" I look at them, seeing Rayne smirk as Romy just nods. Knowing this'll be a lot easier than they think since all I have to do is make the portal, get them settled, then say my good-byes and make the return trip back to Laguna alone.

"We'd like that very much," Romy says.

"And we'd like to leave *now,*" Rayne adds, eyes narrowed. "After all, it's the very least you can do."

I swallow hard. I deserve that, but I still wonder who's more desperate for them to leave, them or me?

I motion toward Rayne as I head for the futon, wondering why neither of them thought to sleep on it instead of the floor. "Come," I say, glancing over my shoulder. "You sit here on my right, and Romy, you sit here." I pat the lumpy cushion. "Now grab my hands and close your eyes, then focus on *seeing* the portal with all of your might. Envisioning that golden shimmer of light as though it's before you. And as soon as the image is clear, I want you to *see* yourself stepping right through, knowing I'm right there beside you, keeping you safe. Okay?"

I peek at them, seeing them nod before we go through the motions, re-creating all the right steps. But just as I step through the light and into that vast fragrant field, I open my eyes and find I'm alone.

"Told you," Rayne says, the second I return. Standing before me, eyes angry, accusing, small, pale hands clutching her plaid skirted hips. "Told you our magick is gone. We're stuck here now with no way to get back. And it's all because we tried to help *you!*"

"Rayne!" Romy shakes her head at her sister, then glances at me with an apologetic look on her face.

"Well, it's true!" Rayne scowls. "I told you we shouldn't risk it. I told you she wouldn't listen. I saw it clear as day. The overwhelming possibility she'd make the wrong choice—*which*, I might add, she *did!*" She shakes her head and frowns. "It went exactly as predicted. And now *we're* the ones paying the price."

*Oh, you're not the only ones,* I think. Hoping they've lost their ability to read minds as well, since I'm immediately shamed by the thought. No matter how much she's annoying me, I know she's right.

"Listen," I say, swallowing hard as I glance between them, needing to defuse this. "I know how bad you want to get back. Trust me, I do. And I'm going to do everything I can to help you." I nod, seeing them glance at each other, two identical faces marred by complete disbelief. "I mean, I'm not exactly sure how I'm going to do it, but just trust that I will. I'll do everything I can to help you get back. And in the meantime, I'll do everything I can to keep you both comfortable and safe. Scout's honor. Okay?"

Rayne looks at me, rolling her eyes and heaving a sigh. "Just get us back to Summerland," she says, arms crossing her chest. "That's all we want. Nothing short of that will do."

I nod, refusing to let her get to me when I say, "Understood. But if I'm going to help you, I'll need you to answer some questions."

They look at each other, Rayne's gaze signaling a silent: *No way,* as Romy turns, nodding at me as she says, "Okay."

And even though I'm not quite sure how to phrase it, it's something I've been wondering for a while now, so I just dive in. "I'm sorry if this offends you, but I need to know—are you guys dead?" I hold my breath, fully expecting them to be mad, or at the very least insulted—pretty much any reaction but the laughter I get. Watching as they fall all over themselves, Rayne doubled over, slapping her knee, as Romy rolls off the futon, practically convulsing. "Well, you can't blame me for asking." I frown, definitely the one who's insulted. "I mean, we *did* meet in Summerland where plenty of dead people hang out. Not to mention how you're both unnaturally pale."

Rayne leans against the wall, fully recovered from her laughing fit and smirking at me. "So we're pale. Big deal." She glances at her sister, then back at me. "It's not like you're exactly rockin' a tan. And yet, you don't see us assuming you're a member of the dearly departed."

I wince, knowing it's true, but still. "Yeah, well, you had an unfair advantage. Thanks to Riley you knew all about me long before we met. You knew exactly who I am and *what* I am, and if I have any hope of helping you, then I'm gonna have to know a few things too. So as much as you may resent it, as much as you may want to resist, the only way we're gonna get anywhere is if you tell me your story."

"Never," Rayne says, staring at her sister, warning her not to rebel.

But Romy ignores her and turns right to me. "We're not dead. Not even close. We're more like—*refugees*. Refugees from the past, if you will."

I glance between them, thinking all I have to do is lower my guard, focus my quantum remote, and touch them for their entire life story to be revealed, but figuring I should at least try to get their version first.

"A long time ago," she starts, peering at her disapproving sister before taking a deep breath and forging ahead. "A *very* long time ago, in fact, we were facing a—" She squinches her brow, searching for just the right word, nodding at me when she says, "Well, let's just say we were about to become victims of a terribly dark event, one of the most shameful times in our history, but we escaped by fleeing to Summerland. And then, well, I guess we lost track of time and we've been there ever since. Or at least until last week when we came to help you."

Rayne groans, dropping to the floor and burying her face in her hands, but Romy just ignores her, still looking at me when she says, "But now our worst fear has come true. Our magick is gone, we've nowhere to go, and no idea how to survive in this place."

"What sort of *persecution* did you flee?" I ask, watching her closely, searching for clues. "And how long ago is *very long ago*? Just what are we dealing with here?" Wondering if their history stretches as far back as Damen's, or if they belong to a more recent past.

They gaze at each other, communicating a wordless agreement that shuts me right out. So I move toward Romy, grasping her hand so quickly she has no time to react. Immediately pulled into her mind—her world—*seeing* the story unfold as though I'm right there. Standing on the sidelines, an unnoticed observer, fully immersed in the chaos and fear of that day, witness to images so horrible I'm tempted to turn away.

Watching as an angry mob swarms their home, voices raised—torches high—their aunt barring the door as best she can, making the portal and urging the twins toward the safety of Summerland.

Just about to step through the portal and join them when the door gives way and the twins disappear. Separated from everything they once knew, having no idea what became of their aunt until a visit to the Great Halls of Learning showed them the torturous trial of false accusations she was forced to endure. Refusing to confess to any kind of sorcery, having taken the Wiccan Rede of *"An it harm none, do what ye will,"* and knowing she'd done nothing wrong, she rebuffed her oppressor and held her head high—all the way to the gallows where she was brutally hung.

I stagger back, fingers seeking the amulet just under my tee, something about their aunt's gaze so eerily familiar, leaving me shaky, unsettled, reminding myself that I'm safe, they're safe—that things like that don't happen these days.

"So now you know." Romy shrugs as Rayne shakes her head.

"Our whole story. Everything about us. Do you blame us for choosing to hide?"

I glance between them, unsure what to say. "I—" I clear my throat and start over. "I'm so sorry. I had no idea." I glance at Rayne, seeing how she refuses to look at me, then over at Romy who solemnly bows her head. "I had no idea you guys escaped *the Salem Witch Trials*."

"Not exactly," Rayne says, before Romy chimes in.

"What she means is we were never tried. Our aunt stood accused. One day she was revered as the most sought-after midwife, and the next, she was rounded up and taken away." She sucks in her breath, eyes welling up as though it were yesterday.

"We would've gone with her, we had nothing to hide," Rayne says, lifting her chin and narrowing her gaze. "And it certainly wasn't Clara's fault that poor baby died. It's the father who did it. He didn't want the baby or its mother. So he did away with them both and blamed Clara. Crying *witch* so loud the entire town heard—but then Clara made the portal, and forced us to hide, and she was just about to join us when—well, you know the rest."

"But that was over three hundred years ago!" I cry, still unused to the idea of an existence that long despite my immortality.

The twins shrug.

"So if you haven't been back since—" I shake my head, the monumental size of this problem just beginning to unfold. "I mean, do you have any idea how much things have changed since you were last here? Seriously. It's like a whole different world from the one that you left."

"It's not like we're idiots." Rayne shakes her head. "Things progress in Summerland too, you know. New people arrive all the time, manifesting the things they're attached to, all the stuff they can't bear to let go."

But that's not what I meant, in fact, not even close. I wasn't just referring to cars versus horse-drawn carriages, and trendy boutiques versus hand sewn—but more their ability to get along in the world—blending in, adapting, not standing out in the glaring way that they do! Taking in their razor-slashed bangs, their large dark eyes and extremely pale skin, knowing their twenty-first-century makeover is far less about a uniform change than a complete and total overhaul.

"Besides, Riley prepared us," Romy says, eliciting a loud groan from Rayne, and my full attention from me. "She manifested a private school and convinced us to enroll. That's where these uniforms came from. She was our teacher, coaching us on all the modern ways, including our speech. She wanted us to return and was determined to prepare us for the trip. Partly because she wanted us to look after you, and partly because she thought we were crazy for missing out on our teens."

I freeze, suddenly grasping a new understanding in Riley's interest in them—one that's got far less to do with me, and everything to do with her. "How old are you guys?" I whisper, looking to Romy for the answer. "Or should I say, how old were you when you first arrived in Summerland?" Knowing they haven't aged a day since.

"Thirteen," Romy says, knitting her brow. "Why?"

I close my eyes and shake my head, stifling a laugh as I think: *I knew it!*

Riley always dreamed of the day she'd be thirteen, a bona fide teenager having finally made it to the important double digits. But after dying at twelve, she chose to hang around the earth plane, living her adolescence vicariously through me. So it only makes sense she'd try to convince Romy and Rayne to return, not wanting anyone else to miss out like her.

And if Clara can find the strength, and Riley the hope, in situations so incredibly dire and bleak, surely I can overcome Roman.

I glance between the twins, knowing they can't stay here on their own or come home to live with Sabine and me, though there is someone who's quite able and ready, if not entirely willing to lend us a hand.

"Grab your stuff," I say, heading for the door. "I'm taking you to your new home."

# thirteen

The second we step outside I realize we'll need a car. And since I'm more interested in speed than comfort, especially after seeing the way the twins cling to each other as they gaze around warily, I manifest something that'll get us there fast and quickly herd them in. Ordering Romy to sit on Rayne's lap as I get myself settled and step on the gas, navigating the streets with surprising skill, while the twins practically hang out the window, gaping at all that we pass.

"Have you guys been inside this whole time?" I glance at them, never having seen anyone react to the beauty of Laguna Beach in quite the same way.

They nod, never once averting their gaze. Squirming in their seat as I pull up to the gate. Allowing the uniformed guard to peer through the window and scrutinize them, before letting us in.

"Where are you taking us?" Rayne eyes me suspiciously. "What's with the guards and big gates? Is this some kind of prison?"

I head up the hill, glancing at her when I say, "Don't you have gated communities in Summerland?" Never actually having seen one myself, but then again I haven't lived there for the last three centuries like they have.

They shake their heads, eyes wide, clearly on edge.

"Not to worry." I turn onto Damen's street and into his drive. "It's not a prison, that's not what the gates are for. They're more to keep people *out* rather than *in*."

"But why would you want to keep people out?" they ask, two childlike voices blending into one.

I squint, having no idea how to answer since it's not like I was raised like this either, all the communities in my old hood were open access. "I guess it's meant to keep people—" I start to say *safe*, but that's not really it either. "Anyway." I shake my head. "If you're going to live here, then you better get used to it. That's pretty much all there is."

"But we're *not* going to live here," Rayne says. "You said this was just a temporary fix until you find a way to get us back, *remember?*"

I take a deep breath and grip the wheel harder, reminding myself how scared she must feel, no matter how bratty she gets.

"Of course it's temporary." I nod, forcing a smile. *Or at least it better be, because if not, someone's going to be extremely displeased.* I climb out of the car and motion for them to follow, saying, "Ready to see your new *temporary* home?"

I head for the door, the two of them close at my heels as I stand right before it, debating whether or not I should knock and wait for Damen to open it or just stride right in since he's probably asleep. And I'm just about to do the latter when Damen swings the door open, takes one look at me, and says, "Are you okay?"

I smile, tacking on a telepathic message of: *Before you say anything—anything at all—just try to stay calm and give me a chance to explain—*his eyes curious, questioning as I say, "Can we come in?"

He moves aside, eyes wide with shock when Romy and Rayne step out from behind me and barrel right into him. Skinny arms wrapped around his waist, gazing up at him adoringly as they squeal, "Damen! It's you! It's really you!" And as nice as this little reunion is, I can't help but notice how their reaction to him, with all the love and excitement, is pretty much the opposite of their reaction to me.

"Hey." He smiles, ruffling their hair and bending down to plant a kiss on the top of their heads. "How long has it been?" He pulls away and squints.

"Last week," Rayne says, complete adoration displayed on her face. "Seconds before Ever added her blood to the antidote and wrecked *everything.*"

"Rayne!" Romy glances between her sister and me, shaking her head. But I just let it go. This is one battle I'll never win.

"I meant *before* that." Damen squints into the distance, trying to remember the date.

They look at him, a mischievous gleam in their eyes when they say, "It was just over six years ago when Ever was *ten!*"

I gape, eyes practically popping out of my head as Damen laughs. "Ah, yes. And I have you two to thank for helping me find her. And since you know how much she means to me, I'd appreciate your kindness toward her. That's not too much to ask—*is it?*" He chucks Rayne under the chin, causing her to smile as her cheeks flush bright pink.

"So to what do I owe this incredible honor?" He leads us

into the still empty living room. "Of being reunited with my long lost friends, who, I might add, haven't aged a day since we met."

They look at each other and giggle, clearly prepared to be charmed by anything he says. And before I can even think of a reply, find the right words to slowly break him in and get him used to the idea of their living with him, they look at each other and shout, "Ever said we could live with you!"

Damen glances at me, smile still planted on his face, as a look of pure horror creeps into his eyes.

"*Temporarily,*" I add, gaze meeting his, sending a barrage of telepathic red tulips his way. "Just until I find a way to get them back to Summerland, or their magick returns, whichever comes first." Tacking on a mental note of: *Remember when you said you wanted to improve your karma, to make up for your past? Well, what better way than to help someone in need? And this way you can keep the house, since you'll need the extra space. It's the perfect solution. Everyone wins!* Nodding and smiling so eagerly I'm like a bobble head doll.

Damen glances first at me, then the twins, laughing and shaking his head when he says, "Of course you can stay. For as long as you need. So what do you say we all head upstairs so you can pick out your rooms?"

I sigh, my perfect boyfriend proving himself even more perfect. Following behind as the twins race up the stairs—happy, giggling, completely transformed now that they're in Damen's care.

"Can we have this room?" They ask, eyes lighting up as they stand in the doorway of Damen's *special* room that's still devoid of his things.

"No!" I answer too quickly, wincing when they turn, eyes narrowed and glaring at me. But even though I feel bad about the negative start, I'm determined to return this room to its normal state, and there's no way I can do that if they're camping in it. "It's taken," I add, knowing it did nothing to soften the blow. "But there's plenty more, this place is huge, you'll see. There's even a pool!"

Romy and Rayne glance at each other before marching down the hall, heads bobbing together, whispering quietly, not bothering to hide their annoyance with me.

*You could've just given it to them*, Damen thinks, close enough to send a charge through my veins.

I shake my head and walk silently alongside him, telepathically replying, *I want to see it filled with your things. Even though they no longer mean anything to you, they mean a great deal to me. You can't just toss out the past—can't just turn your back on the things that defined you.*

He stops, turning to me as he says, "Ever, we are not defined by our things. It's not the clothes that we wear, the cars that we drive, the art we acquire—it's not where we live—but *how* we live that defines us." His gaze bores into mine, as he gathers me into a telepathic embrace, the effect seeming so real, it robs me of breath. "It's our actions that are remembered long after we're gone," he adds, smoothing my hair as his lips telepathically meet mine.

*True.* I smile, enhancing the image he created with tulips and sunsets and rainbows and cupids and all manner of clichéd romantic themes that make us both laugh. *Except that we're immortal*, I add, determined to sway him to my side. *Which means none of that really applies. So with that in mind, maybe we can just—*

But I don't even get to finish before the twins call for us, shouting, "This room! I want this one!"

Since the twins are so used to being together, I was sure they'd want to share the same space and even get bunk beds or something. But the moment they checked out the size of the next room, and the one after that, they each staked their claim and never looked back. Spending the next several hours directing Damen and me to decorate down to their most minute specifications, demanding we manifest beds, dressers, and shelves, only to change their minds, have us empty the room, and start all over again.

But as long as Damen was using his magick, I didn't complain. I was far too relieved to see him manifesting again, even if he was still refusing to manifest anything for himself. By the time we finished, the sun was starting to rise, and I knew I'd better return home before Sabine woke up and noticed I was gone.

"Don't be surprised if I don't make it to school today," he says, walking me to the front door.

I sigh, hating the thought of going without him.

"I can't leave them here on their own. Not until they get settled in." He shrugs, hooking his thumb over his shoulder and pointing upstairs where the twins are finally, mercifully, asleep in their beds.

I nod, knowing he's right, and vowing to get them back to Summerland soon, before they get too comfortable here.

"I'm not sure that's the solution," he says, sensing my thoughts.

I squint, unsure where he's going, but getting an uncomfortable ping in my gut nonetheless.

"I've been thinking—" He cocks his head to the side, thumb tracing his stubble-lined chin. "They've been through a lot—losing their home, their families, everything they've ever known and loved—their lives taken so abruptly, they hadn't had a chance to even live them—" He shakes his head. "They deserve a real childhood, you know? A fresh start in the world—"

I gape, wanting to respond but the words just won't come. Because while I also want them to be happy and safe and all of those things, as far as the rest goes, we're no longer on the same page. I was planning for a short little visit, a couple of days, or at the very worst—weeks. Never once did I entertain the idea of becoming surrogate parents, especially to twins who're just a few years younger than me.

"It was just a thought." He shrugs. "Ultimately, the decision is theirs. It's their life."

I swallow hard and avert my gaze, telling myself this is nothing that has to be settled just yet, heading toward my manifested car when Damen says, "Ever. Seriously? A Lamborghini?"

I cringe, flushing under his gaze. "I needed something fast." I shrug, knowing he's not buying it the second I see his face. "They were scared of being outside, so I needed to get them here quickly."

"And did it need to be shiny and red as well?" He laughs, glancing between the car and me and shaking his head.

I press my lips together and look away, refusing to say anything more. I mean, it's not like I was planning to keep it. I'll get rid of it the second I get home and pull into my drive.

I open the door and climb in, suddenly remembering the thing I meant to ask him before. Taking in the elegant lines of his face as I say, "Hey Damen—how'd you open the door so quickly? How'd you know we were here?"

He looks at me, eyes meeting mine as the smile slowly fades from his face.

"I mean, it was four in the morning. I didn't even have a chance to knock and you were already there. Weren't you asleep?"

And even though a chunk of flashy red metal stands between us, it's as though he's right there, gaze sending shivers over my skin when he says, "Ever, I can always sense when you're near."

# fourteen

After a long day at school without Damen, the second the final bell rings, I get in my car and head for his house. But instead of making a left at the light, I pull an illegal U-turn. Telling myself I should allow him some space, give him a chance to bond with the twins—when the truth is, between their hero worship of Damen and Rayne's glaring animosity toward me—well, I'm just not ready to face them again.

I head toward downtown Laguna, figuring I'll stop by Mystics and Moonbeams, the metaphysical bookstore where Ava once worked. Thinking maybe Lina, the store's owner, can help me find a solution to my more mystical problems without my divulging just what it is that I'm after. Which, considering how suspicious she is, should prove to be quite a feat.

After manifesting the best parking space I can, which in overcrowded Laguna happens to be two blocks away, I stuff the meter full of quarters and make my way toward the door, only to be met by a big red sign reading: BE BACK IN TEN!

I stand before it, lips pressed together as I glance all around, making sure no one is watching as I mentally flip the sign over while making the dead bolt retreat. Silencing the bell on the door as I slip inside and head for the bookshelves, relishing the chance to browse on my own, free of Lina's scrutiny.

The tips of my fingers graze the long row of spines, waiting for some kind of signal, a sudden warming, an itch at the tips, something to alert me to just the right one. But not getting anything, I grab one near the end and close my eyes, pressing my palms to the front and back covers, eager to *see* what's inside.

*"How'd you get in here?"*

I jump, bumping into the shelf just behind me, knocking a pile of CDs to the floor.

Cringing at the mess at my feet, scattered jewel cases everywhere, some of them cracked, as I say, "You scared me—I—"

I drop to my knees, heart racing, face flushing, wondering not just *who* he is but *how* he could've possibly managed to sneak up on me when it should be impossible to do so. A mortal's energy always announces itself long before their actual presence does. So is it possible that he—*isn't* mortal?

I sneak a quick peek as he kneels down beside me, taking in his tanned skin, defined arms, and heavy clump of golden brown dreadlocks spilling over his shoulder and halfway down his back. Watching as he gathers the damaged jewel cases into his hands, searching for some kind of sign that'll out him as an immortal, maybe even a rogue. A face that's too perfect—an Ouroboros tattoo—but when he catches me looking, he smiles in a way that not only displays the most disarming set of dimples perfectly punctuating each cheek, but a set of teeth that are just crooked enough to prove he's nothing like me.

"You okay?" he asks, gazing at me with eyes so green I can barely remember my name.

I nod, standing awkwardly and rubbing my palms on my jeans, wondering why I'm so breathless, unnerved, forcing the words from my lips when I say, "Yeah. I'm—fine." Inadvertently tacking a nervous laugh onto the end that's so high pitched and foolish I cringe and turn away. "I, um—I was just, browsing the merchandise," I add, realizing just after I've said it that I probably have more right to be here than he does.

Glancing over my shoulder to find him gazing at me in a way I can't read, I take a deep breath and pull my shoulders back. "I think the real question is, how'd *you* get in here?" Taking in his sandy bare feet and wet board shorts hanging dangerously low on his hips, averting my gaze before I can see anything more.

"I own the place." He nods, stacking the fallen CDs, the ones that aren't cracked, back onto the shelf before turning to me.

"Really?" I turn, eyes narrowed when I add. "Cuz I happen to know the owner, and you don't look a thing like her."

He cocks his head to the side, squinting in faux contemplation and rubbing his chin as he says, "Really? Most people claim to see a resemblance. Though, I have to admit, I'm with you, never seen it myself."

"You're related to Lina?" I gape, hoping my voice didn't sound as panicked to his ears as it did mine.

"She's my grandmother." He nods. "Name's Jude, by the way."

He offers his hand, long, tanned, fingers extended, waiting for mine. But even though my curiosity's piqued, I can't do it. Despite my interest, despite my wondering why he makes me feel so—flustered and off balance—I can't risk the barrage of knowledge a single touch brings when my psyche's disturbed.

I nod, responding with this stupid, embarrassing sort of half wave, as I mumble my name. Trying not to wince when he gives me an odd look and lowers his hand again.

"So, now that that's covered—" He slings his damp towel over his shoulder, sending a spray of sand through the room. "I'm back to my original question, *what are you doing in here?*"

I turn, feigning sudden interest in a book on dream interpretation when I say, "I'm sticking with my original answer, which was *browsing*, in case you've forgotten. Surely you allow browsers in here?" I turn, meeting his gaze—those amazing sea green eyes reminding me of an ad for a tropical getaway. Something about them so—indefinable—startling—and yet—strangely familiar—though I'm sure I've never seen him before.

He laughs, pushing a tangle of golden dreads off his face and exposing a scar splicing right through his brow, gaze landing just to my right as he says, "And yet, after all the summers I've spent here, watching customers *browse* the merchandise, I've never once seen someone browse quite like you."

His lips pull at the sides, as his eyes study mine. Then I turn, cheeks heating, heart racing, taking a moment to compose myself before turning back to say, "You've never seen someone browse the back cover? That's a little odd, don't you think?"

"Not with their eyes closed." He tilts his head to the side and focuses on the space to my right once again.

I swallow hard, flustered, shaky, knowing I need to change the subject before I sink any deeper. "Maybe you should be more concerned with *how* I got in here instead of what I'm *doing* in here," I say, wishing I could take it back the second it's out.

He looks at me, gaze narrowed. "Figured I left the door open again. Are you saying I didn't?"

"*No!*" I shake my head, hoping he doesn't notice the way my cheeks color and heat. "No, that's—that's exactly what I'm saying. You *did* leave the door open," I add, trying not to fidget, blink, press my lips together, or otherwise give myself away. "*Wide open* in fact, which is not only a waste of air-conditioning but totally—" I stop, my stomach going weird when I see the smile at play on his lips.

"So, a friend of Lina's, huh?" He moves toward the register, dropping his towel on the counter in a wet, sandy *thud*. "Never heard her mention you before."

"Well, we weren't exactly *friends*." I shrug, hoping it didn't look as awkward as it felt. "I mean, I met her once and she helped me with—wait, why did you just phrase it like that? You know, all past tense. Is Lina *okay*?"

He nods, perching on a stool, grabbing a purple cardboard box from a drawer and flipping through a bunch of receipts. "She's on one of her annual retreats. Picks a different one each year. This time it's Mexico. Trying to determine if the Mayans were right and the world will end in 2012. What's your take?"

He looks at me, green eyes curious, insistent, boring right into mine. But I just scratch my arm and shrug, never having heard that particular theory before and wondering if it applies to Damen and me. Is that when we'll head for the Shadowland, or will we be forced to wander a barren Earth—the last two survivors responsible for repopulating the land—only—*irony alert*—if we touch, Damen dies—

I shake my head, eager to escape that particular thread before it can really take hold and mess with my head. Besides, I'm here for a reason and I need to stick with the plan.

"So how do you know her? If you weren't exactly *friends*."

"I met her through Ava," I say, hating the feel of her name on my lips.

He rolls his eyes, mumbling something unintelligible and shaking his head.

"So you know her?" I look at him, allowing my gaze to travel his face, his neck, his shoulders, his smooth tanned chest, making my way down to his navel, before forcing myself to look away again.

"Yeah, I know her." He pushes the box aside, gaze meeting mine. "Just up and disappeared the other day—into thin air from what I can tell—"

*Oh, you don't know the half of it*, I think, carefully watching his face.

"—called her house, her cell, but nothing. Finally did a drive-by to make sure she was okay and the lights were on so it's clear she's been dodging me." He shakes his head. "Left me with a bunch of angry clients, demanding a reading. Who would've thought she'd turn out to be such a flake?"

*Yes, who would've thought? Certainly not the person who was foolish enough to place her deepest darkest secrets right into her greedy, outstretched, hands . . .*

"Still haven't found anyone good enough to replace her though. And let me tell ya, it's pretty much impossible to give readings and take care of the store. That's why I stepped out just now." He shrugs. "Surf was calling and I needed a break. Guess I left the door open again."

His eyes meet mine, sparkling and deep. And I can't tell if he truly believes he left the door open, or if he suspects me. But when I try to peer into his head to see for myself I'm stopped by the wall he's erected to safeguard his thoughts from people like me. All I have to go by is the brilliant purple aura I failed to see before—its color waving and shimmering, beckoning to me.

"So far all I got are a stack of applications from amateurs.

But I'm so desperate to get my weekends back, I'm ready to toss their names in a bowl and pick one just to get it over with." He shakes his head and flashes those dimples again.

And even though part of me can't believe what I'm about to do, the other part, the more practical part, urges me on, recognizing the perfect opportunity when it's standing before me.

"Maybe I can help." I hold my breath as I wait for his reply. But when my only response is a set of narrowed lids accompanied by the slightest curling of lips, I add, "Seriously. You don't even have to pay me!"

He squints even further, those amazing green eyes practically disappearing from sight.

"What I meant was you don't have to pay me all that *much*," I say, not wanting to come off as some weird desperate freak who gives it away for free. "I'll work for just over minimum wage—but only because I'm so good I'll be living off the tips."

"You're psychic?" He folds his arms and tilts his head back, gazing at me with complete disbelief.

I straighten my posture and try not to fidget. Hoping to appear professional, mature, someone he can trust to help run his store. "Yup." I nod, unable to keep from wincing, unused to confiding my abilities to anyone, much less a stranger. "I just sort of *know* things—information just sort of *comes* to me—it's hard to explain."

He looks at me, wavering, then focusing just to my right as he says, "So what exactly *are* you then?"

I shrug, fingers playing with the zipper on my hoodie, drawing it up and down, down and up, having no idea what he means.

"Are you clairaudient, clairvoyant, clairsentient, clairgustance, clairscent, or clairtangency? Which is it?" He shrugs.

"All of the above." I nod, having no idea what half those things mean, but figuring if it's got anything even remotely to do with psychic abilities, then I can probably do it.

"But you're not mediumistic," he says, as though it's a fact.

"I can see spirits." I shrug. "But only the ones that are still here, not the ones who've crossed—" I stop, pretending to clear my throat, knowing it's better not to mention the bridge, Summerland, or any of that. "—I can't see the ones who've crossed *over*." I shrug, hoping he doesn't try to push it since that's as far as I'll go.

He squints, gaze roaming from the top of my pale blond head and all the way down to my Nike clad feet. A gaze that makes my whole body quiver. Reaching for a long-sleeved tee stashed under the counter and yanking it over his head before he looks at me and says, "Well, Ever, if you wanna work here, you're gonna have to pass the audition."

# fifteen

Jude locks the front door then leads me down a short hall and into a small room on the right. I follow behind, hands flexed by my sides, staring at the peace sign on the back of his tee and reminding myself that if he does anything creepy I can take him down quickly and make him regret the day he ever went after me.

He motions toward a padded foldable chair facing a small square table covered by shiny blue cloth, taking the seat just opposite me and propping his bare foot on his knee as he says, "So, what's your specialty?"

I gaze at him, hands folded, focusing on taking slow deep breaths while trying not to squirm.

"Tarot cards? Runes? I Ching? Psychometry? Which is it?"

I glance at the door, knowing I could reach it in a fraction of a second, which might cause a stir, but so what?

"You *are* going to give me a reading, *right*?" His gaze levels on mine. "You do realize that's what I meant by *audition*?" He laughs, displaying a matching set of dimples as he swings his dreads over his shoulder and laughs some more.

I stare at the tablecloth, tracing the bumpy raw silk with my fingers, heat rising to my cheeks when I remember Damen's last words, how he can *always* sense me, and hoping he was just saying that—that he can't sense me *now*.

"I don't need anything," I mumble, still unwilling to meet his gaze. "All I need is a quick touch of your hand and I'm good to go."

"Palmistry." He nods. "Not what I would've expected, but okay." He leans toward me, hands open, palms up, ready to go.

I swallow hard, seeing the deeply etched lines, but that's not where the story lives—at least not for me. "I don't actually read 'em," I say, voice betraying my nervousness, as I work up the courage to touch him. "It's more the—the *energy*—I just—tune into it. That's where all the info is."

He pulls back, studying me so closely I can't meet his eyes. Knowing I need to just touch him, get it over with. And I need to do it *now*.

"Is it just the hand, or—?" He flexes his fingers, the calluses lining his palms rising and falling again.

I clear my throat, wondering why I'm so nervous, why I feel like I'm betraying Damen, when all I'm trying to do is land a job that'll make my aunt happy. "No, it can be anywhere. Your ear, your nose, even your big toe—doesn't matter, it all reads the same. The hand's just more accessible, you know?"

"More accessible than the big toe?" He smiles, those sea green eyes seeking mine.

I take a deep breath, thinking how coarse and rough his hands appear, especially compared to Damen's whose are almost softer than mine. And somehow, even just the thought of that makes this whole moment feel off. Now that our touch is forbidden, just being alone with another guy feels sordid, illicit, *wrong*.

I reach toward him, eyes shut tight, reminding myself it's just a job interview—that there's really no reason I can't land this thing quickly and painlessly. Pressing my finger to the center of his palm and feeling the soft, gentle give of his flesh. Allowing his stream of energy to flow through me—so peaceful, serene, it's like wading into the calmest of seas. So different from the rush of tingle and heat I've grown used to with Damen—at least until the shock of Jude's life story unfolds.

I yank my hand back as though I've been stung, fumbling for the amulet just under my top, noting the alarm on his face as I rush to explain. "I'm sorry." I shake my head, angry with myself for overreacting. "*Normally* I wouldn't do that. *Normally* I'm way more discreet. I was just a little—surprised—that's all. I didn't expect to see anything quite so—" I stop, knowing my inane babbling is only making it worse. "*Normally,* when I give readings, I hide my reactions much better than that." I nod, forcing my gaze to meet his, knowing whatever I say won't hide the fact that I choked like the worst kind of amateur. "Seriously." I smile, lips stretching in a way that can't be convincing. "I'm like the ultimate poker face." Peering at him again and seeing this isn't quite working. "A poker face that is also full of *empathy* and *compassion*," I stammer, unable to stop this runaway train. "I mean, really—I'm just—*full of it*—" I cringe, shaking my head as I gather my things so I can call it a day. There's no way he'll hire me now.

He slides to the edge of his seat, leaning so close I struggle to breathe. "So tell me," he says, gaze like a hand on my wrist, holding me in place. "What exactly *did* you see?"

I swallow hard, closing my eyes for a moment and replaying the movie I just saw in my head. The images so clear, dancing before me, as I say, "You're different." I peer at him, his body unmoving, gaze steady, allowing no clues as to whether or not I'm on track.

"But then, you've always been different. Ever since you were little you've seen them." I swallow hard and avert my gaze, the image of him in his crib, smiling and waving at the grandmother who passed years before his birth now etched on my brain. "And when—" I pause, not wanting to say it, but knowing that if I want the job, then I'd better get to it. "But when your father—*shot himself*—back when you were ten—you thought you were to blame. Convinced your insistence on seeing your mother, who, by the way passed just one year before, somehow sent him over the edge. It was years before you accepted the truth, that your father was just lonely, depressed, and anxious to be with your mother again. Even so, sometimes you still doubt it."

I gaze at him, noting how he hasn't so much as flinched, though something in those deep green eyes hints at the truth.

"He tried to visit a few times. Wanting to apologize for what he did, but even though you sensed him, you blocked it. Sick of being teased by your classmates and scolded by the nuns—not to mention your foster dad who—" I shake my head, not wanting to continue, but knowing I must. "You just wanted to be normal." I shrug. "Treated like everyone else." I trace my fingers over the tablecloth, throat beginning to tighten, knowing exactly how it feels to long to fit in, all the while knowing you never truly can. "But after you ran away and met Lina, who, by the way, is *not* your real grandmother—your *real* grandparents are dead." I look at him again, wondering if he's surprised that

I knew that but he gives nothing away. "Anyway, she took you in, fed you, clothed you, she—"

"She saved my life." He sighs, leaning back in his seat, long tanned fingers rubbing at his eyes. "In more ways than one. I was so lost and she—"

"Accepted you for who you *really are*." I nod, *seeing* the whole story before me, as though I'm right there.

"And who's that?" he asks, hands splayed on his knees, gazing at me. "Who am I *really*?"

I look at him, not even pausing when I say, "A guy so smart you finished high school in tenth grade. A guy with such amazing mediumistic abilities you've helped hundreds of people and asked very little in exchange. And yet, despite all of that, you're also a guy who's so—" I look at him, lips lifting at the corners. "Well I was going to say *lazy*—but since I really do want this job I'll say *laid-back* instead." I laugh, relieved when he laughs along with me. "And given the choice you'd never work another day. You'd spend the rest of eternity just searching for that one perfect wave."

"Is that a metaphor?" he asks, a crooked smile on his face.

"Not in your case." I shrug. "In your case, it's a *fact*."

He nods, leaning back in his chair, gazing at me in a way that makes my stomach dance. Dropping forward again, feet flat on the floor when he says, "Guilty." Eyes wistful, searching mine. "And now, since there are no secrets left, since you've peered right into the core of my soul—I have to ask, any insights into my future—a certain blonde perhaps?"

I shift in my seat, preparing to speak when he cuts me right off.

"And I'm talking the *immediate* future, as in this Friday night. Will Stacia *ever* agree to go out with me?"

"Stacia?" My voice cracks as my eyes practically pop out of my head. So much for the poker face I was bragging about.

Watching as he closes his eyes and shakes his head, those long, golden dreadlocks contrasting so nicely with his gorgeous dark skin. "Anastasia Pappas, aka Stacia," he says, unaware of my sigh of relief, thrilled to know it's some other horrible Stacia and not the one I know.

Tuning in to the energy surrounding her name and knowing right away that it's never gonna happen—at least not in the way that he thinks. "You really want to know?" I ask, knowing I could save him a lot of wasted effort by telling him now, but doubting he really wants to hear the truth as much as he claims. "I mean, wouldn't you rather just wait and see how it plays?" I look at him, hoping he'll agree.

"Is that what you're going to say to your clients?" he asks, back to business again.

I shake my head, looking right at him. "Hey, if they're fool enough to ask, then I'm fool enough to tell." I smile. "So I guess the question is, how big of a fool are you?"

He pauses, hesitates for so long that I worry that I took it too far. But then he smiles, right hand extended as he rises from his seat. "Fool enough to hire you. Now I know why you wouldn't shake hands the first time around." He nods, squeezing my hand for a few seconds too long. "That's one of the most amazing readings I've ever had."

"*One of?*" I lift my brow in mock offense as I reach for my bag and walk alongside him.

He laughs, heading for the door and glancing at me when he says, "Why don't you stop by tomorrow morning, say around ten?"

I pause, knowing there's no way I can possibly do that.

"What? You prefer to sleep in? Join the club." He shrugs. "But believe me, if *I* can do it, *you* can too."

"It's not that." I pause, wondering why I'm so reluctant to tell him. I mean, now that I've got the job what do I care what he thinks?

He looks at me, waiting, gaze adding up the seconds.

"It's just—I have class." I shrug, thinking how *class* sounds so much older than *school*, like I'm in college or something.

He squints, looking me over again. "Where?"

"Um, over at Bay View," I mumble, trying not to wince when I say it out loud.

"The *high school*?" His eyes narrow further, newly informed.

"Wow, you really *are* psychic." I laugh, knowing I sound nervous, stupid, coming clean when I add, "I'm finishing up my junior year."

He looks at me for a moment—too long a moment—then he turns and opens the door. "You seem older," he says, the words so abstract I'm not sure if they were meant for me or for him. "Stop by when you can. I'll show you how to work the register and a few other things around here."

"You want me to sell stuff? I thought I was just giving readings?" Surprised to hear my job description expanding so quickly.

"When you're not giving readings you'll be working the floor. Is that a problem?"

I shake my head as he holds the door open. "Just—just one thing." I bite down on my lip, unsure how to proceed. "Well, two things actually. First—do you mind if I go by a different name—you know, for the readings and stuff? I live with my aunt, and while she's totally cool and all, she doesn't exactly know about my abilities, so—"

"Be whoever you want." He shrugs. "No worries. But since I need to start booking appointments, who do you want to be?"

I pause, not having thought this through until now. Wondering if I should choose *Rachel* after my best friend in Oregon, or something even more common like Anne or Jenny or something like that. But knowing how people always expect psychics to be about as far from normal as it gets, I gaze toward the beach and choose the third thing I see, bypassing *Tree* and *Basketball Court* as I say, "Avalon." Immediately liking the sound of it. "You know, like the town on Catalina Island?"

He nods, following me outside as he asks, "And the second thing?"

I turn, taking a deep breath and hoping he'll listen when I say, "You can do better than Stacia."

He looks at me, gaze moving over my face, clearly resigned to the truth if not exactly thrilled to hear it from me.

"You have a serious history of falling for all the wrong girls." I shake my head. "You do know that, right?"

I wait for a response, some recognition of what I just said, but he just shrugs and waves me away. Still watching as I head for my car, having no idea I can *hear* him when he thinks: *Don't I know it.*

# sixteen

The moment I pull into the drive Sabine calls my cell, telling me to just go ahead and order a pizza for dinner since she has to work late. And even though I'm tempted to tell her about my new job, I don't. I mean, obviously I need to inform her, if for no other reason than to spare me the one she's lined up, but still, there's no way I can admit to getting this *particular* job. She'll think it's weird. Even if I omit all the stuff about getting paid to give readings (and believe me, I'd *never* dream of mentioning that) she'll still think a job at a metaphysical bookstore is strange. Maybe even silly. Who knows?

Sabine's far too reasonable and rational to ever get behind such a thing. Preferring to live in a world that's sturdy and solid, that makes perfect sense, versus the *real* one that is anything but. And while I hate always having to lie to her, I really don't see how I have much of a choice. There's just no way she can ever learn the truth about me, let alone that I'll be giving readings under the code name of Avalon.

I'll just tell her I got a job somewhere local, someplace normal, like a regular bookstore, or a Starbucks perhaps. And then of course I'll have to find a way to back the story up in case she decides to follow up on all that.

I park in the garage and head up the stairs, tossing my bag onto my bed without even looking, then heading for my closet as I yank off my tee. Just about to unzip my jeans when Damen says, "Don't mind me, I'm just sitting here enjoying the view." I cover my chest with my arms, heart beating triple time as Damen lets out a low, sweet whistle and smiles at me.

"I didn't even *see* you. I didn't even *sense* you for that matter," I say, reaching for my tee again.

"Guess you were too distracted." He smiles, patting the space right beside him, face creasing with laughter when I pull on my shirt before joining him.

"What're you doing here?" I ask, not really interested in the answer, just glad to be near him again.

"I figured since Sabine's working late—"

"How'd you—" But then I shake my head and laugh. Of course he knows. He can read everyone's mind, including mine, but only when I want him to. And even though I usually leave my shield down, making my thoughts accessible for him to view, right now I just can't. I feel like I need to explain, tell my side of the story, before he can peek in my head and draw his own conclusions.

"And since you didn't come by after school—" He leans toward me, eyes seeking mine.

"I wanted to give you some time with the twins." I pull a pillow onto my belly and finger the seam. "You know, so you could get used to being together and—stuff—" I shrug, meeting his gaze, knowing he's not buying it, not for a second.

"Oh, we're quite used to each other." He laughs. "I assure

you of that." He shakes his head. "It's been quite a day—very busy and very—*interesting*, for lack of a better word. But we missed you." He smiles, eyes grazing over my hair, my face, my lips, like the sweetest lingering kiss. "It would've been so much better if you'd been there."

I avert my gaze, doubting any of that's the slightest bit true. Muttering under my breath when I say, "I bet."

He touches my chin, making me face him, face masked with concern when he asks, "Hey, what's this about?"

I press my lips together and look away, scrunching my pillow so tight it threatens to burst, wishing I hadn't said anything because now I have to explain. "I'm just—" I shake my head. "I'm just not so sure the twins would agree." I shrug. "They pretty much blame me for *everything*. And it's not like they don't have a point. I mean—"

But before I can finish, I realize something—Damen is *touching me*.

Like *touching me touching me*.

For reals.

No glove, no telepathic embrace, just good old-fashioned skin-on-skin contact—or at least, *almost* contact.

"How'd you—" I look at him, his eyes shining with laughter when he catches me gaping at his bare, gloveless hand.

"You like?" He smiles, grasping my arm and lifting it high, both of us watching as the thin veil of energy, the only thing separating my skin from his, pulsates between us. "I've been working on it all day. Nothing's going to keep me from you, Ever. *Nothing*." He nods, his gaze meeting mine.

I look at him, mind racing with possibilities, of all this could mean. Enjoying the *almost* feel of his skin, separated only by the thinnest shroud of pure, vibrating energy, invisible to everyone but us. And while it does somewhat temper the usual rush of tingle and heat, and while it could never compare to the real thing, I miss him so much—just being with him—I'll take what I can get.

I lean into him, watching the veil expand until it stretches from our heads to our toes. Allowing us to lie together in the way that we used to—or at least *almost* in the way that we used to.

"Much better." I smile, hands roaming his face, his arms, his chest. "Not to mention how it's far less embarrassing than the black leather glove."

"*Embarrassing?*" He pulls away and looks at me, mock outrage displayed on his face.

"Come on." I laugh. "Even *you* have to admit it was a total fashion faux pas. I thought Miles was going to have a seizure every time he saw it," I murmur, inhaling his wonderful, warm, musky scent as I bury my face in his neck. "So how'd you do it?" My lips grazing his skin, longing to taste every last inch. "How'd you harness the magick of Summerland and bring it back here?"

"It's got nothing to do with Summerland," he whispers, lips at the curve of my ear. "It's just the magick of energy. Besides, you should know by now that most everything you can do there, can be done here as well."

I gaze at him, remembering Ava and all the elaborate gold jewelry and designer clothes she used to manifest there, and how upset she always was when they didn't survive the return trip home.

But before I can even mention it, he says, "While it's true that the things manifested there can't be transferred here, if you understand how the magick works, if you truly get how everything is really just made up of energy, then there's no reason you can't manifest the same things here. Like your Lamborghini, for instance."

"I'd hardly call it *my* Lamborghini," I say, cheeks flushing despite the fact that it wasn't so long ago when he had a thing for exotic cars too. "The second I was done with it I sent it right back. I mean, it's not like I *kept* it."

He smiles, burying his hand in my hair and smoothing the ends between the tips of his fingers. "In between manifesting things for the twins, I perfected it."

"What kinds of things?" I ask, moving so I can better see him, immediately distracted by the sight of his lips, remembering how warm and silky they once felt on mine, wondering if this new energy shield will allow us to experience that again.

"It all started with the flat-screen TV." He sighs. "Or, should I say flat *screens* since they ended up requiring one for each of their rooms, plus another two for the den that they'll share. And not long after I got them all hooked up and working, they sat down to watch and not five minutes in they were inundated with images of things they couldn't live without."

I squint, surprised to hear that, since the twins never seemed to care all that much about material things back in Summerland, but maybe that's because material things tend to lose most of their value once you can manifest whatever you want. I guess losing their magick has made them just like anyone else—longing for everything just out of their reach.

"Trust me, they're an advertiser's dream." He smiles, shaking his head. "Falling right into that coveted youth market of thirteen to thirty."

"Except for the fact that you didn't actually *buy* any of those things, did you? You just closed your eyes and made them *ap-*

*pear.* Hardly the same as going to the store and charging it on your credit card. In fact, do you even have a credit card?" Never having seen him even carry a wallet, much less a pile of plastic.

"No need." He laughs, finger skimming the bridge of my nose before his lips meet the tip. "But even though I didn't actually go out and *buy* all of those things as you so generously pointed out . . ." He smiles. "That doesn't make those commercials any less effective, which was really my point."

I pull away, knowing he's expecting me to laugh, or at least say something lighthearted in reply, but I can't. And even though I hate to disappoint him, I still shake my head and say, "Either way, you need to be careful." I shift my body so my gaze can better meet his. "You shouldn't spoil them so much, or make them so comfortable they're reluctant to leave." He squints at me, clearly not following my meaning, so I rush ahead to explain. "What I mean is, you need to remember that living with you is a *temporary* solution. Our main goal is to look after them until we can restore their magick and get them back to Summerland, which is where they belong."

He rolls onto his back and stares at the ceiling. Turning his face toward mine as he says, "About that."

I hold my breath and look at him, my stomach dipping ever so slightly.

"I've been thinking—" He squints. "Who's to say Summerland is where they belong?"

I balk, an argument pressing forth from my lips until he raises his finger and stops it right there.

"Ever, the question as to whether or not they return, well, don't you think that's something they should decide? I'm not sure we're the ones who should be making those choices."

"But we're *not* choosing," I say, voice shrill, unsteady. "That's what they want! Or at least that's what they said the night I found them. They were furious with me, blaming me for the loss of their magick, for stranding them here—or at least Rayne was; Romy—well, Romy was just Romy." I shrug. "But still. Are you saying that's changed?"

He closes his eyes for a moment, before leveling his gaze back on mine. "I'm not sure they even know what they want at this point," he says. "They're a little overwhelmed, excited by the possibilities of being here, and yet too terrified to even step outside. I just think we should give them some time and space and keep our minds open to the possibility of them staying a little bit longer than planned. Or at least until they're fully adjusted, and better able to decide for themselves. Besides, I owe them, it's the least I can do. Don't forget they helped me find you."

I swallow hard and avert my gaze, torn between wanting what's best for the twins while worried about the impact it'll have on Damen and me. I mean, they've been here less than a day and I'm already mourning my access to him, which is a totally selfish way to view two people in need. Still, I don't think you have to be psychic to know that with the two of them around, requiring all kinds of assistance, times like this—when it's just Damen and me—will be severely limited.

"Is that the first time you met? In Summerland?" I ask, seeming to remember Rayne saying something about Damen helping them, not the other way around.

Damen shakes his head, eyes on mine when he says, "No, that was just the first time I'd seen them in a long time. We actually go way back—all the way back to Salem."

I look at him, jaw dropped, wondering if he was there during the trials, though he's quick to dispel that.

"It was just before the trouble started, and I was only passing through. They'd gotten into some mischief and couldn't find their way home—so I gave them a ride in my carriage and their aunt was never the wiser." He laughs.

And I'm just about to make some crappy little comment, something about him spoiling and enabling them from the very start, when he says, "They've suffered an extraordinarily hard life—losing everything they've ever known and loved at a very young age—surely you can relate to that? I know I can."

I sigh, feeling small and selfish and embarrassed that I even needed to be reminded of that. Determined to stick to the practical when I say, "But who's going to raise them?" Hoping it will seem like my concerns are far less about me and more about them. I mean, with all of their unmitigated weirdness, not to mention their totally bizarre history, where would they go? Who could possibly look after them?

"*We're* going to look after them." Damen rolls onto his side and makes me face him again. "*You* and *I*. Together. We're the only ones who can."

I sigh, wanting to turn away, but drawn to the warmth of his all-encompassing gaze. "I'm just not sure we're fit to be parents." I shrug, hand moving over his shoulder, getting lost in his tangle of hair. "Or role models, or guardians, or whatever. We're too young!" I add, thinking it's a good and valid point, and expecting just about any reaction but the laughter I get.

"Too *young*?" He shakes his head. "Speak for yourself! I *have* been around for a while, you know. Plenty long enough to qualify as a suitable guardian for the twins. Besides." He smiles. "How hard can it be?"

I close my eyes and shake my head, remembering my feeble attempts to guide Riley both in human and ghost form, and how I failed miserably. And to be honest, I'm just not sure I'm up for it again. "You have no idea what you're getting into," I tell him. "You can't even begin to imagine what it's like to guide two headstrong, thirteen-year-old girls. It's like herding cats—completely impossible."

"Ever," he says, voice low, coaxing, determined to ease my concerns and chase all the dark clouds away. "I know what's really bothering you, believe me, I do. But it's just five more years until they turn eighteen and head off on their own, and then we'll have the freedom to do whatever we want. What's five years when we have all of eternity?"

But I shake my head again, refusing to be swayed. "*If* they head off on their own," I say. "*If.* Believe me, there are plenty of kids who stick around the house *long* after that."

"Yes, but the difference is, you and I won't let them." He smiles, eyes practically begging me to lighten up and smile too. "We'll teach them all the magick they'll need to gain their independence and get by on their own. Then we'll send 'em off and wish 'em well and go somewhere on our own."

And the way he smiles, the way he gazes into my eyes and smooths my hair off my face makes it impossible to stay mad, impossible to waste any more time on a topic like this when my body's so close to his.

"Five years is nothing, when you've already lived for six hundred," he says, lips at my cheek, my neck, my ear.

I snuggle closer, knowing he's right, despite the fact that my perspective's a little different from his. Having never spent more than two decades in any one incarnation makes five years spent babysitting the twins seem like an eternity.

He pulls me to him, arms locked tightly around me, comforting me in a way I wish could last forever. "Are we good?" he whispers. "Are we finished with this?"

I nod, pressing my body hard against his, having no need for words. The only thing I want now, the only thing that'll make me feel better is the reassuring feel of his lips.

I shift my body so it's covering his, conforming to the bend of his chest, the valley of his torso, the bulk near his hips. Hearts beating in perfect cadence, vaguely aware of the slim veil of energy pulsating between us as I lower my mouth to his—pressing and pushing and kneading together—weeks of longing rising to the surface—until all I want to do is infuse my body with his.

He moans, a low primal sound coming from deep within, hands clutched at my waist, bringing me closer 'til there's nothing between us but two sets of clothes that need to be shed.

I fumble at his fly as he pulls at my tee, breath meeting in short, ragged gasps as our fingers hurry as fast as they can, unable to complete their tasks quickly enough to satisfy our need.

And just as I've unbuttoned his jeans and start to slide them down, I realize we've gotten so close, the energy veil was pushed out.

"Damen!" I gasp, watching as he leaps from the bed, breath coming so heavy and fast, his words are clipped at the end.

"Ever—I'm—" He shakes his head. "I'm sorry—I thought it was safe—I didn't realize—"

I reach for my tee and cover myself, cheeks flushed, insides aflame, knowing he's right, we *can't* take the risk—can't afford to get caught up like that.

"I'm sorry too—I think—I think maybe I pushed it away and—" I bow my head, allowing my hair to fall into my face, feeling small and examined, sure I'm to blame.

The mattress dips as he returns to my side, the veil fully restored as he lifts my chin and makes me face him again. "It's not your fault—I—I lost focus—I was so caught up in you I couldn't maintain it."

"It's okay. Really," I say.

"No it's not. I'm older than you—I should have more control—" He shakes his head and stares at the wall, jaw clenched, gaze far away, eyes suddenly narrowing as he turns back to me and says, "Ever—how do we know if this is even real?"

I squint, having no idea what he means.

"What kind of proof do we have? How do we know Roman's not just playing us, having a bit of fun at our expense?"

I take a deep breath and shrug, realizing I have no proof at all. My eyes meeting his as I replay the scene from that day, all the way to the end where I add my blood to the mix and make Damen drink, realizing the only proof I have is Roman's extremely unreliable word.

"Who's to say this is even legit?" His eyes widen as an idea begins to form. "Roman's a liar—we've no reason to trust him."

"Yeah, but—it's not like we can test it. I mean, what if it's not a big game, what if it *is* legit? We can't take the risk—*can we?*"

Damen smiles, rising from the bed and heading for my desk where he closes his eyes and manifests a tall white candle in an elaborate gold holder, a sharp silver dagger, its blade pointy and smooth, its handle encrusted with crystals and gems, and a gold-framed mirror he sets down beside them, motioning for me to join him as he says, "Normally I would say ladies first—but in this case—"

He holds his hand over the glass and raises the knife, placing the edge to his palm and tracing the curve of his lifeline, watching his blood flow onto the mirror, pooling, coagulating, before closing his eyes and setting the candle aflame. The wound already healed by the time he passes the blade through the blaze, cleansing, purifying, before handing it to me and urging me to do the same.

I lean toward him, inhaling deeply as I quickly slice through my flesh. At first wincing at the sharp stab of pain, then watching fascinated, as the blood pours from my palm and onto the mirror where it slowly creeps toward his.

We stand together, bodies still, breath halted, watching as two ruby red splotches meet, mingle, coalesce—the perfect embodiment of our genetic makeup joining as one—the very thing Roman warned us against.

Waiting for something to happen, some sort of catastrophic punishment for what we've both done—but getting nothing—no reaction at all.

"Well, I'll be damned—" Damen says, eyes meeting mine. "It's fine! Perfectly—"

His words cut short by the sudden spark and sizzle as our blood begins to boil, conducting so much heat a huge plume of smoke bursts from the mirror and fills up the air—crackling and spitting until the blood evaporates completely. Leaving behind only the sheerest layer of dust on a burnt-out mirror.

Exactly what'll happen to Damen if our DNA should meet.

We gape, speechless, unsure what to say. But words are no longer necessary, the meaning is clear.

Roman's not playing. His warning was real.

Damen and I can never be together.

Unless I pay his price.

"Well." Damen nods, struggling to appear calm though his face is clearly stricken. "Guess Roman's not nearly the liar I accused him of being—at least not in this case."

"Which also means he has the antidote—and all I have to do now is—"

But I can't even finish before Damen's cutting me off. "Ever, please, don't even go there. Just do me a favor and stay away from Roman. He's dangerous, and unstable, and I don't want you anywhere near him, okay? Just—" He shakes his head, and runs his hand through his hair, not wanting me to see how distraught he really is and heading for the door as he says, "Just give me some time to figure things out. I'll think of a way."

He looks at me, so shaken by the events he's determined to keep his distance. Manifesting a single red tulip into my newly healed palm in place of a kiss, before heading down the stairs and out my front door.

## seventeen

The next day, when I get home from school, Haven's on my front steps, eyes smeared with mascara, royal blue bangs hanging limp in her face, with a blanketed bundle clutched tight in her arms.

"I know I should've called." She scrambles to her feet, face red and swollen as she sniffs back the tears. "I guess I didn't really know what to do, so I came here." She rearranges the blanket, showing me a solid black cat with amazing green eyes that appears very weak.

"Is he yours?" I glance between them, noticing how both of their auras are ragged and frayed.

"*She.*" Haven nods, fussing with the blanket and raising it back to her chest.

"I didn't know you had a cat." I squint, wanting to help but unsure what to do. My dad was allergic, so we always had dogs. "Is this why you weren't at school today?"

She nods, following me into the kitchen where I grab a bottle of water and pour it into a bowl.

"How long have you had her?" I ask, watching as she places the cat in her lap and brings the bowl to her face. But the cat's not the least bit interested and quickly turns away.

"Few months." She shrugs, giving up on the water and smoothing the top of her head. "Nobody knows. Well, outside of Josh, Austin, and the maid who's sworn to secrecy, but nobody else. My mom would *flip*. God forbid a *real living thing* mess up her designer decorating scheme." She shakes her head. "She lives in my room, mostly under the bed. But I leave the window cracked so she can get out and wander around now and then. I mean, I know they're supposed to live longer if you keep 'em inside, but what kind of life is that?" She looks at me, her normally bright sunshiny aura turned gray with worry.

"What's her name?" I peer at the cat, keeping my voice to a whisper, trying to hide my concern. From what I can *see*, she's not long for this world.

"Charm." The corners of her lips lifting ever so slightly as she glances between us. "I named her that because she's *lucky*—or at least it seemed that way at the time. I found her just outside my window the first time Josh and I kissed. It seemed so romantic." She shrugs. "Like a good sign. But now—" She shakes her head, and looks away.

"Maybe I can help," I say, an idea beginning to form. One I'm not sure will work, but still, from what I can *see* I've got nothing to lose.

"She's not exactly a kitten. She's an old lady now. The vet told me to keep her comfortable for as long as I can. And I totally would've kept her home since she really likes it under my bed, but my mom's decided to redo all the bedrooms even though my dad's threatening to sell, and now the decorator is there, along with a Realtor, and everyone's fighting and the house is a mess. And since Josh is auditioning for this new band, and since Miles is getting ready for his performance tonight, I thought I'd come here." She looks at me. "Not that you were last choice or anything." She cringes, realizing what she just said. "It's just that you're always so busy with Damen and I didn't want to bother you. But if you're busy, I don't have to stay. I mean, if he's coming over or something, I can just—"

"Trust me." I lean against the counter and shake my head. "Damen's—" I stare at the wall, wondering just how to phrase it. "Damen's pretty busy these days. So I doubt he'll be dropping by anytime soon."

I glance between her and Charm, reading her aura and knowing she's even more distraught than she seems. And even though I know it's not right, ethical, or whatever, even though I know it's the circle of life and you're not supposed to interfere, I can't stand to see my friend suffer like this, not when I have a half bottle of elixir sitting inside my bag.

"I'm just—*sad*." She sighs, scratching just under Charm's chin. "I mean, obviously she's lived a good long life and all, but still. Why does it have to be so sad when it ends?"

I shrug, barely listening, mind buzzing with the promise of a new idea.

"It's so weird how like one minute everything's fine—or maybe even not so fine—but still, you're at least *here*. And then the next—*gone*. Like Evangeline. Never to be seen or heard from again."

I drum my fingers against the granite counter, knowing that's not exactly true, but unwilling to refute it.

"I guess I just don't get the point. It's like, why should you bother getting attached to anything if, A: It's never gonna last, and B: It hurts like hell when it's over?" She shakes her head. "Because if everything's finite, if everything has a definite beginning, middle, and end, then why even get started in the first place? What's the point when everything just leads to *The End*?"

She blows her bangs out of her eyes and looks at me. "And I don't mean *death* like—" She nods toward her cat. "Although that's where we all end up—no matter how hard we fight."

I glance between her and Charm, nodding as though I'm right there. Like I'm just like everyone else. Waiting my turn in a long morbid line.

"I mean death in a more *metaphorical* way. In a *nothing lasts forever* way, you know? Because it's true, nothing's built to last. Nothing. *No. Thing.*"

"But Haven—" I start, stopping the second she shoots me a look meant to silence.

"Listen, before you try to sell me all that bright side nonsense you're just dying to spout, name *one* thing that doesn't end." She narrows her gaze in a way that sets me on edge, making me wonder if she knows about me, if she's trying to bait me somehow. But when I take a deep breath and look at her again, it's clear she's battling her own set of demons, not me.

"Can't do it, right?" She shakes her head. "Unless you were going to say *God*, or *universal love*, or whatever, but that's not what I'm talking about, anyway. I mean, Charm is dying, my parents are on the verge of divorcing, and, let's face it, Josh and I are going to end eventually too. And if it's purely an inevitable fact, then—" She shakes her head and wipes her nose. "Well—I may as well take control of the situation and be the one who decides when. Hurt him, before he can hurt me. Because two things are for sure, A: It's going to end, and B: Someone's bound to get hurt. And why should that someone be me?" She looks away, nose runny, lips twisted. "Mark my words, from this point on, I'm Teflon Girl. Everything runs right off me, nothing can stick."

I look at her, sensing this isn't quite the whole story, but willing to take her at her word. "You know what? You're right. You're absolutely right," I say, seeing her look up in surprise. "Everything *is* finite." *Everything but Roman, Damen, and me!* "And you're also right that you and Josh will probably end at some point, and not just because everything *ends* like you said, but because that's just the way it goes. Most high school relationships don't make it past graduation."

"Is that how you see you and Damen?" She picks at Charm's blanket while looking at me. "That you guys won't make it past grad night?"

I press my lips together and avert my gaze, knowing I'm pretty much the world's worst liar when I say, "I—I try not to think about it too much. But what I meant was, just because something ends doesn't mean it's a *bad* thing or that someone's bound to get hurt, or that it should've never happened in the first place, or whatever. Because if each step brings us to the next, then how will we ever get anywhere, how can we ever grow if we avoid everything that might hurt us?"

She looks at me, nodding only slightly, as though she sees my point but won't fully concede.

"So we pretty much have no choice but to continue, to just get out there and hope for the best. And who knows, we might even learn a thing or two along the way." I look at her, knowing I haven't completely sold it, so I add, "I guess what I'm trying to say is, you can't run away just because something won't last. You have to hang in there, let it play out. It's the only way you'll ever advance." I shrug, wishing I could be a little more eloquent, but there it is. "Think about it, if you didn't rescue your cat, if you didn't say *yes* when Josh asked you out—well, there's a lot of wonderful moments you would've missed."

She looks at me, still wanting to argue, but not saying a word.

"Josh is a really sweet guy, and he's crazy about you. I don't think you should throw him overboard so soon. Besides," I say, knowing she hears me but is not truly listening, "you shouldn't make those kinds of decisions when you're feeling so stressed."

"How about moving, then? Is that a good enough reason?"

"Josh is moving?" I squint. I hadn't seen that coming.

She shakes her head, scratching Charm on the spot between her ears when she says, "Not Josh. Me. My dad keeps talking about selling the house, but damn if he'll discuss it with Austin or me."

I look at her, tempted to peer inside her head and see for myself, but sticking to my earlier vow to allow my friends their privacy.

"All I know for sure is that the phrase *resale value* comes up all the time." She shakes her head, looking at me when she says, "But you know what this really means, if any of this is actually true? It means I won't be going to Bay View next year. I won't get to graduate with my class. I won't be going to *any* Orange County high school for that matter."

"I won't let this happen," I say, gaze locked on hers. "There's no way you're leaving. You have to graduate with us—"

"Well, that's very nice and all." She shrugs. "But I'm not sure you can stop it. It's a little out of your league, don't you think?"

I glance between her and her cat, knowing it's not at all *out of my league*. Finding an antidote for Damen? Maybe. Helping my best friend stay in her zip code and save her cat? Not so much. There's plenty I can do. *Plenty*. But still I just look at her and say, "We'll work something out. Just trust me, okay? Maybe you can move in here with me and Sabine?" Nodding as though I mean it, even though Sabine would never have it. But still needing to put something out there, provide some kind of comfort since it's not like I can voice what I'm hoping to do.

"You'd do that?" she squints. "Really?"

"Of course." I shrug. "Whatever it takes."

She swallows hard and gazes around, shaking her head when she says, "You know I'd never take you up on it, but still, it's nice to know that even with all our rough spots you're still my best friend."

I squint, having always assumed it was Miles not me.

"Well, you *and* Miles." She laughs. "I mean, I can have two best friends—an heir and a spare, as they say?" She wipes her nose again, shaking her head when she adds, "I bet I look like crap, right? Go ahead, tell me, I can take it."

"You don't look like crap," I say, wondering why she's suddenly focused on her looks. "You look sad. There's a difference. Besides, does it matter?"

"It does if you're considering whether or not you should hire me." She shrugs. "I've got a job interview, but there's no way I can go looking like this. And it's not like I can bring Charm."

I gaze at her cat, watching the life-force energy slowly slipping away, knowing I have to move fast, before it's too late. "I'll keep her. It's not like I'm going anywhere anyway."

She looks at me, wavering on whether or not she should leave her poor dying cat in my care. But I just nod, coming around to her side of the counter and lifting Charm out of her arms as I add, "Seriously. Just go do what you need to do, and I'll babysit." I smile, urging her to agree.

She hesitates, glancing between me and Charm, then rummages through her oversized bag for a small, handheld mirror, before wetting her finger and clearing the mascara tracks from her cheeks.

"I shouldn't be long." She grabs a black pencil and draws a thick, smudgy line around each eye. "Maybe an hour? Two at the most?" She looks at me, trading the pencil for blush. "All you have to do is hold her and give her some water if she wants. But she probably won't. She doesn't want much of anything now." She coats her lips with a swipe of gloss and rearranges her bangs, before slinging her bag over her shoulder and heading for the door. Climbing into her car as she turns to me and says, "Thanks. I need this job more than you think. Need to start saving some money so I can emancipate myself like Damen. I'm tired of this crap."

I look at her, unsure what to say. Damen's situation's unique. Not at all what it seems.

"And yeah, I know, I probably won't be able to support myself in *quite* the same style as Damen, but still, I'd rather live in some crappy studio somewhere than be subject to my parents' impulsive decisions and whims. Anyway, you sure you're okay with this?"

I nod, hugging Charm tighter, mentally urging her to hold on, just a little bit longer, until I can help.

Haven slides her key into the ignition, the engine turning as she says, "I promised Roman I wouldn't be late. And if I hurry, I might be on time." Checking her appearance in the rearview mirror as she shifts in reverse.

"Roman?" I freeze, my expression one of pure panic but unable to change it.

She shrugs, backing out of my drive as she calls, "He's the one who scored me the interview." Waving as she disappears down the street, leaving me with a dying cat in my arms, and no words to warn her.

# eighteen

"You can't do it," he says, barely having opened the door before he's already shaking his head.

"You don't even know what I'm here for." I frown, hugging Charm tightly to my chest, wishing I hadn't come here.

"The cat is dying and you want to know if it's okay to save it and I'm telling you it's not. You can't do it." He shrugs, reading the situation more than my mind, which I purposely blocked so he can't view my visit to Roman, which would really set him on edge.

"Do you mean *can't* as in *not possible*? Like the elixir won't work on a feline? Or *can't* as in the moral sense, as in *don't play God, Ever?*"

"Does it matter?" He lifts his brow, stepping to the side and allowing me in.

"Of course it matters," I whisper, TV noise drifting down from upstairs, the twins' daily dose of reality shows.

He heads into the den, plopping onto the couch and patting the space right beside him. And even though I'm annoyed by the way he's acting, not even giving me a chance to explain, I still join him, rearranging the blanket, hoping one look at Charm will convince him.

"I just don't think you should jump to conclusions," I say, shifting my body so I'm facing him. "It's not as simple as you think. It's not black or white, it's mostly all gray."

He leans toward me, gaze softening as he moves his thumb back and forth under Charm's whiskered chin. "I'm sorry, Ever. Really." He gazes at me before pulling away. "But even if the elixir did work—which, by the way, I'm not sure it would since I've never tried it on an animal before, but even if it did—"

"Really?" I look at him, surprised to hear that. "You've never had a pet you couldn't bear to part with?" My eyes graze over him, taking him in.

"Not one that I couldn't bear to lose, no." He shakes his head.

I narrow my eyes, not sure how I feel about that.

"Ever, back in my day we didn't keep pets in quite the same way. And after I drank the elixir, I wasn't interested in owning anything that might tie me down."

I nod, catching the way he gazes at Charm and hoping there's room to negotiate. "Fine. No pets. I get it," I say. "But do you get how someone might become so attached to their kitty they can't bear to say good-bye?"

"Are you asking if I know about attachment?" He looks at me, gaze heavy, steady, fixed right on mine. "About love, and the unbearable grief that comes when it's lost?"

I gaze down at my lap, feeling juvenile, foolish. I should've seen that coming.

"There's much more at stake than just saving a cat or granting eternal life—if there even is such a thing in the animal kingdom. The real question is,.how will you explain it to Haven? What will you tell her when she returns only to find the dying cat she left in your care is now miraculously cured—maybe even becoming a kitten again, who knows? How will you possibly explain that to her?"

I sigh, not having thought about that. Hadn't really considered that if it does work, Charm won't just be healed, but physically transformed.

"It's not about it not working—I've no clue about that. And it's not about your right to play God—you and I both know I'm the last one who should judge such a thing. It's more about safeguarding our secrets. And while I know you have only the best intentions at heart, in the end, helping your friend will only ignite her suspicion. Raising questions that can never be answered simply or logically without revealing too much. Besides, Haven's already onto us, or onto something at least. So now, more than ever, it's important for us to lay low."

I press my lips together, swallowing past the lump in my throat, hating that I've got so many amazing tools at my disposal, all of these magical abilities, but unable to use them, to help those whom I love.

"I'm sorry," he says, hand hovering over my arm, hesitating to make contact until the veil comes along. "But as sad as it seems, it really is just the natural course of events. And believe me, animals accept these things far better than people do."

I lean into his shoulder, into his touch, amazed by his power to comfort me no matter how bad things get. "I just feel so bad for her—her parents are always fighting—she might have to move—it's making her question the point of everything. Kind of like I did when my world fell apart."

"Ever—" he starts, gaze soft, lips looming so close I can't

help but press mine against them—the moment cut short when the twins squeal their way down the stairs.

"Damen—Romy won't let me—" Rayne stops, standing before us, dark eyes wider than usual when she says, "Omigod is that a *cat*?"

I glance at Damen. *Since when does Rayne use words like "omigod"?*

But he just shakes his head and laughs. "Don't get too close." He glances between them. "And keep your voice down. This is a very sick cat. I'm afraid she doesn't have very long."

"Then why don't you save it?" Rayne asks, prompting Romy to nod in agreement, the three of us gazing at Damen, our eyes wide and pleading.

"Because we don't do things like that," he says, voice stern and parental. "That's not how it's done."

"But you saved Ever, and she's not nearly as cute," Rayne says, kneeling before me 'til her face is level with Charm's.

"Rayne—" Damen starts.

But she just laughs, glancing between us when she says, "Just joking. You know I'm joking, *right*?"

I look at her, knowing she's not, but not willing to press it. Just about to get up, wanting to get Charm back before Haven returns, when Romy kneels down beside me and places her hand on Charm's head, closing her eyes as she chants a series of indecipherable words.

"No magick," Damen scolds. "Not in this case."

But Romy just sighs, and sits back on her heels. "It's not like it works anyway," she says, still gazing at Charm. "She looks just like Jinx at that age, doesn't she?"

"Which time?" Rayne giggles, nudging her sister as they both start to laugh.

"We may have extended her life a few times," Romy says, cheeks pink as she glances between us, prompting me to look at Damen and think: *See?*

But he just shakes his head. *Again—Haven?*

"Can we get a cat?" Romy asks. "A black kitty like this?" Tugging on his sleeve while gazing at him in a way that's hard to resist. "They're wonderful companions and very good around the house. What do you say? Can we? Please?"

"It'll help us get our magick back," Rayne adds, nodding at him.

I look at Damen, reading his expression and knowing it's as good as done. Whatever the twins want, the twins get. It's as simple as that.

"We'll discuss it later," Damen says, attempting a stern look, but the gesture's empty, everyone knows it but him.

I get up from the couch and head for the door, needing to get Charm back to the house before Haven returns.

"Are you upset with me?" Damen grasps my hand and leads me to my car.

I shake my head and smile. It's impossible to be mad at him, or at least not for very long. "I'm not gonna lie, I was hoping you'd be on my side." I shrug, coaxing Charm into her carrier, before leaning against the door and pulling him close. "But it's not like I don't get your point. I just wanted to help Haven, that's all."

"Just be there for her." He nods, dark gaze on mine. "That's all she really wants from you anyway."

He leans in to kiss me, gathering me into his arms, his hands moving over me and warming me to my core. Pulling away to gaze at me with those deep soulful eyes, the rock to my feather, my eternal partner, whose intentions are so solid and good I can only hope he never learns of my betrayal, reneging on my promise not to visit Roman just after saying I wouldn't.

He cups my face between the palms of his hands and peers into my eyes. Sensing my mood shifts so easily it's as though they are his.

I avert my gaze, thinking about Haven, Roman, the cat, and all the mounting mistakes I can't seem to stop making. Then clearing the thoughts and shaking my head, unwilling to visit that place when I say, "See you tomorrow?" Barely finishing the words before he leans in to kiss me again, a slip of energy pulsating between his lips and mine.

Holding the moment for as long as we can, neither of us willing to break away, until a twin chorus of, "Ew! Gross! Do we really have to watch that?" trails from the window upstairs.

"Tomorrow." Damen smiles, seeing me safely into my car before heading inside.

# nineteen

Everything started out fine. As fine and normal as any other day. I woke up, showered, dressed, stopped by the kitchen to toss some cereal down the sink before chasing it with some OJ I'd swished in a glass—my usual morning routine so Sabine will think I ate the breakfast she made.

Nodding and smiling the whole way to school as Miles yammers on and on about Holt, or Florence, or Holt *and* Florence, as I sit there beside him, stopping, turning, speeding, slowing, chasing yellow lights, waiting for the moment when I can see Damen again. Knowing the mere sight of him will turn all darkness to light, even if the effect is just temporary.

But the moment I pull into the lot the first thing I see is a mammoth-sized SUV parked right next to the space Damen's saving for me. And I mean *mammoth*, as in: big *and* ugly. And something about the sight of Damen leaning against that whale of a car fills me with dread.

"What the *hell*?" Miles gapes. "You give up *riding* the bus so you can *drive* a bus instead?"

I climb out of my Miata, glancing between Big Ugly and Damen, hardly believing my ears when he starts quoting a slew of statistics about its superb safety rating and roomy back seats. I mean, I don't remember him ever once caring about the safety rating when he was chauffeuring me.

*That's because you're immortal,* he thinks, sensing my thoughts as we head for the gate. *But may I remind you, the twins are not, and since they are now in my care, it's my job to keep them from harm.*

I shake my head, gaze narrowed as I try to think of a snappy reply. My thoughts interrupted by Haven who says, "You're doing it again." She crosses her arms and glances between us. "You know, your whole, weird, pseudo telepathy thing."

"Who even cares about that?" Miles screeches. "Damen's driving a bus!" He hooks his thumb over his shoulder, jabbing toward the big, black monstrosity and wincing at the sight of it.

"Is it a bus or a mom car?" Haven squints, shielding her eyes from the sun. Glancing at each of us. "Whatever it is, one thing's for sure, it's tragically middle-aged."

Miles nods, fully warmed up to the subject now. "First the glove and now *this*?" He frowns at Damen, disappointment clouding his face. "I have no idea what you're up to, but dude, you are seriously losing your edge. You're not even close to the rock star you were when you first came to this school."

I glance at him, eyes narrowed in silent agreement. But Damen just laughs, too concerned with the proper care and feeding of the twins to bother with what anyone thinks— including me. And while that's obviously the way a good, responsible, parental-type figure should think, something about it really bugs me.

Miles and Haven continue, teasing Damen about his new,

surprisingly stodgy ways, as I tag along, a sliver of energy pulsating between us as he grabs my hand and thinks, *What's going on? Why are you acting like this? Is this because of the cat? I thought you understood all of that?*

I stare straight ahead, focused on Miles and Haven, sighing loudly as I mentally reply: *It's not the cat. We settled that yesterday. She's back at Haven's, marking her days. It's just—well, it's like, here I am, making myself crazy, trying to find a solution so we can be together, and all you seem to care about is manifesting HDTVs and the world's ugliest babyproof car so you can cart the twins around town!* I shake my head, knowing I need to stop, before I go any further and really have something to regret.

"Everything's changing," I say, not realizing I said it out loud until the words ring in my ears. "And I'm sorry if I'm acting like a brat, but I'm just so frustrated that we can't be together in the way that we want. And I miss you. I miss you so bad I can't stand it." I pause, eyes stinging, throat hot and tight, threatening to close up completely. "And now that the twins are living with you, and with my new job starting and all, well, it's like, we're suddenly thrust into this super stressful, middle-aged life. And trust me, seeing your new car just now didn't help." I peer at him, thinking there's no way I'm riding in that thing. Instantly ashamed when I see him looking at me with such love and compassion I can't help but fold. "I guess I was hoping this summer would be great, you know? I was hoping we could have some fun—just the two of us. But now it's not looking so good. And, just to top things off, did I even mention that Sabine is dating Munoz? *My history teacher?* This Friday night, dinner at eight!" I scowl, hardly believing this pathetic life actually belongs to a supposedly powerful, newly immortal, almost seventeen-year-old girl.

"You got a job?" He stops in place as his eyes search mine.

"Out of everything I just said that's what you're focusing on?" I shake my head and pull him along, laughing in spite of myself.

But he just looks at me, gaze fixed on mine as he says, "Where?"

"Mystics and Moonbeams." I shrug, watching Miles and Haven wave as they turn down the hall and head for class.

"Doing what?" he asks, not ready to drop it just yet.

"Retail stuff, mainly." I gaze at him. "You know, working the register, restocking shelves, giving readings, stuff like that." I shrug, hoping he won't pay much notice to that last part.

*Psychic readings?* He gapes, stopping just shy of our classroom.

I nod, staring longingly as my classmates spill through the door, preferring to join them than having to finish what I started.

"Do you think that's smart? Drawing that kind of attention to yourself?" Back to talking again now that we're alone in the hall.

"Probably not." I shrug, knowing it's most definitely not. "But Sabine insists the discipline and stability will do me some good. Or so she says. She just wants to keep tabs on me. And short of installing a nanny cam, this is the easiest, least invasive way. She even had this horrible, soul-sucking, nine-to-five gig all set up and ready to go, so when Jude said he needed some help around the store, well, I didn't have much choice but to—*what?*" I pause, seeing the look on his face, eyes guarded, hard to read.

"*Jude?*" His eyes narrowing to where I can just barely see them. "I thought you said someone named *Lina* owned the store."

"Lina *does* own the store. Jude's her grandson," I say, only that's not entirely true. "Well, he's not her *real* grandson, it's more like, she looks after him. Helped raise him after he ran away from his last foster home—or—whatever." I shake my head. The last thing I wanted was to start a conversation about Jude, especially with the way Damen's gone high alert. "I thought it might help, you know, allow unlimited access to books and things that might help us. Besides, it's not like I'm working there under my real name. I'm using an alias."

"Let me guess." He peers into my eyes, seeing the answer displayed in my thoughts. "Avalon. Cute." He smiles, but only briefly before he's gone serious again. "But you know how it works, right? It's not like a confessional where you're shielded by a screen. People expect face-to-face contact. They want to *see* you to know whether or not they can trust you. So what exactly are you planning to do when someone you know just happens to walk in for an impromptu tarot card reading? Did you even think about that?"

I frown, wondering why he has to take what I thought was a pretty good deal and turn it into a problem. And I'm just about to deliver some snappy reply, say something like: *Hello? I'm psychic. I'll know before they even get through the door!* when Roman appears.

Roman and—someone else—someone vaguely familiar—someone named Marco who was last seen in a vintage Jaguar, pulling up to his house.

Walking side by side, legs moving swiftly, eyes focused on mine. Roman's gaze taunting, mocking, the proud owner of my dirty little secret.

Damen moves to shield me, gaze on Roman as he thinks: *Stay calm. Don't do a thing. I'll handle this.*

I peer over his shoulder, watching as Roman and Marco barrel toward us like an oncoming train. Gazing at me with eyes so deep, so blue, everything blurs but his moist grinning lips and flashing Ouroboros tattoo. And the last thing I think, before I'm sucked in completely, is that this is my fault. If I'd kept my promise to Damen and stayed away from him, I wouldn't be facing this now.

His energy swirls toward me, tugging, pulling, luring me in, sucking me into a spiral of darkness, bombarding me with images of Damen—the tainted antidote—my ill-advised visit—Haven—Miles—Florence—the twins—all of it coming so quickly I can barely distinguish between them. But the individual images themselves aren't important—it's the whole he wants me to *see*. All of it meant to illustrate one single thing: Roman's in charge now—the rest of us are just puppets, pulled by his strings.

"Mornin', mates!" he sings, releasing me from his grip as my body falls limp against Damen's.

But despite his sweet murmurings as he ushers me away from Roman and into the room, despite the soft reassurances intended to soothe, convinced that we've just dodged a bullet and it's over for now, I happen to know it's only begun.

More is coming.

There's no doubt.

Roman's next shot is aimed solely at me.

# twenty

After lunch I head for Mystics and Moonbeams. Eager to start my on-the-job training, hoping it'll provide a nice distraction from the mess otherwise known as my life.

It was bad enough when Damen kept disappearing between classes so he could check in on the twins, but by lunch, when I assured him I was fine, that Roman wouldn't bother me, and that he should just stay home, I headed for our table only to learn that Haven has boarded the Roman train. Picking apart a vanilla-frosted cupcake while gushing about the *big part* he played in securing her the job at the vintage store, despite her arriving at the interview ten minutes late.

And all I could do was mumble an occasional word of dissent, which didn't go over so well. So after her third excruciatingly dramatic eye roll, after telling me to *relax and unclench* for the umpteenth time, I tossed my uneaten sandwich and made for the gate. Vowing to keep an eye on her, do whatever it takes to keep them from getting together. Just one more item on my growing to-do list.

I pull into the alley, parking in one of two spaces behind the store before heading toward the front, half expecting to find the door locked, figuring Jude couldn't resist the call of killer waves on such a beautiful day, and surprised to find it wide open, with Jude behind the register, ringing a sale.

"Oh hey, here's Avalon now." He nods. "I was just telling Susan about our new psychic reader, and you walk in on cue."

Susan turns, looking me over, scrutinizing, accessing, adding up all the parts in her head. Sure she's aced the equation when she says, "Aren't you a little—*young* to be giving readings?" She gives me a smug look.

I smile, an awkward slanting of lips, as my gaze darts between them, unsure how to respond, especially with the way Jude's looking at me.

"Being psychic is a *gift*," I mumble, nearly choking on the word. Remembering a time, not long ago, when I scoffed at the thought, sure it was anything but. "It's got nothing to do with age," I add, watching her aura flicker and flare, knowing I've failed to convince her. "You either have it, or you don't." I shrug, digging myself a very deep hole.

"So, should I book you a reading?" Jude asks, smiling in a way that's hard to resist.

But not for Susan. Shaking her head and clutching her bag, she heads for the door, saying, "You just give me a call when Ava comes back."

The bell clangs loudly as the door closes behind her. "Well, that went well." I shrug, turning toward Jude and watching him file the receipt before adding, "Is my age going to be a problem here?"

"You sixteen?" he asks, barely glancing at me.

I press my lips together and nod.

"Then you're old enough to work here. Susan's a psychic junkie, she won't resist for long. She'll be on your sign-up sheet before you know it."

"Psychic junkie? Is that anything like a groupie?" I follow him to the office in back, noticing he's wearing the exact same trunks and peace-sign tee as before.

"Can't make a move without consulting the cards, the stars, what have you." He nods. "Though I'm guessing you gathered your share of regulars in the course of all the readings you've given." He glances over his shoulder as he opens the door, eyes narrowed, knowing, in a way I can't miss.

"About that—" I start, figuring I may as well confess since he's obviously on to me anyway.

But he just turns, hand raised, determined to stop me when he says, "Please, no confessionals." Smiling and shaking his head. "If I have any hope of enjoying those huge swells out there, then I don't have the luxury of regretting my decision. Though you might want to rethink that bit about it being a *gift*."

I look at him, surprised to hear him say that since all the psychics I've met, which, okay, pretty much consists of just Ava, but still, most of them think it's most certainly something you're born with.

"I'm thinking of adding some classes to the schedule, psychic development stuff, maybe even throw in some Wicca as well, and trust me, we'll get a lot more sign-ups if everyone thinks they have a fair shot."

"But do they?" I ask, watching as he heads for an extremely messy desk and riffles through a pile of papers near the edge.

"Sure." He nods, picking up a sheet, looking it over, then shaking his head as he swaps it for another. "Everyone has the potential, it's just a matter of developing it. With some it comes easy, they couldn't ignore it if they tried, with others—they have to dig a little deeper to find it. And you? When did you know?"

He looks at me, those sea green eyes meeting mine in a way that makes my stomach dance. I mean, one minute he's talking abstractedly, thumbing through papers as though he's barely minding his words, then the next everything stops, his gaze is on mine, and it's like time has stood still.

I swallow hard, unsure what to say, part of me longing to confess, knowing he's one of the few who would understand, but the other part resists—Damen's the only one who knows my story, and I feel like I should keep it that way.

"Just born with it, I guess." I lift my shoulders, cringing at the way my voice rose at the end. My eyes dart around the room, hoping to avoid the topic as well as his gaze when I add, "So—classes. Who's teaching those?"

He shrugs, tilting his head in a way that allows his dreadlocks to fall into his face. "Guess I will," he says, pushing them back and revealing the scar on his brow. "It's something I've been wanting to do for a while anyway, but Lina's always been against it. I figure I may as well take advantage of her not being here to see if it works."

"Why's she against it?" I ask, stomach settling when he leans back and props his feet on his desk.

"She likes to keep it simple—books, music, angel figurines, with the occasional reading thrown in. Safe. Benign. Mainstream mysticism where no one gets hurt."

"And your way? People get *hurt*?" I study him, trying to pinpoint just what it is about him that sets me on edge.

"Not at all. My goal is to empower people, help them live

better, more fulfilled lives, by accessing their own intuition, that's all." He glances at me, green eyes catching me staring, making my stomach go weird again.

"And Lina doesn't want to empower people?" I ask, feeling all fluttery under his gaze.

"With knowledge comes power. And since power tends to corrupt, she thinks it's too big a risk. Even though I've got no plans to go anywhere near the dark arts, she's convinced they'll find their way in, that the classes I teach will only lead to harder, darker stuff."

I nod, thinking of Roman and Drina and definitely seeing Lina's point. Power in the wrong hands is indeed a dangerous thing.

"Anyway, you interested?" He smiles.

My eyes meet his, unsure what he means.

"In teaching a class?"

I balk, wondering if he's joking or serious, then seeing he's neither, just putting it out there. "Trust me, I don't know the first thing about Wicca, or—or any of it really. I've no idea how it works. I'm better off just giving the occasional reading, and maybe even trying to organize this mess." I gesture toward his desk, the shelves, just about every available surface that's buried beneath a mound of papers and junk.

"I was hoping you'd say that." He laughs. "Oh, and just so you know, I clocked out the moment you walked in. Gone surfing if anyone asks." He gets up, moving toward the surfboard leaning against the far wall. "I don't expect you to get it completely organized or anything, it's too big a mess. But if you could get it into some kind of order, well—" He nods, looking at me. "You just might get a gold star."

"I'd rather have a plaque," I say, pretending to be serious.

"You know, something nice that I can hang on the wall. Or even a statuette. Or a trophy—a trophy would be good."

"How about your own parking space out back? I can probably swing that."

"Trust me, you already have." I laugh.

"Yeah, but this one will have your name on it. Reserved for you only. No one will be allowed to park in it, not even off hours. I'll post a big warning that reads: CAUTION! THIS SPACE RESERVED FOR AVALON ONLY. ALL OTHERS WILL BE TOWED AWAY AT THEIR OWN EXPENSE."

"You'd do that? For reals?" I laugh, eyes meeting his.

He grabs his board, fingers gripping the edge as he heaves it under his arm. "You get this place cleaned up and there's no limit to the rewards that await you. Today Employee of the Month, tomorrow—" He shrugs, tossing his dreads off his forehead and exposing his amazingly cute face.

Our gazes lock, and I know he's caught me again—caught me looking—wondering—thinking he's cute. So I quickly look away, scratching at my arm, fiddling with my sleeve, anything to move past this moment toward something less awkward.

"There's a monitor in the corner there." He nods toward the far wall, back to business again. "*That*, combined with the bell on the door, should alert you to anyone coming in when you're working back here."

"*That*, the bell on the door, and the fact that I'm *psychic*," I say, trying to sound lighthearted, though my voice is a little shaky, having not fully recovered from the awkwardness before.

"Like the way you accessed your powers when I snuck up on you?" he asks, smiling in a nice open way, though his eyes are holding back.

"That was different." I shrug. "You obviously know how to shield your energy. Most people don't."

"And *you* know how to shield your aura." He squints, head cocked to the side, those golden dreadlocks falling halfway down his arm as he focuses in on my right. "But I'm sure we'll get to that later."

I swallow hard, pretending not to notice how his vibrant yellow aura goes a little pink at the edges.

"Anyway, it's all pretty self-explanatory. The files need to be alphabetized, and if you could separate 'em by subject, that'd be great. Oh, and don't bother tagging the crystals or herbs if you're not familiar with them, I'd hate to get 'em confused. Though if you *are* familiar—" He smiles, brow raised in such a way I immediately start scratching my arm again.

I gaze at the gleaming piles of crystals, some of which I recognize from the elixirs I made and the amulet I wear at my neck, but most of which are so foreign they're not even vaguely familiar.

"Do you have a book or something?" I ask, hoping he does since I'd love to learn more about their amazing abilities. "You know, so I can"—*Find a way to sleep with my immortal boyfriend someday*—"so I can get them all tagged properly—and—stuff." I nod, hoping to appear like a hard worker rather than the self-motivated slacker I am. Watching as he drops his surfboard and turns back toward his desk, shuffling through a pile of books and retrieving a small, thick, well-worn tome from the bottom of the stack.

Turning it over in his hands, and gazing at the back when he says, "This has it all. If a crystal's not in it, it doesn't exist. It's also loaded with pictures so you can identify them. Anyway, it should help," he adds, tossing it to me.

I catch it between the palms of my hands, its pages vibrating with life as the contents surge through me. The entire book now imprinted on my brain as I smile and say, "Believe me, it already has."

# twenty-one

I stare at the monitor, making sure Jude has left before taking the seat behind the desk and gazing at the pile of crystals. Knowing the book alone wasn't enough—they need to be handled to be understood. But just as I reach for a large red rock marked by streaks of yellow, my knee knocks against the side of the desk, and my entire body grows itchy and warm—a sure sign that something needs my attention.

I push the chair back and lean forward, peering under the desk, noticing how the sensation grows stronger the lower I go. Following the feeling until I've slid off my seat and dropped to the floor, fumbling around for the source, the tips of my fingers growing unbearably hot the second I touch the bottom left drawer.

I lean back on my heels, squinting at the old brass lock—the kind of deterrent meant to keep honest people honest, and dissuade those who don't know how to manipulate energy like me—closing my eyes as I ease the drawer open, only to find a pile of hanging files that are no longer hanging, an ancient calculator, and a pile of old and yellowed receipts. Just about to close it again when I sense the false bottom beneath.

I scoop up the papers and toss them aside before lifting the hatch and exposing an old, worn, leather-bound tome, its pages curled and fraying like a lost ancient scroll, the words *Book of Shadows* inscribed on its front. I place it onto the desk before me, then sit there and stare. Wondering why someone would go to so much trouble to keep this book hidden—and from *whom*?

Is Lina hiding it from Jude?

Or is it the other way around?

And since there's only one way to find out, I close my eyes and press my palm to its front, planning to read it in my usual way until I'm slammed by a surge of energy so intense, so frenetic, so chaotic—it practically snap crackles my bones.

I'm hurled backward, my chair hitting the wall with such force it leaves a huge dent. The flickering remnants of random images still quivering before me, and knowing full well why it was hidden—it's a book of witchcraft and spells. Divinations and incantations. Containing powers so potent it would be completely catastrophic in the wrong hands.

I steady my breath and stare at the cover, calming myself before I attempt to thumb through it. Fingers twitching, touching only the edges, as I peer at a cursive so small it's nearly impossible to decipher. The bulk of the pages inscribed with all manner of symbols, reminding me of the alchemical journals Damen's father used to keep—carefully written in code in order to protect the secrets within.

I flip to the middle, taking in a fine, detailed sketch of a group of people dancing under a full moon, followed by those of similar people engaged in complex rituals. Fingers hovering above the scratchy old paper and suddenly knowing deep in my bones that this is no mistake. I was meant to find this book.

Just like Roman hypnotized my classmates and put them all under his spell, all I have to do is weave the right incantation to convince him to divulge the information I need!

I turn the page, eager to find the right one, just as the bell on the shop door rings and I peer at the monitor to confirm it. Unwilling to budge 'til I'm sure they're not going to turn right around and leave, that they're truly committed to staying. Watching as the small, slim, black-and-white figure makes her way through the room—nervously glancing over her shoulder as though expecting to find someone there. And just as I'm hoping she'll leave, she goes straight for the counter, places her hands on the glass, and waits patiently.

*Great.* I get up from the desk. *Just what I need—a customer.* Calling, "Can I help you?" before I've even had a chance to turn the corner and see that it's Honor.

The second she sees me she gasps, jaw dropping, eyes widening, appearing almost—*frightened*? The two of us gape at each other, wondering how to move past this.

"Um, do you need something?" I say, voice sounding more confident than I feel, as though I really am in charge around here. Taking in her long dark hair, the recent addition of copper streaks glinting under the lights, realizing I've never seen her alone until now. Never once been confronted by her, just the two of us, without Stacia or Craig.

My mind wanders to the book in the back, the one I left on the desk, the one I need to return to immediately, hoping whatever it is that she wants can be handled quickly and easily.

"Maybe I'm in the wrong place." She pulls her shoulders in,

twisting a silver ring around and around as her cheeks spot bright pink. "I think I—" She swallows hard and glances back at the door, motioning awkwardly as she says, "I think I made a mistake, so I'm—I'm just gonna go—"

I watch as she turns, her aura glowing a tremulous gray as she heads for the door. And even though I don't want to do it, even though I have a potentially life-changing, problem-solving book to return to, I say, "It's not a mistake." She stops, shoulders hunched, looking small and diminutive without the aid of her bully friend. "Seriously," I add. "You meant to come here. And who knows? Maybe I can help."

She takes a deep breath, pausing for so long I'm about to speak again when she turns. "There's this guy." She picks at the hem of her shorts and gazes at me.

"Jude." Sensing the answer without reading her thoughts or touching her skin, just knowing the moment my eyes meet hers.

"Yeah, um, I guess. Anyway, I um—" She shakes her head and starts again. "Well, I was just wondering if he was here. He gave me this." She pulls a crumpled piece of paper from her pocket and lays it flat against the glass, smoothing the creases as she peers up at me.

"He's not here," I mumble, eyes grazing over the flyer advertising his Psychic Development Class level 1, thinking how he wasted no time. "You want to leave a message? Or sign up?" I study her carefully, never having seen her so shy and uncomfortable before—with the ring twisting, eye darting, knee twitching—and knowing it's because of me.

She shrugs, gazing down at the counter as though fascinated by the jewelry inside. "No, um, don't say anything. I'll just come back some other time." She takes a deep breath and pulls her shoulders back, trying to summon some of the usual revulsion reserved just for me, but failing miserably.

And even though part of me wants to soothe her, calm her, convince her there's really no reason to act like this—I don't. I just watch as she leaves, making sure the door closes behind her before heading back to the book.

# twenty-two

"So how was your first day at work?"

I drop onto the couch, kick off my shoes, and prop my feet up on the carved wood coffee table, closing my eyes, and sighing dramatically as I say, "Actually, it was a lot easier than you'd think."

Damen laughs and sinks down beside me. Smoothing my hair off my face when he says, "Then what's with all the fatigue and theatrics?"

I shrug, scrunching down even lower, sinking as deep as I can into the plush, overstuffed cushions, eyes still closed as I say, "I don't know. Maybe it's got something to do with the book I found. It left me feeling a little—*fragmented*. But then, it might have something to do with my surprise visit with—"

"You read a book?" His lips trail down the length of my neck, filling my body with tingle and heat. "As in, the *traditional* way?"

I move closer, throwing my leg over his and snuggling in, eager for the almost feel of his skin. "Believe me, I tried to take the easy way out and just *sense* it instead, but it was like—I don't know—it was the weirdest experience." I look at him, willing his eyes to meet mine, but they remain closed as he buries his face in my hair. "It was like—like the knowledge inside was too powerful to be read in that way, you know? And it gave me this terrible jolt of electricity—like a shock that rattled my bones. Which only made me even more curious, which is why I tried to read it the normal way. Only I didn't get very far."

"Out of practice?" He smiles, lips now at my ear

"More like I couldn't understand it." I shrug. "It's mostly in code. And the parts that are English, well, it was like—olde English. You know, like the kind you used to speak." I pull away and peer at him, smiling when I see the look of mock outrage displayed on his face. "Not to mention the print was really small and it was filled with all these weird sketches and symbols making up spells and invocations, that sort of thing. What—why are you looking at me like that?" I pause, sensing a major energy shift as his body grows tense

"What's the name of this book?" he asks, gaze focused on mine.

I squint, screwing my lips to the side, trying to remember what the fancy gold lettering said. "The *Book of*—Something—" I shake my head, feeling more tired and fragmented than I prefer to let on, especially after seeing the concern on his face.

"*Shadows.*" He nods, wearing a frown. "The *Book of Shadows.* Is that it?"

"So you know it?" I shift, arranging my body until I'm fully facing him, his gaze serious, fixed, as though weighing something he may or may not tell me.

"I'm familiar." He studies my face. "But only with its reputation. I've never had a chance to read it myself. But, Ever, if it's the same tome I'm thinking of—" He shakes his head, disquiet clouding his face. "Well, it contains some extremely powerful magick—magick that needs to be approached with the utmost caution and care. Magick that definitely should not be toyed with, understand?"

"So I guess you're saying it works." I smile, hoping to lighten the mood, but knowing I've failed when he doesn't return it.

"It's nothing like the magick we use. It may seem like it at first, and I suppose that when stripped down to its very essence, it does amount to the same sort of thing. But when *we* evoke the energy of the universe to manifest form, we call upon only the purest and brightest of light with no darkness at all. And even though most magick practitioners or witches are good, *sometimes* when people get involved in witchcraft they get in over their heads, and wind up taking a much darker path, calling on a more malevolent force to get the job done."

I gape, never having heard him even acknowledge a dark force before.

"Everything we do is always based either for the greater good, or our own good. We never do anything to cause any harm."

"I wouldn't say *never*," I mumble, remembering all the times I've beaten Stacia at her own game, or at least tried to.

"Petty schoolyard squabble is hardly what I'm getting at." He dismisses my thoughts. "What I meant was, we manipulate *matter* not *people*. But resorting to spell casting to get what you want—" He shakes his head. "Well, that's a whole other game. Ask Romy and Rayne."

I look at him.

"They *are* witches, you know. Good witches, of course, ones who were taught very well—though unfortunately for them, their schooling was cut a bit short. But take Roman, for instance, he's the perfect example of what can go wrong when one's ego, greed, and insatiable need for power and revenge steer them toward the dark side. His recent use of hypnosis is a prime example of that." He looks at me, shaking his head. "Please tell me you didn't find this book on the shelf—out where just anyone can get it."

I cross my legs and shake my head, fingers tracing the seam on his sleeve. "It was nothing like that," I say. "This copy was— *old*. And I mean, really, *really* old. You know, all fragile and ancient—like it should be in a museum or something. Trust me, whoever it belongs to didn't want anyone to know about it; they went to great lengths to hide it. But you know that can't really stop me." I smile, hoping he'll smile too, but his gaze remains unchanged, worried eyes staring right into mine.

"Who do you think is using it? Lina or Jude?" he asks, using their names so casually you'd think they were friends.

"Does it matter?" I shrug.

He studies me a moment longer, then averts his gaze. Mind wandering to some long-ago place, somewhere I've never been. "So, is that it, then? A brief encounter with the *Book of Shadows*, and you're all tuckered out?" he says, returning to me.

"*Tuckered?*" I lift a brow and shake my head. His odd choice of words never fails to amuse me.

"Too dated?" His lips curve into a grin.

"A little." I nod, laughing along with him.

"You shouldn't make fun of the elderly. It's quite rude, don't you think?" He playfully chucks me under the chin.

"Quite." I nod, quieted by the feel of his fingers straying over my cheek, down my neck, all the way to my chest.

We rest our heads against the cushions and gaze at each other, his hands moving nimbly, deftly, making their way over my clothes, both of us wishing it could lead to something more, but determined to be contented with this.

"So what else happened at work?" he whispers, pressing his lips to my skin, the ever-present veil hovering between us.

"Did some organizing, cataloging, filing—oh, and then Honor came in."

He pulls away, features rearranged into his *I told you so* gaze.

"Relax. It's not like she was looking for a reading or anything. Or at least she didn't seem to be."

"What'd she want?"

"Jude, I guess." I lift my shoulders, inching my fingers under the hem of his shirt, feeling his smooth expanse of skin and wishing I could crawl under there too. "It was weird seeing her alone though. You know, without Stacia or Craig. It's like she was a totally different person—all shy and awkward, completely transformed."

"You think she likes Jude?" His fingers trace the line of my collarbone, his touch so warm, so perfect, barely dimmed by the veil.

I shrug, burying my face in the shallow V of his shirt, inhaling his warm musky scent. Determined to ignore the way my stomach just dipped when he spoke. Having no idea what it means or why I should care if Honor likes Jude, but preferring to push it away nonetheless. "Why? Do you think I should warn him? You know, tell him what she's really like?" My lips pushing into the hollow at the base of his neck, right next to the cord that holds his amulet.

He shifts, rearranging his limbs, pulling away as he says, "If he's as gifted as you say, then he should be able to read her energy and see for himself." He gazes at me, voice careful, measured, overly controlled in a way I'm not used to. "Besides, do we even know what she's *really* like? From what you've described, we only know her under the influence of Stacia. She may be quite nice on her own."

I squint, trying to imagine a nicer version of Honor, but unable to get there. "But still," I say. "Jude has a habit of falling for all the wrong girls and—" I stop, meeting his gaze and sensing that things have taken a definite turn for the worse, though I've no idea why. "You know what? Never mind all that. It's boring and stupid and not worth our time. Let's talk about something else, okay?" I lean toward him, aiming my lips toward the edge of his jaw, anticipating the prickle and scratch of the stubble that grows there. "Let's talk about something that has nothing to do with my job, or the twins, or your ugly new car—" Hoping he was more amused than offended by that. "Something that doesn't make me feel quite so—*old and boring.*"

"Are you saying you're bored?" He looks at me, eyes wide, aghast.

I lift my shoulders and scrunch my face, wishing I could pretend otherwise, but also not wanting to lie. "A little." I nod. "I mean, I'm sorry to say it, but this whole cuddling on the couch while the kids sleep upstairs—" I shake my head. "It's one thing when you're babysitting, but it's a little creepy when the kids are essentially *yours*. I mean, I know we're still adjusting and all—but—well—I guess what I'm trying to say is, it's starting to feel like a rut." I peer at him, lips pressed tightly together, unsure how he'll take that.

"You know how to get out of a rut, don't you?" He jumps to his feet so swiftly he's a shiny, dark blur.

I shake my head, recognizing that look in his eye from when

we first met. Back when things were fun, exciting, unpredictable in every way.

"The only escape is to break free." He laughs, grasping my hand and leading me away.

# twenty-three

I follow him through the kitchen and out to the garage, wondering where he could possibly be taking me since a nice trip to Summerland can be had from the couch.

"What about the twins?" I whisper. "What if they wake and find we're not here?"

Damen shrugs, leading me to his car and glancing over his shoulder as he says, "No worries, they're sleeping soundly. Besides, I have a feeling they'll stay that way for a while."

"And did you have anything to do with that?" I ask, remembering the time he put the entire student body to sleep—including the administrators and teachers—and I'm still not sure how he did it.

He laughs and opens my door, motioning for me to get in. But I shake my head and stand my ground. No way am I riding in the mom mobile—the very embodiment of the rut that we're in.

He looks at me for a moment, then shakes his head and closes his eyes, brows merging together as he manifests a shiny red Lamborghini instead. Just like the one I drove the other day.

But I shake my head again, having no need for a new brand of fun when the old one will do. So I close my eyes and wish it away, replacing it with an exact replica of the shiny black BMW he used to drive.

"Point taken." He nods, waving me in with a mischievous grin.

And the next thing I know we're racing down the drive and onto the street, slowing just enough for the gate to open, before taking Coast Highway in a blur of speed.

I gaze at him, trying to peer into his mind and *see* just where we're going, but he just laughs, purposely erecting his psychic shield, determined to surprise me.

He hops on the freeway and cranks up the stereo, laughing in surprise when the Beatles come on. "*The White Album?*" He glances at me as he navigates the road at near-record speeds.

"Whatever it takes to get you back in this car." I smile, having listened to the story (many times) of his time spent in India learning transcendental meditation right alongside them, back when John and Paul wrote most of these songs. "In fact, if I've manifested it correctly, then that stereo will play nothing *but* the Beatles from now on."

"How am I ever going to adapt to the twenty-first century if you're determined to keep me rooted in the past?" He laughs.

"I was kind of hoping you wouldn't adapt," I mumble, gazing out the window at a blur of darkness and light. "Change is overrated—or at least your more recent changes are. So what do you say? Is she a keeper? Can we banish the big ugly mommy mobile?"

I turn toward him, watching as he exits the freeway and

makes a series of sharp turns before climbing a very steep hill and stopping before a sculpture in front of a huge limestone building.

"What's this?" I squint, knowing we're somewhere in L.A. from the look and feel of the town, but not exactly sure where.

"The Getty." He smiles, setting the brake and jumping out to open my door. "Have you been?"

I shake my head and avoid his gaze. An art museum is about the last place I expected—or even wanted—to go.

"But—isn't it closed?" I glance around, sensing we're the only ones here, other than the armed guards who are probably stationed inside.

"Closed?" He looks at me and shakes his head. "You think I'm going to let something as mundane as that stop us?" He slips his arm around me and leads me up the stone steps, lips at my ear when he adds, "I know a museum's not your first choice, but trust me, I'm about to prove a very good point. One that, from what you just said, clearly needs illustrating."

"What? That you know more about art than I do?"

He stops, his face serious when he says, "I'm going to prove that the world *really is* our oyster. Our playground. Whatever we want it to be. There's no need to ever feel bored or to get into a rut once you understand that the normal rules no longer apply—at least not for us. We can do anything we want, Ever, anything at all. Open, closed, locked, unlocked, welcome, unwelcome—none of it matters, we do *what* we want—*when* we want. There's nothing or no one who can stop us."

*Not entirely true,* I think, ruminating on the very thing we've never been able to do in the past four hundred years, which, of course, is the one thing I really want us to do.

But he just smiles, kissing me on the forehead before grasping my hand, leading me to the door as he says, "Besides, there's an exhibit I'm dying to see, and since there's no crowd it shouldn't take long. And I promise, after, we can go wherever you want."

I stare at the imposing locked doors rigged with the most high-tech alarms that are probably rigged to other high-tech alarms, that are surely rigged to machine gun–wielding guards with their fingers just itching to press the trigger. Heck, there's probably a hidden camera trained on us now, and a *not* amused guard tucked somewhere inside ready to push the panic button under his desk.

"Are you seriously going to try and break in?" I gulp, palms damp, heart clattering against my chest, hoping he's joking even though he clearly is not.

"No," he whispers, closing his eyes and urging me to close mine. "I'm not going to *try*, I'm going to *succeed*. And if you don't mind, you could really help this along by closing your eyes and following my lead." Leaning even closer, lips at my ear when he adds, "And I promise, no one gets caught, hurt, or jailed. Really. Cross my heart."

I peer at him, assuring myself that someone who's lived for six hundred years has survived his share of scrapes. Then I take a deep breath and plunge in. Copying the series of steps he envisions until the doors spring open, the sensors turn off, and the guards all fall into a long deep sleep. Or at least I hope it's long and deep. Long and deep would be good.

"Ready?" He looks at me, lips curving into a grin.

I hesitate, hands shaking, eyes darting, thinking that rut we were in is starting to look pretty good. Then I swallow hard and step in, cringing when my rubber sole meets the polished stone floor, resulting in the most high-pitched, screechy, cringe-worthy sound.

"What do you think?" he says, face eager, excited, hoping I'm enjoying myself as much as he. "I considered taking you to Summerland, but then I figured that's exactly what you'd expect. So I decided to show you the magick of staying right here on the earth plane instead."

I nod, still about as far from excited as it gets but trying to hide it. Scoping out the ginormous room with its tall ceilings, glass windows, and plethora of corridors and halls that probably make it incredibly bright and welcoming in the daytime, but kind of creepy at night. "This place is huge. Have you been here before?"

He nods, heading for the round info desk in the center. "Once. Right before it officially opened. And though I know there's lots of important works to see, there's one exhibit in particular I'm extremely interested in."

He swipes a guest guide off the stand, pressing his palm to the front until the desired location appears in his head. Then dropping it back in its slot, he leads me down a series of halls and up a few stairs, our path lit only by a series of security lights and the glint of the moon shining in through the windows.

"Is this it?" I ask, watching as he stands before a luminous painting titled *Madonna Enthroned with St. Matthew*, body still with awe, expression transformed to one of pure bliss.

He nods, unable to speak as he takes it all in, struggling to compose himself before turning to me. "I've traveled a lot. Lived in so many places. But when I finally left Italy just over four centuries ago, I swore I'd never return. The Renaissance was over, and my life—well—I was more than ready to move on. But then I heard about this new school of painters, the Carracci family in Bologna, who'd learned their craft from the masters, including my dear friend Raphael. They started a new way of painting, influencing the next generation of artists." He motions to the painting before us, face filled with wonder as he softly shakes his head. "Just look at the softness—the textures! The intensity of color and light! It's just—" He shakes his head. "It's just brilliant!" he says, voice tinged with reverence.

I glance between the painting and him, wishing I could see it in the same way as he. Not as some old, priceless, highly regarded picture hanging before me, but as a true thing of beauty, an object of glory, a miracle of sorts.

He leads me to the next one, our hands grasped together as we marvel at a painting of Saint Sebastian, his poor, pale body pierced with arrows—all of it appearing so real I actually flinch.

And that's when I get it. For the first time ever, I can see what Damen sees. Finally understanding that the true journey of all great art is in taking an isolated experience and not just preserving it, or interpreting it, but *sharing* it for all time.

"You must feel so—" I shake my head and press my lips together, searching for just the right word. "I don't know—*powerful*—I guess. To be able to create something as beautiful as this." I peer at him, knowing he can easily create a work with as much beauty and meaning as those that hang here.

But he just shrugs, moving on to the next one as he says, "Other than our art class at school, I haven't painted in years. I guess I'm more of an *appreciator* than a creator now."

"But why? Why would you turn your back on a gift like that? I mean, it *is* a gift, right? There's no way it can be an immortal thing since we've all seen what happens when *I* try to paint."

He smiles, leading me across the room and stopping before a magnificent rendition called *Joseph and Potiphar's Wife*. Gaze searching every square inch of the canvas when he says, "Honestly? *Powerful* doesn't even begin to describe how I feel with a brush in my hand, a blank canvas before me, and a full palette of paint by my side. For six hundred years I've been invincible, heir to the elixir sought by all men!" He shakes his head. "And yet *nothing* can rival the incredible rush the act of creation brings. Of crafting something you just know is destined to be great for all time."

He turns toward me, hand at my cheek. "Or at least that's what I believed up until I saw you. Because seeing you for the very first time—" He shakes his head, eyes gazing into mine. "Nothing can ever compare with that very first glimpse of our love."

"You didn't stop painting for me—*did you?*" I hold my breath, hoping I wasn't the cause of his artistic demise.

He shakes his head, gaze returning to the painting before him as his thoughts travel a long way away. "It had nothing to do with you. It's just—well—at some point, the reality of my situation set in."

I squint, having no idea what that means, or what he could possibly be getting at.

"A cruel reality I probably should've shared with you before." He sighs, looking at me.

I gaze at him, stomach filling with dread, unsure I want to hear the answer when I ask, "What do you mean?" Sensing from the look in his eyes just how much he's struggling with this.

"The reality of living forever," he says, eyes dark, sad, focused on mine. "A reality that seems incredibly vast and infinite and powerful, with no limits in sight—until you realize the truth lurking behind it—the truth of watching your friends all wither and die while you stay the same. Only you're forced to watch it from afar, because once the inequity becomes obvious, you've no choice but to move on, to go somewhere new and start over again. And again. And again." He shakes his head. "All of which makes it impossible to forge any real bonds. And the ironic thing is, despite our unlimited access to powers and magick, the temptation to make a big impact or effect any real change is something that must be avoided at all costs. It's the only way to remain hidden, with our secrets intact."

"*Because—*" I coax, wishing he'd stop being so cryptic and just get to the point. He makes me so nervous when he starts talking like this.

"*Because* drawing that kind of attention guarantees that your name and likeness will be recorded in history, something of which we must work to avoid. *Because* while everyone around you will grow old and die, Haven, Miles, Sabine, and yes, even Stacia, Honor, and Craig—you and I will stay exactly the same, completely unchanged. And, trust me, it doesn't take long before people start to notice how you haven't changed a bit since the day you first met. We can't run the risk of being recognized fifty years from now by a nearly seventy-year-old Haven. Can't afford the risk of having our secret revealed."

He grabs hold of my wrists, gazing at me with such intensity I actually *feel* the weight of his six hundred years. And, like always, when he's troubled like this, my only wish is to whisk it away.

"Can you even begin to imagine if Sabine, or Haven, or Miles discovered the truth about us? Can you imagine what they'd think, what they'd say, what they'd *do*? That's why people like Roman and Drina are so dangerous—they flaunt what they are, completely ignoring the natural order of things.

Make no mistake, Ever, the cycle of life is there for a reason. And while I may have scoffed at that in my youth, feeling quite full of myself for rising above it, I no longer do. Besides, in the end, there's really no fighting it. Whether you reincarnate like our friends, or remain the same like us, your karma will always catch up. And now that I've experienced the Shadowland, I'm even more convinced that life as nature intended it, is the one and *only* way."

"But—if that's what you believe—then where does that leave us?" I ask, a chill blanketing my skin, despite the warmth of his hands. "I mean, to hear you say it, we should lay low, and just live for ourselves, rather than using our incredible powers for any real change. And how can that possibly help your karma if you don't use your gifts to help others? Especially if you do so anonymously?" Thinking of Haven and my hopes of helping her.

But before I can finish, Damen's already shaking his head, looking at me when he says, "Where does that leave *us*? Exactly where we are." He shrugs. "Together. *Forever*. As long as we're very, very careful and continue to wear our amulets, that is. And as for using our powers? Well, I'm afraid it's much more complicated than simply righting all wrongs. While we may judge things as good or bad, karma *doesn't*. It's a simple case of like gets like, the ultimate balancing act, nothing more, nothing less. And if you're determined to fix every situation *you* deem as bad, or difficult, or somehow unsavory, then you rob the person of their own chance to fix it, learn from it, or even grow from it. Some things, no matter how painful, happen for a *reason*. A reason you or I may not be able to grasp at first sight, not without knowing a person's entire life story—their cumulative past. And to just barge in and interfere, no matter how well-intentioned, would be akin to robbing them of their journey. Something that's better not done."

"So let me get this straight." An edge creeping into my voice I don't try to hide. "Haven comes to me and says, *my cat is dying.* And even though I'm pretty sure I can fix it, I don't because it would result in too many questions I could never explain and draw undue suspicion. Fine, I get it. I don't like it, but I get it. But when she says, *my parents might be divorcing, I might have to move, and it feels like my entire world is caving in*—telling me this with no inkling whatsoever that I'm in the perfect position to help her, to maybe even *reverse* some of those things by—I don't know." I shrug, feeling totally frustrated now. "But anyway, my point is, something like that happens to *our* good friend and you're telling me we can't help? Because it would mess with her journey, or her karma, or whatever it is that you said? I mean, explain to me how that helps *my* karma by keeping the goods to myself."

"I advise you to not get involved," he says, turning back toward the painting and away from me. "Haven's parents will continue to fight no matter what you do, and even if you miraculously paid off her house, thinking you could save it"—he looks over his shoulder, giving me a pointed look, sensing that's exactly what I planned to do—"well, they'd probably end up selling it so they could split the proceeds and end up moving anyway." He sighs, voice softening when he looks at me and adds, "I'm sorry, Ever. I don't mean to sound like some jaded old man, but maybe I am. I've seen far too much and made so many mistakes—you've no idea how long it took me to learn all these things. But there really is a season for everything— just like they say. And while our season may be eternal, we can never let on."

"And yet, how many famous artists painted your portrait? How many gifts did you receive from Marie Antoinette?" I shake my head. "I'm sure those portraits lived on! I'm sure someone kept a journal and put your name in it! And what about your modeling days in New York? What about that?"

"I don't deny any of it." He shrugs. "I was vain, full of myself, a textbook narcissist—and boy did I have fun." He laughs, face transforming into the one I know and love, the sexy Damen, the fun Damen, so opposite of this forebearer of doom. "But you've got to understand, those portraits were all privately commissioned, even back then I knew better than to allow them to be publicly displayed. And as for the modeling, it was just a few pictures for a small-time ad campaign. I quit the next day."

"So why did you stop painting? I mean, it seems like a great way to record an unnaturally long life." My head beginning to spin from all of this.

He nods. "The problem was my work was becoming very well known. I was exalted, and believe me, I exalted in my exaltedness." He laughs and shakes his head. "I was painting like a madman, completely obsessed, uninterested in anything else. Amassing a very large collection that drew far too much attention to myself before I properly realized the risk, and then—"

I look at him, heart crashing when I *see* the image unfold in his head. "And then there was a fire," I whisper, *seeing* violent, orange flames rise into a darkened sky.

"Everything was destroyed." He nods. "Including, for all appearances anyway, *me.*"

I suck in my breath, meeting his eyes, unsure what to say.

"And before they could even extinguish the flames, I was

gone. Traveling all over Europe, fleeing from place to place like a nomad, a gypsy, a vagabond, even changing my name a few times until enough time had passed and people started to forget. Finally settling in Paris, where, as you know, we first met—and, well, you know the rest. But, Ever—" He looks into my eyes, wishing he didn't have to say it, but knowing it's necessary to put it into words, even though I already know what comes next. "All of this is to say that at some point—not long from now—you and I will have to move."

And the moment he says it, I can hardly believe I hadn't thought of it before. I mean, it's so obvious, hiding right in plain sight. And yet somehow I was able to ignore it, look the other way, pretending it would be different for me. Which just shows you what denial can do.

"You probably won't age much past this," he continues, hand smoothing my cheek. "And trust me, it won't be long before our friends start to notice."

"Please." I smile, desperate to add a little lightness to this dark, heavy space. "May I remind you that we live in *Orange County*? A place where plastic surgery is practically the norm! Nobody ages here. Seriously. Nobody. Heck, we can carry on just as we are for the next hundred years!" I laugh, but when I look at Damen, see the way his eyes peer into mine, it's clear the gravity of the situation trumps my small joke.

I head for the bench in the center of the room, plopping onto it as I bury my face in my hands. "What do I tell Sabine?" I whisper, as Damen sits beside me, slipping an arm around me and easing my fears. "I mean, it's not like I can fake my own death. That crime-scene investigation stuff's a little more advanced than it was in your day."

"We'll deal with it when the time comes," he says. "I'm sorry, I should've mentioned this before."

But when I look into his eyes, I know it wouldn't have mattered. Wouldn't have made the least bit of difference. Remembering the day when he first presented the whole idea of immortality to me, how careful he was to explain that I'd never cross the bridge, never be with my family again. But I went for it anyway. Pushed the thought right out of my way. Figuring I'd find some kind of loophole, discover a way to work around all of that—willing to convince myself of just about anything if it meant being with him for eternity. And it's no different now.

And though I have no idea what I'll say to Sabine, or how I'll even begin to explain our sudden desertion to our friends, in the end, all I want is to be with *him*. It's the only way my life feels complete.

"We'll enjoy a good life, Ever, I promise you that. You'll never experience any lack, and you'll never be bored again. Not after realizing the glorious possibilities of all that exists. Though aside from you and me—all of our outside connections will be extremely short lived. There's just no getting around it, no *loophole* like you think. It's a necessity, pure and simple."

I take a deep breath and nod, remembering when I first met him and how he said something about being bad at good-byes. But he just smiles, responding to my thoughts when he says, "I know. You'd think it'd get easier, right? But it never really does. I usually find it easier to just disappear and avoid them altogether."

"Easier for *you* maybe, though I'm not so sure about those you've left behind."

He nods, rising from the bench and pulling me up alongside him. "I'm a vain and selfish man, what can I say?"

"That's not what I meant—" I shake my head. "I just—"

"Please." He looks at me. "There's no need to defend me. I know what I am—or at least what I used to be."

He gets up, leading me away from the paintings he came here to see. Only I'm not ready to go. Not yet. Anyone who's forfeited their greatest passion, just simply walked away like he has, deserves a second chance.

I let go of his hand and shut my eyes tightly, manifesting a large canvas, a wide selection of brushes, a comprehensive palette of paints, and whatever else he might need, before he can stop me.

"What's this?" He gazes between the easel and me.

"Wow, it really has been a long time if you can't even recognize the tools of the trade." I smile.

He peers at me, gaze intense, unwavering, but I meet it with equal strength.

"I thought it might be nice for you to paint alongside your friends." I shrug, watching as he grabs a brush from the table, turning it over in the palm of his hand. "You said we could do anything we want, *right*? That the normal rules no longer apply? Wasn't that the point of this trip?"

He looks at me, expression wary but yielding.

"And if that's the case, then I think you should paint something *here*. Create something beautiful, grand, everlasting, whatever you want. And as soon as you're finished, we'll mount it alongside your friends. Leaving it unsigned, of course."

"I'm far past the point of needing my work to be recognized," he says, looking at me, eyes filled with light.

"Good." I nod, motioning toward the blank canvas. "Then I

expect to see a work of pure inspired genius with no ego in-volved." Hand on his shoulder, giving him a nudge when I add, "You should probably get started though. Unlike us, this night is finite."

# twenty-four

I glance between the painting and Damen, palm pressed to my chest, at a complete loss for words. Knowing whatever I say could never describe what's before me. Absolutely no words will do.

"It's so—" I pause, feeling small, undeserving, definitely not worthy of an image so grand. "It's so *beautiful*—and *transcendent*—and"—I shake my head—"and no way is that *me!*"

He laughs, eyes meeting mine when he says, "Oh it's you all right." Smiling as he takes it all in. "In fact, it's the embodiment of all your incarnations. A sort of compilation of the *you* of the last four hundred years. Your fiery hair and creamy skin hailing straight from your life in Amsterdam, your confidence and conviction from your Puritan days, your humility and inner strength taken from your difficult Parisian life, your elaborate dress and flirtatious gaze lifted straight from your London society days, while the eyes themselves—" He shrugs, turning toward me. "They remain the same. Unchanging, eternal, no matter what guise you wear."

"And now?" I whisper, gaze focused on the canvas, taking in the most radiant, luminous, glorious, winged creature—a true goddess descending from the heavens above, eager to bestow the Earth with her gifts. Knowing it's quite possibly the most beautiful image I've ever seen, but still not getting how it could really be me. "What part of me is taken from now? Other than the eyes, I mean."

He smiles. "Why your gossamer wings, of course."

I turn, assuming he's joking until I see the serious expression marking his face.

"You're quite unaware of them, I know." He nods. "But trust me, they're there. Having you in my life is like a gift from above, a gift I surely don't deserve, but one I give thanks for every day."

"Please. I'm hardly that good—or kind—or glorious—or even remotely angelic like you seem to think." I shake my head. "Especially not lately, and you know it," I add, wishing I could hang it in my room where I could see it every day, but knowing it's far more important to leave it right here.

"You sure about this?" He glances between his beautiful un-signed painting and those of his friends.

"Absolutely." I nod. "Imagine all the chaos that'll ensue when they find it professionally framed and mounted on this wall. And I mean the *good* kind of chaos, by the way. Besides, just think of all the people who'll be called upon to study it, trying to determine just where it came from, how it got here, and who could've possibly created it."

He nods, glancing at it one last time before turning away. But I grab his hand and pull him back to me, saying, "Hey, not so fast. Don't you think we should name it? You know, add a little bronze plaque like the other ones have?"

He glances at his watch, more than a little distracted now. "I've never been much good at titling my work, always just went with the obvious. You know: *Bowl of Fruit*, or *Red Tulips in a Blue Vase*."

"Well, it's probably better not to name it *Ever with Wings, Angelic Ever*, or anything remotely like that. You know, just in case someone does recognize me. But how about something a little more—I don't know—*story like*? Less literal, more figurative." I tilt my head and gaze at him, determined to make this work.

"Any suggestions?" He looks at me briefly, before his gaze begins to wander.

"How about—*enchantment*—or *enchanted*—or—I don't know, something like that?" I press my lips tightly together.

"*Enchantment*?" He turns toward me.

"Well, you're obviously under some kind of spell if you think that resembles me." I laugh, watching his eyes light up as he laughs along with me.

"*Enchantment* it is." He nods, back to business again. "But we need to make this plaque quick—I'm afraid we—"

I nod, closing my eyes and envisioning the plaque in my head, whispering, "What should I use for the artist—*anonymous* or *unknown*?"

"Either," he says, voice hurried, anxious, eager to move on

Choosing *unknown* because I like the sound of it, I lean forward to inspect my work, asking, "What do you think?"

"I think we better run!"

He grasps my hand and pulls me alongside him, moving so fast my feet never once touch the ground. Racing down the long series of halls, taking the stairs as though they're not even there. The entry door just within view when the whole room goes bright and the alarm begins to sound.

"Omigod!" I cry, panic crowding my throat as he picks up the pace.

Voice hoarse and ragged when he says, "I didn't plan on staying so long—I—I didn't know—" Stopping as we reach the front door just as the steel cage descends.

I turn to him, heart crashing, skin slick with sweat, aware of the footsteps behind us, the shouts ringing out. Standing mutely beside him, unable to move, unable to scream, his eyes closed in deep concentration, urging the complex alarm system to go dormant again.

But it's too late. They're already here. So I raise my arms in surrender, ready to accept my fate, when the steel cage ascends and I'm yanked out the door and toward the blooming fields of Summerland.

Or at least I envisioned Summerland.

Damen envisioned us safely ensconced in his car, heading toward home.

And so we find ourselves in the middle of a busy highway instead—a slew of speeding cars honking and skidding as we scramble to our feet and hurry to the side, gazing all around and catching our breath as we try to determine where we are.

"I don't think this is Summerland," I say, glancing at Damen as he breaks into a laugh so contagious, it gets me going as well. The two of us huddled on the side of a litter-strewn highway, in some undetermined location, falling all over ourselves.

"How's *that* for breaking out of a rut?" He gasps, shoulders shaking as we continue to laugh.

"I almost had a heart attack back there—I thought for sure we'd—" I catch my breath and shake my head.

"Hey now." He pulls me near. "Didn't I promise I'd always look after you and keep you from harm?"

I nod, remembering the words, but unfortunately the last few minutes are still etched on my brain. "How about a car then? A car would be good about now, don't you think?"

He closes his eyes, transferring the BMW from *there* to *here*, or maybe he manifested a brand new one instead, it's impossible to tell since they both look the same.

"Can you even imagine what those guards thought when first *we* and then the *car* disappeared?" He holds the door open and ushers me in, adding, "The security cameras!" before closing his eyes and taking care of them too.

I watch as he pulls into traffic, a happy grin spread wide across his face. Realizing he's actually enjoying this. That those last few minutes of danger got him even more excited than the painting did.

"It's been a while since I pushed it like that." He glances at me. "But just so you know, I'm holding you partly responsible. After all, you're the one who convinced me to linger."

I look at him, eyes grazing over his face, really taking him in. And even though my heartbeat may never return to normal again, it's been far too long since I've seen him like this—this— *happy*—this—*carefree*—this—*dangerous*—in the way that first made him attractive to me.

"So what's next?" He slaloms through the traffic, hand on my knee.

"Um, home?" I look at him, wondering what could possibly top an outing like that.

He looks at me, clearly game for more. "Are you sure? Because we can stay out as long as you like, I don't want you to get bored again."

"I think I underestimated *bored*." I laugh. "I'm starting to see how it has its place."

Damen nods, leaning toward me and pressing his lips to my cheek, almost rear-ending an Escalade the second he takes his eyes off the road.

I laugh, pushing him back toward his seat. "Really. I think we pushed our luck enough for one night."

"As you wish." He smiles, squeezing my knee as he turns back toward the road, focused on home.

# twenty-five

Even though I'd hoped to be long gone by the time Munoz swung by to pick up Sabine, the second I pull into my drive I glance at my rearview mirror only to find him right there behind me.

Early.

Ten minutes early in fact.

The same ten minutes I'd earmarked for racing home from work and changing into something properly somber, before fleeing the scene and heading for Haven's front yard where Charm's memorial service will be held.

"Ever?" He climbs out of his shiny silver Prius, jangling his keys and squinting at me. "What are you doing here?" He tilts his head as he approaches, enveloping me in a cloud of Axe bodyspray.

I sling my bag over my shoulder, slamming my car door much harder than planned. "Funny thing. I—um—I actually *live* here."

He looks at me, face so still I'm not sure he heard until he shakes his head and repeats, "You *live* here?"

I nod, refusing to say anything more.

"But—" He gazes around, taking in the stone façade, the front steps, the recently clipped lawn, the beds of flowers beginning to bloom. "But this is Sabine's house—*isn't it?*"

I pause, tempted to tell him *no*, that this faux Tuscan, Laguna Beach McMansion isn't Sabine's house at all. That he's obviously made some kind of mistake and ended up at my house instead.

But just as I'm about to, Sabine pulls right up beside us. Jumping out of her car with way too much enthusiasm when she says, "Oh! Paul! So sorry I'm late—the office was crazy and every time I tried to leave something else got in the way—" She shakes her head, gazing up at him in a way that's far too flirtatious for a first date. "But if you could just give me a minute, I'll run upstairs and change so we can get going. It shouldn't take long."

*Paul?*

I glance between them, noting her happy, lilting, singsongy tone, and not liking the sound of it; not liking it at all. It's too intimate. Too forward. She should be forced to call him Mr. Munoz like we do at school. At least until the end of tonight, after which, of course, they'll mutually decide to go their separate ways . . .

He smiles, raking his hand through his longish, wavy brown hair, like the worst kind of show-off. I mean, just because he has exceptionally cool hair for a teacher, doesn't mean he should flaunt it like that.

"I'm a few minutes early," he says, gaze locked on hers. "So please, take as much time as you need. I'm fine talking with Ever here."

"So you've met?" Sabine rests her overstuffed briefcase against her hip, glancing between us.

I shake my head, blurting, "No!" before I can stop. Unsure if I'm saying *no* to her question, or to this whole situation. But still, there it is, an unequivocal *no*, and I've no plans to rescind it. "I mean, yeah, we've met and all but—just now." I pause, their eyes narrowed, as confused as I am as to where this is going. "What I mean is, it's not like we knew each other *before* or anything." I peer at them, knowing I've only confused them more. "Anyway, he's right. You should just—um—go upstairs and get ready—and—" I jab my thumb toward Munoz since there's no way I'm calling him *Paul,* no way I'm calling him anything. "And we'll just hang here until you're ready." I smile, hoping to keep him outside, on the driveway, far from my den.

But unfortunately, Sabine's manners are much better than mine. And I've barely finished the sentence before she shakes her head and says, "Don't be ridiculous. Come inside and relax. And, Ever, why don't you order yourself a pizza or something since I haven't had time to get to the store."

I follow, lagging behind as much as I can without literally dragging my feet. Partly in protest, and partly because I can't risk bumping into either of them, not trusting my quantum remote to bar me from a sneak peek of their date.

Sabine unlocks the front door, glancing over her shoulder as she says, "Ever? Okay? You're good with the pizza?"

I shrug, remembering the two slices of vegetarian Jude left me, which I proceeded to tear into little bits and flush down the toilet as soon as he left. "I'm good. I grabbed a little something at work." I meet her gaze, thinking this just might be the perfect time to tell her, knowing she won't freak with Munoz (*Paul!*) standing nearby.

"You got a *job*?" She gapes, all wide-eyed and slack jawed right there in the entryway.

"Um, yeah." I pull my shoulders in and start scratching my arm even though it doesn't itch. "I thought I told you, no?"

"*No.*" She shoots me a look that's loaded with meaning—none of it good. "You definitely failed to mention it."

I shrug, picking at the hem of my shirt, trying to appear unconcerned. "Oh, well, there it is. I'm officially employed." Chasing it with a laugh that, even to my ears, rings false.

"And just where did you *get* this job of yours?" she asks, voice lowered, gaze following Munoz as he heads into the den, eager to avoid all the bad mojo I've so brilliantly introduced.

"Downtown. At a place that sells books and—stuff."

She squints.

"Listen," I say. "Why don't we discuss this later? I'd hate for you guys to be late or anything." I glance toward the den where Munoz is hunkered down on the couch.

She glances at the den, expression grim, voice low and urgent when she says, "I'm glad you found a job, Ever, don't get me wrong. I just wish you would've told me, that's all. We'll need to find a replacement for you at work now, and—" She shakes her head. "Well, we'll talk about this later. Tonight. When I get back."

And even though I'm *thrilled* to learn that her plans with Munoz do *not* extend to the morning, I still look at her and say, "Um, here's the thing. Haven's cat died, and she's having this memorial service, and she's really upset, which means it could run really late, so—" I shrug, not bothering to finish, allowing her to fill in the blanks that I've left.

"Tomorrow then." She turns. "Now go talk to Paul while I change."

She runs up the stairs, briefcase swinging, heels pounding, as I take a deep breath and make for the den, taking my place behind a big, sturdy armchair, hardly believing it's come to this.

"Just so you know, I'm not calling you *Paul*," I say, taking in his designer jeans, untucked shirt, hipster watch, and shoes that are way too cool for any teacher to wear.

"That's a relief." He smiles, gaze light and easy, resting on mine. "Might get kind of awkward at school."

I swallow hard, fiddling with the back of the chair, unsure just where I'm expected to take it from here. Because even though my entire life is undeniably weird, being forced to make entertaining banter with my history teacher who knows one of my biggest secrets takes it to a whole new level.

But apparently I'm the only one who's uncomfortable around here. Munoz is completely relaxed, sitting back on the coach, foot resting on knee, the absolute picture of ease. "So what exactly *is* your relationship to Sabine?" he asks, arms spread wide across the cushions.

"She's my aunt." I study him, checking for signs of disbelief, confusion, surprise, but all I get is an interested gaze. "She became my legal guardian when my parents passed away." I lift my shoulders and look at him.

"I had no idea. I'm so sorry—" He scrunches his face, voice fading as sadness fills up the space.

"My sister died too." I nod, caught up in it now. "As did Buttercup. She was our dog."

"Ever—" He shakes his head in the way people do when they can't even begin to imagine what it's like to be you. "I—"

"I died too," I add, before he can finish. Not wanting to hear his awkward condolences, struggling to find just the right words when the truth is, those words don't exist. "I died right alongside them—but only for a few seconds, and then I was—" *brought back, resurrected, given the elixir that grants eternal life—* I shake my head. "Well, then I woke up." I shrug, wondering why I just confessed all of that.

"Is that when you became psychic?" His gaze is unwavering, fixed right on mine.

I glance toward the stairway, making sure Sabine's nowhere near, then I glance at Munoz and just nod.

"It happens," he says, neither surprised nor judgmental, more matter of fact. "I've read up on it a bit. It's a lot more common than you'd think. A lot of people come back changed or altered in some way."

I gaze down at the chair, fingers tracing along the top of the cushion, glad for the information but realizing I have no clue how to respond.

"And from the way you're fidgeting and glancing at the stairs every five seconds, I'm guessing Sabine doesn't know?"

I look at him, trying to lighten the mood when I say, "So who's psychic now? Me or you?"

But he just smiles, searching my face with a new understanding that, thankfully, erases the look of pity that lived there before.

We stay like that, him looking at me, me studying the chair, the silence lingering for so long I finally shake my head and say, "Trust me, Sabine wouldn't understand. She'd—" I dig the toe of my sneaker into the carpet's tight weave, unsure just where to take it from here but knowing it's imperative that I make myself clear. "I mean, don't get me wrong, she's a great person, really smart, and a super successful lawyer and all, but it's like—" I shake my head. "Well, let's just say she's a big fan of

black and white. She's not so big on gray." I press my lips together and look away, knowing I've said more than enough,
but needing to make one final thing clear. "But please don't tell
her about me—okay? I mean, you won't—will you?"

I peer at him, holding my breath as he considers, taking his
time as Sabine heads down the stairs. And just when I'm sure I
can't take another second he says, "We'll make a deal. You stop
cutting class and I won't say a word. How's that?"

*How's that? Is he kidding? He's practically blackmailing me!*

I mean, I know I'm not in the best position—especially since
I'm the only one with something to lose, but still. I glance over
my shoulder, seeing Sabine pause in front of the mirror, double-
checking her teeth for stray lipstick tracks, as I turn toward
him and whisper, "What does it matter? There's only a week
left! And we both know I'm getting an A."

He nods, rising from his seat, a smile widening his cheeks
as he takes in Sabine, though his words are directed at me.
"Which is why you have no good reason *not* to be there, right?"

"To not be where?" Sabine asks, looking way too beautiful
with her smoky eye makeup, fluffy blond hair, and an outfit
that Stacia Miller would probably sell a kidney for if she were
twenty years older.

I start to speak, not trusting Munoz not to blow my cover,
but he jumps right in, voice overpowering mine when he says,
"I was just telling Ever to get on with her plans. There's no
need to stick around and entertain me."

Sabine glances between us until her gaze rests on *Paul*. And
even though it's nice to see her looking so relaxed and happy
and eager to get the night going, the second he places his hand
on the small of her back and leads her toward the front door, it's
all I can do not to hurl.

# twenty-six

By the time I get to Haven's, everyone's gathered, looking on as Haven stands just outside the window where she first found her cat, saying a few words in Charm's memory, while hugging a small urn to her chest.

"Hey," I whisper, sidling up beside Damen and glancing at the twins. "What did I miss?"

He smiles, looking at me as he thinks: *Some tears were shed— some poems were read—* He shrugs. *Though I'm sure she'll forgive your lateness—eventually.*

I nod, deciding to show Damen the reason for my lateness— presenting the entire debacle in full Technicolor glory. Watching as Haven sprinkles Charm's ashes over the ground as the images from just a few moments before stream from my mind to his.

He slides his arm around me, comforting me in just the right way, placing a full bouquet of red tulips briefly into my hands—careful to make it appear and disappear before anyone sees.

*Was it really that bad?* He glances at me as Haven hands the urn to her little brother Austin, who scrunches his nose and peers inside.

*Worse.* I shake my head, still wondering why I chose to confide in Munoz—of all people.

I move closer, leaning my head on his shoulder as I add: *And the twins? What are they doing here? I thought they were afraid to go outside?*

They stand beside Haven, faces identical with their solemn dark eyes and razor-slashed bangs—but the similarities end there, having ditched their usual private school uniforms for ones of their own. With Romy striving for the all-American wholesomeness of a J. Crew catalog model, while Rayne's look hails straight from the Hot Topic aisles with her edgy black minidress, torn black tights, and towering platform Mary Jane shoes. Though I doubt they actually shopped at those stores. Not when Damen can just manifest for them.

He shakes his head, arm tightening around me as he responds to my thoughts. *Nope, that's where you're wrong. They're venturing out. Eager to explore the world outside of TV, magazines, and my Crystal Cove gated community.* He smiles. *Believe it or not, they chose those outfits themselves. Even paid for them too. Using the money I gave them, of course.* He looks at me. *Just think, yesterday the mall, today a cat funeral, and tomorrow—who knows?* He turns, smiling in a way that lights up his face as Haven says a final farewell to the cat practically no one here knew.

"Shouldn't we have brought something?" I ask. "You know—flowers or something?"

"We did." Damen nods, lips grazing my ear when he adds, "Not only did we bring those flowers over there"—he points to a giant bouquet made of colorful spring blooms—"but we also made a very generous, though *anonymous*, donation to the ASPCA in Charm's memory. I thought she'd appreciate that."

"Helping people *anonymously?*" I gaze at him, taking in the slant of his brow, the curve of his lips and longing for them to press against mine. "I thought you were against all of that?"

He looks at me, obviously misconstruing the words I'd meant as a joke. But just as I'm about to explain, Josh motions for us to come over.

He peers at Haven, making sure she can't hear, before turning to us, saying, "Listen, I need your help. I messed up."

"How?" I squint, even though the answer just appeared in my head.

He crams his hands into his pockets, dyed black hair falling into his eyes when he says, "I got her a kitten. This guy in my band—well, his girlfriend's cat just had a litter and I thought it might help her get over Charm so I took the black one—but now she won't even talk to me. Says I don't understand. She's seriously mad."

"I'm sure she'll come around, just give her some time, and she'll—"

But he's already shaking his head. "Are you kidding? Did you hear her just now?" He glances between us. "The way she went on and on about how Charm was one of a kind, how she can never be replaced." He shakes his head and looks away. "That was for *me,* make no mistake."

"Everyone feels that way after losing a pet. I'm sure if you—" I stop, gazing into eyes so defeated I know I'm not making a dent.

"No way." He lifts his shoulders, looking at her, the loss clear on his face. "She meant it. She's sad about Charm, mad at me, and now I've got this kitten in the backseat of my car and no idea what to do with it. I can't bring it home, my mom'll kill me, and Miles can't take it because of the whole Italy thing, so I thought maybe you guys would want her." His gaze darts between us, silent but pleading.

I take a deep breath and glance toward the twins, knowing they would love nothing more than a pet of their own, especially after the way they reacted to Charm. But what becomes of it once their magick's restored and they head back to Summerland? Is it possible to bring the cat with them? Or will she become our responsibility?

But when they turn, the two of them gazing at me, Romy's face lifting into a smile while Rayne's drops to a scowl, I know I need all the help I can get where they're concerned, and a cute little kitten might be a good start.

I look at Damen, knowing the moment our eyes meet that we're on the same page.

We head for Josh's car as he says, "Let's have a look."

"Omigod! Are you serious? She's seriously ours? For reals?" Romy cradles the tiny black kitten and glances between us.

"She's all yours." Damen nods. "But you should thank Ever, not me. It was her idea."

Romy looks at me, a grin spread wide across her face as Rayne twists her mouth to the side, pursing her lips in a way that makes it clear she's sure she's being played.

"What should we name her?" Romy glances between us before focusing solely on Rayne. "And don't say Jinx the second, or Jinx squared, or anything like that, because this kitty deserves her own name." She hugs the kitten tight to her chest, planting a kiss on the top of her tiny black head. "She also deserves a much better fate than the other Jinx had."

I look at them, about to ask what happened when Rayne says, "That's all in the past. But Romy's right, we need to find the perfect name. Something strong and mystical—something truly worthy of a kitty like this."

We sit, the four of us sprawled across the various chairs and couches in Damen's oversized den. Damen and I sharing a cushion, limbs entwined as our minds sift through long lists of suitable names until I clear my voice and say, "How about Luna?" I glance between them, hoping they'll like it as much as I do. "You know, like the Latin word for *moon*?"

"Please." Rayne rolls her eyes. "We know what *Luna* means. In fact, I'm pretty sure we know way more Latin than *you*."

I nod, struggling to keep my voice calm and composed, refusing to rise to her bait, when I add, "Well, I was thinking that since they say cats are connected to the moon and all—" I stop, taking one look at her face and knowing there's no point in going on, she's dead set against it.

"You know, it used to be said that cats were the children of the moon," Damen says, determined not only to rescue me, but also to prove, once and for all, why I'm worthy of their respect. "Because like the moon, they both come to life at night."

"Then maybe we should name her Moon Child," Rayne says. Nodding when she adds, "Yes, that's it! Moon Child. It's *so* much better than *Luna*."

"No it isn't." Romy gazes down at the sleeping cat in her lap, stroking the narrow space between her ears. "Moon Child's all wrong. Lumpy. Too much. A name should be only *one* word. And this kitty is clearly a *Luna* to me. Luna. That's what we're calling her then?"

She glances between us, counting three nodding heads, and one that refuses to budge just to spite me.

"Sorry, Rayne." Damen clasps my hand, a sliver of energy the only thing that separates his palm from mine. "I'm afraid the majority rules in this case." He nods, closing his eyes as he manifests an exquisite velvet collar of the deepest purple that instantly appears around Luna's neck. Romy and Rayne gasping, eyes shining with delight when he manifests a matching velvet bed. "Perhaps you should place her there now," he says.

"But we're both so comfortable like this!" Romy whines, not wanting to part with her pet.

"Yes, but we also have lessons to get to, don't we?"

The twins glance at each other, then rise simultaneously, carefully placing Luna in her new bed and hovering at its edge, making sure she's sleeping comfortably, before turning back to Damen, ready to begin. Taking the seats just across from him, ankles crossed, hands folded in laps, more obedient than I've ever seen them. Ready for whatever Damen's got planned.

*What's this about?* I shift as we untangle our limbs.

"Magick." He nods, glancing between them. "They need to practice daily if their powers are to return."

"How do you practice?" I squint, wondering if it's anything like the classes Jude's planning to teach. "I mean, are there exercises and tests, like in school?"

Damen shrugs. "It's really more a series of meditations and visualizations—though far more intense and of a much longer duration than the ones I put you through on our first journey to Summerland, but then, you didn't require as much. Even though the twins hail from a long line of very gifted witches, I'm afraid that as it stands now, they're back to stage one. Though I'm hoping that with regular practice, they'll recapture their abilities in reasonable time."

"How long is *reasonable*?" I ask. When what I really mean is: *How soon do we get our life back?*

Damen shrugs. "Few months. Maybe longer."

"Would the *Book of Shadows* help?" Realizing just after it's out, that I shouldn't have said it. Damen's expression is not at all happy, though the twins are now poised on the edge of their seats.

"*You* have the *Book of Shadows*?" Rayne says, as Romy just sits there and gapes.

I glance at Damen, seeing he's none too pleased, but since the book could very well help them as much as I hope it can help me, I say, "Well, I don't exactly *have* it, but I have access to it."

"Like for real? Like a *real Book of Shadows*?" Rayne phrases her words like a question, though her gaze tells me she's sure it's a fake.

"I don't know." I shrug. "Is there more than one?"

She looks at Romy, shaking her head and rolling her eyes before Damen can say, "I haven't seen it, but from Ever's description, I'm sure that it's real. And quite powerful too. Too powerful for you at the moment. But maybe later, after we've progressed through our meditations we can—"

But Romy and Rayne are no longer listening, their attention focused solely on me as they rise from their seats and say, "Take us there. Please. We need to see it."

# twenty-seven

"How will you get in?" Romy whispers, edging up alongside me and gazing at the door, a wary expression crossing her face.

"Duh!" Rayne shakes her head. "It's easy for them. All they have to do is unlock the door with their minds."

"True." I smile. "But having a key is handy too." Jangling it so they can see before inserting it into the lock. Careful to avoid Damen's gaze, though it's not like I need to see to know he disapproves.

"So this is where you work," Romy says, stepping inside and gazing around. Moving lightly, gingerly, as though she's afraid to mess anything up.

I nod, placing my finger against my lips in the international sign for *shush* as I lead them toward the back room.

"But if the store's closed, and we're the only ones here, then why do we have to *shush*?" Rayne asks, her high-pitched voice practically bouncing off the walls, wanting me to know that while she's pleased that I'm about to show her the *Book of Shadows* it doesn't extend much further than that.

I open the door to the back office and motion them inside, telling them to sit, while Damen and I consult in the hall.

"I don't like this," he says, eyes dark, focused on mine.

I nod, very well aware of that but determined to stand my ground.

"Ever, I'm serious. You have no idea what you're getting into. This book is powerful—and in the wrong hands—dangerous as well."

I shake my head, saying, "Listen, the twins are familiar with this brand of magick, much more so than you and me. And if they're not worried, then how bad could it be?"

He looks at me, refusing to budge. "There are better ways."

I sigh, wanting to get started and frustrated to be dealing with this. "You act like I'm going to introduce them to evil spells or make them bad witches with warts and black hats, when all I want is the same thing as you—for them to get their power back." Careful to shield my mind so he can't hear the unspoken part, the real truth behind this visit—that I spent most of yesterday at work struggling to make sense of the book to no avail—that I need help if I've any hope of convincing Roman to hand over the antidote. Knowing it's better unsaid. Damen would so not approve.

"There are better ways of doing this," he says, voice patient but firm. "I have their lessons mapped out, and if you'll just give it the time to—"

"How much time? Weeks, months, a year?" I shake my head. "Maybe we can't afford to waste that kind of time, did you ever think of that!"

"*We?*" His brows merge as his gaze studies mine, a hint of understanding forming in his eyes.

"We, them, whatever." I shrug, knowing I better move on.

"Let me just show them the book and see if it's even the real deal. I mean, we don't even know if it really works, maybe my reaction was—well, maybe that was just *me*. Come on, Damen, please? What could it hurt?"

He looks at me, convinced it could hurt plenty.

"Just one quick look—only to determine if it's real or not. Then we'll head right back home and get started with your lesson, okay?"

But he doesn't say anything. Just nods and motions me in.

I head for the chair on the other side of the desk, settling in and leaning toward the drawer when Rayne says, "Just so you know, we heard *everything*. Our hearing is exceptional. Maybe you should stick with telepathy instead."

Determined to ignore her, I place my hand on the lock, closing my eyes as I open it with my mind, flicking a quick glance at Damen as I rummage inside. Digging past the pile of papers, the folders, and tossing the calculator aside, before reaching the false bottom, grabbing hold of the book, and plopping it onto the desk. Fingers tingling, ears buzzing from the energy it contains.

The twins rush forward, gazing upon the ancient tome with more reverence than I've ever seen from them before.

"So, what do you think? Is it real?" My gaze darts between them, so breathless I can barely form the words.

Romy tilts her head, face quizzical, until Rayne reaches forward and opens to the very first page. The two of them gasping, twin intakes of breath, as their eyes grow wide and they take it all in.

Rayne perches on the edge of the desk, angling the book so it faces her and her sister, as Romy leans across her lap, tracing her fingers along the series of symbols—markings that are completely indecipherable to me—though from the way their lips move makes perfect sense to them.

I glance at Damen standing directly behind them, his face belying any emotion as he watches the twins mumble and giggle, jostling each other in excitement as they flip through the pages.

"So?" I say, unable to take the suspense and needing a verbal either way.

"Real." Rayne nods, eyes still focused on the page. "Who ever put this together knew their stuff."

"You mean, there's more than one?" I squint, glancing between them, barely able to meet their eyes under their lush fringe of lashes and jagged-cut bangs.

"Sure." Romy nods. "There's tons. *Book of Shadows* is just a generic title for a *spell book*. They think the name originated due to the fact that the books had to be kept hidden, in the shadows so to speak, because of their content."

"Yeah," Rayne cuts in, "but some also say it's because they were often read and written by candlelight, which casts shadows as you know."

Romy shrugs. "Either way, they're written in code to avoid the danger of falling into the wrong hands. But the truly powerful ones, the ones like this"—she stabs the page with her index finger, which is newly painted ballet slipper pink—"are extremely rare and hard to find. Hidden away for the very same reason."

"So it's powerful? *And real?*" I repeat, needing it confirmed one more time.

Rayne looks at me, shaking her head like I'm too dense to be believed, while her sister nods, saying, "You can actually *feel* the energy of the words on the page. It's quite powerful, I assure you."

"So, you think it'll be useful then? You think it might help us—*you*—with your needs?" Eyes darting between them, hoping they'll say *yes* while carefully avoiding Damen's gaze.

"We're a little rusty—" Romy starts. "So we can't say for sure—"

"Speak for yourself," Rayne says, flipping back toward the front until finding the page that she wants. Repeating a stream of words I can't even begin to understand as though it's her native tongue. "See that?" She waves her hand in the air, laughing as the lights flicker on and off. "I wouldn't exactly call that *rusty*."

"Yes, but since they were supposed to burst into flames, you're still a long ways away," Romy says, arms folded, brow raised.

"Burst into flames?" I glance at Damen. He was right, this is dangerous in the wrong hands—their hands.

But Romy and Rayne just laugh, falling all over themselves when they say, "Psych! We totally psyched you! Ha!"

"You are too gullible to be believed!" Rayne adds, seizing any chance to make a fool of me.

"And you guys have been watching *way* too much TV," I say, slamming the book shut and moving it away.

"Wait! You can't take that! We *need* it!" Two sets of hands frantically reaching and grasping my way.

"It doesn't belong to me. So it's not like we can take it home or anything," I say, holding it just out of reach.

"But how will we get our magick back if you hide it like that?" Romy's face drops to a pout.

"Yeah," Rayne adds, shaking her head. "First you make us leave Summerland and now—" Stopping only when Damen raises his hand to silence them.

"I think it's best you put that away," he says, eyes on mine, jaw clenched tight. "Now," he adds, with new urgency.

I nod, thinking he's more upset than I thought, taking a stand and insisting I stick to our deal. Until I follow his gaze to the monitor and watch as a dark blurry figure walks in.

# twenty-eight

I slide the drawer open, frantically shoving the book inside as a soft thud of footsteps makes their way down the hall.

Barely getting it closed before Jude sticks his head in and says, "Working late?"

He steps into the room and offers his hand to Damen who hesitates, taking a moment to size him up, before offering his own. Even after releasing Jude's grip his gaze remains focused, unmoving, his mind far away.

"So, what's going on here? Is this take-your-family-to-work day?" Jude smiles, though it doesn't quite reach his eyes.

"No! We were just—" I swallow hard, having no idea what comes next, meeting his deep knowing gaze and quickly looking away.

"We were looking at your *Book of Shadows*," Rayne says, arms folded, eyes narrowed. "And we were wondering where you got it?"

Jude nods, lips lifting at the corners when he says, "And you *are*?"

"Romy and Rayne." I nod. "They're my—" I glance at them, wondering how to explain them.

"Nieces," Damen says, gaze locked on Jude. "They're staying with me for a while."

Jude nods, glancing at Damen briefly before returning to me. Moving just shy of the desk as he says, "Well, if anyone could find it, it's you."

I swallow hard, glancing at Damen who continues to eye Jude in a way I've never seen from him before. Like his entire being is on a full-scale alert—posture stiff, features controlled, eyes narrowing to the deepest, darkest points, all the while taking him in.

"Am I fired?" I ask, laughing a little, but mostly I'm serious.

Jude shakes his head. "Why would I fire my very best psychic? My only psychic!" He smiles. "Funny, that book's been in the drawer since last summer and yet no one found it 'til now." He shrugs. "So what's your interest in it anyway? I thought you weren't into magick and stuff?"

I swivel back and forth in my seat, uncomfortable, squirmy, especially with the way Damen keeps looking at him. "I'm not, but the twins are very much into—"

"Wicca," Damen says, placing a protective hand on each of their shoulders. "They're interested in learning more about Wicca, and Ever thought this book might help. Though obviously, it's far too advanced."

Jude looks at Damen, slowly taking him in. "Looks like I just got my second and third sign-up for class."

"There's another?" I say, quickly, without thinking, glancing briefly at Damen and feeling an inexplicable flush rise to my cheeks.

Jude shrugs. "If she shows. Seemed pretty interested though."

*Honor.* I know it without even peering into his mind. Honor's the first sign-up, and I've no doubt she'll show.

"Class?" Damen asks, hands still on the twins, gaze darting between Jude and me.

"Psychic Development level one." He shrugs. "With a small emphasis on self-empowerment and magick. I'm thinking we should start soon, maybe even tomorrow. Why wait?"

Romy and Rayne look at each other, eyes blazing with excitement. But Damen shakes his head saying, "No."

Jude looks at him, face easy, relaxed, not the least bit daunted. "Aw come on, I won't even charge. I'm new at this anyway, so it's a good chance for me to try it all out and see what works and what doesn't. Besides, it's just a simple introductory course, nothing heavy, if that's what you're worried about."

Their eyes meet, and even though I know the *heavy* part is pretty much Damen's number-one concern, it's clearly not his *only* concern.

· No, this sudden edginess, this uncharacteristic guardedness, has something to do with Jude.

And me.

Jude and me together.

And if I didn't know better, I'd think he was jealous. But I do know better, and, unfortunately, that sort of behavior is relegated only to me.

The twins plead with him, large brown eyes gazing into his. "Please!" they say, voices high-pitched, intertwining. "We *really, really, really* want to take this class!"

"It'll help us with our magick!" Romy nods, smiling as she tugs on his hand.

"And get us out of the house so Ever can't complain about your lack of privacy anymore!" Rayne adds, managing to insult me even as she aims to convince.

Jude looks at me, brows raised in amusement, but I quickly look away, holding my breath until I hear Damen say, "We'll get there on our own, you need to be patient." His words final, leaving no room to negotiate.

Jude nods, shoving his hands deep into his pockets as he gazes between us. "No worries. If you change your mind, or just want to stop by and monitor, feel free. Who knows, maybe you'll learn something?"

Damen's eyes narrow ever so slightly, but still it's enough to persuade me to stand up and say, "So, I'm still on the schedule tomorrow?"

"Bright and early." Studying me closely as I maneuver around the desk and into the welcoming crook of Damen's arm. "I won't be in until later," he adds, moving for the seat I just vacated and settling in. "So if that girl—" He squints, looking at me.

"Honor." I nod.

Seeing Damen gape in surprise as Jude laughs and says, "Wow, you really are psychic. Anyway, if she comes in, tell her we'll start sometime next week."

# twenty-nine

"Your boyfriend seems cool." Jude looks at me, leaning on the edge of the counter, coffee mug in hand.

"That's because he *is* cool." I nod, thumbing through the appointment book, seeing I'm booked for a two o'clock, followed by a three, a four, and a five—and relieved to see that the names aren't even slightly familiar.

"So he *is*—your boyfriend, then?" He takes a quick sip of his drink, eyeing me from over the top of the cup. "I couldn't be sure. Seems kind of *old*, you know?"

I slam the book shut and reach for my water, even though I'd really prefer a gulp of immortal juice instead. But ever since Roman showed up I vowed to cut back on my public consumption. "We're in the same class." I shrug, returning his gaze. "Which would make us the same age, no?" Hoping to avoid further scrutiny by phrasing it like that.

But Jude continues to stare, gaze deepening when he says, "I don't know, does it?"

I swallow hard and look away, heart beating overtime as I think, *Does he sense something too? Is he onto us?*

"Could mean he was held back—for—" He smiles, those sea green eyes sparkling, full of light. "Several decades—at least?"

I lift my shoulders, determined to ignore the insult if that's what it was. Reminding myself that Jude's not just my boss—providing a job that gets Sabine off my back—but also the keeper of the *Book of Shadows*, a tome I desperately need to get to again.

"So, how'd you meet Honor?" I ask, leaning down to tinker with the jewelry display. Rearranging the silver chains with their gemstone pendants, tucking the price tags away. Hoping to appear nonchalant, blasé, as though I'm just filling up the silence and not because I care.

He leaves his cup on the counter and disappears into the back, fiddling with the stereo system until the room fills with the sound of crickets and rain, the same CD he plays every day. "I was hanging a flyer over at this place." He returns to the counter and points to the name on his cup.

"Was she alone or with someone?" I squint, imagining Stacia egging her on, making her approach him, as some kind of dare.

He looks at me, eyes searching my face for so long I avert my gaze and busy myself with the rings, organizing them by color and type, as he continues to study me.

"Didn't notice." He shrugs. "She just asked about the class so I gave her a flyer to take with her."

"Did you talk? Did she tell you *why* she's interested?" Blowing my cover as a person who's only mildly curious the moment the words escape.

He squints, gaze deepening as he says, "Said she's having

boyfriend problems and wanted to know if I knew any good spells she could cast."

I gape, unsure if he's joking, until he laughs.

"What's with all the interest? She try to steal your boyfriend or something?"

I shake my head, shutting the jewelry case and meeting his gaze when I say, "No, her best friend did."

Jude eyes me, voice careful when he says, "And was she successful?"

"No! Of course not!" Cheeks flushing, heart racing, knowing I answered too quickly to ever be believed. "But that doesn't stop her from trying," I add, knowing that was no better.

"*Doesn't* stop her, or *didn't* stop her? She still at it?" He lifts his cup and takes a long pull, his gaze never once leaving my face.

I shrug, still trying to recover from my previous outburst. Knowing I'm the one who started all this.

"So, you in the market for a spell of your own? Something that'll keep the girls away from Damen?" Brow raised, voice giving no hint if it was a joke.

I shift on my stool, unnerved by the weight of his gaze, not liking the sound of Damen's name on his lips.

"Guess that explains your sudden interest in the *Book of Shadows*," Jude says, refusing to let it go.

I roll my eyes and move away from the counter, not caring if it's an insubordinate act. This conversation is over. I'm making that clear.

"Is this going to be a problem?" he asks, his voice carrying a tone I can't read.

I stop just shy of the bookshelf, unsure what he's referring to. Turning to read his sunshiny aura, and still not having a clue.

"I know you don't want people to know about you, and now there's some girl from your school dropping in . . ." He shrugs, allowing me to fill in the rest.

I shrug too, realizing the list of people who know my psychic secret is really starting to grow. First Munoz, then Jude, and soon Honor, which means Stacia will follow (though she already suspects anyway)—and then of course there's Haven who proclaims to be "onto" us as well. And the awful part is—all of this can be traced back to me.

I clear my throat, knowing I have to say something though I've no idea what. "Honor's not—" *nice, pleasant, kind, decent, at all what she seems*—but the truth is, that more describes Stacia. Honor's much more of an enigma to me.

Jude looks at me, waiting for the finish.

But I just turn away, face obscured by a chunk of blond hair when I say, "Honor's not someone I know all that well."

"Guess that makes two of us." He grins, tossing back the last of his coffee before crumbling his cup and projecting it toward the trash where it lands with a thud. His gaze seeking mine when he says, "Though she does seem a little lost and unsure, and that's exactly the kind of person we try to help around here."

By six, my fifth client, a last-minute walk-in, is gone for the day, and I'm in the back room smoothing my hair from the black wig I decided to wear.

"Better." Jude nods, glancing up from his computer briefly, before returning to his work. "The blond suits you. That black was a little harsh," he mumbles, tapping the keyboard and shaking his head.

"I know. I looked like a severely anemic Snow White," I say, looking at Jude as we laugh.

"So, what'd you think?" he asks, back to his computer screen.

"I liked it." I nod, moving away from the mirror and closer to the desk where I perch on the edge. "It was good. I mean, some of it was kind of depressing and all, but it's nice to be able to help someone for a change, you know?" Watching his fingers move across the keyboard so fast my eyes can hardly keep up. "Because honestly, I wasn't so sure. But I think it went okay. I mean, you didn't get any complaints or anything—did you?"

He shakes his head, squinting as he shuffles through a stack of papers at his side. "Did you remember to shield yourself?" He takes a moment to gaze up at me.

I lift my shoulders, having no idea what he means. The only *shielding* I've ever done is the kind that shuts off everyone's energy, which would make it pretty much impossible to give a reading.

"You need to protect yourself," he says, pushing away his laptop to better focus on me. "Both before and after a reading. Has no one ever shown you how to leave yourself open while still shielding yourself from unwanted attachments?"

I shake my head, wondering if that's even necessary for an immortal like me. Unable to imagine anyone's energy being strong enough to drag me down, but it's not like I can share that with him.

"Would you like to learn how?"

I shrug, scratching my arm as I glance at the clock, wondering how long it'll take.

"It won't take long," he says, reading my expression, already moving away from the desk. "And it really is important. Think of it like washing your hands—it releases all the negative stuff your clients carry with them, making sure it can't contaminate your life."

He motions for me to take one of the seats as he perches on the adjacent one, regarding me seriously as he says, "I would guide you through a meditation that'll help strengthen your aura—but since I can't actually *see* your aura, I have no idea if it needs strengthening."

I press my lips together and cross my right leg over my left, shifting uncomfortably in my seat, unsure how to respond.

"Sometime you'll have to tell me how you hide it like that. I'd love to learn your technique."

I swallow hard and nod slightly, as though I might just do that someday, but not now.

Keeping his voice low and smooth, almost to a whisper, he says, "Close your eyes and relax, breathing slowly and deeply as you picture a swirl of pure golden energy with each intake of breath, followed by a swirl of dark mist with each outtake. Breathing in the good—ridding yourself of the bad. Continuing this cycle again and again, allowing only good energy to work its way through your cells, until you feel cleansed and whole and ready to begin."

I do as he says, reminded of the grounding meditation Ava once put me through, concentrating on my breath, keeping it slow, steady, and even. At first feeling self-conscious under the weight of his gaze, knowing he's studying me closer than he would if my eyes were open, but soon, I'm pulled into the rhythm—pulse calming, mind clearing, concentrating on nothing but breathing.

"Then, when you're ready, imagine a cone of the most brilliant, golden white light reaching down from the heavens and descending upon you—growing and expanding in size until it bathes you completely—surrounding your entire being and allowing no lower energies or negative force fields to creep in—keeping all your positivity fully intact, safe from those who might leech it."

I open an eye, peeking at him, never having thought of someone trying to steal my chi.

"Trust me," he says, waving his hand, motioning for me to close my eyes and return to the meditation again. "Now imagine that same light as a powerful fortress, repelling all darkness while keeping you safe."

So I do. Seeing myself in my mind, sitting on that chair, with a cone of light extending from above and moving down past my hair, over my tee, and well past my jeans to my flip-flops below. Enveloping me completely, keeping the good stuff in, and the bad stuff out—just like he said.

"How does it feel?" he asks, voice much closer than I expected.

"Good." I nod, holding the cone of light in my mind, keeping it steady and bright. "It feels warm and—welcoming—and—good." I shrug, more interested in enjoying the experience than rooting around for just the right word.

"You need to repeat that every day—but this is the longest it should ever take. Once you've imprinted yourself with the cone of light, all you need to do to maintain it is a few of those deep cleansing breaths, followed by a quick image of you sealed by the light, and you're good to go. Though it's not a bad idea to renew it now and then—especially since you're about to become very popular around here."

He places his hand on my shoulder, palm flat and open, fingers splayed across the cotton of my tee, the sensation so shocking, so jolting, the images so revealing, I jump to my feet.

"Damen!" I cry, voice hoarse, scratchy, as I turn to find him at the door, watching me—watching *us*.

He nods, gaze meeting mine in what, at first seems his usual loving way—filled with a complete and total reverence for me. But the longer it holds, the more I sense something behind it. Something dark. Troubling. Something he's determined to keep.

I move toward him, clasping his hand as it reaches toward mine, aware of the protective shield of energy that hovers between us—an energy I was certain no one could see, until I notice Jude squinting.

I peer at Damen, unable to determine the big hidden thing in his gaze, wondering what he's doing here, if he somehow sensed this.

His arm tightens around me, pulling me near when he says, "Sorry to interrupt, but Ever and I have somewhere to be."

I gaze up, drinking him in—the smooth planes of his face, the swell of his lips—the tingle and heat strumming from his body to mine.

Jude rises and follows us into the hall, saying, "Sorry. Didn't mean to keep her so long." His hand reaching toward me, glancing my shoulder then falling away as he adds, "Oh, I forgot—the book! Why don't you take it, it's not like I need it around here."

He turns back toward the desk, about to retrieve it from the drawer, and even though I'm tempted to grab it and run, with the way Damen stiffens as Jude's aura grows brighter—well, it's beginning to feel like a test. And it's all I can do to force the words past my lips when I say, "Thanks, but not tonight. Damen and I have plans."

Damen's energy relaxes, returning to normal as Jude's gaze

dances between us. "No worries," he says. "Another time."
Holding the gaze for so long, I'm the first to turn away.

Leading Damen out the door and onto the street, determined to shake off Jude's energy, along with the thoughts and
images he unwittingly shared.

# thirty

"So you kept it." I smile, settling into his BMW, happy to see he's kept it in place of Big Ugly.

He looks at me, eyes still serious but voice light when he says, "You were right. I went a little overboard with the whole safety thing. Not to mention, this is a *much* better ride."

I gaze out the window, wondering what sort of adventure he's planned, but figuring he wants to surprise me as usual. Watching as he pulls onto the street and weaves through the traffic until we're clear of all cars and he picks up the speed. Pushing the gas and accelerating so quickly, I have no idea where we're going, until we're already there.

"What's this?" I gaze around, amazed by his ability to always do the least expected thing.

"I figured you'd never been here." He opens my door and takes my hand. "Was I right?"

I nod, taking in a barren desert landscape, dotted only by the occasional shrub, a mountainous backdrop, and thousands of windmills. Seriously thousands. All of them tall. All of them white. All of them turning.

"It's a windmill farm." He nods, hoisting himself onto the trunk of his car and dusting off a space for me to sit too. "It produces electricity by harnessing the wind. In just one hour it can make enough electricity to run a typical household for a month."

I glance all around, taking in the turning blades and wondering what the significance could be. "So, why'd we come here? I'm a little confused."

He takes a deep breath, gaze far away, expression wistful when he says, "I find myself drawn to this place. I guess because I've borne witness to so much change during the last six hundred years, and harnessing the wind is a very old idea."

I squint, still not getting its importance, but definitely sensing there is one.

"Despite all the technological changes and advances I've seen—some things—things like this—remain pretty much the same."

I nod, silently urging him on, sensing something much deeper in his words, but knowing he's choosing to dole them out slowly.

"Technology advances so quickly, making the familiar obsolete at an increasingly rapid pace. And while things like fashion may seem to advance and change, if you live long enough, you realize it's really just cyclical—the readapting of old ideas made to seem new. But while everything around us seems to be in a constant state of flux—people at their very core remain exactly the same. All of us still seeking the things we've sought all along—shelter, food, love, greater meaning—" He shakes his head. "A quest that's immune to evolution."

He looks at me with eyes so deep and dark, I can't imagine what it's like to be him. To have witnessed so much, to know so much, to have done so much—and yet, despite what he thinks, he's not the slightest bit jaded. He's still full of dreams.

"And once the basics are covered, once we've secured food and shelter, we spend the rest of our time just looking to be loved."

He leans toward me, lips cool and soft as they brush my skin—fleeting, ephemeral, like a sweet desert breeze. Pulling away to gaze at the windmills again when he says, "The Netherlands is known for their windmills. And since you did spend a lifetime there, I thought you might want to visit."

I squint, thinking he surely misspoke. We've no time for that trip—*do we?*

Watching as he smiles, gaze growing lighter as he says, "Close your eyes and come with me."

# thirty-one

We tumble forward, hands clasped together as we land with a thud. Taking a moment to look around when I say, "Omigod—this is—"

"Amsterdam." He nods, eyes narrowing as he adjusts to the mist. "Only not the real Amsterdam, the Summerland version. I would've taken you to the real one, but I figured this trip was shorter."

I gaze all around, taking in the canals, the bridges, the windmills, the fields of red tulips—wondering if he created that last part for me, then remembering how Holland is famous for its flowers—especially its tulips.

"You don't recognize it, do you?" he asks, studying me carefully as I shake my head. "Give it some time, you will. I've recreated it from memory, how I remember it back in the nineteenth century when you and I were last there. It's a pretty good copy if I say so myself."

He leads me across the street, pausing long enough to allow an empty carriage to pass, before continuing to a small storefront, its door wide open, as a lively crowd of faceless people gather inside. Watching me carefully, eager to see if a memory's sparked, but I move away, wanting to get a feel on my own, trying to picture the former me in this place—the red-haired, green-eyed me—walking among these white walls, wood floors at my feet, gazing at the line of paintings dotting the perimeter as I weave through the patrons who begin to fade at the edges before strengthening again. Knowing that Damen's responsible for keeping them here, having manifested their very existence.

I move along the walls, assuming this is a re-creation of the gallery where we first met, though disappointed to find it not the least bit familiar. Noting how all the paintings blur and fade until they're completely imperceptible, except for the one just before me, the only one that's intact.

I lean forward, squinting at a girl with abundant titian hair—a luxurious blend of reds, golds, and browns contrasting so beautifully with her expanse of pale skin. Painted in a way so tangible, so smooth, so inviting—it's as though one could step in.

My gaze roams the length of her, seeing she's nude though strategically covered. The ends of her hair damp and conforming, tumbling over her shoulders and hanging well past her waist, while her hands are folded, resting atop a pink flushed thigh turned slightly in. Though it's the eyes that grab me, made of the deepest green and holding a gaze so direct, so open, as though staring at a lover, not the least bit ashamed at having been caught in this state.

My stomach twitches, while my heart begins to flutter, and even though I'm aware of Damen standing right there beside me, I can't look at him. Can't include him in this. Something is creeping upon me, the birth of an idea tugging, nudging, demanding to be known. And before I've even blinked, I *see* it. As sure as I see the gilt frame surrounding the canvas, I know that the woman is *me*!

The prior *me*.

The Dutch *me*.

The artist's muse *me* who fell for Damen the night we met in this gallery.

But the thing that disturbs me, the thing that keeps me quiet and still, is the sudden realization that the unseen lover she gazes upon *isn't* Damen.

It's somebody else.

Someone unseen.

"So you recognize her." Damen's voice smooth, matter-of-fact, not the least bit surprised that I do. "It's the eyes, right?" He peers at me, face very close when he adds, "The color may change, but their essence stays the same."

I glance at him, taking in the lush fringe of lashes that nearly obscure the wistfulness of his gaze—prompting me to quickly turn away.

*How old was I?* Not trusting my voice with the words. The face appearing unlined and youthful, though the confidence is that of a woman, not a girl.

"Eighteen." He nods, continuing to study me. Gaze pushing, probing, wanting me to be the first one to say it, pleading for me to just speak up—to spare him this task. Following my gaze to the painting as he adds, "You were beautiful. Truly. Just like this. He captured you so—*perfectly*."

*He.*

*So there it is.*

The edge in his voice speaking volumes—revealing everything his words only hint at. He knows the identity of the artist. Knows it wasn't him I unclothed myself for.

I swallow hard, eyes narrowing as I try to make sense of the black, angular scrawl at the bottom right corner. Deciphering a series of consonants and vowels, a combination of letters that mean nothing to me.

"Bastiaan de Kool," Damen says, gazing at me.

I turn, my eyes meeting his, unable to speak.

"Bastiaan de Kool is the artist who painted this. Painted *you*." He turns toward the portrait, eyes roaming over it again, before returning to me.

I shake my head, feeling light, woozy—everything I once thought I knew—about me—about us—the entire foundation of our lives suddenly gone tenuous and weak.

Damen nods, there's no need to press it. Both of us recognizing the truth displayed right before us.

"In case you're wondering, it was over before the paint even dried. Or at least that's what I convinced myself of—" He shakes his head. "But now—well, I'm no longer sure."

I gape, eyes wide, uncomprehending. What could this painting—this century-old version of me—have anything to do with us—the way we are now?

"Would you like to meet him?" he asks, gaze shadowed, distant, difficult to read.

"Bastiaan?" The name oddly comfortable on my lips.

Damen nods, willing to manifest him if I'll only agree. But just as I'm about to refuse, he places his hand on my arm and says, "I think you should. It only seems fair."

I take a deep breath, focusing on the warmth of his hand as

he closes his eyes in deep concentration, summoning a tall, rangy, slightly disheveled guy from what was once empty space. Letting go of my arm as he moves away, allowing me plenty of room in which to study, observe, before we run out of time and he fades.

I move toward him, walking slow, wide circles around this blank, hollow stranger—this bright, empty, creation—soulless, unreal.

Noting his traits in an offhand way—the height making him appear even slighter, the hint of lean, sinewy muscle lightly padding his bones—the clothes that are clean and of decent quality and cut, hanging slightly off kilter, the skin so pale and flawless it nearly matches my own, while his hair is dark, wavy, brushed to the side, a good chunk of bang falling heavily into a startling pair of eyes.

I gasp, forcing the air into my lungs as he soon fades away, hearing Damen say, "Would you like me to refresh him again?" Obviously hating to do so, but willing to oblige if I ask.

But I just continue to stand there, staring into a swirl of vibrating pixels that soon vanish completely. Knowing I don't need him revived to know who he is.

*Jude.*

The guy who was standing before me, the Dutch artist who went by the name of Bastiaan de Kool in the nineteenth century—has now reincarnated into this century as Jude.

I reach for something to steady me, feeling shaky, empty, off balance. Realizing too late that there's nothing to catch me, until Damen quickly moves to my side.

"Ever!" he cries, voice so urgent it resonates to my core, his arms tightening around me, shielding me in a way that feels just like home. Manifesting a soft, plushy couch where he guides me to sit, his gaze hovering over me, anxious, unnerved, having no intention of upsetting me like this.

I turn, holding my breath as my eyes meet his, afraid of finding something different, something changed, now that it's all laid out in the open. Now that we both know it wasn't always just him.

That there was once someone else.

And I know him today.

"I don't—" I shake my head, feeling embarrassed, guilty, as though I've somehow betrayed him by unknowingly seeking him out. "I'm not sure what to say—I—"

Damen shakes his head, his hand at my cheek, drawing me near. "Don't think that," he says. "None of this is your fault. You hear me? *None of it.* It's just karma." He pauses, gaze holding mine. "It's just unfinished business—so to speak."

"But what could be unfinished?" I ask, having an inkling of an idea of where this is going and refusing to take part in that journey. "That was over a hundred years ago! And like you said, it was over before the paint even—"

But before I can get there, he's shaking his head, hand on my cheek, my shoulder, my knee, as he says, "I'm no longer so sure about that."

I look at him, fighting the urge to pull away. Wishing he'd stop. Wanting to leave. No longer liking it here.

"It seems I've interfered," he says, face hard, judgmental, though it's a judgment reserved only for him. "It seems I have a habit of intruding on your life, meddling in decisions that should've been yours. Pushing a fate that"—he pauses, jaw clenched, gaze steady, though his lip quivers in a way that reveals the price of all this—"that was never meant to be yours—"

"What are you talking about?" I cry, voice high, urgent, sens-ing the energy surrounding his words, and knowing it's about to get worse.

"Isn't it obvious?" He looks at me, the light in his eyes frac-tured into millions of bits—a kaleidoscope of darkness that may never be fixed.

He rises from the couch in one quick, sinuous move until he's filling the space just before me. But before he can speak, before he can make things even worse, I rush ahead when I say, "This is ridiculous! All of it! Everything! It's destiny that's brought us together again and again. We're soul mates! You said it yourself! And from what I've learned, that's exactly how it works—soul mates find each other, time and again, against all odds, no matter what!" I reach for his hand but he's slipped just out of reach, pacing before me, avoiding my touch.

"Destiny?" He shakes his head, voice harsh, gaze cruel, but all of it directed inwardly. "Was it destiny when I purposely roamed the earth in search of you—over and over again—unable to rest until I'd found you?" He stops, eyes meeting mine. "Tell me Ever, does that sound like destiny to you? Or something that was forced?"

I start to speak, lips parting wide though no words will come, watching as he turns toward the wall and stares at the girl. That proud and beautiful girl whose gaze moves right past him—toward somebody else.

"Somehow I was able to ignore all of this, push it aside for the last four hundred years, convincing myself it was our fate, that you and I were meant to be. But the other day, when you dropped by after work, I sensed something different—a shift in your energy. And then last night, at the store—I *knew*.

I stare at his back, the solid square of his shoulders—his

lean, muscled form. Remembering how he acted so strangely, so formal, and thinking how it all makes perfect sense.

"The moment I saw his eyes, I knew." He turns, his gaze meeting mine. "So tell me, Ever, tell me the truth, was it not the same way with you?"

I swallow hard, wanting to look away, but knowing I can't. He'll misread it, assume I'm holding back. Remembering the moment Jude caught me alone in his store, the way my heart raced, my cheeks flushed, along with the odd, nervous dance in my gut. One moment I was fine and the next—a mess. And all because Jude's deep sea green eyes met mine . . .

It couldn't mean—

Couldn't possibly—

*Could it?*

I rise from the couch, moving toward him 'til our bodies are mere inches apart. Wanting to assure him, assure *me*. Find a way to prove that none of it meant anything.

But this is Summerland. And thoughts are energy. And I'm afraid he just witnessed mine.

"It's not your fault," he says, voice hoarse, rough. "Please don't feel bad."

I shove my hands in my pockets, pushing as deep as they'll go, determined to steady myself in a world that's no longer stable.

"I want you to know how sorry I am. And yet—" He shakes his head. "*Sorry* just doesn't cut it. It's woefully inadequate, and you deserve better than that. I'm afraid the only thing I can do now—the only thing that'll make things right, is to—"

His voice breaks, prompting me to lift my face until it's even with his. The two of us standing so close the slightest move forward could easily bridge the gap.

But just as I'm about to make the leap, he backs away, gaze steady, features drawn tight, determined to be heard when he says, "I'm stepping aside. It's the only thing I can do at this point. From this moment on, I will no longer interfere with your fate. From this point on, every move toward your destiny is yours and yours alone to make."

My vision goes blurry, throat hot and tight. Surely he can't mean what I think?

*Can he?*

Gazing upon him as he stands before me, my perfect soul mate, the love of my lives, the one person I was sure was my shelter now leaving my side.

"I've no right to barge into your life in the way that I have. Never giving you the chance to choose for yourself. And you know what the worst part is?" He looks at me, eyes filled with such self-loathing I'm pressed to look away. "I wasn't even noble enough, wasn't even man enough, to play fair." He shakes his head. "I used every trick in the book, all the powers at my disposal to annihilate the competition. And while I've no way to change the past four hundred years—nor the immortality I've forced upon you—I'm hoping that now—by stepping aside—I'll allow you some smidgen of freedom in allowing you to choose."

"Between you and *Jude*?" I gape, voice rising to the point of hysteria, wanting him to say it. Just say it. Quit dancing around it and get to the point.

But he just continues to stand there, world-weary gaze focused on mine.

"Well, there is no choice! No choice at all! Jude is *my boss*—he's not the least bit interested in me—or I in him!"

"Then you fail to see what I see," Damen says, as though it's a fact—some large, solid object parked right before me.

"That's because there's nothing to *see*. Don't you get it? All I see is *you!*" I gaze at him, vision blurry, hands shaky, feeling so awful and empty as though each breath just might be my last.

But as soon as I've said it, Damen highlights the painting again. Causing it to glow in a way that can't be ignored. But even though he thinks it's significant, that girl is a stranger to me. My soul may have once occupied her body, but it's no longer home.

I start to speak, wanting to explain that, but no words will come. Only a long piercing wail that courses from my mind to his. A sound that means *please* and *don't*—a sound without end.

"I'm not going anywhere," he says, immune to my plea. "I'll always be close, somewhere nearby. Able to sense you, keeping you safe. But as for the rest—" He shakes his head, voice defeated, sad, but determined to be heard. "I'm afraid I can no longer—I'm afraid I'll have to—"

But I won't let him finish, can't let him finish, cutting right in when I cry, "I've already tried a life without you, when I went back in time, and guess what? Fate sent me right back!" Gaze blurred by tears, but I don't turn away. I want him to see it. Want him to know exactly what his misguided altruism is costing me.

"But, Ever, that doesn't mean you were meant to be with me, maybe you were sent back to find Jude, and now that you have—"

"Fine," I say, refusing to let him finish, not when I have plenty more evidence proving my case. "Then what about the time you held your hand close, making me focus on our tingle and heat, claiming that's exactly how it feels between soul mates? What about *that*? Did you not mean it? Are you taking it back?"

"Ever—" He shakes his head and rubs his eyes. "Ever, I—"

"Don't you get it?" I shake my head, sensing his energy,

knowing it won't make the least bit of difference but continuing anyway. "Don't you *see* that I only want *you*?"

He brings his hand to my cheek, fingers so soft and loving—a cruel reminder of what I'll no longer have—his thoughts traveling the distance from his head to mine, pleading with me to understand, to give it some time.

*Please don't think this is easy for me. I had no idea how painful it is to act without the slightest hint of self-interest—maybe that's why I never tried before?* He smiles, attempting a bit of levity that I refuse to accept. Wanting him to feel as awful and empty as me. *I robbed you of ever seeing your family again—put your very soul at risk—*his gaze narrows on mine—*But, Ever, you've got to listen, you must understand, it's time for you to choose the one thing you still can—without interference from me!*

"I've already chosen," I say, voice wooden, weary, too tired to fight. "I chose you and you can't take it back." I look at him, knowing my words are useless, he's fixed on his plan. "Damen, seriously, so I knew him hundreds of years ago in a country I haven't visited since. Big deal! *One life*—out of how many?"

He looks at me for a moment, then closes his eyes, voice barely a whisper as he says, "It wasn't just one life, Ever." Fading the gallery though keeping the windmills and tulips as he manifests a whole world before me—several worlds in fact—Paris—London—New England—all lined up in a row, placed right in the middle of Amsterdam where we both stand. Worlds that stay true to their time—the architecture, the clothing—all indicative of their period—yet devoid of their citizens—populated only by three.

Me in all of my guises—a lowly Parisian servant—spoiled London society girl—daughter of a Puritan—with Jude always beside me—a French stable boy—a British Earl—a fellow parishioner—each of us different, changing, though the eyes are the same.

And I watch, focusing on one vignette at a time, the scene playing before me like a well-staged play. My interest in Jude always waning the moment Damen comes on the scene—just as magical and mesmerizing as he is today, using all of his tricks to steal me away.

I stand there, breathless, no idea what to say. All I know is that I want it to fade.

I face him, understanding why he feels like he does, but knowing it doesn't make the least bit of difference. Not to me. Not where my heart is concerned.

"So you've made up your mind. Fine. I don't like it, but fine. But what I really need to know is just how long are we talking here? Couple days? A week?" I shake my head. "Just how long will it take for you to accept the fact that no matter what happens, no matter what you may think or say, no matter how unfair the fight may have seemed, I choose you. I've *always* chosen you. For me there's *only* you."

"This isn't something you can attach a date to—you've got to give yourself time, time to release your attachment to me— time to move on—"

"Just because you're determined to do this, just because you want to *make things right* despite what I say, just because you invented the game doesn't mean you make all the rules. Because if you're truly intent on letting me choose, then I choose until the end of today."

He shakes his head, eyes appearing the slightest bit lighter, and if I'm not mistaken, tinged with a hint of relief.

And in that moment, I *know*—a glimmer of hope that makes

my heart soar. He hates this just as much as I do. I'm not the only one around here in need of an end date.

"The end of the year," he says, jaw clenched in a way that tells me he's trying to be noble, gallant, ridiculously so. "That should allow plenty of time."

I shake my head, barely allowing him the chance to finish when I say, "By the end of *tomorrow*. I'm sure I'll have my decision by then."

But he's not having it, refusing to even negotiate, saying, "Ever, please, we've our whole lives ahead of us if that's what you choose. Trust me, there's really no hurry."

"The end of next week." I nod, voice tightening, wondering how I'll possibly make it 'til then.

"The end of the *summer*," he says, the words final as his gaze meets mine.

I stand before him, unable to speak. Thinking how the summer I've been anticipating since we first got together— imagining three months of frolic and fun in the Laguna Beach sun—has quickly deteriorated into the loneliest season.

Knowing there's no more to say, I move away. Ignoring his hand reaching for mine, wanting to make the return trip together.

If he's so determined for me to choose my own path, then I choose to start now. By leaving the gallery and heading onto the street, making my way through Amsterdam, Paris, London, and New England, without once looking back.

# thirty-two

The moment I turn the corner, I run. Feet moving so quickly, it's as though I can outrun Damen, the gallery, everything, all of it. The cobblestone first fading to pavement then grass, running past all of my usual Summerland haunts, determined to manifest one of my own—a place where Damen can't go.

Making my way to the top of the wooden bleachers at my old school, facing the scoreboard that reads *"GO BEARS!"* and claiming the seat in the far right corner where I tried my first (and last) cigarette, where I kissed my ex-boyfriend Brandon for the very first time, and where my former friend Rachel and I once reigned supreme, giggling and flirting in our cheerleading outfits, totally unaware of just how complicated life can be.

I place my feet on the bench right before me and bring my head to my knees, choking back great, shoulder-heaving sobs as I try to make sense of what happened. Sniffling into a handful of manifested tissues as I gaze bleary eyed at a football field crowded with faceless, nameless players running through their practice drills as their hair-tossing girlfriends gossip and flirt from the side. Hoping such a familiar, normal scene will somehow provide the comfort I need—then making it fade when I only feel worse.

This is no longer my life. No longer my fate.

Damen's my future. There's no doubt in my mind.

Even though I get all jumpy and nervous whenever Jude's near, even though there's an undeniable *something* whenever we meet—it doesn't mean anything. Doesn't mean he's The One. It's merely the effect of our past familiarity, a subconscious recognition, no more.

Just because he played a part in my history doesn't mean he has a role in my future other than *boss* at a summer job I never would've gone looking for if Sabine hadn't made me. So how can I possibly be at fault? How can this possibly be anything other than just a weird coincidence, a pesky part of my past that, through no fault of mine, refuses to die?

I mean, it's not like I went looking for this—right?

*Right?*

But even though my heart knows the truth, I can't help but wonder just what we once meant to each other.

Did I really emerge from a lake not caring if he saw the nude me? Or was that portrait taken straight from his overactive imagination?

Which only leads me to more questions—ones I'd prefer to ignore, like:

*Was I not really a virgin for the last four hundred years like I thought?*

*Did I actually sleep with Jude and not Damen?*

*And if so, is that why I feel so shy and weird around him now?*

I gaze at the empty field before me, turning it into the Roman Coliseum, the Egyptian Pyramids, the Acropolis in

Athens, the Grand Bazaar in Istanbul, the Opera House in Sydney, St. Mark's Square in Venice, the Medina in Marrakech—watching the scenery whirl and change, becoming all the places I hope to visit someday, knowing only one thing for sure:

I've got three months.

Three months without Damen.

Three months of knowing he's out there, somewhere, but unable to touch him, access him, be with him again.

Three months in which to learn enough magick to solve all our problems and get him back for good.

Knowing more than I've ever known anything—that he alone is my future, my destiny, no matter what came before.

I focus back on the scenery, the Grand Canyon morphing into Machu Picchu, which becomes the Great Wall of China, knowing there's plenty of time for this later, but for now, I've got to go back.

Back to the earth plane.

Back to the store.

Hoping to catch Jude before he closes up shop, needing him to teach me, once and for all, how to read that book.

# thirty-three

All week I avoided Sabine. I didn't think it was possible, but between school, my new job, and Miles's final *Hairspray* performance, I was pretty much scot-free until the moment I'm about to toss my breakfast down the sink.

"So." She smiles, sidling up beside me, dressed in workout clothes and glistening with the glow of good health and sweat. "Don't we have something to talk about? A conversation you've worked hard to delay?"

I reach for my glass and shrug, unsure what to say.

"How's your new job? Everything okay?"

I nod, easy, noncommittal, as though I'm far too interested in chugging this juice to respond.

"Because I can probably still squeeze you in on that internship if you'd like—"

I shake my head and finish the remains, including the pulp. Rinsing my cup and placing it into the dishwasher as I say, "Not necessary." Catching the expression on her face and adding, "Really. It's all good."

She studies me, gaze intense, really taking me in. "Ever, why didn't you mention that Paul was your teacher?"

I freeze, but only for a moment before I turn my attention to a bowl of cereal I have no interest in eating. Grabbing a spoon and swirling the contents around and around as I say, "Because *Paul* with the cool shoes and designer jeans *isn't* my teacher. *Mr. Munoz* with the dork glasses and pressed khakis *is*." I lift the spoon to my mouth, carefully avoiding her gaze.

"I just can't believe you didn't say anything." She shakes her head and frowns.

I shrug, pretending I don't want to speak with my mouth full, when the truth is, I don't want to speak.

"Does it bother you? That I'm dating your teacher?" She squints, sliding the towel off her neck and pressing it to her forehead.

I stir the cereal around and around, knowing there's no way I can eat any more, not after she's started all this. "As long as you don't talk about me." I study her closely, reading her aura, her body language, noting the way she just shifted uncomfortably, and stopping just short of peering into her head. "I mean, you don't talk about me, *right*?" I add, gaze fixed on hers.

But she just laughs, averting her eyes as a flush blooms on her cheeks. "Turns out we've got much more in common than that."

"Yeah? Like what?" I mash my spoon against my cereal, displacing my frustration onto my Froot Loops and turning them into a soggy, rainbow-colored mess. Wondering if I should break the news to her now or save it for later. The startling revelation that this love match won't last—not according to the vision I saw of her paired up with some cute, nameless guy who works in her building—

"Well, for starters we're both fascinated by the Italian Renaissance—"

I look at her, fighting the urge to roll my eyes. Having never heard her mention that and I've lived with her for nearly a year.

"We both love Italian food—"

*Oh yeah, definitely soul mates. The only two people who actually like pizza and pasta and stuff drenched with red sauce and cheese . . .*

"*And* as of Friday, he'll be spending quite a bit of time in my building!"

I stop. Stop everything. Including breathing and blinking, so I can stand there and gape.

"He's working as an expert witness on a case that—"

Her lips keep moving, hands gesturing, but I stopped listening a few sentences back. Her words drowned by the sound of my own crashing heart, accompanied by the silent scream that crowds everything out.

*No!*

*It can't be.*

*Can't. Be.*

*Can it?*

Remembering the vision that night in the restaurant—Sabine getting together with a cute guy who works in her building—a guy, who, without the glasses I didn't even recognize as Munoz! Knowing immediately what this really means—this is it—her destiny—Munoz is The One!

"You okay?" Her hand reaches for mine as concern clouds her face.

But I pull away quickly, avoiding her touch. Swallowing hard as I paste a smile onto my face, knowing she deserves to be happy—heck, even *he* deserves to be happy. But still—why do they have to be happy together? Seriously, out of all the men she could date, why does it have to be my teacher, the one who knows my secret?

I look at her, forcing a nod as I drop my bowl in the sink, fleeing for the door as I say, "Yeah—it's all good, seriously. I just—I don't want to be late."

# thirty-four

"Hey, it's Sunday we don't even open 'til eleven." Jude props his surfboard against the wall and squints.

I nod, barely glancing away from the book, determined for it to make sense.

"Need help?" He tosses his towel on a chair and moves around the desk until he's standing behind me.

"If it involves more of this handy dandy code translator you made," I tap the sheet of paper beside me, "or anything even resembling your long list of meditations, then no thanks, I've had all I can take. But if you're finally going to tell me how to read this thing, without assuming the lotus position, picturing beams of white light, and/or making me imagine long, spindly roots growing from the soles of my feet and extending deep into the earth, then yes, by all means, go ahead and try." I slide the book toward him, careful to touch only its edge, catching a quick glimpse of his amused face, that tropical gaze, the spliced brow, before looking away.

He places his hand on the desk and leans toward the book,

fingers splayed against the old, pockmarked wood, body so close I can feel the push of his energy merge into my space. "There's another way that might work. Well, for someone with your gifts anyway. But the way you handle that thing, only touching the edges, keeping your distance, it's pretty clear you're afraid."

His voice drifts over me, soothing and calm. Prompting me to close my eyes for a moment and allow myself to feel it, *really* feel it, without trying to stop it or push it away. Eager to prove Damen wrong, report back that I gave it a fair shot and there's not a single trace of tingle or heat to be found. Even though Jude *likes* me—likes me in the same way I like Damen and Damen likes me—even though I *saw* it in the vision he unwittingly showed me that day—it's one-sided. All about him, not the slightest bit reciprocated by me. The only thing I'm getting is a decrease in stress and anxiety, a serenity so languid, so relaxed, it soothes my jangled nerves, and—

He taps me on the shoulder, yanking me out of my reverie and motioning for me to join him on the small couch in the corner where he balances the book on his knees. Urging me to place my hand on the page, shut my eyes, clear my head, and intuit the message inside.

At first nothing happens, but that's because I'm filled with resistance. Still smarting from the last energy slam that practically fried my insides and left me tired and fragmented for the rest of the evening. But the second I decide to let go and give in, to just trust in the process and allow the buzz to flow through me, I'm overcome with a barrage of energy that's surprisingly, almost embarrassingly personal.

"Getting anything?" he asks, voice low, gaze fixed on me.

I shrug, turning to him when I say, "It's like—it's like reading someone's diary. Or at least that's what I'm getting—you?"

He nods. "Same."

"But I thought it would be more like—I don't know, like a book of spells. You know, a different one on each page."

"You mean a *grimoire*." He smiles, displaying two amazing dimples and charmingly crooked front teeth.

I frown, unfamiliar with the word.

"It's like a recipe book for spells, containing very specific data—dates, times, ritual performed, results of the ritual, that sort of thing. Strictly business, nothing but the facts."

"And this?" I tap my nail against the page.

"More like a journal, as you said. A highly personal account of a witch's progress—what she did, why she did it, how she felt, the results, et cetera. Which is why they're often written in code, or Theban like this."

My shoulders droop as I screw my lips to the side, wondering why every bit of progress I'm about to make actually results in two giant steps back.

"You were looking for something more specific? A love spell perhaps?"

I peer at him, eyes narrowed, wondering why he just said that.

"Sorry." He shrugs, eyes grazing my face, lingering on my lips for a few seconds too long. "Seems like trouble in paradise with the way you and Damen are avoiding each other these days."

I close my eyes for a moment, forcing the sting to retreat. It's been one week. One week without Damen—his sweet telepathic messages—his warm and loving embrace. The only hint that he even exists is the fresh supply of elixir I found in my fridge. An elixir he must've slipped in while I slept, taking every precaution to get the job done before I could wake. Each passing hour so painful, so agonizing, so lonely—I've no idea how I'll get through the summer without him.

Jude's energy shifts, his aura pulling back just as a sensitive shade of blue flickers at the edges. "Well, whatever you seek," he says, back to business again. "You'll find it in here." He thumps the page with his thumb. "You just have to give it some time to take it all in. It's a very detailed account, and the content goes pretty deep."

"Where'd you find it?" I take in the spray of dreadlocks hitting just shy of his lips. "And how long have you had it?" I add, suddenly needing to know.

He shrugs, averting his gaze. "Picked it up somewhere—some guy I once knew." He shakes his head. "It was a long time ago."

"Vague much?" I smile, giving a sort of half laugh he fails to return. "Seriously. You're only nineteen—how long ago could it have been?" I study him closely, remembering the time I asked the same question of Damen—well before I knew what he was. A sudden chill pricking my skin as I take him in, the crooked teeth, the scar marking his brow, the tangle of dreadlocks falling into those familiar green eyes—assuring myself he's merely someone I knew from my past, that he's nothing like me.

"Guess I'm not so big on tracking time," he says, the laugh that follows uncommitted, forced. "I try to live in the moment—the now. Still, must've been four—maybe five years ago—when I first started getting into this stuff."

"And did Lina find it? Is that why you hide it?"

He shakes his head, face flushing when he says, "As embarrassing as it is to admit, she came across a poppet I'd made and completely freaked out. Thought it was a voodoo doll. Misread the whole thing."

"Poppet?" My gaze fixed on his, having no idea what that is.

"A sort of magical doll." He shrugs, embarrassed gaze meeting mine. "I was a kid, what can I say? I was misguided enough to think it would convince a certain girl to like me."

"And did it?" I hold my breath, studying him carefully, wondering why those simple words cause a ping in my gut.

"Lina destroyed it before it could work. Just as well." He shrugs. "Turns out she was trouble."

"Your usual type." The words rushing forward before I can stop them.

He looks at me, eyes glinting. "Old habits die hard."

We sit like that, eyes locked, breath halted, the moment growing, stretching, until I finally break away and return to the book.

"I'd love to help you," he says, voice low and deep. "But I get the feeling your journey's too private for me."

I turn, about to speak, when he adds, "No worries. I get it. But if it's spell casting you're after, there are a few things you should know." His gaze meets mine, making sure he has my full attention before he goes on. "One, it's a last resort—only to be used when all other avenues are exhausted. And two, spells are really just recipes for change, to get what you want, or alter a certain situation that needs—altering. But in order for it to work, your goals have to be clear—you need to visualize the outcome you want and direct all of your energy toward it."

"Like manifesting," I say, wishing I hadn't when I see his gaze change.

"Manifesting takes too long—magick's more immediate—or at least it can be."

I press my lips together, knowing better than to explain how manifesting can also be instantaneous once you understand how the universe works. But then again, you can't manifest what you don't know, making the antidote, among other things, strictly off limits.

"Think of this like a giant cookbook." He taps the page with his nail. "One with liner notes." He smiles. "But nothing in here is fixed, you can alter the recipes to suit your own needs, and choose your own set of tools accordingly—"

"Tools?" I look at him.

"Crystals, herbs, elements, candles, phases of the moon—that kind of thing."

I think back on the elixirs I made, just before I went back in time, having thought of it more in terms of alchemy than magick, though I guess in some ways, it's pretty much the same thing.

"It also helps if you cast your spell in verse."

"Like a poem?" I look at him, startled. Maybe this isn't going to work after all. I pretty much suck at that kind of thing.

"Doesn't have to be Keats, just something that rhymes and has some sort of meaning for what you want it to do."

I frown, feeling disheartened before I even begin.

"And, Ever—"

I look at him.

"If you're wanting to cast a spell on a person, you might want to rethink it. Lina was right. If you can't convince someone to see things your way, or cooperate with you, by using more mundane means, there's a pretty good chance it's not meant to be."

I nod and look away, knowing that may be true for some situations, but not mine.

Mine is different.

# thirty-five

"I stopped by your work." Haven studies me closely, gaze moving from my hair, to the black silk cord holding my amulet, just barely visible at the base of my tee, before settling back on my face.

I nod briefly before returning my attention to Honor, watching as she laughs with Stacia and Craig and the rest of the A-list crew as though everything were normal—but it's not. Not for her. She's dipping into magick now—a serious student of *the craft*, according to Jude. All without her ringleader's consent.

"Thought maybe we could grab lunch or something, but the hot guy behind the counter said you were busy." Fingers picking at the frosting on her chai-latte cupcake, gaze never once straying from me.

Miles looks up from his phone, brows merged, eyes darting between us. "Excuse me? There's a hot guy and nobody informed me?"

I turn toward them, Haven's words just now making an

impact. *She went to my work! She knows where I work! What else might she know?*

"Oh, he's hot all right." Haven nods, still looking at me. "*Muy caliente*, for sure. But apparently Ever's determined to keep it a secret. Didn't even know he existed 'til I saw for myself."

"How'd you know where I work?" I ask, trying to keep it casual, nonchalant, not let on just how alarmed I really am.

"The twins told me."

*This just went from bad to even worse.*

"I ran into them at the beach. Damen's teaching them to surf."

I smile, but it's a feeble one that feels false on my face.

"Guess that explains why you didn't tell us about your new job—you didn't want your best friends moving in on your hottie coworker."

Miles stares at me, abandoning his texting for something far juicier.

"He's my *boss*." I shake my head. "And it's not like it's a secret or anything, I just haven't had a chance to mention it, that's all."

"Yes, because our lunchtime chats are so scintillating you just couldn't squeeze it in. Please." Haven rolls her eyes. "*So* not buying it."

"Um, hello? Descriptors would be nice about now!" Miles leans forward, face eager, eyes darting between us.

But I just shrug, watching as Haven smiles and sets down her cupcake, brushing the crumbs from her black denim lap as she says, "Picture the tannest, most aqua-eyed, hot-bodied, rockin' the golden dreadlocks, laid-back surfer boy, hottie of the entire McHottie clan that you can even possibly imagine—then times it by ten and that's *him*."

"Seriously?" Miles gapes, staring at me. "Like, for reals?"

I sigh, tearing my sandwich to shreds as Haven says, "Trust me, words cannot describe the extreme measure of hotness. The only ones who can even come close are Damen and Roman, but then, they're pretty much in a class by themselves, so they don't really count. How old is he anyway?" She looks at me. "Seems too young to be a boss."

"Nineteen." I shrug, not wanting to talk about work, Jude, or pretty much anything else on that list. This is exactly the kind of thing Damen warned me about. The kind of thing I need to avoid. "Speaking of hotties, how's Josh?" I smile, making for a pretty awkward segue but hoping it'll work.

Watching her aura waver and flare as she focuses on her cupcake and says, "It ended the second he tried to give me the kitten. You should've seen him, smiling as though it was some miraculous gift." She rolls her eyes and rips her cupcake in half. "I mean, seriously. How clueless can you get?"

"He was just trying to be nice—" Miles starts, but Haven isn't having it.

"*Please*." She scowls. "If he truly understood what I was going through, he never would've pushed some Charm replacement on me. Some adorable kitty that's only real destiny is to die once I've grown extremely attached to her so I can experience the maximum amount of pain and suffering."

Miles rolls his eyes as I say, "It doesn't always have to be like that—"

But she cuts right in. "Oh really? Name one thing—one *living* thing—that doesn't either die or leave you or both? Last time I asked you that question, you choked. So, Miles, you with the rolling eyes and smirking lips, go ahead, knock yourself out, name one thing that—"

Miles shakes his head, hands raised in surrender, hating all confrontation and gladly forfeiting the game before it can start.

Haven smirks, satisfied with our combined failure when she says, "Trust me, all I did was beat him to the chase. It would've ended eventually anyway."

"Well." Miles shrugs, returning to his text. "For what it's worth, I liked him. I thought you were good together."

"Then you date him." Haven smirks, tossing a cupcake sprinkle his way.

"No thanks. Too skinny and cute." He smiles. "Now Ever's boss on the other hand—"

I glance at Miles, checking his aura and seeing he's mostly joking—*mostly.*

"His name's Jude." I sigh, resigned to the conversation coming full circle again. "And as far as I can tell he only likes girls that don't like him back, but you're welcome to take your best shot." I close my lunch pack, zipping it shut with an uneaten apple, bag full of chips, and a shredded sandwich inside.

"Maybe you should invite him to my going away party," Miles says. "You know, so I can treat myself to a nice long good-bye." He brushes his hand through his cropped brown hair and laughs.

"About that—" Haven says, eyes partially obscured by the false eyelashes she's been experimenting with. "My mom just tore up the den—like *literally* tore it up. Carpet ripped out, furniture cleared, walls knocked down—which, on the one hand, is nice since there's no way they can sell the house when it's all ripped up like that, but it also means there's no way we can party at my house so I was hoping—"

"Sure." I nod, met by two faces so shocked I'm ashamed. Realizing their regular visits to my house, our Friday-night pizza eating, Jacuzzi-soaking ritual, ended the moment Damen entered my life. But now that he's gone—or at least determined to stay away for a while—maybe it's time to start up again.

"You sure Sabine won't mind?" Miles asks, voice hopeful but cautious.

I shake my head. "As long as you don't mind Munoz dropping by, it's all good." I roll my eyes.

"Munoz? You mean *the history teacher*?" They gape. My two best friends looking as shocked and bug-eyed as I was when I first found out.

"They're *dating*." I nod, knowing as much as I hate it, I certainly can't stop it.

Haven pushes her royal blue bangs off her face and leans toward me. "Wait—let me get this straight, your aunt Sabine is dating the hottie history teacher?"

"Who's hot for teacher now?" Miles laughs, nudging her arm.

But Haven just shrugs. "*Please*. Don't act like you haven't noticed. I mean, as far as old guys go, especially ones who wear glasses and khakis, he's smokin'."

"Please don't call him *smokin'*." I laugh in spite of myself. "And just so you know, at night he ditches the specs and swaps the Dockers for designer denim."

Haven smiles, rising from the bench. "That's it then. Party at your house. *This* I've *got* to see."

"Is Damen coming?" Miles slips his phone in his pocket, eyeing me carefully.

"Um—I don't know—maybe." I shrug, pressing my lips together and scratching my arm so fervently I may as well wear a sign that says: HEY—CHECK ME OUT! I'M LYING! "I mean, he's pretty busy these days looking after the twins and all—"

"Is that why he's blown off school all week?" Haven asks.

I nod, mumbling some nonsense about taking his finals early, but my heart isn't in it, and it shows. Seeing them nod in assent, but only to appease me, their eyes and auras say otherwise, they're not buying a word of it.

"Just make sure Jude's there," Miles says, the mere mention of his name making my stomach dance.

"Yeah, I'll need him as a backup in case my date doesn't work out like I hope." Haven smiles.

"You have a date?" Miles and I both say, voices blending as we take a moment to gawk.

"Who?" I ask.

Just as Miles says, "That was fast!"

But Haven just smiles, waving over her shoulder as she heads for class, singing, *"You'll see!"*

# thirty-six

Since I kept my promise to Munoz by attending history (which was way more awkward for me than it was for him), and since I made no such promise to any of my other teachers, I skip the rest of the day and head for the store.

My thoughts drifting to Damen as I cruise Coast Highway, visualizing him so clearly he manifests in the seat right beside me. Gazing at me with those dark, smoldering eyes, lips parted, enticing, as he presses a spray of red tulips onto my lap—causing an ache so palpable, I banish him well before he can fade. Knowing a manifest Damen will never do. Not when the real one is out there—somewhere—waiting for three months to end.

But I can't wait. I *refuse* to wait. The only way to rid myself of this hollow empty feeling is to get Damen back. And the only way to do that is to crack Roman's code. Get my hands on that antidote once and for all and then all of my problems are solved.

But short of returning to his house, I've no clue where to find him. Like Damen, he's pretty much blowing off the last days of school.

I pull into the alley and claim the small space in back, storming through the door with such speed and force, Jude glances up in confusion as I head behind the counter and reach for the appointment book.

"Trust me, if I'd known you were ditching, I would've scheduled some readings, but as it stands, I got nothing."

"I'm not ditching," I mumble, even though we both know I am. "Okay, maybe I am." I shrug, glancing at him. "But it's the last week of school so it's really no biggie. You won't tell anyone, will you?"

He dismisses the thought with a wave of his hand, lifting his shoulders as he says, "Just wish I'd known. I would've brought my board."

"You can still get it." I head for the shelves and begin rearranging some books. Wanting to put some distance between us so I can avoid the enticing wave of calm his proximity brings. "Seriously," I add when I see he's not moving. "I'll keep an eye on the place."

He looks at me, gaze steady, focused on mine. "Ever—" he starts.

I look at him, sensing where this is going and eager to dispel any fears before he can get there. "You don't have to pay me," I say, arms loaded with books. "I'm not here for the overtime. In fact, I don't even care if you pay me at all."

He narrows his gaze for one beat, then two. Tilting his head to the side when he says, "You really don't, do you?"

I shrug and return all the books, taking a moment to line them up perfectly before answering, "Nope, I really don't." Feeling good to unburden yet another illusion of mine, no matter how small.

"Exactly what *are* you here for?" he asks, voice catching in a way I can't help but notice. "The book?"

I turn, feeling all nervous and squirmy as my gaze settles on his. "Is it that obvious?" I lift my shoulders, forcing a laugh.

Relieved when he smiles and jabs his thumb over his shoulder as he says, "Go ahead, have fun. I won't tell Damen what you're up to."

I shoot him a look making it clear I'm over the Damen jokes, until I see that he's serious.

"Sorry." He shrugs. "But it's pretty clear he's not into it."

I shrug, neither confirming nor denying. There's no way I'm discussing Damen with him. Heading for the back room and settling in at the desk, just about to unlock the drawer with my mind when I see that he's followed.

"Oh, um, I forgot that it's locked," I mumble, feeling false and ridiculous as I motion toward the drawer, knowing I'm the worst actress ever but still going through the motions.

He leans in the doorway, shooting me a look that makes it clear he's not buying it. "Didn't seem to stop you the last time," he says, voice low and deep. "Or even the first time I found you in the store."

I swallow hard, unsure what to say. Admitting my abilities is breaking Damen's most cardinal rule. The weight of Jude's gaze heavy on mine as I say, "I can't—I—"

He lifts a brow, knowing I very well can.

"I can't do it in front of *you*," I finish, knowing it's foolish to keep up this ruse.

"Does this help?" He places a hand over each eye and grins.

I gaze at him for a moment, hoping he won't peek through his fingers, then I take a deep breath and close my eyes too, *seeing* the lock spring open, before retrieving the book. Placing it on the desk as he takes a seat, head cocked to the side, foot balanced on his knee when he says, "You know, you're pretty special, Ever."

I freeze, fingers hovering above the ancient tome, heart beating overtime.

"I mean, your *gift* is special." He looks at me, eyes squinting, shoulders lifting, the color on his cheeks deepening as he adds, "I've never met anyone with abilities like yours. The way you absorb information from a book, a person—and yet—"

I gaze at him, throat tight and hot, sensing the beginnings of something I'd rather avoid.

"And yet—you've no idea of who stands beside you. Right beside you, in fact."

I sigh, wondering if this is the moment when he thrusts a pamphlet at me and goes into full-blown testimony mode, but he just motions to my right, smiling and nodding as though someone's right there. But when I turn to look, all I get is blank space.

"At first I thought for sure you'd arrived in this store to teach me." He smiles, reading my expression when he adds, "You do know there's no such thing as coincidence—the universe is far too precise for random events. You came here for a reason, whether you realize it or not, and—"

"I was led here by Ava," I say, uncomfortable with where this is going and wanting it to stop. "And I returned to see Lina not *you*."

But he just nods, completely unfazed. "And yet, you returned at a time when Lina wasn't here, making it possible for you to find *me*."

I shift in my seat and focus on the book since I can't look at him. Not after what he just said. Not after my trip to Amsterdam with Damen.

"Ever hear the phrase *when the student is ready the teacher appears?*"

I shrug, glancing at him briefly before looking down again.

"We meet the people we're supposed to when the time is just right. And even though I'm sure I have plenty to learn from you, I'd really like to teach you something if you'll let me—if you're open to learning."

I can feel his gaze, heavy and intense, and knowing my options are few, I just shrug. Seeing him nod and look to my right, tilting his head as though someone's there.

"There's someone who wants to say hello," he says, gaze fixed on that spot. "Though she warns me you're skeptical so I'll have to work extra hard to convince you."

I stare at him, neither blinking nor breathing. Thinking that if this is a joke—if he's tricking me in some way—then I'll—

"Does the name Riley mean anything to you?"

I swallow hard, unable to speak. My mind speeding backward, searching every conversation we've ever had, looking for the moment when I might have revealed that.

He looks at me, patient, waiting. But I just nod, unwilling to offer anything more.

"She says she's your sister—your younger sister." Giving me no time to reply when he adds, "Oh, and she's brought someone with her—or rather—" He smiles, pushing his dreads off his face as though to *see* better. "Or rather some*thing*—it's a dog—a yellow—"

"Lab," I say, almost involuntarily. "That's our dog—"

"Butterball." He nods.

"*Cup*. Butter*cup*." Eyes narrowing, wondering how he got that one wrong if Riley's truly standing beside him.

But he just nods, going on to say, "She says she can't stay long since she's keeping quite busy these days, but she wants you to know that she's with you, a lot more than you think."

"Really?" I fold my arms and lean back in my seat. "Then why doesn't she show herself?" I frown, abandoning my vow to keep silent and indulging my frustration with her. "Why doesn't she *do* something to make herself known?"

Jude gives a half smile, lips quirking the tiniest bit when he says, "She's showing me a tray of—" He pauses, squinting as he continues, "brownies. She wants to know if you enjoyed them?"

I freeze, remembering the brownies Sabine made a few weeks ago, and how the smallest piece was marked with my initial, the largest with Riley's, just like she used to do back when my mom used to make them—

I look at Jude, throat so tight no words can get past. Struggling to compose myself as he says, "She also wants to know if you enjoyed the movie—the one she showed you in—"

*Summerland*. I close my eyes, fighting back tears, wondering if my blabbermouth sister is going to tell him about *that*, but he just shrugs, and ends it right there.

"Tell her—" I start, voice so hoarse and scratchy I'm forced to clear my throat and start again. "Tell her *yes* to everything— all of it. And tell her that—that I love her—and miss her—and to please say hi to Mom and Dad—and that she really needs to help me find a way so I can talk to her again—because I need—"

"That's where I come in," he says, voice quiet, subdued, eyes seeking mine. "She wants me to be our go-between since she can't speak directly to you—at least not outside of your dreams. Though she wants you to know she can always hear you."

I look at him, skepticism taking over again. *Our go-between?* Would Riley really want that? Does that mean she trusts him? And if so, *why?* Does she know about our past? And what's that about our dreams—last time she appeared in my dream it was more like a nightmare. A riddle-filled nightmare that didn't make any sense.

I look at Jude again, wondering if I can trust him—if he's somehow making this up? Maybe the twins told him—maybe he Googled the accident and—

"She's leaving," he says, nodding as he smiles and waves good-bye at my supposedly invisible sister. "Would you like to say anything before she goes?"

I grip the sides of my seat, gazing down at the desk as I struggle to breathe. The space feeling suddenly cramped, confined, as though the ceiling is dropping as the walls cave in. Having no idea if I can trust him, if Riley is here, if any of this is even real.

All I know is that I need to get out of here.

Get some air.

His voice calling after me as I spring from the desk and bolt for the door—having no idea where I'm headed, but hoping it's vast, open, far from *him.*

# thirty-seven

I run out the door and head for the beach, heart racing, mind spinning, forgetting to slow down to a more normal speed until I'm already there. Toes tipped toward the water, a cloud of sand and bewildered people left in my wake. Each of them squinting and shaking their heads, telling themselves they imagined it, couldn't possibly be. No one can run that fast.

No one who appears as normal as me.

I abandon my flip-flops and wade farther in, at first stopping to roll the hem of my jeans, then deciding not to care when a wave comes and wets them to my knees. Just wanting to feel something—something tangible, physical—a problem with an obvious fix. Unlike the kind I've been wrestling with.

And though I'm no stranger to loneliness, I've never felt quite as lonely as this. I've always had someone to go to. Sabine—Riley—Damen—my friends—but now with my entire family gone, Sabine busy with Munoz, my boyfriend on a break, and friends I can't confide in—what's the point?

What's the point of having these powers, the ability to manipulate energy and manifest things, if I can't manifest the one thing I really want?

What's the point of seeing ghosts when I can't see the ones who actually mean something to me?

What's the point of living forever if I'm forced to live it like this?

I go deeper, 'til I'm up to mid-thigh, never having felt so alone on such an overcrowded beach, so helpless on such a bright and sunny day. Refusing to budge when he comes up from behind, grasping my shoulder and trying to pull me away from the waves. Enjoying the slam of water as it wets my skin, the ceaseless push and pull, luring me in.

"Hey." His eyes narrowed against the sun as he studies me closely, refusing to loosen his grip 'til he's sure I'm okay. "What do you say we head back inside?" Voice calm, careful, as though I'm fragile, delicate, capable of doing just about anything.

I swallow hard and hold my ground, gaze fixed on the horizon when I say, "If you were joking—if you were in any way playing me—" I shake my head, unable to finish, but the threat is implied.

"Never." He squeezes tighter, holding me steady, pulling me up and over a small oncoming wave. "You read *me*, Ever. That very first day. You know what I can do—what I can *see*." I take a deep breath, about to speak when he adds, "And just so you know, she's been with you several times since. Not every time, but most of them. Though this is the first time she spoke."

"And why is that?" I turn, gaze meeting his. Having no real reason not to believe, but needing to be as sure as I can.

"I guess she wanted to build a little trust." He shrugs. "Not unlike you."

I look at him, gaze into those sea green eyes, the truth laid open, bared for me to see. He's not lying, not at all playing, certainly not making it up. He really does see Riley, and his only agenda is to help.

"I think this is why we found each other." He nods, voice lowered to almost a whisper. "I wonder if Riley arranged this?"

*Riley or—something else—something greater than us?* I stare at the ocean, wondering if he recognizes me like I recognize him. If he feels the ping in the gut, the prickle of skin, the strange yet familiar *pull*—the same things I feel? And if so, what does it mean? Do we really have unfinished business—karma that must be addressed?

*Is there really no such thing as coincidence?*

"I can teach you," he says, gaze like a promise he wants to fulfill. "There's no guarantee—but I can try."

I remove myself from his grip and wade farther in, not caring that my bottom half's soaking while the rest of me's dry.

"Everyone has the ability. Just like everyone's psychic—or at the very least intuitive. It's just a matter of how open one is, how willing to let go and learn. But with your gifts—there's no reason why you can't learn to see her too."

I glance at him, but only briefly, something's caught my attention—something that—

"The trick is to raise your vibration—getting it to a level where—"

We don't see the wave until it's already cresting, leaving us no time to duck dive or at the very least run. The only thing keeping me from a complete and total wipeout are Jude's incredibly fast reflexes and the strength of his arms.

"You okay?" he asks, gaze boring into mine.

But my attention's elsewhere, drawn to that warm wonderful pull, the familiar loving essence that only belongs to one person—only belongs to *him*—

Watching as Damen cuts through the water, board tucked under his arm, body so sculpted, so bronzed, Rembrandt would weep. Water sluicing behind him like a hot knife through butter, cleanly, fluidly, as though parting the sea.

My lips part, desperate to speak, to call out his name and bring him back to me. But just as I'm about to, my eyes meet his and I see what he sees: me—hair tangled and wet—clothes twisted and clinging—frolicking in the ocean on a hot sunny day with Jude's tanned strong arms still wrapped around me.

I release myself from Jude's grip, but it's too late. Damen's already seen me.

Already moved on.

Leaving me hollow, breathless, as I watch him retreat.

No tulips, no telepathic message, just a sad, empty void left behind in his place.

# thirty-eight

Jude follows me out of the water and halfway down the beach, calling after me, trying to keep up, finally surrendering when I cross the street and head toward the store where Haven works.

I need to talk to someone, confide in a friend. Put it all out there and unburden myself, no matter the cost.

Immune to the weight of my soaking wet jeans, the slap of fabric, my clinging, damp tee—not even thinking about manifesting something dry to wear until I get to the door and find Roman there.

"Sorry, no shoes, no shirt, no service." He smiles. "Though I must say, I *am* enjoying the view."

I follow his gaze all the way down to my chest, covering it with my arms when I see how my top has gone pretty much see-thru.

"I need to talk to Haven." I start to push past him only to be blocked once again.

"Ever, please. This is a classy establishment. Maybe you should come back when you're a little more—*pulled together.*"

I peer over his shoulder, catching a glimpse of a fairly large space so opulent, so packed with stuff, it's like the inside of Genie's bottle. Crystal chandeliers hanging from the rafters, iron sconces and framed oil paintings marking the walls, while the floors are covered with colorful, woven, overlapping rugs as antique furnishings butt up against rack after rack of vintage clothing and tall glass display cases filled with trinkets and jewelry.

"Just tell me if she's here." I glare, patience running thin as he looks me over and smirks. Trying to tune into her energy and assuming he's blocking me when I don't get very far.

"Maybe yes—maybe no. Who's to say?" He reaches into his pocket and retrieves a pack of cigarettes, offering one to me. But I just roll my eyes and make a face, seeing him squint as he brings his lighter to the tip, inhaling deeply then exhaling as he says, "Fer chrissakes, Ever, live a little! Immortality is *wasted* on you!"

I frown, making a show of waving the smoke out of my face when I say, "Who owns this place?" Realizing I've never noticed it before and wondering what his connection could be.

He takes a long drag, eyes narrowed, catlike, as he looks me over from my head to my feet. "You think I'm joking but I'm not. No self-respecting immortal would ever be seen looking like *that*." He wags a finger at me. "And yet—and yet—feel free to keep the top—just be sure to change all the rest." He leers, grinning at me in the most predatory way.

"Who owns this place?" I repeat, peering inside again, an idea beginning to form. This isn't just any old vintage store. These are Roman's own personal goods. The stuff he's hoarded through the last six hundred years, doling them out diligently, selling at just the right time—a dealer of antiquities.

He squints, exhaling in a series of smoke rings as he says, "A friend owns it. It's of no concern of yours."

I narrow my gaze, knowing better. This is his store. He's Haven's boss, the one who signs her checks. But not wanting to let on I just say, "So you've made a friend. How sad for them."

"Oh, I've made plenty." He grins, taking another deep pull before tossing the butt and stomping it out with his shoe. "Unlike you, I don't alienate people. I don't *hoard my gifts* so to speak. I'm a populist, Ever. I give the people what they want."

"And what's that?" I ask, part of me wondering why I'm still here, dripping water onto the sidewalk, shivering in my wet jeans and see-thru tee only to engage in this useless, go-nowhere banter, while the other part's stuck, unable to move.

He smiles, deep blue eyes boring into mine as he says, "Well, they want what they want now, don't they?" His deep guttural laugh, almost like a growl, sending chills over my skin. "It's not too hard to decipher. Perhaps you'd like to venture a guess?"

I peer over his shoulder, sure I saw something move. Hoping it's Haven but finding the same girl I saw at his house that night—the night I was foolish enough to stop by. Her eyes meeting mine as she makes her way around the counter and approaches the door where we stand—all raven black hair, coal black eyes, and smooth dark skin—a beauty so exotic it robs me of breath.

"While it's been nice chatting with you, Ever, I'm afraid it's time for you to move along. No offense, darlin', but you're looking a bit—*unkempt*. Bad for business to have you loitering here. Might drive away all the customers, you understand? Though if it's bus change you need—" He fishes around in his pocket, coming up with a handful of quarters arranged on his palm. "I've no idea how much these things cost—haven't had to ride one since—"

"Since six hundred years ago," I say, narrowing my gaze. Watching the girl stop and turn the second Roman wiggles his fingers, a signal for her to back away. A gesture someone else might've missed, but not me. Seeing her stop and head into a back room I can't see.

I turn, knowing I've no business here. Roman's voice calling out from behind me as I make my way down the street, shouting, "There were no buses six hundred years ago! You'd know that if you'd quit ditching history!"

But I just continue, refusing to play, almost to the corner when he reaches out and grips me with his mind: *Hey, Ever— what do the people want? You might want to ponder that one, could be the clue that leads you to the antidote.*

I stumble, hands seeking the wall, fighting to steady myself as the sound of Roman's voice crowds my head. His lilting accent singing:

*We're not so different you and I. We're very much the same. And it won't be long now, darlin', 'til you'll get the chance to prove it. Won't be long now 'til you finally pay the price.*

Laughing heartily as he releases me and sends me on my way.

# thirty-nine

The next day I head to work as though nothing happened, determined to get past that awkward embrace on the beach, not to mention a shared past that Jude not only has no recollection of, but that never came to fruition for a reason.

A reason named *Damen*.

But even though I rushed, Miles and Haven still managed to beat me, as they both lean on the counter, flirting with Jude.

"What're you doing?" I ask, struggling to keep the panic to a minimum while glancing between the three of them—a triumphant Haven, a gleaming-eyed Miles, and a more than a little amused Jude.

"Spilling your secrets, exaggerating your flaws, oh, and inviting Jude here to my going away party—you know, in case you forget to." Miles laughs.

I glance at Jude, cheeks flaming, unsure what to say. Still gazing at him when Haven adds, "And as luck would have it, he's free that day!"

I make my way around the counter as though that's perfectly fine, as though I couldn't care less that the guy I've apparently spent the past several centuries hooking up with—the same guy my soul mate is convinced I have unfinished business with—will be partying in my living room in just a few days.

Haven picks up the flyer advertising Jude's Psychic Development class and waves it in front of my face. "And how come you never mentioned this?" She frowns. "This kind of thing is right up my alley. You know how I'm totally into this stuff." She turns to smile at Jude.

"Sorry, but I really didn't." I shrug, dropping my bag under the counter and grabbing the stool next to Jude. Refusing to go along with something that's not even remotely true, and wondering just how soon I can convince them to leave.

"Well, I am. Have been for a while now." She lifts her brow, looking at me in a way that dares me to refute it, but I refuse to bite. "Luckily, Jude said he'd try to squeeze me in," she adds with a smirk.

I shoot him a look, a quick, hard, fleeting look, watching as his shoulders pull in ever so slightly as he shrugs and heads for the back room. Returning a moment later with his board hitched under his arm, waving at the three of us as he heads out the door.

"I can't believe you kept him a secret!" Miles says, the second Jude's gone. "That's the *worst* kind of selfish! Especially when you already have a hottie of your own!"

"I can't believe you kept *this* a secret," Haven says, still gripping the flyer. "You're lucky he's letting me in!"

"*I'm* lucky?" I shake my head. The last thing I need is Haven developing any hidden psychic abilities when she intuits too much already—or at least where Damen and I are concerned. "Besides, class already started, which is why he said he'd *try* to fit you in." Knowing I'll do whatever it takes to turn that *try* into a *can't*. "And what about work? Won't it interfere?"

She shakes her head, eyes narrowed, my opposition making her more determined than ever. "Nah, they're good with my schedule—won't be a problem."

"They?" I glance at her briefly, before reaching for the appointment book, thumbing through it in an attempt to appear blasé, uncommitted, when the truth is, I've gone high alert.

"The powers that *be*." She laughs, looking at me. "My bosses, whatever."

"Is Roman one of your bosses?" I glance at her briefly before turning the page.

"Um, hello? He's in high school, remember?" She shakes her head and glances at Miles, the two of them exchanging a look I prefer not to read.

"I stopped by yesterday." I study her closely, peering at her aura, her energy, stopping just shy of peeking into her head. "Roman said you weren't there."

"I know, he told me. Guess we just missed each other." She shrugs. "But even though you think we've changed the subject, we haven't. So tell me, what's up with you and this class?" She stabs the flyer with her purple-painted nail, gaze narrowed on mine. "Why don't you want me to take it? Is it because you like Jude?"

"No!" I glance between them, knowing it was too quick, too forceful, and only raised their suspicions. "I'm still with Damen," I add, even though it's not really true. But how can I admit it to them when I can't even admit it to myself? "Just because he's never at school doesn't mean—" I stop and shake my head, knowing it's better to end it right here. "But just so you know, Honor's enrolled, and I pretty much figured you wouldn't want to be in the same class as her." My gaze fixes on hers, hoping that'll stick.

"Seriously?" She and Miles both gape, four brown eyes taking me in.

"What about Stacia? And Craig?" Haven asks, ready to forget all about it if the entire Mean Team is in.

And even though I'm tempted to lie, I shake my head and say, "No, just her. Weird, huh?"

Haven's aura flickers and flares, weighing the pros and cons of developing her psychic skills alongside a bully like Honor. Looking around the store as she says, "So what exactly do you do here? Do you give readings and stuff?"

"Me? No!" I press my lips together and reach for the box of receipts, flipping through them for no other reason than to avoid her piercing gaze.

"So who's this Avalon chick? She any good?"

I freeze, eyes darting between them, unable to speak.

"Um, hello? Earth to Ever! The sign, right behind you, the one that says: BOOK YOUR READING WITH AVALON TODAY!" She shakes her head. Only half joking when she says, "Jeez, you really do just slide by on your good looks, don't you?"

"Sign me up!" Miles says. "I'd love a reading with Avalon. Maybe she can tell me where all the hotties hang out in Florence." He laughs.

"Sign me up too." Haven nods. "I've always wanted a reading, and I could really use one about now. Is she here?" She glances around.

I swallow hard. I should've known it would come to this. Damen warned me of this very thing.

"Um, hello?" Haven waves, exchanging a look with Miles.

"We'd like to book a reading, please. I mean, you do work here, *right?*"

I reach under the counter, grasping the book, flipping through it so quickly the dates and names are a blur of black letters on white. Slamming it shut and stashing it away again when I say, "She's booked."

"O—*kay.*" Haven narrows her gaze, totally onto me now. "Then how about tomorrow?"

I shake my head.

"The next day."

"Still booked."

"Next week."

"Sorry."

"Next *year.*"

I shrug.

"What's your deal?" She squints.

I pause, seeing how they're both staring at me, convinced I'm either holding something back, have completely lost it, or both. Knowing I need to do what I can to dispel that when I say, "I just don't think you should waste your money. She's not all that great. We've had some complaints."

Miles shakes his head, looking at me when he says, "Way to close a deal, Ever."

But Haven's unmoved, gaze fixed on mine, head nodding slowly as she adds, "Well, I'm sure this isn't the only place where I can get a reading. And for some reason, for some *strange, unknown* reason, now I'm more determined than ever." Slinging her bag over her shoulder and grabbing Miles's hand, pulling him alongside her as she heads for the door and says, "I don't know what's going on with you, but you've been acting really strange. Stranger than usual." Glancing over her shoulder and shooting me a loaded look I prefer not to interpret. "Seriously, Ever, if you're into Jude, then just say so. Though you might want to tell Damen first—he deserves the courtesy, don't you think?"

"I'm not into Jude." I shrug, trying to appear calm, even, but failing miserably. Besides it's not like it matters, they're already convinced. Everyone's convinced. Everyone but me. "And trust me, there's nothing going on except finals, planning for Miles's party, and all—the usual—*stuff*—" My voice trailing off, knowing not one of us is buying it.

"Then where's Damen? How come he never comes around anymore?" Haven asks, as Miles stands beside her and nods. Allowing me a few seconds to answer before adding, "You know, friendships are supposed to work both ways. Give and take. Based on *trust*. But for whatever reason, you think you need to act perfect all the time. Like nothing ever goes wrong in your perfect, pretty life. Like nothing ever bothers you or drags you down. And I'm here to tell you that believe it or not, Miles and I will still love you even if you have an imperfect moment. Heck, even if you have an imperfect *day*, we'll still sit with you at lunch and text you in class. Because, trust us, Ever, it's not like we're buying your perfect act anyway."

I take a deep breath and nod. It's all I can do. My throat is so hot and tight there's no way I can speak.

Knowing they're waiting, both of them, standing by the door, willing to stay if I'll just say the word, find the courage to open up and trust them enough to unburden myself for a change.

But I can't. Who knows how they'd react, and I have enough to deal with already.

So I just smile and wave and promise to catch up with them later. Trying not to wince as they roll their eyes and leave.

# forty

I'm in the back room, hunched over the book when Jude comes in, surprised to find I'm still here.

"I saw your car parked out back and wanted to make sure you're okay." He pauses in the doorway, eyes narrowed, taking me in, before dropping onto the chair just opposite the desk where he studies me some more.

I gaze up from the book, eyes bleary as I glance at the clock, surprised to see how late it's gotten, surprised to see I've been here so long.

"I guess I got a little caught up." I shrug. "It's a lot to slog through." Closing the cover and pushing it aside as I add, "And most of it useless."

"You don't have to pull an all-nighter, you know. You can take it home if you want."

I think about home, and the message Sabine left for me earlier, informing me of her plans to cook dinner for Munoz, making home pretty much the last place I want to be at this point.

"No thanks." I shake my head. "I'm done." Realizing I mean it in every possible way.

For a book that once held such promise, all I've read so far are location spells, love spells, and a dubious cure for warts with inconclusive results—nothing about reversing the effects of a tainted elixir—or how to get a certain someone to divulge the only thing I really need to know.

Nothing that holds the slightest bit of promise for me.

"Can I help?" he asks, reading the defeat in my gaze.

I start to shake my head, knowing he can't. But then I think better. *Maybe he can?*

"Is she here?" I stare at him, holding my breath. "Riley—is she around?"

He looks to my right, then shakes his head. "Sorry." He shrugs. "Haven't seen her since—"

But even though his voice fades, we both know how it ends. He hasn't seen her since yesterday, just before Damen caught us embracing on the beach—a moment I prefer to forget.

"So how exactly do you teach someone to—you know—see spirits?"

He looks at me for a moment, rubbing his chin as his eyes study mine. "I can't necessarily teach someone to *see* them." He leans back in his seat, propping his bare foot on his knee. "Everybody's different—with different gifts and abilities. Some are naturally clairvoyant—able to *see*, or clairaudient—able to *hear*, or clairsentient—"

"Able to *sense*." I nod, already knowing where this is going and eager to get to the good stuff—the juice—the part that helps *me*. "So what are you then?"

"All three. Oh, and clairscent too." He smiles, a quick easy grin that practically lights up the room and makes my stomach go all weird again. "You probably are too. All of those I mean. The trick is to get your vibration raised high enough, then I'm sure—" He looks at me, knowing he lost me at *vibration* and adding, "Everything is energy, you know that, right?"

The words bringing me back to that night on the beach just a few weeks before, when Damen said the very same thing, about energy, vibrations, all of it. Remembering how I felt then, so afraid of confiding what I'd done. Naïve enough to think that was the worst of my problems, that it couldn't get any worse.

I gaze at Jude, his mouth still moving as he goes on and on, explaining energy, vibration, and the ability of the soul to live on. But all I can think about is the three of us, Damen, me, and him—wondering how we truly do fit.

"What do you think of past lives?" I ask, cutting him off. "You know, reincarnation. Do you believe in that stuff? Do you think people really have leftover karma they need to work out, again and again until they get it just right?" Holding my breath, wondering how he'll respond, if he has any recollection of us, who we once were.

"Why not?" He shrugs. "Karma's pretty much king. Besides, wasn't it Eleanor Roosevelt who said she didn't think it would be any more unusual for her to show up in another life, than the one she was in now? You think I'm gonna quash old Eleanor?" He laughs.

I sit back, studying him, wishing he knew about our tangled past. If for no other reason than to get it all out in the open, put it right there on the table, so I could report back to Damen and prove that it's over. And figuring maybe it's my job to get the ball rolling, I take a deep breath and say, "Have you ever heard of someone named Bastiaan de Kool?"

He looks at me, squinting.

"He was—Dutch—an artist—he painted—and—*stuff*—" I shake my head and look away, feeling foolish for bringing it up. I mean, what exactly am I supposed to follow that with? *Well, just so you know, Bastiaan was you, several hundred years ago—and the person you painted was me!*

Seeing him sit there before me, lips quirked, shoulders lifted, clearly unaware of what I'm getting at. And short of escorting him to Summerland and re-creating the gallery, neither of which I'm going to do, there's no way to continue. I'll just have to sit this one out. Wait until my three lonely months are up.

I shake my head, determined to put it behind me and get down to the business at hand. Looking at him and clearing my throat when I say, "So, how exactly does one raise their vibration?"

By the time we're done, I'm no closer to talking to dead people than I was before I started. At least not the dead person I'm actually interested in. Though plenty of other disincarnates made themselves known, but I pretty much blocked them all out.

"It takes practice." He locks the front door and leads me to my car. "I sat in a weekly spirit circle for years before my powers fully returned."

"I thought you were born with it?" I squint.

"I was." He nods. "But after blocking it out for so long, I had to really work to develop it again."

I sigh, unable to see myself joining a séance group and wishing there was an easier way.

"She visits you in your dreams, you know."

I roll my eyes, remembering that one crazy dream, and knowing no way was that her.

But he just looks at me, nodding when he says. "Of course she does. They always do. It's the easiest way to get through."

I look at him, leaning against my car door, key in hand as my eyes travel his face. Knowing I should go, say good night and be on my way, but for some reason I'm unable to move.

"The subconscious mind takes over at night, freeing us of all the usual restrictions we put on ourselves, all the things we block out, telling ourselves it can't happen, that mystical things aren't really possible, when the truth is, the universe is magical, and mysterious, and much grander than it seems, with only the thinnest veil of energy separating us from them. I know it's confusing with the way they communicate in symbols—and to be honest, I'm not sure how much of that is us—the way we arrange information—or them, and the restrictions on just how much they're allowed to share."

I take a deep breath, my whole body shivering though I'm not really cold. Spooked is more like it. Spooked by his words, his presence, the way he's making me feel. But not cold. In fact, not at all.

Wondering what Riley could've meant with the glass prison, the way I could see Damen, but he couldn't see me. Trying to view it as though it's an assignment for English, like symbolism in a book. Wondering if it means that Damen's misguided, can't see what's in front of him? And if so, what does *that* mean?

"Just because you can't *see* something doesn't mean it doesn't exist," he says, his voice the only sound in this still and quiet night.

I nod, feeling like I should know that better than anyone as

Jude stands before me, going on and on about dimensions, the afterlife, and how time's just a made-up concept that doesn't really exist, and I can't help but wonder what he'd do if I gave him a treat. Just grabbed his hand, closed my eyes, and took him to Summerland to show him just how deep it really goes—

He catches me, catches me looking. My gaze roaming his smooth dark skin, golden dreadlocks, the scar splicing his brow, until finally meeting those sea green eyes, so deep, so knowing, I quickly look away.

"Ever—" he groans, voice low, thick, as he reaches for me. "Ever—I—"

But I just shake my head and turn away, climbing into my car and backing out of the space. Glancing into my rearview mirror to find him still standing there, still looking after me, his longing displayed in his gaze.

Shaking my head and focusing back on the road, telling myself that particular past, the things I once felt, have nothing to do with my future.

# forty-one

Originally the party was supposed to be Saturday, but with Miles leaving early next week, and with so much to do between now and then, we moved it to Thursday, the last day of school.

And even though I know better, even though I'm fully aware that Damen is a man of his word, I'm still disappointed when I walk into English and find he's not there.

I glance at Stacia, her eyes narrowing, lips smirking, extending her foot as I try to move past, as Honor sits beside her, playing along despite the fact that she can barely meet my eyes—not with the secret we share.

And as I take my seat and gaze around the room, one thing is clear—everyone has a partner, a friend, someone to talk to—everyone but me. Having spent the better part of the year befriending someone who refuses to show, his seat beside mine, woefully empty.

Like a big block of ice where the sun used to be.

So as Mr. Robins yammers on and on about stuff no one

really cares about, including him, I distract myself by lowering my shield and aiming my quantum remote at all of my classmates, filling the room with a cacophony of color and sound, remembering how my life used to be—my life before Damen when I was constantly overwhelmed.

Tuning in to Mr. Robins who's looking forward to the moment the final bell rings so he can enjoy a nice long summer free of us, then Craig who's planning to break up with Honor by the end of the day so he can make the most of the next three months. And over to Stacia who still has no memory of her brief time with Damen, though she's definitely still into him. Having recently discovered where he surfs, she's planning to spend the summer in a revolving collection of bikinis, determined to start senior year on his arm. And even though it bugs me to see that, I force myself to shrug it off and move on to Honor, surprised to see her agenda's full—having nothing to do with Stacia or Craig—and everything to do with her growing interest in *the craft*.

I narrow my focus, tuning everyone out in order to better *see* her, curious to know what's driving this sudden interest in magick, assuming it's some harmless crush on Jude, and surprised to *see* it's nothing like that. She's tired of being the shadow cast by the spotlight, the *B* that follows the *A*. Tired of life on the second rung, and is planning the day when the tables are turned.

She glances over her shoulder and looks right at me, eyes narrowing as though she knows what I *see* and dares me to stop her. Still holding the look when Stacia nudges her arm, looks at me, and mouths the word *freak*.

I roll my eyes, starting to turn away when she swings her hair over her shoulder and leans toward me, looking me over when she says, "So, what happened to Damen? Did your spell stop working? Did he find out you're a witch?"

I shake my head and lean back in my seat, legs crossed, hands folded on my desk, projecting a picture of absolute calm as I shoot her a look so long and deep she can't help but squirm. Convinced I'm the only witch in the room, having no idea that her minion has her own magick coup planned.

Flicking my gaze back toward Honor, sensing her defiance, a newly summoned strength she never exhibited before, our gaze holding, stretching, until I finally look away. Telling myself it's none of my business—I've no right to interfere in their friendship—no right to intrude.

Shutting out all the color and sound as I glance down at my desk, doodling a field of red tulips onto my notebook, having *seen* more than enough for one day.

When I get to history Roman is there, loitering just outside the door as he talks with some guy I've never seen before. The two of them stopping the moment I approach, turning toward me to get a good look.

I reach for the door just as Roman blocks it, smiling when my hand accidentally skims his hip, and laughing even harder when I cringe and pull away. His deep blue eyes meeting mine when he says, "Have you two met?" He nods toward his friend.

I roll my eyes, wanting only to get to class and get it over with, put this whole miserable junior year behind me and fully prepared to knock him out of my way if I have to.

His tongue clucking inside his cheek when he says, "*So* unfriendly. Seriously, Ever, your manners are *lacking*. But far be it from me to force it. Some other day perhaps."

He nods at his friend, prompting him to leave, and I'm just about to barge into class when I glimpse something on the periphery—the lack of an aura—the physical perfection—and I'm sure if I looked hard enough I'd find an Ouroboros tattoo to confirm it.

"What are you up to?" I say, my gaze switching to Roman. Wondering if his *friend* is one of the long-lost orphans, or some unfortunate soul he's more recently turned.

Seeing the smile that widens his cheeks when he says, "It's all part of the riddle, Ever. The one you'll be called upon to solve very soon. But for now, why don't you just head inside and brush up on your history. Trust me." He laughs, opening the door and waving me in. "There's no need to hurry. Your time will come soon."

# forty-two

Even though I told Sabine she could invite Munoz to the party, she's smart enough to recognize a halfhearted offer when she hears it—so luckily for us, they made other plans.

I ready the house with all things Italian—platters of spaghetti, pizza, cannelloni—balloons that are red, white, and green—and a profusion of paintings—manifested replicas of *Primavera* and *Birth of Venus* by Botticelli, Titian's *Venus of Urbino*, Michelangelo's *Doni Tondo*, as well as a life-sized statue of *David* out by the pool. All the while remembering the time Riley and I decorated the house for that fateful Halloween party—the night I kissed Damen—the night I met Ava and Drina—the night that changed everything.

Pausing to glance around and take it all in before heading for the couch and assuming the lotus position. Closing my eyes and concentrating on raising my vibration just like Jude taught me, missing Riley so much I've committed to my own séance circle, determined to practice a little each day until she appears.

Quieting my mind of all the usual chatter and noise, keeping myself open, alert to all that surrounds me. Hoping for some sort of shift, an unexplained chill, a whisper of sound, some sort of signal to prove that she's near—but getting only a stream of bossy ghosts who are nothing like the sassy, twelve-year-old sister I seek.

And I'm just about to call it quits when a tremulous form starts to shimmer before me—leaning forward, straining to *see* it—when two high-pitched voices say, "What're you doing?"

The second I see them I spring to my feet, knowing *he* brought them, and hoping I can still catch him before he leaves.

My flight halted when Romy places her hand on my arm, shaking her head when she says, "We took the shuttle and walked the rest of the way. I'm sorry. Damen's not here."

I glance between them, breathless, bereft, struggling to compose myself when I say, "Oh. So, what's up?" Wondering if they're here for the party, if Haven somehow invited them.

"We need to talk to you." Romy and Rayne glance at each other before focusing on me. "There's something you need to know."

I swallow hard, eager for them to spill it, tell me just how unhappy and miserable Damen's become—regretting his decision to separate—desperately wanting me back—

"It's about Roman," Rayne says, eyes hard on mine, reading my expression if not my thoughts. "We think he's making others—other immortals like *you*."

"Except not really like *you*." Romy adds. "Since you're nice and not at all evil like him."

Rayne shrugs and looks all around, not quite willing to include me in that.

"Does Damen know?" I glance between them, wanting to fill up the room with his name, shout it over and over again.

"Yeah, but he won't do anything." She sighs. "Says they have every right to be here so long as they don't pose a threat."

"And do they?" My eyes dart between them. "Pose a threat?"

They look at each other, communicating in their own silent twin speak before turning to me. "We're not sure. Rayne's starting to get some of her *feeling* back—and sometimes it seems like my visions might be returning—but it's pretty slow going—so we were wondering if we could maybe have a look at the book. You know, the *Book of Shadows*, the one you keep at the store. We think it might help."

I look at them, eyes narrowed, suspicious, wondering if they're truly concerned about Roman's minions or just trying to play me against Damen to get what they want. And yet, there's no doubt it's true. From last count, there were three new immortals in town, all connected to Roman. All possibly up to no good. Though it's also true they've done nothing to prove that so far.

But still, not wanting them to think I'm a total pushover I say, "And Damen's okay with this?" The three of us looking at each other, the three of us knowing he's not.

They glance at each other in silent communion before turning to me. Rayne taking the lead when she says, "Listen, we need help. Damen's way is too slow, and at this rate, we'll be *thirty* before our powers return, and I'm not sure who wants that less—us or *you?*" She shoots me a look and I shrug, making no move to refute it since we both know it's true. "We need something that'll work, give quicker results, and we have nowhere to turn but to you and the book."

I glance between them, then look at my watch, wondering if I can get to the store, get them the book, and make it back in time for the party, which, considering how fast I move, and that the party's still hours away, it's clear that I can.

"Run, walk, whatever it takes." Rayne nods, knowing it's as good as done. "We'll wait for you here."


I head for the garage, at first thinking a run would be nice, if nothing else it makes me feel strong and invincible and not quite so inadequate against the problems I face. But since it's still light out, I drive instead. Arriving at the store to find Jude locking up early, key stuck in the door as he says, "Aren't you supposed to be throwing a party?" He squints, gaze moving over me, taking in my tee, shorts, and flip-flops.

"I forgot something." I nod. "It'll just take a sec—so—go ahead—no worries—I can lock up."

He cocks his head, aware that something's up but still opening the door and waving me in. Trailing behind, right on my heels, watching from the doorway as I open the drawer and lift the secret latch. Just about to retrieve the book when he says, "You're never gonna believe who came in today." I glance at him briefly, then open my bag, shoving the book deep inside when he adds, "Ava."

I freeze, eyes seeking his.

"Tell me."

He nods.

I swallow hard, stomach like a Ping-Pong ball, bouncing furiously as I find my voice again. "What did she want?"

"Her job, I guess." He shrugs. "She's been freelancing—wants something more stable. Seemed pretty surprised when I told her I'd hired you instead."

"You told her? About *me*?"

He shifts uncomfortably, from one foot to the next, looking at me when he says, "Well, yeah. I figured since you guys were friends and all—"

"And what did she do? When you told her? What *exactly* did she say?" Heart beating overtime, eyes never once leaving his.

"Nothing, really. Though she seemed pretty surprised."

"Surprised that I was *here*—or surprised that you hired me? Which surprised her *more*?"

He just stands there and squints, hardly the answer I need.

"Did she mention anything about *Damen*—or *me*—or *Roman*—or say anything else? Anything at all? You have to tell me *everything*—leave *nothing* out—"

He backs into the hall, hands raised in mock surrender. "Trust me, that was pretty much it. She split after that, so there's nothing to tell. Now come on, let's go. You don't want to be late to your own party, do you?"

# forty-three

Even though Jude offered to follow me home and help set things up, I didn't want him to know I'd gotten the book for the twins. So I made up some bogus excuse about needing plastic cups and asked him to stop by the store to get some, preferably red, white, and/or green, then I broke the speed limits all the way home where I handed over the goods.

"First—some ground rules," I say, holding onto the book despite two sets of hands clamoring for it. "I can't just give this to you, since it doesn't belong to me. And you can't take it home since Damen will freak. So the only way to get around all of that is for you to study it here."

They glance at each other, obviously not liking it but all out of options.

"Have you read it?" Romy peers at me.

I shrug. "I tried to intuit it, but I didn't get much. It's more like a diary than anything else."

Rayne rolls her eyes and reaches for it again, as her sister says, "You need to look deeper, read between the lines."

I glance between them, not understanding.

"You're skimming the surface. The book's not only written in the Theban code, the words themselves are a code."

"It's a code within a code," Rayne says. "Protected by a spell. Didn't Jude tell you?"

I freeze, glancing between them, thinking he most certainly did not.

"Come, on, we'll show you," Romy says, her twin grabbing the book as we head up the stairs. "We'll give you a lesson."


I leave the twins in the den, the two of them still hunched over the book, as I head for my walk-in closet and reach for the box stashed up high on the shelf. Retrieving my assortment of crystals and candles, oils and herbs, all the stuff that's left over from the elixirs I made just before the blue moon, and manifesting whatever's left on the list, which turns out to be sandalwood incense, and an athame—a double-edged knife with a jewel-encrusted handle much like the dagger Damen made.

Getting it all laid out and organized before slipping out of my clothes and removing my amulet. Placing it on a shelf next to the metallic clutch purse Sabine gave me a couple months back, knowing the deep V in the dress I plan to wear offers no place to hide the assortment of stones. Besides, after the ritual I'm planning to do, I'll no longer need it.

No longer need anything.

Thanks to Romy and Rayne I've been handed the key I've sought all along. And all it required was a password of sorts, the three of us forming a circle with the book in the center, hands clasped, eyes closed, each of us repeating a verse that went:

*Within the world of magick—resides this very tome*
*To which we are the chosen—returning to our home*
*Within the realm of mystics—we shall now reside*
*Allowed to glimpse upon this book—and see what lies inside*

The two of them beside me as I pressed my palm to its front, simultaneously frightened and fascinated when the book opened in a flurry of pages until resting on just the right one.

I knelt down before it, hardly believing my eyes. What was once a series of convoluted, hard-to-read code had become a simple recipe stating just what I need to get the job done.

I drop my dirty clothes in the hamper and reach for the white silk robe I rarely wear but that'll be perfect for the ritual. Carrying it into the bathroom where I fill up the tub for a nice long soak, which, according to the book, is the first important step in any ritual. Not only for cleansing the body and releasing the mind of all distracting negativity and thought, but also allowing time to reflect on the spell's intent, the outcome one wishes to see.

I lower myself in the water, sprinkling a dash of sage and mugwort and adding a clear quartz crystal stone to aid in my quest and center my vision, closing my eyes as I chant:

*Cleanse and reclaim this body of mine*
*So that my magick may properly bind*
*My spirit reborn, now ready for flight*
*Allowing my magick to take hold tonight*

All the while visualizing Roman before me, tall, tanned, and golden-haired, deep blue eyes gazing into mine as he apologizes for the terrible inconvenience he's caused, begging forgiveness and offering aid, willingly handing over the antidote to the antidote, newly enlightened to the error of his ways.

Replaying the vision again and again until my skin's gone all pruney and it's time to move on. Stepping out of the bath and into my robe, cleansed and purified and ready to proceed as I assemble my tools and light the incense, passing the knife through the smoke three times, as I say:

*I call upon Air to cast out any dark energies from this athame*
*Allowing only the light to remain*
*I call upon Fire to blaze away all negativity from this athame*
*Allowing only the good to remain*

Repeating the verse for the rest of the elements, calling upon Water and Earth, to cast out all dark and leave only light, concluding the consecration by sprinkling salt over the knife and calling upon the highest of magical powers to see that it's done.

Cleansing and consecrating the room as I walk three times around it, waving my incense as I say:

*I walk this circle thrice around*
*To consecrate and empower this ground*
*Evoking the power and protection of thee*
*Drawing their magical powers to me*

Forming a magick circle by sprinkling salt onto the floor, not unlike Rayne did with Damen just a few weeks before. Taking my place in the center and envisioning a cone of power rising around me as I arrange my crystals, light my candles, and anoint myself with oil, calling upon the elements of Fire and Air to aid in my spell, then closing my eyes until a white silk cord and a replica of Roman manifests right before me.

*Where you go my spell will follow*
*Where you hide my spell will find*
*Where you rest my spell will lie*
*With this cord your actions cease*
*With my blood your knowledge released*
*With this spell I bind thee to me*

Raising my athame and slicing it across my palm, tracing the curve of my lifeline as a rush of wind sweeps through the circle and an applause of thunder claps overhead. My hair whipping about as I squint against the swirling gale, my blood letting onto the cord until it's soaked and red. Rushing to secure it around Roman's neck, my gaze fixed on his, willing him to provide what I seek, before banishing him as though he never appeared.

I rise, body shaking, sweating, elated to know that it's over and done. Just a matter of time before the antidote to the antidote is in my possession and Damen and I join as one.

The wind begins to slow as the snap crackle of electricity starts to abate, and I'm collecting the stones and snuffing the candles when Romy and Rayne burst through the door, mouths open, eyes wide, as they stand there and gape.

"What have you done?" Rayne cries, gaze darting from my magick salt circle, to my collection of tools, to my blood-covered knife.

I look at them, gaze steady and secure, as I say, "Relax. It's over. I fixed it. And now it's just a matter of time before everything is put right again."

About to step out of the circle when Romy shouts, "Stop!"

Hand held before her, eyes blazing as her sister adds, "Don't move. Please, just trust us this time and do what we say."

I pause, glancing between them, wondering what could possibly be the big deal. The spell worked. I can *feel* its energy still thrumming inside me, and now it's just a matter of time until Roman appears—

"You've really done it this time," Rayne says, shaking her head. "Don't you know that the moon is *dark*? You're never supposed to do magick on the dark moon—*never*! It's a time for contemplation, meditation, but you *never, ever,* practice unless you're practicing the *dark arts*."

I glance between them, wondering if she's serious, and if so, what difference it could possibly make. If the spell worked, it worked. The rest is just details. *Right?*

Her twin chiming in to add, "Who did you call upon to aid you?"

I think back on my rhyme, the one I was pretty proud of for making up on the fly, recalling the line: *Evoking the power and protection of thee,* and repeating it to her.

"Great," Rayne says, closing her eyes and shaking her head.

Romy standing beside her, frowning as she adds, "During the dark moon, the goddess is absent while the queen of the underworld takes over. So in other words, instead of calling upon the light to work your spell, you asked the dark powers to aid you."

*And to bind Roman to me!* I gape, eyes wide, darting between the two of them, wondering if there's a way to reverse it, quickly, easily, before it's too late!

"It *is* too late," they say, reading my face. "All you can do now is wait for the next moon phase and try to reverse it. *If* it can be reversed."

"But—" The word dying on my lips as the enormity of my situation starts to sink in. Remembering Damen's warning from before, how sometimes when people get involved in witchcraft they get in over their head and wind up taking a much darker path . . .

I gaze at the two of them, unable to speak. Watching Rayne shake her head angrily as her sister looks at me and says, "All you can do now is cleanse yourself and your tools, burn your athame, and hope for the best. And then, if you're lucky, we'll let you out of the circle so all the bad energy you've conjured can't escape."

"If I'm *lucky*?" I look at them, stomach sinking. *Is she serious? Is it really that bad?*

Gaze darting between them as Romy says, "Don't push it. You've no idea what you've started."

# forty-four

Miles and Holt arrive together, and when they take one look at the decorations, Miles totally flips.

"I don't even have to go to Florence now that you've brought Florence to me!" He hugs me to him, quickly pulling away when he says, "Sorry, I forgot how you hate to be touched."

But I just shake my head and hug him again, feeling pretty good despite Romy and Rayne standing before me like the Great Wall of Pessimism—all raised brows, folded arms, and twisted lips—while I performed a quick but thorough grounding/protection meditation, picturing strong beams of white light penetrating my skull and flowing through my body, in an attempt to ward off at least some of the damage they're convinced that I've done.

But the truth is, I don't see the point. After the initial burst of empowerment, just after the binding spell was completed, everything returned to normal again. The only reason I even went through with their guided meditation is because they were acting so freaked, it was the only way to calm them down. But now I'm thinking it was all just a big misunder-standing—a complete overreaction on their part.

I mean, I'm immortal, gifted with strength and power they can't even begin to imagine. So while performing a magical ritual during the dark moon may pose danger to *them*, I seriously doubt it makes the slightest bit of difference for *me*.

And no sooner have I gotten Miles and Holt their drinks when the bell rings again, and again, and before I know it, my house is filled with pretty much every member from the *Hairspray* cast and crew.

"Huh, guess he's not Haven's date after all, unless they're arriving separately?" Miles says, nodding toward Jude as he enters the room laughing that good-natured laugh and helping himself to some virgin sangria, before taking off with Holt and leaving us alone together.

"Nice send-off." Jude nods, gazing around. "Makes me want to go somewhere too."

I look at him, smiling vaguely, wondering if he notices anything different about me, a change of energy, a new sense of empowerment—

But he just smiles, raising his cup as he says, "Paris." He takes a sip and nods. "I've always wanted to go to Paris. London and Amsterdam too." He shrugs. "Pretty much any of the great European cities would do."

I swallow hard and try not to gape. Wondering if he somehow knows—if it's buried deep within his subconscious, trying to surface. I mean, why else would he list all the significant places of our past?

He looks at me, green eyes on mine, holding the moment so long I clear my throat and say, "Huh. And here I had you pegged as the eco-adventure type. You know, Costa Rica,

Hawaii, Galapagos —seeker of the perfect wave and all that." Knowing that laugh at the end did nothing to hide my sudden bout of nervousness, just about to follow with something equally dumb when he looks past my shoulder and says, "Incoming."

I turn to find Haven, practically dwarfed by the tall, lithe, beautiful girl from the store where she works, on one side, and Roman on the other, while the immortal from the hall today at school walks just behind them. Three gorgeous, auraless, and pretty much soulless, immortal rogues Haven inadvertently invited into my home.

I swallow hard, eyes narrowed on Roman, fingers at my throat, seeking the amulet I chose not to wear, and reminding myself that I no longer need it. I'm in charge now. I summoned him here.

"Figured you'd have plenty of room and food." Haven smiles, hair newly dyed to the darkest of browns with a platinum streak that curves down the front, having ditched her usual emo look for one that's even edgier yet vintage—like a post apocalyptic vintage if there is such a thing. And all it takes is one look at the dark beauty beside her, her spiky hair, multi-pierced lobes, delicate lace-corseted dress paired with black leather boots, to know who spawned this latest makeover of hers.

"I'm Misa." The girl smiles, voice betraying the faintest trace of an accent that's unrecognizable to me. Her hand reaching for mine as I brace for the chill, the familiar jolt of ice water swarming my veins confirming my suspicion, though failing to tell me if she's one of the orphans, or more recently turned.

"And of course you know Roman." Haven smiles, lifting her hand so I can see it entwined with his.

But I refuse to react. Refuse to give anything away. I just nod and smile, as though it doesn't bother me at all.

Because it doesn't.

It's just a matter of time now 'til Roman's handing over the cure and doing my bidding. That's the only reason he's here.

"Oh, and this is Rafe." She nods, jabbing her finger toward the glorious rogue just behind her.

Same group of rogues the twins were talking about, minus Marco, the one with the Jaguar who doesn't seem to be here. And even though I've no idea what they're up to, what their agenda could possibly be, if they're hanging with Roman, the twins have every right to be worried.

Haven heads for the den, eager to introduce Misa and Rafe to her friends, as Roman lags behind, grinning at me.

"I'd almost forgotten how good you can look when you put a little effort behind it." He smiles, gaze gliding over my turquoise blue dress, hovering at the deep V of the neck, the expanse of bare skin where my amulet should be. "Guess this must be the reason," he nods, motioning toward Jude. "Since we know it wasn't for me, and Damen doesn't seem to be around much these days, does he? What happened, Ever? You forfeit your quest?"

I swallow hard and steady my gaze, taking in the tousled hair, designer board shorts, leather flip-flops, and long-sleeved tee, nothing about him appearing the slightest bit different, and yet we both know it is. That gleam in his eye, his lascivious gaze, his attempt to embarrass me—it's all just a front, a bit of bravado, trying to save face before he hands over the goods.

"So, you pouring?" He nods toward the punch bowl filled with nonalcoholic sangria. "Or is this a help-yourself situation?" Eyeing the bowl in a way that sets me on edge.

"I don't think you'd like it." I shrug, gaze fixed on his when I add, "Not your kind of drink."

"Good thing I brought my own." He winks, raising his glass bottle and stopping just shy of his lips, tilting it toward Jude when he says, "Wanna try? Takes the edge off. Guarantee you that."

Jude squints, entranced by the sparking, pearlescent liquid Roman jiggles before him. And I'm just about to intervene when Romy and Rayne barrel down the stairs, halting when their eyes meet Roman's, knowing I'm responsible for his being here.

"Well, if it isn't the Catholic school twins." Roman smiles, cheeks spread wide as he takes them in. "*Love* the new look! Especially you—you little punk goddess." He nods at Rayne, prompting her to turn away as he takes in her short dress, ripped stockings, and black patent-leather Mary Jane shoes.

"Go back upstairs," I tell them, wanting to get them as far from Roman as I possibly can. "And I'll—"

About to say that I'll be there in a minute, when Jude steps in, nudging my arm when he says, "Why don't I take them home?"

And even though I'm not thrilled with the idea of him going to Damen's, sure that Damen will like it even less, there's really nothing else I can do. As long as Roman's in my house, I'm pretty much stuck here too.

I follow them to the door, Rayne tugging my sleeve, pulling me down to her level when she says, "I don't know what you've done, but something *very bad* is brewing."

I look at her, about to refute it, tell her it's nothing like that, it's all under control, but she just shakes her head and adds, "Changes are coming. Big changes. And this time, you better choose right."

# forty-five

By the time Jude returns I'm out by the pool, watching the blond, tanned, physically glorious, golden-boy Roman splashing around and inviting everyone to jump in and join him.

"Not a fan?" Jude says, sitting beside me and eyeing me closely.

I frown, watching Haven's aura light up like the Fourth of July, glowing brighter and brighter as she clings to his back as he dips underwater, having no idea that he isn't really her date like she thinks. I'm the one who brought him here. He's bound to me now.

"Is it concern for your friend, or—something else?"

I fidget with the crystal horseshoe bracelet on my wrist, the one Damen gave me that day at the track, turning it around and around, as I narrow my eyes. Wondering what's taking so long. If the spell truly worked (and I *know* it did), then why don't I have the antidote now? Why is he delaying?

"So, the twins—they okay?" I ask, tearing my gaze away from the pool and focusing on Jude.

My eyes meeting his when he says, "Damen might've been right about the book being too strong for them."

I press my lips together, hoping Damen doesn't know I went behind his back and interfered with his lesson plan.

"No worries." Jude nods, reading my face. "Your secret's safe. I didn't even mention it."

I sigh in relief. "Did you see him—Damen?" I ask, throat tightening, heart clenching, the mere mention of his name turning my insides to mush, imagining how he must've felt to find his nemesis of the past several lives, the very same guy I embraced on the beach, standing on his front porch, Romy and Rayne at his side.

"He was out when I got there, and the twins were so freaked I waited 'til he got back. That's some place he's got."

I press my lips together, wondering what he saw, if the twins gave him a tour, if Damen's special room is restored.

"I think he was surprised to find me watching TV in his den, but once I explained, it went fairly well."

"Fairly?" I raise my brow.

He shrugs, looking at me, gaze so direct, so open, it's like a lover's embrace.

Prompting me to turn away, voice shaky, unsteady when I say, "So how did you explain it?"

His cool breath on my cheek as he leans in and whispers, "I told him I found them at the shuttle stop and decided to give them a ride. No harm done, right?"

I take a deep breath and focus on Roman, watching as he hoists Haven onto his shoulders so she can dogfight with Miles. Splashing and playing, and, on the surface anyway, engaging in nothing but good clean fun—until Roman turns, and time seems to stop. His eyes meeting mine, gleaming, mocking, as though he knows what I've done. And before I can blink he's back to playing again, making me question if I really did see what I thought.

"No. No harm done," I say, a terrible ache invading my gut, wondering just what it is that I've started.

# forty-six

After Miles's third failed attempt to get me to dive in, he finally gets out, moving toward me as he says, "Hey, what gives? I know you got your bikini on—I can see the straps!" Laughing when he pulls me off the lounge chair and hugs me tightly to him, whispering, "Have I *ever* told you how much I love you, *Ever*? Have I? Ever, *Ever*?"

I shake my head and pull away, glancing at Holt just behind him, rolling his eyes and tugging on Miles's arm, trying to convince him to leave me alone and quit dripping on me.

But Miles won't have it, he's got something to say and won't stop 'til it's done. Throwing a wet arm around my shoulder as he leans all over me and slurs, "I'm *shlo shlerious*, Ever. Before you came to this school—it was just me and Haven. But then— from the moment you *shlowed* up at our table—it became me and Haven and *you*." He looks at me, head bobbing, struggling to focus, as he grips me tighter and fights to keep his balance.

"Wow—that's really—*deep*." I glance at Holt, the two of us stifling a laugh as we each wrap an arm around Miles and lead him into the kitchen for some coffee. Getting him settled at the breakfast bar just as Haven and her three immortal friends come in.

"You guys leaving?" I squint, seeing they're back in their clothes, wet towels in their hands.

Haven nods. "Misa and Rafe have to work tomorrow, and Roman and I have an appointment."

I look at Roman, holding his gaze. *How can he be leaving when he hasn't given me what I want? Hasn't even begun to grovel, beg, and ask my forgiveness like I visualized?*

*How can he be leaving when it goes against my plan?*

I follow them to the door, heart racing as I take in the tilt of his chin, the gleam in his gaze, and I know it's not good. Something's gone wrong. Terribly wrong. Even though I cast the spell exactly like the book said, from the look in his eyes, and the curl of his lips, it's clear the goddess and queen have both failed me.

"Where are you going?" I squint, trying to peer into his energy but not getting anywhere.

Haven looks at me, brow raised, smile on her face as Roman throws his arm around her shoulder and says, "Private party. But there's room for you, Ever. Maybe you can stop by a little later, you know, when you're done here."

My eyes meet his, holding his gaze until I break away and focus on Haven again. And even though I promised I wouldn't do it, I peer right through her aura and into her mind, eager to see what's lurking in there, what's really going on, but not getting very far before I'm stopped, run up against a brick wall someone's placed in my path.

"You *all right?*" Roman asks, squinting at me, as he opens the door. "You look a little—*peaked.*"

I take a deep breath and narrow my gaze, about to say something more when Jude comes up and says, "Someone just hurled on the rug."

And even though my attention's only pulled for a moment, it's still long enough for them to exit. Roman glancing over his shoulder, looking at me when he says, "Sorry to bail on you, Ever. Though I'm sure we'll meet later."

## forty-seven

I was expecting it to be Miles, but it turns out he's fine. Helping to mop up the mess as he smiles and says, "And *that's* what you call acting. *Viva Firenze!*" He pumps his fist in the air.

"So really, you're fine?" I hand him a clean towel, feeling bad for making him go through the motions when as soon as everyone leaves, I'll just make it vanish and manifest a new one. "You're not drunk?"

"Not at all! But the point is, you *thought* I was."

I shrug. "The slurring, the loss of balance—all the signs were present and accounted for."

He rolls up the towel, about to hand it to me when Jude appears by my side and takes it instead. "Laundry?" he asks, brow raised.

But I just shake my head and point toward the trash, looking at Miles as I ask, "So who did it, who brought the booze?"

"Oh, no." He shakes his head and holds up his hands. "I'm sorry to break it to you, Ever, but this little get-together you organized, is also what's known as a *party*. And even if you don't serve it, it'll still find its way in. You'll get no information from me." He clamps his lips shut, pulling the imaginary zipper that seals them, before adding, "I say you just ditch this old thing." He points at the rug. "Seriously, I'll help roll it up. All we have to do is move the furniture around and Sabine won't even notice it's gone."

But I just shake my head, this vomit-covered rug is the least of my concerns now that Roman's no longer playing along. Taking Haven on some mysterious *appointment* I can't seem to crack, and what was that bit about us meeting up later? Was that a reference to the binding spell—or—*something else*?

Miles leans in to hug me, gathering me into his arms and giving me a really tight squeeze when he says, "Thanks for the party, Ever. And even though I don't know what's going on between you and Damen, I have one thing to say and I hope you'll listen and take me seriously. Ready?" He quirks his brow and pulls away.

I shrug. My mind preoccupied, in some other place.

"You deserve to be happy." He nods, gaze intense, focused on mine. "And if Jude makes you happy, then you shouldn't feel bad about that." He waits, waits for me to respond in some way, but when I don't he adds, "Party's pretty much over once someone hurls, right? So we're gonna bolt. But we'll get together before Florence, okay?"

I nod, watching as he and his friends all head for the door, calling, "Hey, Miles, did Haven or Roman mention where they're going?"

Miles looks at me, brows merged when he says, "Fortune-teller."

I squint, stomach sinking though I've no idea why.

"Remember the other day when she wanted to book one?"

I nod.

"She mentioned it to Roman and he arranged a private reading."

"This—*late*?" I look to my wrist to confirm the time though I'm not wearing my watch.

But Miles just shrugs and heads for the car, making me wonder if I should head out too. Try to catch up with Roman and Haven and make sure she's okay. But when I try to tune in to her energy again, I don't get very far. In fact, I don't get anything at all.

About to try again when Jude comes up and says, "You really need to ditch that rug. Smells awful."

I nod, distracted, unsure what to do.

"You know what helps?"

"Coffee grounds," I mumble, remembering how my mom used it once when Buttercup ate something bad and got sick in Riley's room.

"Well, yeah, that, but I was thinking more like getting *away* from the stench. Always works for me."

I look at him, his face lighting into a smile.

"Seriously." He slips his arm through mine and leads me outside. "What's the point of going to all that trouble, going all out with the decorations and food, doing all that you can for your friend's going-away pool party, when you spend the entire night on the sidelines, watching, observing, but not once diving in?"

I look away. "The party was for Miles, not me."

"Still." Jude shakes his head, gazing at me in a way that sends a flood of calm through my system. "You're looking a little stressed, and you know what kills stress, don't you?" I glance at him, seeing him smile when he says, "Bubbles."

"Bubbles?"

He points at the spa. "Bubbles." Face serious, gaze fixed on mine.

I take a deep breath and look at the Jacuzzi, warm, welcoming, and yes, bubbling too. Watching as Jude grabs some towels and sets them by the edge, and figuring I've got nothing to lose, that it just might help clear my head enough to come up with a new plan, I turn my back and yank off my dress. A silly bout of modesty since I'll be half naked soon, but still, facing him would feel too much like undressing.

Too much like the girl in the painting.

He heads for the edge and dips a toe in, eyes going wide in such a way that I can't help but laugh.

"You sure about this?" I wrap my arms around my waist like I'm cold, when really I'm just trying to fend off his gaze. *Seeing* the way his aura sparks and flames as he takes me in, the way his cheeks flush when he quickly looks away.

"Definitely." He nods, voice thick, rough, watching as I step into the Jacuzzi, at first wincing against the hot water then slowly easing in. Immersed in heat and bubbles, thinking this may be my smartest move yet.

I close my eyes and lean back, muscles loosening, relaxing, when Jude says, "Got room for one more?"

I squint, watching as he removes his shirt, taking in his expanse of chest, defined abs, trunks that hang low on his hips, making my way back up past his dimples and all the way to his eyes, two aqua pools I've known through the years. Watching as he moves forward, just about to step in when he remembers his phone in his pocket and drops it onto the towel.

"Whose decision was this?" He laughs, cringing against the steam and heat as he sits down beside me and stretches his legs, his foot accidentally landing on mine and letting it rest for a moment before pulling away. "Yeah, this is the life," he says, tilting his head back and closing his eyes, then peeking at me when he adds, "Please tell me you use this all the time, that you don't just forget it's here 'til someone coaxes you in."

"Is that what's happening? I'm being coaxed?"

He smiles, that relaxed, easy grin lifting his face and lighting his eyes. "Seems like you needed a little convincing. I don't know if you've noticed, but you can be a little intense."

I swallow hard, wanting to look away, look anywhere but at him, but unable to leave his gaze.

"Not that there's anything wrong with that—being intense that is—"

His gaze deepens, boring into mine, luring me closer like a fish on his line, his face looming so near I close my eyes to meet it. Tired of fighting, tired of repeatedly pushing him away. Assuring myself it's only a kiss. Jude's kiss. Bastiaan's kiss. Hoping it'll tell me, once and for all, if Damen's fears are in any way real.

His wave of calm energy comforting, tempering, as his lips part and his hand finds my knee, leaning toward each other, mouths about to merge when his ringing phone breaks our trance.

He pulls away, annoyance stamped on his face. "Should I get it?"

"I'm off duty." I shrug. "You're psychic, you tell me."

He stands, turning toward his towel as I take in his form, the squared shoulders, the sharp V of his waist, stopping when I catch a glimpse of something at the small of his back. Something round, dark, barely discernible, but still—

He turns, facing me again, brows merged, hand over his other ear, when he says, "Hello?" and then, "*Who?*"

Smiling at me and shaking his head, but it's too late.

I've seen it.

The unmistakable shape of a snake eating its own tail.

The Ouroboros.

The mythical symbol claimed by Roman's tribe of immortal rogues, tattooed right on the small of Jude's back.

I reach for my amulet, fingers fumbling but finding only skin. Wondering if this is somehow connected to my spell gone bad, if Roman has somehow arranged this.

"Ever? Yeah, she's here—" He looks at me, making a face as he adds, "O-*kay* . . ."

He looks at me, arm extended, trying to pass on the phone.

But I just ignore it, moving out of the Jacuzzi so fast he shakes his head and blinks.

Grabbing my dress and yanking it over my head, feeling it dampen and cling to my skin, as my eyes blaze on his, wondering what the hell he's up to.

"It's for you," he says, climbing out of the spa and trying to pass it again.

"Who is it?" I ask, voice barely a whisper. Mentally reciting the list of all seven chakras and their corresponding weaknesses, and trying to determine his.

"It's Ava. Says she needs to speak to you. You okay?" He squints, head cocked to the side, concern clouding his face.

I step back, unsure of what's happening but knowing it's a long way from good. Going straight past his aura and trying to peer into his mind, but not getting much of anything thanks to the shield that he built.

"How'd she get your number?" I ask, gaze fixed on his.

"She used to work for me—remember?" He shrugs, hands in the air. "Ever—seriously—what's this about?"

I look at him, heart racing, hands shaking, assuring myself I could take him if it comes to that. "Set the phone down."

"What?"

"Set it down. Right there," I point to a lounge chair, my gaze never once leaving his. "Then walk away quickly; don't come anywhere near."

He shoots me a look but does as I say. Backing toward the spa as I pick up the phone, still holding his gaze.

"Ever?" The voice is clipped, urgent, and definitely belongs to Ava. "Ever, I need you to listen, there's no time to explain." I stand there, numb, shell-shocked, still staring at Jude as she says, "Something's happened to Haven—she's in trouble— barely breathing—we're—we're gonna lose her if you don't get to Roman's right away."

I shake my head, trying to make sense of it. "What're you talking about? What's going on?"

"I just need you to get here—now—*hurry*—before it's too late!"

"Call nine-one-one!" I shout, hearing a muffled sound, a struggle of sorts, then Roman's smooth voice moves in.

"There'll be none of that, luv," he purrs. "Now be a good sport and get over here quick. Your friend wanted to see a fortune- teller, and now, unfortunately, her future's not looking so bright. She's hanging by a thread, Ever. *A thread,* I tell you. So do the right thing and come over. Seems it's time for you to solve the riddle."

I drop the phone and make for the gate, Jude following be- hind, begging me to explain. And when he makes the mistake of grabbing my shoulder, I turn and smack him so hard he flies through the yard and crashes into the lounge chairs.

Gaping at me in a tangle of limbs and outdoor furniture,

struggling to stand as I glance over my shoulder and say, "Grab your stuff and get out of here. I don't want to see you when I return."

Plunging through the gate and breaking into a run, hoping I can reach Haven before it's too late.

# forty-eight

I run.

Past cars, houses, stray dogs and cats. Legs moving, muscles pumping, carrying me forward with hardly a thought. My body moving like a well-oiled machine with shiny new parts. And even though it's only seconds, it feels like hours.

Hours since I last saw Haven.

Hours 'til I'll see her again.

And the second I get there I see *him*. Arriving at the same time as I do.

The mere sight of him causing everything to fade—of no possible consequence now that he's standing before me.

My heart caving as my mouth goes dry, overcome with such longing, I can't even speak—gazing upon my sweet, wonderful Damen—more glorious than ever under the glow of the streetlights. The sound of my name on his lips, so charged, so loaded, it's clear he feels the same.

I move toward him, pent-up emotions rising to the surface, bubbling over, I've so much to tell him, so much to say. The words fading the second we meet and my body's overtaken by tingle and heat—wanting only to melt into him, to never be separated again—

His hand at my back, propelling me closer, as Roman opens the door, glances between us, and says, "Ever, Damen, so glad you could make it."

Damen charges the door, pinning Roman to the wall as I slip right past and head for the den, eyes seeking Haven only to find her stretched out across the couch, pale, unmoving, and from what I can tell, barely breathing.

I rush toward her, dropping to her side as I grasp her wrist, fingers seeking her pulse like I once did at Damen's.

"What did you do to her?" I glare at Ava who's crouched right beside her, knowing she's working with Roman, they're on the same team. "What. Did you. Do?" I repeat, knowing a swift kick to her root chakra, the center for vanity and greed, would take her down in an instant if it should come to that. Wondering if Damen's already done the same, plunging his fist into Roman's sacral center, and no longer caring if he did.

Not after what they've done to my friend.

Ava looks at me, face pale against her wavy auburn hair, brown eyes wide and pleading, reminding me of something—something I've no time to grasp—when she says, "I didn't do anything, Ever. I swear. I know you don't believe me, but it's true—"

"You're right, I don't believe you." My focus back on Haven, pressing my palm to her forehead, her cheek, her skin cold and dry as her aura grows dimmer, darker, and her life-force energy slips away.

"It's not what you think—they booked me for a reading—said it was for a party—and when I showed up—this is what I found—" She gestures toward Haven and shakes her head.

"But of course you showed up! It's your dear friend Roman after all." I gaze at Haven, searching for signs of abuse, but I can't see a thing. She looks peaceful, unaware, clueless to the fact that she's not long for this world. Well on her way to the next one, the Summerland, unless I can stop it.

"I tried to help—tried to—"

"So why didn't you? Why'd you call Jude instead of nine-one-one?" I glare at her as I reach for my bag, my phone, remembering too late that I came here without it, manifesting a new one just as Roman storms into the room.

I look past him for Damen, my heart lurching when I don't find him.

But Roman just laughs, shaking his head as he says, "Moves a bit slower than me. He *is* older, you know!" Snapping the manifested phone out of my hand when he adds, "Trust me, luv. It's well beyond that. Seems your friend had herself a very potent cup of belladonna tea—" He motions toward a fine china cup on the table, its contents recently drained. "Also known as deadly nightshade in case you're not familiar, and she's so far along, she's way beyond medical help. No, the only one who can save her now is *you*."

I narrow my gaze, unsure what he means, seeing Damen now standing behind him, eyes guarded, troubled, as they look into mine. And I know he's trying to tell me something, send a telepathic message I can't seem to grasp. Getting only the faintest echo of sound, but unable to determine the words.

"This is it, Ever." Roman smiles. "The moment you've been

waiting for!" He sweeps his arms wide, motioning toward Haven as though she's the grand prize.

I glance between him and Damen, still trying to receive Damen's message, but nothing will come.

Roman's eyes roaming over me, slowly taking me in, my bare feet, damp, clinging dress, wetting his lips as he says, "It's real simple, darlin', simple enough for even you to decipher. Remember the day you came to my house and we talked about the price?"

I glance at Damen, catching a flash of alarm, disbelief, hurt, before quickly looking away.

"Oops!" Roman lifts his shoulders and covers his mouth as he glances between us. "Sorry. Forgot your unauthorized visit was our dirty little secret. Guess you'll just have to forgive my indiscretion, what with the life and death circumstances we're in. So just to catch you up to speed"—he nods at Ava and Damen—"Ever swung by my house looking to broker a deal. Seems she's extremely eager to bed her hunky boyfriend." He laughs, his gaze landing on Damen as he heads behind the bar, reaching for a cut crystal goblet and filling it with elixir as Damen fights to stay calm.

I take a deep breath but stay put. Knowing it won't make the slightest bit of difference if Roman's dead or alive, either way he's still in control. His game. His rules. And I can't help but wonder how long he's been at it—how long I've been fooling myself that I'm actually making progress when I'm just blindly following along. Just like the vision he showed me at school, all of us are under his rule.

"Ever—" Damen looks at me, telepathy no longer working, forced to voice his thoughts to the room. "Is this true?"

I swallow hard and look away, not looking at either of them when I say, "Just get to the point."

"Always in such a hurry." Roman shakes his head and clucks his tongue against his cheek. "Seriously, Ever, for someone with nothing but time, it doesn't make the slightest bit of sense. But fine, I'll play, so tell me, any clues, any ideas as to where this all leads?"

I gaze at Haven, barely breathing, barely hanging on, unwilling to admit that I have no idea what he wants, no clue as to what's going on.

"Remember the day when you came to see me at the store?"

Damen shifts, I can *feel* his energy shift, but I just shake my head, glancing over my shoulder, eyes narrowed when I say, "I went to see Haven, you just happened to be there."

"Details." Roman waves it away. "It's the riddle I'm getting at. Remember the riddle I presented you with?"

I sigh, grasping Haven's hand in mine—cold, dry, and still—not a good sign.

"*Give the people what they want.* Remember when I said that?" He pauses, waiting for me to respond, but when I don't he adds, "The question is—what does it *mean*, Ever? Exactly what *do* the people want? Any clues?" He lifts his brow and waits, nodding when he adds, "Try stepping out of yourself for a moment and take a more populist view. Go ahead, give it a whirl, try it on for size, see how it fits. It's quite unlike the elitist view you and Damen hold, I assure you of that. No hoarding of the gifts where I stand—I share them freely. Or at least with those I deem deserving."

I turn, turn until I'm facing him, suddenly beginning to understand. Voice hoarse, barely discernible when I say, "No!"

Glancing between Roman and Haven as the truth of what he wants, the *price* he insists on, becomes clear.

*No!*

My gaze locked on Roman's, as Ava and Damen remain silent, clueless as to what's truly transpiring here.

"I won't do it," I tell him. "There's no way you can make me."

"Wouldn't dream of it, luv. Where's the fun in that?" He smiles, slow, lazy, like the Cheshire cat. "Just like you can't make me do *your* bidding with pathetic attempts at mind melds and the dark forces you so recently called upon." He laughs, wagging his finger at me as he adds, "You've been a very naughty girl, Ever. Messing with magick you don't understand. Never realized when I sold the book all those years ago it'd end up in your hands. Or maybe I did?" He shakes his head. "Who's to say?"

My eyes meet his, the truth of his words hitting me at full speed. *Jude.* Is he the one who sold the book to Jude? And if so, are they in this together?

"Why are you doing this?" I narrow my gaze. No longer caring that Damen's now privy to my long list of betrayals, or what Ava's thinking off in her corner, focusing only on him and me—as though we're alone in this creepy, Godforsaken room.

"Well, it's really rather simple." He smiles. "You're so set on drawing lines, setting yourself apart—so now's your chance to really lay it down, now's your chance to prove you're nothing like me. And if you succeed, if you can prove beyond a doubt that we're nothing alike, well then, I'm fully prepared to give you what you want. I'll hand over the antidote to the antidote, the cure to the cure, and you and Damen can proceed to the honeymoon suite and have at it. It's what you've dreamed of all along, right? It's what you've been scheming for all this time. And all you have to do to get it is to let your friend die. If you let Haven die, the happily ever after is yours, satisfaction guaranteed—more or less."

"No." I shake my head. "*No!*"

"No to the antidote or the happily ever after? Which is it?" He glances between his watch and Haven, smiling as he adds, "Tick-tock, time to decide."

I move toward Haven, her breath coming hollow, frail, as Ava sits nearby, shaking her head, and Damen—my eternal love—my soul mate—the guy I've failed in so many ways—pleads with me not to do the very thing I'm inclined to.

"If you hesitate for too long, she dies. And if you bring her back, then, well, it can get a little messy, as you well know. But if you save her now, just slip her the elixir, well, she'll wake up feeling fine. Better than fine. And, the best part is, she'll stay that way *forever*. Which, after all, is *exactly* what the people want, isn't it? Eternal youth and beauty. Everlasting good health and vitality. No old age, no illness, no fear of death. An infinite horizon with no end in sight. So, which will it be, Ever? Stick to your high-minded, elitist, self-serving views, prove you're nothing like me, continue to hoard all the goods, say good-bye to your friend—and the antidote is yours. Or—" He smiles, gaze fixed on mine. "Save your friend. Give her the backstage pass to the sort of strength and beauty she could only dream of before. The very thing she's always longed for, the very thing *everyone* longs for. You don't *have* to say good-bye. It's entirely up to you. But, like I said, daylight's burning, so you might wanna hurry."

I take in her pale, fragile face, knowing I'm responsible, completely to blame. Vaguely aware of Damen beside me, urging,

"Ever, baby, please listen, you *can't* do it. You *can't* save her." Unwilling to look at him when he adds, "You *have* to let her go—it's *not* about us—not about us being together—we'll find a way, I promised you that. You know the risk this brings—you know you *can't* do this—not after experiencing the Shadowland," he whispers. "You can't resign her to *that*."

"Ooh! The *Shadowland*—sounds *scary!*" Roman laughs and shakes his head. "Don't tell me you're still meditating, mate? Still trekking the Himalayas searching for meaning?"

I swallow hard and look away, ignoring them both. Mind crowded with arguments, both for and against, as Ava adds, "Ever. Damen's right."

I glare at her, the woman who betrayed me in the very worst way. Leaving Damen vulnerable and exposed after promising to look after him, a willing partner in Roman's game.

"I know you don't trust me, but it's not what you think. Listen, Ever, please, I don't have time to explain, but if you won't listen to me, then listen to Damen, he knows what he says, you can't save your friend, you have to let her go—"

"Spoken like a true rogue," I hiss, remembering how she took off with the elixir, which I've no doubt she drank.

"It's not what you think," she says, "it's nothing like that."

But I'm no longer listening, my attention returning to Roman, now by my side, jiggling the goblet of elixir, the liquid flashing, sparking, as he swirls it around and around, warning me the time has come, it's time for me to choose.

"Haven wanted her fortune told, and who better to tell it than you, *Avalon?* Too bad Jude's not here, or we could really have ourselves a party—or wake—depending on how things work out. What happened, Ever, you two looked pretty tight last time I checked."

I swallow hard, my friend now hanging by a string. A string I can either cut—or—

"Hate to rush you, but it's the moment of truth. Please don't disappoint Haven, she was so looking forward to her reading. So what's it going to be? What do the cards say? Does she live—or does she die? The future is yours to decide."

"Ever," Damen says, hand on my arm, veil of energy hovering insistently between us, one more reminder of my mounting mistakes. "You can't do it, *please*. You know it's not right. As hard as this is, you've no choice but to say good-bye."

"Oh, there's a *choice*." Roman jiggles the bottle again. "Just how far are you willing to go to maintain your ideals and get the one thing you most want in the world?"

"Ever, *please*." Ava leans toward me. "This is all wrong, it's against the law of nature. You *have* to let her go."

I close my eyes. Unable to act—unable to move—I can't do this—I can't make this choice—he can't make me do this—

Roman's voice hovering over me when he says, "So I guess that's it then." He sighs and moves away. "Good for you, Ever, you proved your point. You're nothing like me. Nothing at all. You're a true elitist, a person of lofty ideals, higher mind, and now you get to sleep with your boyfriend too! Well done! And to think all it cost is the life of your friend. Your poor, sad, lost friend, who only wanted what everyone else wants— what you already have and are in the perfect position to share. Congratulations—should I say?"

He heads for the hall as I kneel before Haven, face streaming with tears as I gaze at my friend. My sad, lost, confused friend who didn't deserve any of this, who's always paying the price for befriending me. Damen's and Ava's murmuring voices beside me, a lullaby of promises, promising me I'll get through it, that I did the right thing, that it'll all be okay.

And then I see it, the silver cord that attaches the body to the soul. Having heard about it but never actually *seeing* it until now. Watching as it stretches so thin it's ready to snap—send my friend far from here and straight into Summerland—

I spring to my feet, ripping the bottle from Roman's grasp, and forcing Haven to drink.

Immune to the cries all around me, Ava's piercing gasp, Damen begging me to stop, and Roman's one-man applause accompanied by his loud vulgar laugh.

But I don't care about that.

I only care about *her*.

Haven.

I can't let her go.

Can't let her die.

Can't say good-bye.

Cradling her head in my arms and making her drink—the color instantly returning to her cheeks as she opens her eyes and gazes at me.

"What the—?" She struggles to sit, and looks all around. Squinting when she glances between me, Ava, Damen, and Roman, and says, "Where am I?"

I stare at her, mouth open, but with no idea what to say. Knowing that this is how Damen must've felt with me, only this is much worse.

He didn't know about the death of the soul.

I did.

"Damen and Ever decided to join us, luv, and guess what? The future's looking brighter than ever!" Roman swoops in beside me and helps her to her feet, winking at me when he adds, "You weren't feeling so well, so Ever gave you some juice, thinking a little *sugar* might perk you right up—and damn if it didn't work. And now, Ava, be a luv, and go fetch us some tea, would ya? There's a new pot on the stove."

Ava gets to her feet, willing me to meet her gaze as she heads for the hall. But I won't. Can't. Can't look at anyone. Not after what I've just done.

"Glad to know you're on board, Ever." Roman pauses just shy of the door. "It's like I said—you and I—we're the same. Bound to each other for all of eternity. And not because of the spell, darlin'—but because it's our fate—our destiny. Think of me as yet another soul mate." He laughs, voice a whisper when he adds, "There, there, luv, don't look so shocked. I, for one, am not the least bit surprised. You've never once strayed from the script. At least not so far."

# forty-nine

Damen leans toward me, his gaze like a hand on my arm, warm, inviting, luring me in. "Ever, please, look at me," he says.

But I just continue to stare at the ocean, the water so black I can't even see it.

Black ocean, dark moon, and a friend who's headed for the Shadowland, thanks to me.

I climb out of his car and head for the edge, staring down the steep cliff at the darkness below. Drawn to the pull of his energy as he comes up behind me, hand on my shoulder, pulling me close to his chest as he says, "We'll get through this— you'll see."

I turn, needing to see him, wondering how he can say such a thing. "How?" I start, voice so frail it's as though it belongs to somebody else. "How will we do that? You gonna make her an amulet and insist she wear it every day?"

He shakes his head, eyes boring into mine when he says, "How can I make Haven wear hers when I can't even convince you to wear yours?" His fingers drift to my neck, my chest, tracing the space where the crystals should be. "What happened?"

I turn, unwilling to look even worse in his eyes by explaining how I removed it, so overconfident in my misguided spellcasting attempt I set it aside.

"What am I supposed to tell her?" I whisper. "How can I possibly explain what I've done? How do you tell someone that you've given them eternal life, but if by chance they die, then their soul will be lost?"

Damen's lips looming close, warming my ear when he says, "We'll find a way—we'll—"

I shake my head and move away, staring into the black, avoiding his gaze. "How can you say that? How can you—"

He comes up beside me, his mere presence heating my skin as he says, "How can I what?"

I swallow hard, unable to say it, to put into words all that I've done. Allowing myself to be pulled into his arms, held tightly to his chest, wishing I could crawl right inside him, curl up next to his heart and stay there forever—the safest shelter I could ever know.

"How can I forgive a girl who loves her friend so much she can't bear to let her go?" He tucks my hair behind my ear and lifts my chin, making me face him. "How can I forgive a girl who sacrificed the one thing she's wanted all this time, all these *years*? Forfeiting the immediate hope of us being together so her friend could *live*? How can I forgive *her*, you ask?" He looks at me, eyes searching mine. "It's easy. Did I not make a similar choice when I first made you drink? And yet, what you did was so much bigger, motivated only by love, while my own actions weren't quite so pure. I was far more interested in alleviating my suffering." He shakes his head. "Convincing myself I did it for you, when the truth is, I was selfish and greedy, always interfering, never allowing you to choose for yourself. I brought you back for *me*—it's clear to me now."

I swallow hard, wishing I could believe him—that my decision was noble. But this is different. What I did was entirely different. I knew about the Shadowland, he didn't.

Looking at him as I say, "And that's all fine until she's in trouble again, then the death of her soul is on *me*."

He gazes past me, out to an invisible ocean sending a continuous crash of waves to the shore. Both of us knowing there's nothing more to say. No words that can remedy this.

"It wasn't—" I pause, feeling stupid for bringing it up now, in light of everything else, but still wanting him to know. "It wasn't what you think—about me and Jude—that day on the beach—" I shake my head. "It wasn't what it seemed." His jaw tightens, his grip loosens, but I bring him back to me, having much more to say. "I think he's an immortal. A rogue, like Roman." Damen stares at me, eyes narrowed when I add, "I saw his tattoo, right on the small of his back—" Then realizing how that sounds, that I was actually in a position to get a close-up look at his bare lower back, I add, "He was in his trunks and we were in the spa—" I shake my head, this isn't helping. "It was a whole thing for Miles's going-away party—and—anyway, when Ava called, he turned and reached for the phone and I saw it. The snake eating its own tail. The Ouroboros. Just like Drina had, like the one Roman wears on his neck. Same thing."

"Is it *just* like Roman's?"

I squint, unsure what he means.

"Did it flash? Move? Fade in and out of view?"

I swallow hard, and shake my head, wondering what

difference it could make. I mean, sure I only saw it for a few seconds, no more than a glimpse, but still—

He sighs and moves away, sitting on the hood of his car when he says, "Ever, the Ouroboros itself isn't evil. Far from it. Roman and his tribe have distorted the meaning. It's actually an ancient alchemical symbol, signifying creation out of destruction, eternal life—that sort of thing. Plenty of people have 'em, and the only thing it proves is that Jude has a thing for body art. Body art, and *you*."

I move toward him, wanting him to know that it's not at all reciprocated. How could it be with Damen in the picture?

Realizing he heard my thoughts when he pulls me close and presses his lips to my ear. "You sure? It's not the flashy car and magick tricks that won you over?"

I shake my head and nuzzle closer, aware of the veil that hovers between us, thrilled our telepathy is working again. Fearing I'd somehow broken it when we were back in that room.

*Of course it's working again*, he thinks. *Fear separates—makes us feel alone—disconnected—while love—love does just the opposite—it unites.*

"It's always been *you*," I say, needing to say the words out loud where we can both hear them. "Just *you*. No one but *you*." I gaze into his eyes, hoping the wait is over, that we can forgo our three-month deal.

He cradles my face in his hands and presses his lips against mine. His warm loving presence the only answer I need. The only answer I want.

Knowing there's so much more to discuss—Roman, Haven, the twins, Jude, the *Book*, Ava's return—but knowing it can wait. For now I just want to revel in being with him.

Sliding my arms around his neck as he pulls me onto his lap, the two of us gazing out at something so dark, so vast, so infinite, so eternal, we both know it's there—and yet we can't even see it.

*Read on for a preview of the next book in*
*Alyson Noël's Immortals series*

# Dark Flame

*Now available from St. Martin's Griffin*

"What the *fug*?"

Haven drops her cupcake, the one with the pink frosting, red sprinkles, and silver skirt. Her heavily made-up eyes searching mine as I glance around the busy plaza and cringe. Instantly regretting my decision to come here, foolish enough to think a trip to her favorite cupcake place on a nice summer day would be the best place to break the news. Like that little strawberry cake would somehow sweeten the message. But now I'm just wishing we'd stayed in the car.

"Inside voice. *Please.*" I aim for a light delivery but end up sounding like a cranky old schoolmarm instead. Watching as she leans forward, tucks her long, platinum-streaked bangs back behind her ear, and squints.

"Excuse me? But are you for real? I mean, here you drop a major bomb on me—and I mean *major*—as in my ears are still ringing and my head is still spinning and I kind of need you to repeat it just to make sure you really did say what I think—and your only concern is that I'm *talking too loud*? *Are you kidding me?*"

I shake my head and glance all around, slipping into full-on damage control mode as I lower my voice and say, "It's just—nobody can know. It's *got* to remain secret. It's *imperative*," I urge, realizing too late that I'm talking to the one person who's never been able to keep anyone's secret, much less her own.

She rolls her eyes and slams back in her seat, muttering under her breath as I take a moment to study her closely, dismayed to see the signs already present: her pale skin is luminous, clear, practically poreless as well, while her wavy brown hair with the blond streak in front is as shiny and glossy as a high-end shampoo ad. Even her teeth have gone straighter, whiter, and I can't help but wonder how this happened so quickly, with only a few sips of elixir, when it took so much longer for me.

My eyes continue to graze over her as I take a deep breath and dive in. Forgoing my usual promise not to eavesdrop on my friend's innermost thoughts, while I strain to get a better look, a glimpse of her energy, the words she's not sharing—sure that if snooping ever was warranted, it's now.

But instead of my usual front-row seat, I'm met by a rock-solid wall that bars me from entering. Even after I casually slide my hand forward and tap my fingertips against hers, feigning interest in the silver skull ring she wears, I get nothing.

Her future is hidden from me.

"This is just so—" She swallows hard and looks around, taking in the bubbling fountain, the young mom pushing a stroller while yelling into her cell phone, the group of girls exiting a swim shop with armfuls of bags—looking just about anywhere but at me.

"I know it's a lot to take in—*but still*—" I shrug, knowing I've got to make a better case but not quite sure how to do it.

"*A lot to take in?* Is that how you see it?" She shakes her head and drums her fingers against the armrest of her green metal chair as her gaze slowly sweeps over me.

I sigh, wishing I'd handled this better, wishing I could do something to make it go away, but it's too late for that. I've no choice but to deal with this mess that I made. "I guess I was hoping that's how *you'd* see it." I shrug. "Crazy. I know."

She takes a deep breath, face so still, so placid, it's impossible to read, and I'm just about to speak, just about to start begging forgiveness, when she says, "Seriously? You made me an immortal? Like—*for reals?*"

I nod, stomach a jumble of nerves as I sit up straighter and pull my shoulders back, bracing for the blow that's surely headed my way. Knowing that whatever she gives, be it verbal or physical, I've no choice but to take it. I deserve nothing less for wrecking her life as she knows it.

"I'm just—" She sucks in her breath and blinks several times, her aura invisible, offering no clue to her mood, now that I've made her like me. "Well—I'm in a total state of shock. I mean, seriously. I don't even know what to say."

I press my lips together and drop my hands to my lap, worrying the crystal horseshoe bracelet I always wear as I clear my throat and say, "Haven, listen, I'm so sorry. *So—very—very—sorry.* You have no idea. I just—" I shake my head, knowing I should cut to the chase but feeling like I need to explain my side of things—the impossible choice I was forced to make—how it felt to see her so pale, so helpless, teetering on the verge of death, every shallow breath quite possibly her last—

But before I can even begin she leans toward me, eyes wide and fixed on mine. "Are you *insane?*" She shakes her head. "You're actually *apologizing,* when I'm just sitting here, so psyched, so totally gobsmacked, I can't even imagine how I'll ever repay you!"

*Huh?*

"I mean, this is just *so* fugging cool!" She grins, bouncing up and down in her seat, face lighting up like a thousand-watt bulb. "It's seriously the coolest fugging thing that's ever happened to me—and I owe it all to *you!*"

I gulp, nervously glancing around, unsure how to react. This is not what I expected. Not what I prepared for. Though it's pretty much exactly what Damen warned me about.

Damen—my best friend—my soul mate—the love of my lives. My amazingly gorgeous, sexy, smart, talented, patient, and understanding boyfriend who knew this would happen and begged to come along for this very reason. But I was too stubborn. Insisting I do it alone. I'm the one who *turned* her— I'm the one who made her drink the elixir—so I'm the one who should explain. Only it's not going at all like I thought. Not even close.

"I mean, it's like being a vampire, right? Minus the blood-sucking?" Her sparkling eyes eagerly search mine. "Oh, and without all the coffins and sun avoidance too!" Her voice rises with glee. "This is *so* amazing—like a dream come true! Everything I've ever wanted has finally happened! I'm a vampire! A beautiful vampire—but without all the gruesome side effects!"

"You're not a vampire," I say, voice dull, listless, wondering how it got to this point. "There's no such thing."

*Nope, no vampires, no werewolves, no elves, no fairies—just immortals, whose ranks, thanks to Roman and me, are quickly multiplying . . .*

"And how can you be sure of that?" Haven asks, brow raised.

"Because Damen's been around a lot longer than I have," I say. "And he's never met one—or met anyone who's met one. We figure the vampire legends all stem from immortals, only with a few big distortions—like the bloodsucking, not being able to go out in sunlight, and the whole being allergic to garlic thing." I lean toward her. "It's all been added on for extra drama."

"Interesting." She nods, though her mind is clearly elsewhere. "Can I still eat cupcakes?" She motions toward the dented strawberry mess, one side caved in, flattened against its cardboard container, while the other side remains fluffy, begging to be eaten. "Or is there something else I'm supposed to—" Eyes going wide, giving me no time to reply before she slaps the table and squeals, "Omigod—it's *that juice,* isn't it? That red stuff you and Damen always drink! That's it, huh? *So,* what are you waiting for! Hand it over already, let's make it official—I can't wait to get started!"

"I didn't bring any," I say, seeing her face drop in disappointment as I rush to explain. "Listen, I know you think it sounds really cool and all—and some of it is, there's no doubt about that. I mean, you'll never grow old, never get zits or split ends, you'll never have to work out, and you might even grow taller—who knows? But there's other stuff too—stuff you need to know—stuff I have to explain in order to—" My words are halted by the sight of her jumping out of her chair so quickly and gracefully she's like a cat—yet another immortality side effect.

Hopping from foot to foot as she says, "Please. What's to know? If I can jump higher, run faster, never age or fade away—what else could I possibly need? Sounds like I'm good to go for the rest of eternity."

I glance around nervously, determined to curb her enthusiasm before she does something crazy—something that'll draw the kind of attention we cannot afford. "Haven, please. Sit. This is serious. There's more to explain. *A lot* more," I whisper, the words harsh, brutal, but having no effect whatsoever. She just stands there before me, shaking her head and refusing to budge. So drunk on her new immortal power she skips past defiant and heads straight for belligerent.

"*Everything* is serious with you, Ever. *Every—single—thing* you say and do is just *so* dang serious. I mean, *seriously,* you hand me the keys to the kingdom then demand I stay put so you can warn me about the dark side? How crazy is that?" She rolls her eyes. "Come on, unclench a little, would ya? Let me try it out, take it for a test drive, see what I'm capable of. I'll even race you! First one to make it from the curb to the library wins!"

I shake my head and sigh, wishing I didn't have to do it, but knowing a little telekinesis is in order. It's the only thing that'll put an end to all this and show her who's really in charge around here. Narrowing my eyes, I focus hard on her chair, driving it across the pavers so fast it buckles her knees and forces her to sit.

"Hey—that hurt!" She rubs her leg and glares.

But I just shrug. She's immortal, it's not like she'll bruise. Besides, there's plenty more to explain and not enough time if she continues like this, so I lean toward her, making sure I have her full attention when I say, "Trust me, you can't play the game if you don't know the rules. And if you don't know the rules, someone's bound to get hurt."

# Ever's little sister, Riley gets her own series!

### alyson noël
#1 NEW YORK TIMES BESTSELLING AUTHOR OF
the immortals

## Radiance

Riley has crossed the bridge into the afterlife—a place called Here, where time is always Now. She has picked up life where she left off when she was alive—but she soon learns that the afterlife isn't just an eternity of leisure. . . .

## AVAILABLE SEPTEMBER 2010

For free downloads, hidden surprises, and glimpses into the future, visit www.ImmortalsSeries.com.

SQUARE
FISH